STEEL

The Cartographer Book 2

AC COBBLE

Cobble Publishing LLC

Coldlands

Rhenar

Finavir

Tralla

United Territories

Enhover

Vendari Islands

Inchun

Westlands

Arching
Atolls

Farawk

Southlands

Darklands

The Known World
Year 982
Duke Oliver Wellesley

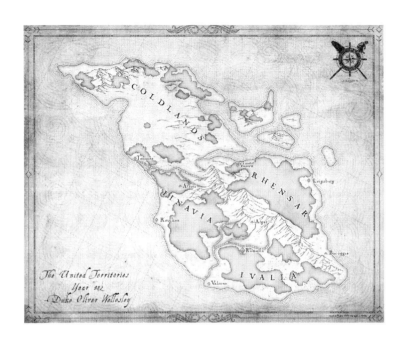

COLDLANDS

RHENSAR

Totonna

Vassen

Leigsburg

Anne

FINAVIA

Rouchan

Aigın

Romalla

Baroggia

IVALLA

Valerno

The United Territories
Year 842
Duke Oliver Wellesley

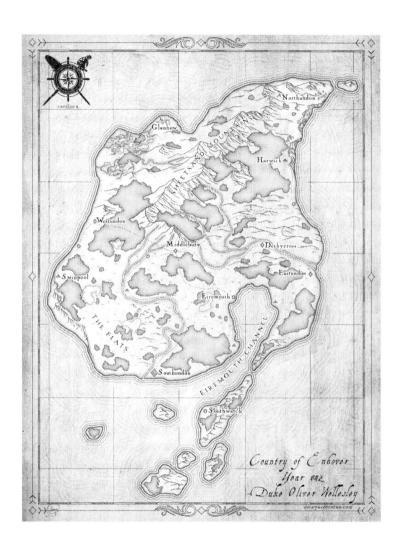

Country of Enhover
Year 842
Duke Oliver Wellesley

KEEP IN TOUCH AND EXTRA CONTENT

THANKS FOR CHECKING out the book! You can find larger versions of the maps and custom artwork on my website accobble.com. While there, sign up for the newsletter to get the free prequel novella and short stories. One email a month, never spam, unsubscribe anytime.

I save the best stuff for Patreon (patreon.com/accobble). If you want exclusive updates, pre-publication access to the books, and a chance to steer future projects, that is the place to be.

Happy reading!
AC

THE CARTOGRAPHER I

THE MAN HELD HIS GAZE. Only his flat, brown eyes were visible beneath the black, silk mask. His voice was deep, and cracked with the strain of speaking in a slow, solemn rasp. "Welcome, aspirant. Tonight, we renounce our primitive selves, our realistic selves, and our moral selves. Are you ready to set them aside and become one with the spirit Seheht?"

Oliver drew a deep breath and touched his chest, his pointer and thumb forming a circle, the other three fingers sticking out straight.

The masked man nodded and opened the door.

Oliver rolled his eyes behind the man's back before walking inside. His skin crawling, he passed his masked and cloaked guide. Each step brought a tremor of apprehension and disbelief. The theatrics seemed so… theatrical, but he had to consider the possibility the masked man was a sorcerer, even if it did seem a bit unlikely in that particular case. Surely a sorcerer wouldn't be made to guard the door?

Regardless, Marquess Colston and Isisandra Dalyrimple had been true practitioners, and they had been associated with the Feet of Seheht. Anyone at the meeting could be upon the dark path.

He shivered, thinking of the grim horror he'd experienced just weeks before in Derbycross. He couldn't let the theatrics and play-acting distract him. Any of these people might be dangerous.

But the man at the door made no movement toward Oliver when he passed. He did nothing threatening at all, in fact. He simply closed the door as Oliver crossed the threshold, presumably to wait out in the hall until the next aspirant formed the correct symbol and gained entry.

Briefly, Oliver wondered what would happen if someone arrived at the mansion in the correct attire, passed down that plain stone corridor, and couldn't make the proscribed hand sign. Would they merely turn the person around, or deal with it in some other way?

He hadn't thought to ask his cousin Lannia what would happen if her instructions failed, but it didn't matter. He'd made it inside the Feet of Seheht, the secret society Isisandra Dalyrimple had been a member of, and where maybe she and her mentor Marquess Colston had learned the dark arts they'd utilized deep beneath Derbycross. As Oliver stood before the entrance to a large open ballroom, he forced himself to breathe slow, to still his racing heart.

The room was dimly lit. Shrouded fae light barely illuminated two dozen figures moving slowly about the tile-floored room. All of them were dressed similar to Oliver in flowing black, silk robes and masks that hid everything but their eyes. Scattered throughout the room were tables filled with slender glasses of sparkling Finavian wine. There were cushions and low-slung tables in other sections that held knee-high, glass vases, sprouting twisting, tentacle-like tubes that released slow tendrils of thick, white smoke. He watched as one of the robed figures bent and sucked from a tube and then stood, exhaling a billowing cloud. Syrup of the poppy.

Behind him, the door opened again, and he turned to see another aspirant standing directly behind him, waiting to enter.

The person stood there patiently for a moment then grunted and waved at him.

Coughing into a gloved hand, Oliver shuffled out of the way, and the newcomer passed by, surveying the room and then marching to one of the tables and collecting a glass of wine.

Oliver found a strategic location and watched as several more arrivals came in the door, each of them quickly finding their way to the wine tables or clustering around the water pipes. No one spoke, as Lannia had instructed was procedure. Instead, they shuffled about, eyeing each other surreptitiously and, in short time, becoming rather intoxicated.

In the far corners of the room, black-robed shapes gathered, pawing at each other. Lannia had told him that after the ceremonies, it wasn't unusual for an orgy to begin. At higher ranks within the society, they were part of the practice. He'd asked Sam, and she confirmed that sexual rites were rumored to be used in a variety of sorcerous rituals. They could be used to bind an aspirant to the society, she'd told him, among other things. He'd thought that his attention-seeking cousin had merely been trying to impress him with her wanton youth. It seemed she hadn't lied, though, and some of the attendees were getting started early.

He steeled himself, thrilled and disgusted by the idea he might witness such deviant behavior. Stand against the wall, pretend you're one of those who likes to watch, Lannia had advised him, before cheekily adding some other suggestions if the watching grew too wearisome. Sam, straight-faced, had suggested he join in but not complete the act. Do not stand out, leave no material behind, she'd insisted.

Hoping the silk mask hid his curdled grimace, he grabbed a glass of wine, raised it to his lips, and then set it back down. Poppy syrup was not just smoked, and there was no telling what members of a secret sorcerous society may have drugged the wine with.

A gong sounded. It was mere minutes before midnight and the start of the winter solstice. The figures in the room moved slowly toward the far side, though those in the corner took some encouraging, and several robes were adjusted as they walked to join the group. Oliver fell in behind the throng, noting that through the entrance, several more masked people had entered and lined the back wall.

At the far end of the ballroom, a short man was holding a mallet. He stood beside a metal gong that shined brilliantly even in the dim light. The gong was adorned with an upside-down, five-pointed star — the symbol of Seheht. It was set upon a dais beside a waist-high altar that was covered with purple velvet cloths and gleaming silver implements. A dagger, a bowl, and a mirror.

Behind the altar and the gong, a huge, silver star hung upside down against a plain stone wall. Both it and the symbol on the gong were identical to the star on the cover of the black leather-bound book Oliver and Sam had found in Isisandra's effects. He had no doubt now that the Book of Law, as Sam had called it, had originated from this organization.

Another door opened, and from behind the altar, two figures emerged. They moved slowly, as if they were counting their steps, like players on the stage at the cheaper theatres. Cloaked and hooded like everyone else, these two sported silver, inverted-star emblems that hung around their necks on delicate chains.

One of the figures settled in front of the altar and raised its arms skyward. The gong sounded again, and a woman began to speak, her voice artificially low, echoing around the sparsely furnished stone-and-tile room. "Welcome, aspirants to the Feet of Seheht."

The voice sounded familiar, and he suspected he'd met the woman at some function or another, but with her forced, low pitch, he couldn't place her. He let a hand drift up to check that his mask was in place. If he recognized her voice, then she would surely recognize his face if she saw it.

The gong sounded again, and the woman glanced back at the mallet-holder. Oliver caught a barely perceptible shrug. The woman turned to address the crowd. "I, ah, I am the most high priestess of our order. Tonight, I will induct you into— as long as you pass the test of membership, you will be inducted into our order."

Around him, Oliver felt the crowd shifting uncomfortably. The woman did not strike him as an experienced master of sorcery, real or imagined, and evidently, he wasn't the only one. The woman's speech had the hallmarks of the worst type of acting, and as the gong-banger struck again, the woman attempted to awe them by raising her voice and her arms even higher.

"Founded over three hundred years ago, our ranks are steeped in wisdom and knowledge obtained from the greatest sorcerers in Enhover's history. Those ancient adepts studied at the feet of the spirits known as the dark trinity, and their forbidden knowledge has been passed down for generations, from elder, to priest, to acolyte. We, ah, we follow Seheht—"

"Where is Colston?" barked an annoyed voice in the crowd.

The room fell silent as they all waited on the answer.

"Our membership is a secret," declared the woman, finally dropping her arms to her side and peering into the crowd, looking for the man who had interrupted her.

"You're not the elder, are you?" questioned the man, shuffling irritably, making no efforts to hide. "You can try to keep his identity a secret if you like, but the man recruited half of us in this room. We know who he is, and I suspect I'm not alone in wondering where he is."

"This is not—" began the woman.

"I'm a member of half a dozen societies in Enhover and even Rhensar," interjected the man from the crowd. "I've never been to an induction ceremony without the elder present. Do you even have the rank to initiate us?"

"He is… Our elder is not here tonight," admitted the woman, twisting her hands together in front of her. "He's been, ah, not present for some weeks. Our mission continues, though, and the Feet of Seheht will continue to delve the secrets of this world and the next. If the marquess— if the elder does not reappear, we will elect a new elder. In time for our initiation rite we will have new leadership, if necessary. Do not fear. There is no cause for concern."

Her assurances were cut off by a loud snort from the man in the crowd.

Underneath his mask, Oliver smirked. Evidently, he was the only one in the room who knew Marquees Colston would not be returning to the Feet of Seheht, ever. He was glad that, so far, it seemed none of the minions even realized the man was dead.

Oliver frowned. They didn't know the man was dead. A suspected group of sorcerers didn't know that, weeks ago, their leader had passed the barrier to the underworld. These people, purportedly in the business of summoning the spirits of the dead, did not know what had happened to Colston. Oliver's heart sank. All of the work to follow the one clue that they had, and these fools were just play-acting. A true cabal of sorcerers would know by now that their leader had perished. Oliver was wasting his time.

Frustrated complaints rose from the crowd, and the woman demanded they quiet. Raising her voice to an unceremonious shout, she declared that the aspirant ritual would continue. A man turned to leave, but several cloaked figures had gathered around the back door and they crossed their arms, signaling that despite the complaints, no one would be leaving.

The gong-banger swung his mallet again, and the sonorous vibrations stilled the rustling crowd. There were a few muttered complaints around the man who had spoken out, but the rest of the aspirants quieted. They knew Marquees Colston and may have had some interest in the secrets he promised, but Oliver guessed most had come to the Feet of Seheht for the wine, the poppy syrup, and the orgy.

Oliver looked around, wondering how he could get out of there and salvage the rest of his night. These were not illicit sorcerers plotting to tear down the government of Enhover. These were bored peers and merchants looking for a little excitement. Joining this organization and moving up through the ranks was going to take him years to learn all of their secrets, and he was quickly becoming sure that they had few worth keeping.

The man at the gong banged it with his mallet again.

Shaking his head, Oliver turned, glancing back toward the blocked door and the milling cloaked figures around it, wondering if there was a way he could slip away unnoticed. The woman on the dais had begun speaking again, and this time, the crowd let her continue her farcical performance.

Between her declarations about the wondrous power of Seheht and the zealous gong-banger's activities, a wave of sound washed over Oliver as he studied the available doors in the room. Just two of them, which was disappointing, and both were blocked by masked and robed figures. Against the walls, he saw plain stone covered with hanging black silk. If the mansion was like most in the neighborhood, one of the walls should have a bank of windows looking out onto the carriage courtyard. Perhaps he could slip out that way, behind the hanging?

He frowned.

Nearly imperceptible, the black silk over the far wall masked a subtle glow. Light from the carriage court, he assumed, but shadows moved through it, as if backlit by the lights. The silk curtain waved, stirred by a wind that didn't touch the rest of the room. A window left open?

He glanced back toward the way he'd entered and saw one of the cloaked figures at the door fiddling with it. When the figure moved away, Oliver gasped. A dull iron lock hung from the door handle.

His eyes darted back to the silk curtain and he saw it stir again, a shape pressing against it. Supernatural or mundane, he didn't wait to learn. The exit had been locked, and someone was sneaking in through the window. Whatever it was, he didn't think it was part of the planned ceremony.

Moving quickly, Oliver stepped to the closest table, one set with long-stemmed wine glasses. He gripped one in his fist, and as the mallet-wielder smacked the gong again, he cracked the glass against the edge of the table, snapping off the cup, leaving him with a spike of broken glass in his fist. A few robed aspirants turned to him curiously, but Oliver ignored them, his gaze darting between the silk curtain and the two doors.

The curtain parted, and a dozen men dressed in simple work-man's garb came pouring into the room. They clutched a variety of tools and implements that wouldn't be out of place on the streets of Westundon. Their faces were unmasked. Oliver took that as a sign they didn't intend to leave witnesses to what was about to happen.

Grunting, he sprinted toward the door behind the dais, the only exit that wasn't locked and wasn't blocked by a dozen armed men.

Instead of a dozen, he saw it was just one. As he approached, and shouts of surprise rose behind him, the mallet-wielder stepped away from his gong and made to block the door. Beneath his mask, Oliver saw the man's eyes showed no surprise at the sudden interruption. He'd been ready for this. Whether the man was a member of the Feet of Seheht or part of the group that was attacking the society, Oliver didn't know. He just knew the man was blocking his one chance at escape.

Shouts of alarm turned to pain and terror behind him. Oliver launched himself at the mallet-wielder, speeding behind the woman who'd been intoning their welcome.

His opponent raised the steel-headed mallet, but Oliver didn't give him time to draw it back for a swing. He crashed into the man, one arm smacking painfully against the handle of the club, the other whipping up and jabbing the stem of the broken wine glass into the man's neck.

Startled eyes met Oliver's as sharp glass punctured the man's throat.

Oliver shoved him out of the way and cursed vehemently when he saw an iron lock hanging from the door handle. Without pause, he dove after the man he'd just stabbed in neck and snatched the mallet from his hands. The man, kicking and thrashing in the throes of his dying, raised no objection. He was solely focused on gripping his neck, trying to stem the spurts of blood that squirted out of the puncture wound.

Oliver smashed the mallet against the lock, snarling when it didn't snap from the blow. He swung again and again, battering the mallet against the stubborn iron. Behind him, he could hear shouts and shrieks as the unarmed aspirants of the Feet of Seheht tried to defend themselves against a dozen assassins. Knowing there was no chance against the armed men, Oliver frantically battered the lock.

"What are you doing?" cried the woman who'd led the ritual earlier. She had stepped off the dais and was crouching beside him.

Ignoring her, he swung again. He smiled to himself as the hasp finally broke. He yanked the remains of the lock away and glanced over his shoulder.

The woman who'd claimed to be the high priestess stared at him open-mouthed. The rest of the room was filling with violence and mayhem. Black-clad aspirants were falling before their attackers. A few of them had hefted tables or the glass water pipes and were trying to defend themselves. Oliver could see in an instant that their attackers were practiced and determined. These were men who'd faced combat before, and they operated as a coordinated unit. As he watched, two of them closed on a man gripping one of the tall tables that had held the wine. The aspirant twisted and turned, but his assailants split and surrounded him. He could only swivel helplessly as they closed on him.

Oliver didn't bother to watch the end. Instead, he opened the door and rushed through, calling over his shoulder to the shocked woman, "Come with me or die."

Shaking herself, she darted after him.

Oliver slammed the door shut. There was no lock on the other side, though, and no way to secure it. Cursing under his breath, he started off down the hallway and found a well-dressed corridor that wouldn't have been out of place in his own home. It was richly decorated and shouted the wealth of the owners.

"How do we get out of here?" he demanded, turning to the woman.

"What happened in there?" she babbled.

"You were attacked!" he exclaimed. "Can you… can you do something about it?"

She stared at him, eyes blank beneath her mask.

"Can you use sorcery to fight back?" he growled.

"Sorcery… That's not… It's not possible in Enhover anymore," spluttered the woman. "We're scholars, not—"

Grumbling, Oliver grabbed her wrist and dragged her after him up a flight of stairs. He didn't know where they led, but anywhere was better than the room behind them. He was certain now that he knew her, but there was no time to wrack his brain and recall how. Now, the only thought was flight. At the top of the stairs, he found a long, dark hallway, and at the end, he spotted a pair of huge, mahogany doors. The front doors to the mansion, he thought. They should lead to the street. He didn't bother to ask the panic-stricken woman as he was becoming convinced she knew even less about the Feet of Seheht and their chapter house than he did.

"I don't understand," complained the woman. "Who were those men? Why did they attack us?"

Ahead of them, Oliver heard glass shattering. He stopped, paralyzed with indecision in the middle of the hallway.

"What is— The library!" screamed the woman.

She jerked her hand from his grasp and charged forward, heading toward an opening beside the doors. A growing orange and red glow shined on her black, silk robes.

Oliver snarled a curse as he heard more shattering glass. Their attackers were not content to merely slay everyone on the bottom floor. They were going to burn the mansion to the ground.

He called after the woman, "We have to get out of here!"

She didn't respond. She was transfixed, staring into the open room where he assumed the society's library was quickly going up in flames. Books, manuscripts, the type of knowledge he was seeking, none of it known for its resistance to fire.

Suddenly, he heard the sounds of running boots from the floors above. Attackers or other victims, he didn't know. There was no time to wait, no time to seek what he'd come to find. Besides, if the woman or her fellows had known real sorcery, they'd be using it now.

Oliver spun, hoping the rear of the building offered an easier exit than the front. Somewhere out there, someone was tossing incendiaries into the broken windows. He had no desire to catch one on his way out the door.

In the back, he found staff quarters, storage rooms, and other spaces that didn't attract the presence of the society's members. Fortunately, they also were not yet attracting the interest of their assailants. Unfortunately for the woman Oliver had left in the hallway, she did. He heard her pained, warbling scream as he finally found the rear of the building.

He kicked open a locked shutter and peered out. Below him, flame and smoke poured out of the windows on the basement level. An alley ran behind the building, and on opposite ends, he saw figures moving about, guarding against escape. They'd soon be joined by the fire brigade and curious citizens, he hoped.

One of the figures saw him and pointed, shouting. They began to mill about, arguing amongst themselves.

Oliver could feel the heat of the fire below him growing. The assassins in the alleyway had no way to approach him on the second floor, but he was stuck. He looked behind him, and while he didn't see anyone yet, he could hear men moving about, ransacking and burning the place. If they found him, he'd be cornered. He had no weapons, no way to call for help. He glanced out again and saw more shapes appearing at the ends of the alleyway.

The fire brigade or more attackers?

Wishing it didn't feel like such a foolish decision, he clambered up onto the windowsill and then jumped down, falling through a haze of smoke and fire. He landed heavily in the dirty cobblestone alleyway. On the front side of the building, there was a wide tree and mansion-lined boulevard. Behind the buildings, though, it was a maze of narrow streets used by servants, delivery men, and refuse-takers. At the end of the alley, he could see the watchers shifting in agitation and then starting to come toward him. They must have seen him drop from the window. He guessed they'd have orders to leave no witnesses.

He darted across the alley, clambered up a pile of discarded crates, and flopped over a wall into the garden of a building across the way. Some public offices, he thought, perhaps a barrister or physician, but he didn't take time to look. He ran through the back to the carriage yard, checking his mask and robes to ensure they were still in place, that his identity was still secret. He knew he looked strange, covered from head to toe in black silk, but he had to move quickly to gain distance between himself and the attackers. There was no time to make himself appear less suspicious.

Running into the night, half an hour past midnight, he saw a mechanical carriage rumbling ahead of him. He sprinted after it and leapt to catch onto the back of it where a footman would have ridden if his master was inside.

Oliver had no idea where the carriage would take him, but he had to go somewhere.

THE PRIESTESS I

"Another?" asked the barman.

"Why not?" she replied.

He grabbed her mug and turned, pulling on his tap and spilling a frothy golden liquid into the container. When he sat it down, his eyes stayed locked on the book she had open in front of her.

"What?" she said, glaring at him.

"I'm not sure the old man would approve," remarked the barman. "Your kind is meant to destroy that knowledge, are you not?"

"To defeat your enemy, you must know them first," she replied. "I read that somewhere."

"No you didn't."

She snorted. "Maybe not, but someone probably wrote it. If we do not understand what we're up against, how can we defeat it? How can we even know what we're supposed to be fighting? You say Thotham would disapprove, but he learned more about sorcery than anyone I've ever known. He walked the dark path as far as he was able. He had to walk it to do his job."

Andrew grunted, shaking his head. "And how did that go for him?"

She glared at the barman.

Holding up his hands, the man muttered, "I can see I won't convince you, but know this. The dark path is difficult to walk, but even more difficult to turn from. Once you've gone far enough, you may not be able to come back."

"What do you know about the dark path and the people we pursue?" questioned Sam.

"I'm a simple pub owner," replied Andrew, scratching at his short beard. "I don't know what's in those pages any more than I know what King Edward had for breakfast this morning, but I do know what is not in there. The old man is gone, girl. He's gone, and reading that book won't bring him back. What you seek is not down this path, and if you're not careful, you're going to find something that is better left undiscovered."

"I know he's gone," she snapped, "but if he was here, he'd be doing exactly as I am. Our purpose, his purpose, was defeating sorcery. We cannot do that if we do not learn about it. Maybe if he'd had access to this book and time to study it, he wouldn't have died."

Andrew stared at her for a moment and then moved away, muttering darkly under his breath.

She snorted. If the man kept his nose out of her business, he'd have no reason to be upset by it. She knew Thotham wasn't coming back. Trying to decipher the leather-bound grimoire on the bar wouldn't change what had happened, but it was all she could think to do. Her mentor had died pursing his mission, trying to battle the shadowy memory of what he'd seen in his prophecy. He would want her to finish what he'd started, but without his guidance, where else was she to turn? The Book of Law may hold the answers she was seeking, and she'd be foolish to ignore it.

In his prophecy, Thotham had described a tree of darkness spreading out from Enhover, a deep root of sorcery in the one place it was supposed to be impossible. It was all as obscure as the mysterious diagrams and script she'd been mulling over. Since she'd put Duke in the carriage and returned to the pub, she'd done nothing but drink and try to tease out some meaning from the grimoire.

Not for the first time, she wondered if Isisandra Dalyrimple had been able to read the ancient manuscript. The Book of Law, stamped with the symbol of the Feet of Seheht. The sorceress had carried it in her personal effects for a reason, Sam was certain. There was something within those cryptic pages worth learning. Maybe tonight, Duke would find something they could use, some paradigm that would help untangle the ancient terms and language of the book.

She wasn't hopeful, though. Even if the ranks of the Feet of Seheht held the secrets they sought, the society was unlikely to hand them out to aspirants at the first meeting. Still, there could be something, and she was glad the nobleman had agreed to pursue it. Without him, she'd be entirely lost.

She picked up her ale mug and took a sip, looking down at the thin ink that covered the pages in front of her. An old dialect of Darklands script, she was pretty sure. Frozen hell. Duke or no Duke, she was entirely lost.

She closed the grimoire and glanced around the pub. An hour after midnight, it wasn't crowded, but it wasn't empty, either. A few men were drinking heavily and tossing daggers at a painted target on the wall. Another man was passed out a dozen paces away with his forehead flat against the rough plank table. A pair of men were sharing a nearly empty bottle of murky brown liquor, and half a dozen were clustered together in a corner booth, laughing uproariously at a joke one of them had told. They were armed heavily. Perhaps security for a merchant who had no livery or perhaps privateers. Either way, they were solely focused on their own jests, and despite the weaponry, she sensed no threat from them.

She frowned. There were no women in the room except for her.

Waving Andrew over, she asked him quietly, "Why are there no women here?"

"You're here," he mentioned.

"Aside from me, why are there no women?"

He stroked his beard, flattening it down from where his furious scratching earlier had tangled it. "There are never any women here."

"Why is that?" she wondered.

"Is there a man in here you couldn't best in a fight?" questioned Andrew.

She brushed a strand of jet-black hair behind her ear and replied, "Probably not."

The barman nodded, satisfied.

"What does that have to do with anything?" she wondered.

"You can out-drink and out-fight every man in here," he explained. "You've probably slept with more women than any two of them combined. You've traveled farther, you've seen stranger things than most, and if I needed a new bottle opened and I was struggling with it, I'd ask for your help before any of those louts. By the way some judge these things, you're more man than any of the rest of them. You don't have a penis, though, of course."

"No, I don't have a penis," she agreed. "I'm not sure if you're trying to compliment me or insult me, Andrew."

He smirked. "The patrons of my bar aren't here because the chairs are comfortable or the decoration is attractive. They didn't come because it's convenient or even that the other clientele is worth talking to. If I had latrines, they wouldn't be cleaned, not by me at least. No, these fellows come here because I've got the best drink in Westundon. That's the only reason anyone comes here, and I've learned over my years, that's not enough for the fairer sex."

She sipped her drink and set it down. "You do have good ale, but I think you'd sell a lot more of it if you enticed a few women inside. Not everyone heads to the pub just to drink, you know?"

"In here they do," replied Andrew. "Find yourself a man, if you want some entertainment. They didn't come for softer company, but not a one'a them would turn it down."

"I prefer women," she remarked.

"Aye," he replied, "I know. I also know a man'll do the job. Probably be a lot easier to talk them into it, too. Where's that chap, Walpole? You scare him off?"

"Walpole has done the job, but I've had better," she claimed. "A lot better."

"That's my point," declared Andrew. "When you prefer a good lay to a good drink, you go and find yourself another pub. When drinking is what's on your mind, the doors of the Befuddled Sage are always open. That, my girl, is why there are no women here. This establishment is for drinking. Woman wants a man, or a man wants a woman, they'll go somewhere else. I promise the best drinks in Westundon and that's all. Everyone knows women want a little decoration on the walls, maybe some better lighting, a place to empty their bladders other than the alley out back. They want to talk to people. Here, it's just about the drink."

Sam snorted, taking another sip.

"Fancy another before your nobleman gets back?" asked Andrew.

She turned and gazed over the other patrons in the pub. "Why not? Not much else to do in here, is there?"

Grinning, the barman poured her another, and she sat quietly, unwilling to reopen the Book of Law, but finding it impossible to shift her focus away from it. She sat silently for half an hour, nursing her ale, watching the room. None of it changed until a new group entered, four men, covered in soot, looking like they needed a stiff drink.

"Barman," called one of them, "a bottle of gin and four cups."

Andrew nodded and then gestured to their torn and smoke-fouled clothing. "A fire?"

"Aye," confirmed the man. "Some rich peer's mansion. Whole

thing burned like a pitch-covered torch. Can't for the life of me imagine what he was storing in there. In less than a turn of the clock, it was just fire-blackened stone. Craziest thing I've seen since I joined the brigade, a big mansion like that burning so fast. He must have been a lamp oil merchant and was saving on warehouse expenses. Stupid way to die, if you ask me."

A second man snorted. "Aye, that or something darker. It smelled funny in there, you know? Like meat over the fire, 'cept not like any meat my missus cooks."

"Well, with a big mansion like that, there could have been some staff trapped inside or even the peer himself," said the first man. "Not that you'd have much luck identifying what they was now. Peer or pauper, they're all the same after that fire."

The second grunted. "Maybe. Must'a been a lot of 'em to stink it up like that. You could smell it a block away."

"Where was this fire?" asked Sam quietly.

The first man eyed her up and down, his gaze lingering on her hips, on the kris daggers hanging there. Then, he looked to her face and answered, "About eight blocks north of here. Normally outside of our territory, but they called in fire brigades from five different boroughs to deal with it. Didn't want the peers and the merchants getting their mansions damaged, I suppose. Fine by me. We get paid a bonus anytime we have to venture outside of our district."

Sam slid off the stool, collecting the Book of Law and sticking it into the satchel she had Duke's clothing in. She didn't expect him back at their meeting point for another hour, but a mansion, just eight blocks north... She had to find out.

"Careful out there, Sam," murmured Andrew. "It's dark tonight."

She nodded curtly and then slipped out the open door. On the damp night air, she could already smell the smoke.

THE CARTOGRAPHER II

HE STAGGERED against the wall of the building, his breath coming in ragged gasps. He'd been running flat out for half an hour, panicked that he would accidentally stumble into the attackers who'd struck the Feet of Seheht. That many of them, assaulting a crowded building so blatantly, would stop at nothing if they knew he'd been inside.

And there was little chance they wouldn't know he'd been inside. He was prancing around in the society's flowing black silk robes and mask. Inside of the chapter house, they'd felt silly. Running through the dark streets of Westundon in the middle of the night, they were ludicrous. But while he felt a fool, there wasn't much to be done about it. Sam had his clothing, and if someone did see him, he'd be glad of the mask.

He'd leapt off the mechanical carriage a league and a half from his brother's palace and even farther from his own estate in the city. He'd considered racing toward either place, no matter how absurd he would feel banging on the gates, but he realized that if the attack on the Feet of Seheht had been directed at him, then Sam was in grave danger. He'd zigzagged across Westundon, heading back toward the Befuddled Sage. Now he was within two blocks, leaning against the wall, watching Sam's unmistakable kris-adorned hips as she hurried down the dark alley toward him.

"What happened?" she whispered.

"Fire, attackers," he gasped.

"Attackers?"

"Everyone is dead," he explained between breaths. "The pub, what—"

"Nothing," assured Sam. "There's been no disruption at all. I came to find you because members of the fire brigade came in. They said a mansion had burned. Duke, they reported that there were no survivors. Is that... is that true?"

"There's at least one," he said, finally catching his breath and standing upright, "but maybe only one. They locked the doors and tried to corner us in the basement. I got out, but the fires had already started. I didn't see anyone else escape. Sam, I need to change."

She glanced at his clothing and nodded curtly. "My apartment."

"They may look for us there," he warned.

Shaking her head, she took his hand and led him back the way he'd come. "We can avoid the main streets this way. I don't think they'll come for us at my place. If they wanted to find me, they would have at the Befuddled Sage. Remember, we both went in there. If this was directed at either one of us personally, they would have had to follow you to the meeting. They would have known I was inside the pub. I don't think either of us were the targets tonight."

He was silent for a moment before responding. "If not me, then you think it was the society itself they were attacking? Some rival organization taking the opportunity to destroy the Feet of Seheht?"

"A rival or someone inside," she muttered.

"Someone inside?" he questioned.

Sam grunted, stopping him behind a building and removing a key from her vest to open the door. She led him in, and they were quiet until they entered her apartment and fastened the bolt behind them.

"Colston performed real sorcery," she said, turning to him. "We saw that. Isisandra Dalyrimple knew real sorcery as well, though I suspect she learned it from her parents instead of the Feet of Seheht. What if when she arrived back in Enhover, she sought out a mentor and found Colston? He had true power and took her on knowing that she was skilled as well. Sorcerous knowledge is prized and protected. Even if he was the superior, it's possible she knew things he did not. It's likely that few others in the society were true sorcerers. Maybe none of them."

Oliver shook his head. "Someone had that book before Isisandra. Someone taught Colston. Members of the Feet of Seheht had occult knowledge, even if I didn't see it tonight."

"What if there was someone who ranked higher than the elder?" mused Sam.

"Higher than the elder?"

"They could have attacked tonight to cover up their involvement in the society," she speculated. "The elder may have been only a figurehead, albeit one with knowledge and skill. The true master could still be out there and is destroying anyone who would lead us to him."

"Or her," grumbled Oliver.

Sam smirked. "Or her. We think this all started when someone found out Hathia Dalyrimple was returning to Enhover with an object tainted by the spirit Ca-Mi-He. It wasn't her daughter, and it wasn't the elder who killed her, right? It had to be either a rival or a superior. Which do you think makes more sense, that some rival was able to guess what she was up to on the other side of the world, or that a superior in the society learned of what she'd done? For all we know, she could have told this person herself and was going to meet them, but then paid the ultimate price for her candor."

Oliver grunted. "I'm not thinking straight, Sam. It sounds plausible."

"The attack tonight wasn't directed at us," continued Sam, pacing across the narrow space in her apartment. "I'm certain of it. They killed Hathia and took the tainted dagger she'd brought to Enhover. They killed Governor Dalyrimple, they killed Captain Haines, and they killed Standish Taft. If we hadn't done the work for them, I wonder if they would have allowed Marquees Colston and Isisandra to survive? Now, they're cleaning up the remaining loose ends. Duke, as we suspected, there's another sorcerer out there. They're slaughtering anyone who might lead to them."

"Where does that leave us?" wondered Oliver, rubbing a hand over his hair, checking the knot in the back. "The only thread we had to follow died tonight in the chapter house."

Sam nodded and smacked a fist against the wall.

Oliver sat slumped in one of Sam's two chairs, staring down at his hands. They'd speculated that there might be another sorcerer or several. It was why Oliver had taken the risk of infiltrating the Feet of Seheht. But somehow, it hadn't occurred to him that there may be someone who was the superior of both Colston and Isisandra. The thought was terrifying, and he would have had trouble believing it except what else explained the attack? Who, other than an insider, would be aware the society was meeting? Who would have the motivation to kill everyone who attended, burning the evidence? It was too much of a coincidence to believe the attack was unrelated to what happened in Derbycross, and if it was related, it was too much to believe it was someone unaffiliated with the society.

In the end, though, it didn't much matter whether it was a superior cleaning up loose ends or a lieutenant getting spooked by their missing elder. Someone wanted to eradicate any evidence the society existed, someone who could only be involved in sorcery. The problem was, they now had no leads, no resources. Nothing. They'd lost Sam's mentor Thotham. They'd—

"Ivalla," declared Oliver suddenly, inspiration hitting him like a bolt of lightning. He looked up at Sam. "You have to go to Ivalla, to the Church there. You need to find the cardinal or this council you've told me about. Find more priests like you and Thotham. There have to be more. You said the Church sent someone to Archtan Atoll after we'd left. Who are they? Where are they? That's who we need, Sam. Let's find someone experienced in hunting these bastards."

She crossed her arms over her chest and admitted, "I've never been to the Church in Ivalla. I don't even know where to start with the Council of Seven. Their practices are a secret, even amongst churchmen. You cannot simply knock on the door and ask to speak to them. Thotham was the one who always communicated with the rest of the organization. He kept me out of it. What if there was a good reason for that, Duke?"

Oliver stood and crossed the small room to her. He put a hand on her shoulder. "In the short time I knew him, I learned to respect your mentor. He was dedicated and knowledgeable. Ask yourself what he would do in our circumstances."

She glanced at the corner of the room where Thotham's rune-covered spear leaned against the wall. The spear, the steel tip reflecting the light of the fire, was infused with his soul.

Oliver didn't understand it, and it sounded a bit like mumbo jumbo to him, but he knew the weapon gave her comfort. He gestured to the spear. "Can he..."

"Can he speak to me from a hunk of wood and steel? No, but..." She went and collected the weapon, running her hands along its length. "Thotham, if you can hear me, can you give me some sign that I should travel to Ivalla?"

Oliver stood silently, watching her.

She looked back at him and shrugged.

"If there's no sign, does that mean..." he trailed off, not sure what he was asking.

"I don't know what it means, but I can't think of any reason not to try and find another Knife of the Council," she admitted. "We have no leads in Enhover, nowhere else to turn. We know someone is out there, though, and I will stop them. I will. I just have to figure out who they are. Going to Ivalla, finding another Knife, I suppose that's as good a step as any."

"I'll go with you," offered Oliver. "We can take the Cloud Serpent. I don't know much about this council or the Church, but whatever way I can help, I will."

"No," replied Sam, running her hands over the spear, "you stay here. I can move within the shadows, outside of our enemy's notice. You and your involvement in this hunt are impossible to hide. Word of what we did in Derbycross must have been on the lips of every peer. If you were to go to Ivalla and began asking around for priest-assassins to take care of a sorcerer problem you have, well, that'd spread quickly, wouldn't it? Remember, it was a priest who attacked Thotham in Middlebury. If they have associates in the Church in Middlebury, then surely they do in Ivalla as well."

Oliver grunted. He wanted to argue, but she was right. If he visited the Church in Ivalla, there'd be no hiding it.

Sam continued, "Our enemies operate in secrecy, and so should we. I will go to Ivalla and find the Council of Seven. You stay here. Go to your brother's parties, spend time with the Child twins, do some cartography or whatever it is you do for the Company. Act like nothing is wrong, but watch. When the time comes, and we have the help we need, we'll make our move."

Oliver grimaced. "It feels wrong, you going into danger and me living in luxury."

Sam grinned. "I'm an unknown apprentice to a dead man no one remembered anyway. You're the son of the king. You've been publicly investigating sorcerous practices. They haven't come after you yet, but that doesn't mean they never will. You are in danger, Duke."

"Don't act like no one knows you were in Derbycross with me," he chided. "You may not be as prominent as I amongst the social set, but our enemies will be watching you just as closely."

She shrugged.

He ran his hand back over his hair, feeling the leather thong that tied it back. Their enemies might be watching her, but so what? If he traveled to Ivalla, word of it would be all over. The spirit-forsaken papers might even report on it. If they had any chance of avoiding notice, it had to be her alone. Sighing, he said, "It's a plan, then. What now?"

She glanced at the dark window beside the fireplace of her small room. "First, we need to sleep. Then, I need to find a way to Ivalla."

"And I need to live normally and not raise suspicion," he said, nodding, pinching his chin. "I'll keep my eyes open and learn what I can. If there's anything I can help with, you just have to ask."

"Good," said Sam, her shoulders tense, her face serious. "Duke, I need to borrow some money."

HE STUMBLED INTO HIS ROOMS, DAWN'S GLOW JUST BEGINNING TO lighten the windows. He kicked his boots off, shrugged out of his jacket, and tossed it over the back of a chaise in the sitting room. Still stripping, he made his way toward his bedchamber, fighting back a jaw-cracking yawn.

"M'lord," hissed a quiet voice.

He turned, raising an eyebrow at his valet, Winchester. The man was holding a silver coffee service, staring at him in confusion.

"What?" asked Oliver.

"Were you not… Are you just returning home?" queried the valet. "I thought you'd been here asleep all night."

"Where I've been is none of your concern," Oliver grumbled.

"I disagree, m'lord," remarked Winchester crisply. "If I don't know where you are, how can I plan your attire? How can I arrange your breakfast?" The valet lifted the coffee service to make his point.

"I'm sorry, Winchester," mumbled Oliver, turning back to his bedchamber. "It was a long night, and I need some sleep."

"You're not going on the hunt this morning?" prodded the valet. "You're supposed to meet your brother at the south carriage court in two turns of the clock, aren't you?"

"Ah, frozen hell."

THE PRINCE I

He eyed his brother askance, shaking his head. "Really, Oliver, you forgot about the hunt today? Viscount Brighton is an ideal match for our cousin, he's a potential member of our family. Is this the welcome you want to give the man?"

"I didn't forget," muttered Oliver, rubbing the stubble on his chin and wincing, "but if the man wants Lannia's hand, then she's the one who ought to be welcoming him. She or William."

"William is busy," claimed Philip, "and the viscount rarely makes it to Southundon. Our uncle asked me to receive Brighton here, show him around, and get a feel for whether Lannia would agree to be courted by him. She's our cousin, Oliver. We have a responsibility to ensure she marries well."

"If the viscount rarely makes it to Southundon, he's not a good match for our theatre-loving cousin, brother," challenged Oliver. "Besides, you are here, so I don't see why I need to be as well."

Philip rolled his eyes. "If I can be here, then so can you. You know Lannia far better than I. If at the end of today, you don't feel the viscount is right for her, then so be it. I'm not going to listen to your opinion on the man, though, until you've actually met him."

Oliver sighed and leaned against the back of the mechanical carriage they were waiting beside. Around them, Philip's guard was shifting restlessly. Viscount Brighton was a quarter hour late, and it was rare someone was late for an appointment with the prince. It was unheard of if that person wasn't Oliver.

"There she is," said Oliver, nodding toward the entrance of the courtyard.

Lucinda Wellesley, Philip's wife, was descending into the gravel-strewn yard. She was adjusting her skirts, cut short for the hunt, displaying the dark leather boots on her feet. They crunched on the gravel in the carriage court as she strode toward the men.

"Well, now he's in trouble," grumbled Philip, nodding toward his wife and forcing a smile onto his lips.

"All packed and ready?" she asked, her bright grin taking in Philip and Oliver. "It's a bit crisp, don't you think, to be waiting outside of the carriage? You didn't have to do it on my account, husband. Shall we depart for the hunt?"

Philip shook his head. "We are packed, but the viscount has not yet joined us."

Lucinda pursed her lips and glanced at Oliver.

"Don't blame me!" he protested. "I'm here."

"Looking rather worse for wear," suggested the princess, eyeing the duke up and down. "Long night last night, Oliver?"

The younger Wellesley simply shrugged. "I'm here."

Philip turned to the guards and instructed, "Go find the viscount, will you? Tell him the princess is ready to depart."

A man nodded and dashed off toward the same stairwell Lucinda had arrived from.

"Not there, man!" said Philip. "The viscount is staying in the guest quarters."

"He may not be," called a high-pitched voice.

"Shackles," said the prince, looking in surprise to see his chief of staff. "What do you mean?"

"I'm afraid there was a fire in the city late last night, m'lord," declared the man, holding a thin slip of parchment that Philip recognized as a scrip from the palace's glae worm station. "It was a mansion long owned by the Colston family, burned to the bare stone. I'm sure you recall the marquess has not been seen in weeks."

"You're telling me his house burned down last night?" wondered Philip, glancing at his brother.

Three weeks prior, Oliver had killed Marquess Colston beneath Dalyrimple Manor in Derbycross. Rather than explaining to the Congress of Lords that the man was a sorcerer, they'd simply done nothing. It was common knowledge that the marquess was missing, but only a handful of close confederates knew why. After consultation with his father, Philip had decided not to tell his chief of staff, Herbert Shackles. There were some things the man did not need to know.

"Not his house, no, ah…" stammered the prince's chief of staff. He glanced at Lucinda. "The building was associated with a society…"

"The Feet of Seheht?" questioned Philip. "The chapter house burned?"

"I believe it may have, m'lord," replied Shackles. "I'm not familiar with the society, but it seems there was a gathering there last night, m'lord. According to my sources, several peers and prominent merchants were inside. The fire brigades have so far only been able to confirm that bodies were found. They're all unidentifiable. My assumption, m'lord, is that news of missing individuals will soon trickle in."

The chief of staff looked nervously at the princess.

"My wife is not delicate," chided Philip. "How many have they found?"

Swallowing, Shackles continued, "The fire didn't die down enough for the men to enter and begin searching until nearly dawn. They're still digging out corpses, but already they've found several dozen bodies. I'm told there could be at least that many more."

"Several dozen?" gasped Lucinda, a hand covering her mouth.

Oliver shifted restlessly, and Philip glanced at him out of the corner of his eye. His youngest brother had been up to his neck in the investigation of the Dalyrimples. Even when instructed to leave the investigation to the professionals, he'd continued. Was he still pursuing leads? Philip had to admit, if he was, the Feet of Seheht was a logical place to look for sorcerers. Did Oliver know something?

"You think Viscount Brighton was there?" Lucinda asked Shackles.

The chief of staff shrugged. "I am not sure, m'lady, but a minor peer visiting Westundon for the first time in years when it just so happens there is a ceremony for this society? And now he's late to an appointment with the prince? It's only a guess, but…"

Philip grunted. "How did the fire start?"

Shackles responded, "There were no witnesses until the blaze was out of control, m'lord. By then, it was too late to determine the original cause. Perhaps some part of a ritual?"

"No," declared Philip. "The Feet of Seheht uses no fire in their aspirant ceremonies."

His little brother stared at him open-mouthed. He met Oliver's look and nodded. It'd been years since he'd been inside of the chapter house, but he doubted much had changed in that time. The members of the Feet of Seheht were a lot of things, but they were not arsonists. However the fire started, it wasn't intentional. Not on their part, at least.

Lucinda murmured, "Philip, I don't think you should…"

He waved a hand dismissively and continued, "We will let the fire marshal investigate the fire. Shackles, I'd like you to quietly ascertain the health of the minor peers. See if you can determine who is missing. If the bodies are unable to be identified, at least that will give us some clue as to who they might be. Those families will be facing significant embarrassment if word gets out about what was happening inside of the mansion."

"There were several peers scheduled to join you on the hunt today, m'lord," mentioned Shackles.

Philip nodded. "Lucinda and I will continue to the country estate and inform the group that the hunt is cancelled. While there, we can determine who is missing and who is not. Rumors will fly in that group, and it's best if we're there to quell them in person. Shackles, inquire discreetly in the city, and be sure not to start any whispered mutterings. Reach out to the staff of those who you suspect might have been involved. Track down Adelaide Boughton, but do not be obvious about it. Perhaps send a messenger to fetch her secretary. The countess was in from Swinpool this week, but I do not know where she was staying."

"You think she was—" began Shackles.

"Adelaide," muttered Oliver under his breath. "That's why she was familiar."

Philip and Shackles both turned to him.

Oliver looked back at them in surprise. "Sorry, I hadn't heard that name in years. She was in Westundon last night, you said?"

Philip eyed his brother suspiciously. Oliver knew more than he was sharing, but Philip had his secrets as well. Secrets which neither Shackles nor Oliver needed to hear.

Instead of responding to his brother, he took a safer route and changed the subject. Looking back to his chief of staff, he instructed, "Keep in touch with the fire marshal and send me a transmission on the glae worm filament the moment you have any information."

Herbert Shackles nodded curtly.

"You," said Philip, turning to his little brother, "do some digging around the palace. There are a number of peers visiting and several begged off attending the hunt this morning. It could be because they had plans which would have kept them awake most of the night."

"Who?" wondered Oliver.

Before Philip could respond, the princess interjected, "The Childs, for one. You are familiar with the family, yes, Oliver? Do you know of any late night plans they may have had?"

Philip watched as his little brother blanched. Oliver, despite his reputation as a rake, truly did care for the girls. As far as the prince knew, they weren't involved in the Feet of Seheht, but their father and uncle had been members of another society years earlier. If the twins were following in those footsteps…"

"The elder family members have been known to, ah, to attend functions such as these," murmured Philip. "Nothing to do with Colston, as far as I know, but—"

"But if someone was going to be the star of an orgy, it'd be one of those two," snapped Lucinda.

"That's unfair," protested Philip, leaning close and whispering so none of the guards could overhear. "The girls enjoy themselves, but no more than you did in your youth, wife."

"Do you have any reason to believe they were there last night?" questioned Oliver, stepping close to Lucinda, concern lowering his voice.

The princess tugged on her gloves and then hugged herself, making much of the cool air in the courtyard, but she did not respond.

"Do you?" pressed Philip.

"You know the history of the baron and his brother as well as I," declared Lucinda, "and you know how hard the family has been looking for Nathaniel. There is nothing they would stop at to get closure. Perhaps in Colston's entourage, they might have sought—"

"Oliver will check into it," interjected Philip, cutting his wife off before she said too much. "You're right. The Child's have been devastated, and it would not be out of character for Josiah."

Oliver's face darkened. "Both brothers, in such a short time…"

"Aria Child asked to attend the hunt today," mentioned Lucinda. "I had the servants arrange a carriage for her, and I believe it is that one over there. I imagine she would have rested well before the hunt. The game she's interested in gives a more vigorous chase than silver fox. She'll have to stay rested if she means to edge out her sister. Neither of those girls has ever been on time to anything, but perhaps if Aria deigns to arrive, she can save us the trouble and tell us about her father."

Oliver glanced at the waiting carriage. "Aria Child's?"

"Is someone calling for me?" lilted the girl.

Philip smirked as his brother jumped in surprise.

"Have you seen your father this morning, Aria?" questioned Lucinda.

"Yes," she said, slowing her walk, glancing around the group in confusion. "I breakfasted with him and my sister just a turn of the clock past."

Oliver let out a sigh of relief.

"There was a fire in the city last night. We believe some peers may have been trapped inside the building," said Lucinda. "I thought… Your father may know some of the victims. Regardless, the hunt is cancelled until we identify who is missing. I suppose we'll need to make notifications to their families once we find out."

Aria Child crossed her arms under her breasts, pushing them tantalizingly high. Philip, wondering how conscious the display was, could see a broad expanse of pale flesh pebbled by the chill air. He craned his neck closer until his wife's sharp elbow dug into his ribcage.

"That's too bad," purred Aria, her eyes fixed on Oliver. "I was hoping for a hard ride today. It can be so difficult to find suitable exercise in the city."

"I'm sure you'll manage," remarked Lucinda crisply.

"Yes, I suppose I will," responded Aria, giving the princess a wicked, predatory smile.

"Come, Philip," said Lucinda, grabbing his arm and turning up her nose. "Let's go inform the others."

He nodded, his eyes darting between Aria and Oliver. "While you're here, brother, make the rounds, inquire around, will you?"

Oliver nodded acknowledgement as Philip ducked inside the carriage.

Settling down on one of the padded benches, the prince eyed his wife. Her lips were pursed and she was glaring out the window.

He told her, "I don't understand why you dislike those girls."

"I do not like you staring at them," claimed Lucinda, turning her glare toward him.

He snorted. "A look, that is all. It's never bothered you in the past. What is it about those two?"

His wife looked back out the window as the carriage lurched into motion.

"Is it because Oliver is bedding them?" wondered Philip.

"Oliver?" questioned Lucinda, not turning to face him. "Why would it have anything to do with him?"

He snorted.

"Oliver is a boy," said Lucinda. "He plays with his toys as boys do. I am not jealous of any woman who finds herself in his bed."

"One might be forgiven for thinking such," remarked the prince, forcing himself to breathe evenly. "There was a time…"

"Why would I be jealous?" asked Lucinda, looking back to Philip and letting her full lips curl into a smile. "I'm married to the prince, the future king. You, m'lord, are the finest catch that Enhover has produced in a generation. There's no place I'd rather be than in this carriage with you."

Philip leaned back as the mechanical carriage rumbled out of the court onto the cobblestone-paved city streets. "Why concern yourself with the Child twins, then?"

Lucinda did not answer for a long moment. Then finally, she responded, "As I said, Oliver is a boy with his toys. I imagine those two have quite a bit of fun with him, but one day, he will find new toys. He'll move on as he always does. I'm afraid those girls have nothing but heartbreak in their future. I've tried to warn them, but they won't listen."

"Perhaps," said Philip, "but I think they've consummated the fling with eyes wide open. Those girls are no innocent, wilting daisies, wife. If anyone is in for a surprise, I think it will be Oliver. I'm told the baron is rather anxious following his brother's disappearance. He's been inquiring about suitable prospects for his daughters. If Oliver isn't careful, one of those girls is going to truss him up like a fattened hog and drag him thrashing and protesting down the aisle. But until then, they seem to be enjoying themselves."

"Your brother is quite the adventurer," replied Lucinda. "I'm sure that is exciting for a young woman."

"Are you?" asked Philip. When she didn't respond, he leaned forward and tugged the curtain shut over their small window. "It's a turn of the clock until we reach the country estate. What do you think, a little adventure?"

"I told you true," declared Lucinda with a laugh, her hands moving up to the laces of her blouse. "There is no place I'd rather be than right here."

THE CARTOGRAPHER III

OLIVER WOKE up staring at the plush, embroidered draperies that hung from the posters of his bed. He hated the things. It made him feel like he was sleeping inside one of his grandfather's old formal jackets, but evidently, it was expected that a peer's bedchamber be decked in enough of the thick brocade to clothe a small village. That, or Winchester had some cousin who made the damned things.

He sat up, a fist covering a yawn. Through the open door of his bedchamber, he saw firelight flickering in his sitting room. It was dark outside, and he was disoriented for a moment until he remembered what, and who, he'd been doing earlier that day. Evidently, she hadn't left. It seemed she was unwilling to allow any interlopers onto her territory once she'd claimed his rooms.

He'd spent days avoiding the Child twins, but earlier in the courtyard, he'd been so exhausted he couldn't figure a way to slip away from Aria's company. He'd nearly been too exhausted once they'd made it to bed, but he had rallied. Recalling the fervent, frantic exercise, he believed he'd accounted himself well.

Sighing, he didn't bother to dress and walked to the open door of the sitting room. "Still here?"

"I am," she said, turning so that a long, pale leg stretched along the chaise, the light of the fire reflecting on her smooth skin. She looked to be wearing one of his shirts and nothing else. "Is that a problem? Are you expecting company?"

"No, I'm not," he said. "No plans at all, actually."

"Perfect," she said, a smile curling her lips.

"Well," he admitted, running a hand over his head, "Philip asked me to check around and see if anyone was missing, but I've got Winchester on it. Gossiping with the servants, he'll get it done in half the time I could."

"I know," she replied. She pointed toward a covered tray on his table. "I asked him to bring us something to eat. Fruits, cheese, and I believe a little bread and nuts. They sent wine as well."

"Winchester knows my needs."

"Speaking of needs, you were rather lethargic this morning," she complained.

"I was up all night," he said and then held up a hand when she opened her mouth. "Not with another woman, Aria."

She pouted until he offered her a glass of wine and brought her a bite of cheese and bread. Aria accepted the wine gracefully then opened her mouth for the cheese and bread. She wrapped her lips around his fingers and let her teeth press against his skin.

Grunting, he moved back to the table and poured his own wine, a chill pebbling his bare torso away from the fire.

"Now that you've slept all day, perhaps you're ready to be up all night again?" she asked.

He sipped his wine and studied her.

"I'm not going to let you off as easy as I did this morning," she warned.

"You rarely do," he said, stepping toward her.

She held up a hand. "Not yet. This morning, you reeked of smoke, and you bled a little bit onto your sheets. We'll get you cleaned up, first."

"I bled?" he wondered, looking down at himself.

"Your elbow," she advised.

"Ah," he said, turning his arm to see a dark crimson scab. He must have gotten it scrambling away from the burning mansion the night before. "Just a shallow scrape."

"Every time I see you, you have a new scar," remarked Aria. "It's a bit exciting, I have to admit, but it's a bit scary as well. What were you doing last night, Oliver?"

"Business of the Crown, I'm afraid. I can't speak of it. If, ah, if the smoky smell bothers you…"

"Winchester is keeping water on boil for a bath," she said. "Ring him, and he'll bring it up."

Oliver did as she instructed, and in short time, a pair of porters were sloshing steaming water into a large copper bath placed in front of the fire. Oliver ate and drank, watching the baroness as she watched him.

Winchester ducked his head into the room, and Oliver asked for a report.

"Aside from the viscount, no one significant is missing from the palace, m'lord," he said. "They're either here or off at the country manor with your brother. There are some worrying updates about those staying in the city, though. A few minor peers, mostly younger sons and daughters. I don't believe anyone you're closely acquainted with, though I'm afraid you may know some of them. A few merchants have been reported missing, but those updates are passing through the city watch before they come to the palace, so our information is incomplete. In addition to Viscount Brighton, Adelaide Boughton is missing. Fortunately, the countess is the only one with a seat in the Congress of Lords who we cannot locate, but of course the viscount meant to court your cousin."

"Lannia won't notice his absence," Oliver said and then waved off Winchester.

Adelaide Boughton. The moment his brother had said the name, Oliver had known they wouldn't be able to find the countess. The slow intonation she'd been speaking atop the dais had masked her voice, but it was her, he had no doubt. No, the only question was why had his brother known to check on her. What was Philip hiding?

With Winchester and the porters out of the room, Aria said, "With my uncle gone, my father is becoming rather nervous. This new incident will do nothing to calm him. He's not going out, not making his usual appointments. There's no one left to continue the Child name unless Isabella or I find a prospect that will bear the family crest. A merchant with Company shares but no title might suit my father's needs."

"You're telling me that you intend to be formally courted?" asked Oliver.

"No, I'm telling you I intend Isabella to be formally courted," she responded, her chin held high. "I told you, Oliver, you will not be done with me so easily."

"I see," he mumbled, looking away.

A rap on the door and the two porters topped off the water in the tub.

Winchester returned with them and asked, "Your bath is ready, m'lord. Shall I assist?"

"I believe I can handle that tonight, Winchester," declared Aria, standing from the chaise and setting her wineglass down. "Oliver seems to have injured himself last night, and I believe a tender hand may help bring him back to health."

Oliver swallowed.

Aria pulled his shirt over her head and tossed it to the valet. "There's a bloodstain on the elbow, Winchester."

"I, ah, I'll see to the laundry then," muttered the man, his eyes falling to his feet.

"I think that's best," agreed Aria. "I can take it from here."

Sighing, Oliver refilled his wine and walked across the room like a prisoner to the gibbet. He settled into the hot tub. He wouldn't lie to himself, he was looking forward to the baroness' soft hands on his body, but this talk of her father and the family crest made the skin on his back crawl. Both of the twins' beauty hid a ruthless determination to get what they wanted. He'd been tugged back and forth between them often enough to admit without false arrogance that he was what they wanted. With discussion of prospects and courting looming, he couldn't help but worry how they'd try to sink their claws into him.

"You seem nervous, m'lord," whispered the baroness into his ear.

"Do you really mean to bathe me, Aria?"

She knelt beside the tub. "Of course, m'lord." She pushed him deeper into the water, then her hands, slick with soap, roamed his body.

She'd told him the truth, he knew. She had no intention of letting him go, and he wasn't sure that was such a bad thing, as long as Isabella could be convinced to find company elsewhere. Aria was a match his brother and father would both approve.

But the hunt for the sorcerers, the risks he was taking, he couldn't let her…

The thought fled his mind as Aria set down the soap and stepped into the tub, settling down on top of him.

THE PRIESTESS II

SHE EYED the derelict building with a burning itch of trepidation. It'd been years since she'd been inside. Years since she'd spoken to any of the scoundrels who frequented the place. Years since she'd axed the side of her hand into a woman's throat and then stormed out, unsure if the woman had lived or died.

She imagined the woman had lived, but Sam had woken in a sweat for months after the incident, gasping and worrying that she hadn't. There'd been no news of a killing in the district, which was no surprise. News rarely escaped the flimsy door or wax paper-covered windows of the Lusty Barnacle.

The Lusty Barnacle, such a stupid name. Half brothel, half pub, and half gambling den. The fact that three halves didn't equal one whole said everything that needed to be known about the place. It was an exhilarating mixture of everything that a priestess wasn't supposed to be involved in. It'd been fun, years ago, when she'd last found pleasure rebelling against the expectations of her mentor and the Church. Live in the full current of life, he'd told her. Well, she had. Looking back on that time now, it'd been rather exhausting.

Steeling herself, she stepped toward the crooked door that marked the only public entrance to the wobbling den of depravity.

Briefly, as her hand rested on the rusted tin doorknob, she wondered if those she sought would still be there after so many years. Then, she decided they had nowhere else to go. Like her, there was nowhere else in Westundon that they fit in.

She tugged open the door, the thin boards scraping across the threshold as she pulled on it in frustrating fits. A wave of smoke from cheap tobacco and expensive poppy syrup washed over her. She could smell the spilt ale on the floor and the spilt semen on the floors above. Had Duke been there, she would have claimed it smelled like him every time he went out with one of the baronesses, but it wasn't true. No level of natural wickedness smelled quite like the Lusty Barnacle. Such a stupid name.

Taking a last breath of fresh air, she stepped inside. The interior of the place seemed unchanged, suspiciously so. Scores of intoxicated patrons reveled around the large, open room. Tables and chairs, in various states of disrepair, were scattered about, but only a few of them were in use. In fact, in several places, people were sprawled out on the floor rather than risking the rickety, apt-to-collapse furniture.

Fires were roaring at both ends of the room, adding their own layer of smoke due to the poor ventilation. A number of targets had been painted on the walls for throwing darts or knives, but the wood was so pitted and scarred that it was difficult to see how anyone could determine whether they'd hit a mark.

That didn't seem to bother those who were playing the games, and the noxious smoke didn't bother those who were busy producing more of it. They hadn't come for the ambiance, she supposed. Many had come for the poppy syrup, which, as far as she knew, was still illegal in Enhover. Had a watchman deigned to set foot within a city block of the dilapidated building, they certainly would have smelled the sweet haze, and even if they couldn't, they were as likely to find a patron under the influence of the poppies as one who was not.

Though, to be fair, there were plenty of those, too. Ale poured like a river back behind the sticky, splinter-studded bar, and for many, that was enough. It was how the Lusty Barnacle had gotten started, she'd been told. Cheap ale and the even cheaper women.

Half a dozen of those women, flimsy clothing doing more to show their bodies than hide them, made their way through the stumbling crowd. After a brief negotiation, they would drag potential customers to the back stairs where they'd lead them up to one of the curtained rooms filled with beds so stained with sweat and sex that it made Sam sick just thinking about it. If the women found someone too intoxicated to handle the other end of the transaction, they'd simply dip their fingers into the unfortunate's purse and take their fee unnoticed. The girls at the Lusty Barnacle always got paid.

Sam made her way to the back bar where she knew the ale would be shockingly decent. Clean ale, dirty women. That had been the slogan they'd come up with later, after a few years in operation. Sam wondered what Andrew, the barman at the Befuddled Sage, would think of such a thing.

"Ale," she said, leaning against the bar and placing her elbows carefully on the counter to avoid the jagged splinters that stuck up from it.

A man, bald head reddened by either the drink or the sun, yellow-painted tin hoops dangling from his ears, turned and hauled on a tap, splashing frothy ale into a mug. The man's arms were as thick as her legs, and his open vest showed hard slabs of muscle. It looked like he spent his days hauling merchandise down at the docks rather than hauling on the taps. She told him as much.

He snorted. "I pull the taps when they ask me. I toss out the drunks when I feel like it. Don't think they hired me 'cause I could pour a clean head, do ya?" He flexed an arm like he was applying for a job all over again.

"What does one have to do to get tossed out of this place?" she wondered, glancing at the raucous crowd behind her.

"They'll get there," he said with a laugh. "Your first time here? It'll probably be your last."

"First time in a couple of years," she admitted. "I'm afraid I've moved on, but I came back to see some old friends."

He nodded. "I just started six moons ago, but already I can tell ya friendships don't last long in this place, girl. If you want my advice, you're wasting your time."

"Is Goldthwaite around?" asked Sam.

The barman eyed her but didn't answer.

"How about Lagarde?"

"She went back to Finavia," said the man, leaning on the bar and peering at her curiously.

"She's alive, then?"

He frowned at her. "Of course she's alive."

"That's good to hear," muttered Sam. "Pass a word to Mistress Goldthwaite for me, will you?"

"You looking to get hired on, girl?" wondered the barman. "Something wrong with you?"

"There's nothing wrong with me," said Sam, trying her ale and then glaring at the man. "Why?"

"If nothing is wrong with you, why do you want to work here?" he pressed. "A girl like you could earn pounds sterling in one of the nicer flesh shops. These girls make shillings and pence. Often as not, they're paid in poppy."

"Pence?" questioned Sam. "Surely..."

"Hand job," replied the barman, making the motion with his fist.

"Oh..." mumbled Sam. "No, I'm not looking to get hired. Will you tell Goldthwaite that Sam is here?"

"Not looking to get hired?" pressed the barman, shaking his head like he was catching her in a lie. "You want to work here, you gotta try out. Wait a quarter turn, and I'll have my break. I'll give you a go, and if you're good, the mistress will get my recommendation. You're not diseased, are you? If you are, you may as well leave now. I won't give it a go, and the mistress won't take you on even if I swore on the Church's shining golden circle that you were the best I'd ever had. You got to get that sorted, first, girl, if you're sick."

"I'm not diseased."

"Quarter turn then," said the barman, nodding confidently.

"She's going to cut off your twig and berries and feed them to you, Rance," claimed a honeyed voice.

"What?" barked the man, his eyes darting between a newcomer and Sam.

"The last person who tried to get her to lay on her back never spoke again," claimed the woman, leaning beside Sam on the bar. "You ever wonder why Lagarde couldn't talk? It's cause of this girl."

"Lagarde was a woman," growled the barman.

"Aye," agreed the newcomer, "and if Sam would do that to a woman, I'd hate to think of what she'll do to you."

The barman snarled, bowing up like a sail filled with a fresh wind. His muscles stood out in sharp relief underneath smooth skin, and his hands flexed, ready to grab her throat, she supposed. Sam wondered how she'd so quickly gotten off on the wrong foot, though, it always seemed to happen that way in the Lusty Barnacle.

"Stab his ball with one of your daggers," suggested the fallen woman who was leaning on the bar beside her. The woman offered a grin, showing a flashing golden tooth beside two missing ones.

"What?" exclaimed Sam and Rance at the same time.

"He's got two of 'em, and a man only needs one," continued the woman. "Stab one of his balls, and Goldthwaite'll be down here in a flash."

"I'll man the bar, Rance," interjected a sultry voice.

The three of them turned to see a middle-aged woman clad in diaphanous silks, the silhouette of her voluptuous body clearly visible beneath the thin material. She walked behind the bar with the confidence and grace of a woman who knew what everyone around her was thinking, and she liked it.

"Rance, go up and attend to Earl Resault," instructed the mistress. "I'm afraid Daphanae isn't what the man is looking for this evening."

"I, ah…"

"Rance," breathed Mistress Goldthwaite. "There's no need to try and look tough in front of our guest Samantha. She knows what goes on in this place and knows that everyone working under my roof has their price. Go attend to Earl Resault. I expect him to leave fully satisfied, Rance. Fully satisfied."

The barman, and evidently sometimes rent boy, stomped angrily toward the back stairwell.

"Earl Resault will pound that attitude out of him," promised Mistress Goldthwaite before turning to Sam. "I believe, girl, that I told you if I ever saw you again, I'd have you killed."

"That was years ago," replied Sam. "A lot has changed since then."

"Has it?" wondered the mistress, tilting her head and studying Sam. "Lagarde was never the same, you know? She never worked upstairs after that and recently went back to Finavia to be with her family. She was the best I'd ever hired behind the bar and second only to me on the mattress. Losing her cost me customers, Samantha, high-paying peers and merchants."

"No one lays on their back forever, Goldthwaite," said Sam. "Sooner or later, she was going to leave, whether or not I punched her in the neck."

"In her day, Lagarde could do things with her mouth that was the stuff of dreams, her clients would tell me," replied Goldthwaite. "They and I both could live with her never speaking again, but after you struck her, her throat was so swollen she could barely swallow a spoonful of soup, much less a—"

"She should have known better," snapped Sam, glaring at the mistress. "You knew better, once."

"Time heals all wounds, I suppose," replied Goldthwaite airily, only a slightly higher pitch in her voice showing she understood the implicit threat in Sam's remark. "I find now I only somewhat want to see you bleed."

"None of your toughs can handle me," said Sam, holding Mistress Goldthwaite's gaze. "If you send them at me, you'll only get them killed. Then, you really will have something to regret."

The mistress laughed, a light tinkling sound of mirth that seemed precariously out of place in the rough tavern. Sam had forgotten just how quickly the slippery woman could shift.

The mistress grinned at her. "I forgot how much I loved your spirits-blessed confidence, Samantha. What is it you want?"

"I want to see your daughter," replied Sam.

Goldthwaite scowled at her.

"I didn't know where to look for her, so I came here."

"You broke her heart," said the mistress. "I won't let you—"

"There are easier ways to get laid," interrupted Sam. "I'm not looking for that. I'm— I need to get a tattoo. A new one."

"She doesn't do those anymore," declared Goldthwaite. "It's too dangerous, for one, and two, I won't allow it."

"It's important," pleaded Sam. "I wouldn't ask if it wasn't."

"She doesn't do that work anymore," stated the mistress again.

"She remembers how to, doesn't she?" asked Sam. "It is her decision, Goldthwaite. Not yours, not mine. Tell me where she is and let her decide."

"What in the frozen hell are you two talking about?" asked the prostitute, leaning against the bar, her eyes darting between the two women like she was watching a championship match on the racquet courts.

"Go find yourself a man," instructed Goldthwaite, not bothering to look at the prostitute. When the woman opened her mouth to protest, the mistress shot her a hard glare, and the fallen woman scampered off without further comment. Turning back to Sam, Goldthwaite offered, "Want a real drink?"

"Why not?" drawled Sam. "I'm not going anywhere until we talk."

"I will not tell you where my daughter is," advised Goldthwaite. "You want a real drink and a talk, we can have it. We'll remember the better times, and if we can't think of any, we won't speak at all. Then, when you've finished your drink, you'll leave."

"No, I won't," insisted Sam.

The mistress stared at her, her jaw bunched, her eyes hard with determination.

"You're worried the Church will find her," said Sam. "What if someone else did, someone worse?"

"Worse?" questioned Goldthwaite. "Who is worse than that murdering mentor of yours?"

"He's dead," said Sam. "Killed in battle with a pair of sorcerers."

"There's no proper sorcery in Enhover anymore. Everyone knows that," snapped Goldthwaite. "You Church folk know it, too, but still you track down innocent men and women. Haul 'em off or kill 'em right there. How many guiltless lives has your Church ruined because you've been trained to do a task the world no longer needs?"

Sam held the older woman's gaze. "Thotham is dead. I was there, Goldthwaite. Sorcery, true sorcery, is not gone from Enhover. I don't care what Bishop Yates and his new Church say."

"And what's that got to do with my daughter?" snapped Goldthwaite. "They — you — will hunt her like a rabid dog."

"If someone could kill Thotham, what do you think they would do to Kalbeth? She's a target, Goldthwaite, for the Church and for anyone on the dark path. You know that is true."

"You and that old man have brought nothing but trouble for us," complained the mistress.

"He brought you her," said Sam, gripping the edge of the bartop.

"Whatever you think is happening, Samantha, it has nothing to do with us," stated the mistress. "I want nothing to do with you or anything you're involved in."

"Kalbeth wouldn't agree," stated Sam. She leaned forward. "Goldthwaite, I witnessed my mentor killed in a battle with

horrors that not even he had ever imagined. I've seen the muti-
lated bodies of dozens who were sacrificed to the dark powers.
Surely, you've read the papers. You know enough to understand
what you're seeing. The murders up in Harwick, the attack on
Duke Wellesley in Swinpool, last night when Marquess Colston's
mansion was burned to the ground with a few dozen peers
inside... Goldthwaite, I tell you this truly, it is all connected. You
want to know what happened last night? Someone is cleaning
house, killing anyone who could be a threat. Kalbeth does not
walk the dark path. I know that and you know that, but do you
think someone who is willing to burn down the mansion of a peer
would care? Do you think they'll take time to talk to the girl and
understand her motivations are pure, as Thotham and I did?"

Goldthwaite snorted. "Took time to understand her motivations? The both of you used her, he for what she was capable of,
and I seem to recall all you were interested in was getting between
her legs. I never worried about her safety until you came back into
her life."

Sam smirked. "Getting between her legs. Aye, there's some
truth to that. You of all people understand."

The mistress yanked a clear glass bottle of amber liquid off her
shelf and produced two battered tin cups from beneath the bar.
She filled the two cups to the rim and claimed, "Best pour I keep
in the house."

"I don't want to hurt her," assured Sam. "Others do."

Not speaking, Goldthwaite snatched her drink and downed it
in three gulps. Sam sipped at hers, waiting.

Finally, the mistress shook her head angrily. She snapped,
"Four Sheets Inn. Up in the scrivener's district. 'Bout as far from
here as I could bring myself to put her. Finish your drink, girl, and
if I see you again, I may not be inclined to be so polite."

Sam drank slowly, watching the mistress as she moved about
the bar, refilling customers and sorting out the dirty cups and
misplaced bottles the barman Rance had left behind. Sam took her
time because Goldthwaite had spoken the truth. The liquor slid

down her throat and warmed her gullet. It surely was the finest whiskey a place like this could get its hands on, but also, Sam waited to ensure the mistress wouldn't rush out and put a price on her head. It had happened once before, and Goldthwaite needed a few moments to consider what she was going to do when Sam stepped out of the door.

Eventually, it seemed, she decided. Goldthwaite leaned close to Sam and said, "Go on, then. Tell her I said hullo."

Nodding, Sam tossed back the rest of her drink and made her way through the crowd of fallen women and drunks.

Outside, mist lay over Westundon like a thick blanket. She was startled to feel damp flakes of snow falling against her skin. The city wasn't used to snow. Westundon didn't deal with it well. It'd be hell to get out of Enhover if the harbor showed any signs of freezing. A freeze would make the long journey to Ivalla that much longer.

Sighing, she started off toward the scrivener's district. One thing at a time.

THE CARTOGRAPHER IV

"Alexander," Oliver declared, "my twenty-percent share was based on the Company providing all of the transportation and manpower for the expedition. Now that my own assets are involved, I expect a larger percentage of the reward. You cannot ask for my resources without adequate compensation."

Finance Director Alexander Pettigrew frowned, his fingers drumming restlessly on the finely carved desk. It was Director Randolph Raffles' desk and had been a gift from the Company when he'd been named a director. The map carved into the surface was hopelessly inaccurate, Oliver knew, but no one had asked his opinion when it had been commissioned. Evidently, the price of that commission was sufficient that not even Raffles himself was interested in a recreation with a realistic depiction of the Company's territory.

A curious relic and rarely seen since Raffles preferred to conduct his business at his club, but Director Pettigrew was a notorious teetotaler, and there was no sense dragging the man from Company House to the Oak & Ivy for a cup of tea.

"Oliver," replied the Company's finance director, "twenty percent is the richest share we've ever awarded an individual involved in any expedition. Surely, you don't mean to—"

"The richest share, as it should be, no?" interrupted Oliver. "I paid my freight. I am the one who secured an escort from the royal marines. I am the one who convinced my father to extend our exclusive trading charter to the west. I am the one who will be leading this mission, and now, I'm the one who will be providing the assets and manpower. Why, tell the spirits, do you believe I should not be entitled to a larger share of this expedition? Would you rather continue without my involvement, without the royal marines and exclusive rights for the next fourteen years? You know as well as I that there are cabals merchants in Southundon prepared to officially organize and petition the Crown for a charter."

"The prime minister has already granted our exclusive petition," mumbled Pettigrew, his fingers tracing the rough outline of the Westlands carved into the surface of Raffles' table.

The finance director found a small knob meant to represent the Company's one colony on the far continent. Oliver watched the man's finger trace the location. He didn't bother to tell the finance director that in reality, the location of the compound was over one hundred leagues north of where the woodworker had fancifully placed it.

"William has granted the petition," agreed Oliver, "but Baron Josiah Child is one of my father's oldest friends. He's been angling to expand his New Enhover Company's trading footprint for years now. With a sad story about his missing brother and the Crown's inability to solve the crime, how do you think the man's chances fair at getting our charter revised to a joint expedition instead of exclusive rights?"

Director Pettigrew snorted. "I'm well aware of the Child family's attempts to influence your own. Josiah, his brother if he ever resurfaces, and of course the twins. It's common knowledge, Oliver, that it is not just King Edward who, shall we say, is well acquainted with the Childs."

Oliver grinned at the older man.

"Please explain," continued Pettigrew, his voice rising in

timbre and a finger raising to point skyward, "why would granting you a larger share of the expedition help with this influence problem?"

"Aria and Isabella Child both have a one percent share of the Company's expedition to the Westlands," explained Oliver. "If the charter remains exclusive, it is worth far more to them than if it is termed a joint expedition, even if their father is the one heading the competition. If the charter is opened to the New Enhover Company, it will be open to anyone, after all. There are dozens of other interested parties who'd leap at the chance to sponsor travel to the Westlands. With small effort, I believe I can convince Josiah to stay out of the Westlands trade and allow his daughters to collect income with no risk to the family holdings. It's simple business. Why take the risk and step between the Company and the Crown if the Childs already stand to profit? When Josiah understands the girl's shares are contingent on my continued approval, I believe he'll withdraw his own petition quickly."

Frowning, Director Pettigrew questioned, "You mean to bribe the Childs with Company shares? The board of directors will never allow Josiah Child a voting interest."

"The shares have already been allocated," remarked Oliver. "Both girls have subsidiary rights to my own shares. Five percent each. They stand to benefit financially, but I retain the voting block. Their stake will increase when mine does. The paperwork is filed at Company House in Southundon, Pettigrew. As my fortunes improve, so will theirs. The value of the charter staying exclusive will be apparent."

Oliver held the finance director's gaze, refusing to back down from his demand for additional compensation, hoping his eyes didn't betray a flutter of uncertainty. It seemed everyone knew of Oliver's tryst with the twins, and while the Child family collecting additional Company shares would bring a smile to the baron's face, it was possible the man might decide an even larger allocation was in the offing if he could foist one of the twins on Oliver in a permanent match.

It wasn't good business, asking a man for a favor while bedding both of his daughters.

"I must have missed the notification of ownership change," muttered the finance director. "Was a transmission sent to my office?"

Director Raffles coughed and nodded. "It was sent on the wire some weeks ago, Alexander."

"Pardon me," said Oliver, frowning at Pettigrew. "As finance director, I would imagine you would review every transfer of ownership. Is this something you've assigned to a deputy, or perhaps you're behind on your work due to your travels? Is it wise, Director, for you to be in Westundon with your responsibilities unattended back at the capital?"

Alexander Pettigrew flushed. "Boy, I take my—"

Director Raffles smacked a hand down on the table. "Frozen hell, Pettigrew. Oliver's right. You ought to be personally reviewing any transfer of shares! You ought to have sewed up the issue with the New Enhover Company months ago, and when you came to ask the son of the king to supply his own airship and another contingent of his father's marines, you damn well should have been prepared to offer a larger stake in the expedition!"

Red-faced, the finance director glared at Raffles.

"What is really happening in the capital, Alexander?" questioned Raffles.

The three men were silent for a long moment. Oliver studied the visiting finance director, wondering what it was the man was hiding. Randolph Raffles had known Pettigrew for years, and if Raffles thought something was amiss, then something was.

Finally, Pettigrew admitted, "There's been some tension from the situation with Governor Dalyrimple."

"Tension?" pressed Raffles, piercing his old friend with a steady, blue-eyed gaze.

"Pierre de Bussy, Finavia's governor in the tropics, he heard about the unpleasantness," mumbled Pettigrew, his eyes fixed on the carved wooden table in between the men. "He's been writing to Edward and William, questioning the Company's governance in the region. Worse, he tracked down Cardinal Langdon, and now the cardinal is sending envoys to Edward. You both know the king and how well he takes to that type of interference."

"And?" asked Raffles.

"And the king has demanded the Company provide adequate security in the tropics. With the corsairs taking prizes, our governor turning out to be a…"

"Sorcerer," interjected Oliver.

Pettigrew swallowed and continued, "Edward wasn't happy you were at risk, m'lord. He felt the Company should have been monitoring our agent more closely. He's threatened to take an active role of governance of the colonies if we do not… I won't describe it as the king did, but he was rather blunt."

"I'm sure he was." Oliver laughed.

"It's not a laughing matter, m'lord," complained Pettigrew. "The Company's board of directors is nervous, nervous for the first time since I've had a seat at the table. This is about more than a simple share allocation in the Westlands. There are political and commercial complexities like nothing I've seen in my career. We cannot simply wave our hands and adjust our calculations. We must consider all factors."

"Oh, I understand how you are nervous about these developments," remarked Oliver, standing and placing his fists on the table so he loomed over the finance director. "If my father decides to intervene, the impact to the Company's books would be bleak. I quite expect you'd be the first man sacked if that were to happen. My father taking an interest in Company business is rather less of a concern for me, though, you understand? Whichever way it went, I stand to benefit as a member of the Wellesley family or as a shareholder of the Company."

Pettigrew swallowed, his loose jowls wobbling as little tremors rocked him. "Crown involvement in Archtan Atoll would mean—"

"I have no shares in Archtan Atoll," reminded Oliver. "As a

Company man, I suppose I could speak to my father, convince him the board has all in order, and the incident I was so deeply involved in was overblown. I think I may be a bit more persuasive with my father than either Governor de Bussy or Cardinal Langdon. That's asking a rather lot of me, though, don't you think? Particularly given you've already made a request for my assistance with no consideration, and particularly since having my father involved could open far more opportunities for me personally. King Edward has rarely become interested in commercial affairs. I daresay he'd be glad to appoint me as a steward for whatever involvement he deems necessary. Isn't that an interesting thought?"

"We just don't have the airships available," mumbled Pettigrew. "What resources we have, we're devoting to reinforcing our presence around the atoll. If we're to proceed, it must with the Cloud Serpent."

Oliver snorted.

"Give him a thirty-percent share, Pettigrew," instructed Raffles. "This is foolish."

The finance director did not respond.

Raffles frowned. "What?"

"With the threat of intervention, there's been some concern that already the Wellesleys are too deeply involved in our affairs," croaked Pettigrew. "Some on the board feel that what we need is fewer Crown entanglements, not more."

Oliver stood straight and laughed out loud. Pettigrew stared down at his hands. Raffles shook his head in consternation.

"Director, you have a decision to make," declared Oliver. "One way or the other, the Company's affairs will be deeply entwined with that of the Crown. There's no way around it. You want Crown protection, you want the royal marines, you get the royal line as well. Your choice, Director, is which royal do you want to be entangled with? You and the board of directors can do business with me or with my father."

Squirming in his seat, Pettigrew refused to meet Oliver's look.

"You'll get thirty percent, Oliver," declared Raffles. "I'll accompany Alexander back to Southundon and make sure of it."

"That's unnecessary," whispered the finance director.

"You will handle it?" questioned Raffles. "Alexander, the duke is right. The Company and the Crown have long enjoyed a symbiotic partnership. Perhaps the Company's directors wish otherwise, but it's the man on the throne who gets to decide when that relationship is over. For the sake of my own bank ledger, I do hope the board can be convinced to make the right decision."

"They will be," agreed Pettigrew, his head bowed.

"Then I think it's best you leave now and go do it," instructed Raffles.

"If-If the share is allocated..." stammered the finance director.

"When I have the signed papers that my stake is increased to thirty percent, with consideration for the Child twins, then the Cloud Serpent will be ready to sail. I will ensure my father stays out of it, and I promise you, Pettigrew, he will listen to me before de Bussy or Langdon."

The finance director stood and half-bowed, catching himself and offering a trembling hand which neither Raffles nor Oliver deigned to shake. When Pettigrew finally scurried out of the office, presumably out of Company House and to the rail station, Raffles shook his head and turned to Oliver.

"A drink at the Oak & Ivy?" he asked. "I do think he'll get the directors sorted, and I've no doubt you can talk your father down, but I'm worried about Cardinal Langdon. I didn't know the extent of his involvement, and I don't like it. The Crown may not be the only entity he's trying to manipulate."

Oliver ran a hand back over his hair, staring at the doorway Pettigrew had exited. "The cardinal hasn't been involved in Crown or Company business in years, right?"

"That's what concerns me," replied Raffles.

"Let's go get that drink, Director."

"My apologies about Pettigrew," said Director Randolph Raffles, sinking into the plush, overstuffed leather chair. "The man is getting daft in his later years. His son handles most of his responsibilities, I've heard."

"I thought Pettigrew was your friend," remarked Oliver, sitting opposite the director.

"He was before I earned a seat at the director's table," guffawed Raffles.

He gestured to an attendant and ordered a Finavian sparkling wine while Oliver ordered a red varietal from Ivalla. The attendant also dropped off a small pouch at the elbow of the director.

He pulled out his carved ivory pipe and a sack of shredded tobacco leaf. "The smoke won't bother you, will it?"

"If it does, we're in the wrong room," observed Oliver.

The director winked.

While Raffles packed his pipe, Oliver studied the smoking room of the Oak & Ivy. So early in the afternoon, there were few others inside. This time of day, the crowd was in the tea room.

"Have you ever considered joining?" wondered Raffles, evidently noting Oliver's look.

Oliver shrugged. "Members must have at least forty winters under their belts, no?"

The director smirked. "Not in your case."

The attendant returned and Oliver picked up the wine glass the liveried man left. He sipped it, tasting the rich bouquet, dark stone fruit and pepper. He looked to Raffles. "Tell me about Pettigrew."

It was Raffles turn to shrug. He inhaled and then blew out a steady stream of pipe smoke. "The man was quite sharp a few decades ago, but I believe the numbers have gotten beyond him. He was appointed before we discovered the levitating islands of Archtan Atoll, Imbon, the Westlands, all of it. The Company was a straightforward trading concern, then. As long as we paid our taxes on time, we rarely had any interaction with the Crown. We certainly never had to deal with the headaches that come with colonial occupation. We petitioned the Crown from time to time, of course, but it was never turned back on us. I'm afraid the role of finance director in this new environment is beyond Alexander Pettigrew's capabilities, and it wouldn't surprise me if the director most concerned with Crown involvement is actually him."

"What's to be done about it, then?" wondered Oliver.

"We need another man nominated to fill the position, after the directors vote Pettigrew out, that is," mused Raffles. "He'll retain his shares but only as a passive owner and not a managing partner. Plenty for him to support his estate and dowry off his daughters, but not the sums he's become accustomed to."

"I've never paid much attention to Company politics," admitted Oliver.

"You're a son of the king," replied Raffles. "You've never needed to pay attention to it."

"Interceding with my father, supplying my own assets on expedition... Perhaps it is time I gave it more of my attention," mused Oliver.

"Perhaps," agreed Raffles. "If you mean to have an active role, you should know which strings you're pulling, which boats you're rocking. These last few weeks, though, I wondered if the Company was still what held your interest."

Oliver frowned.

"Once a man gets a taste for a certain kind of adventure, it's difficult to turn from it, I've always thought."

"Are you talking about Isisandra Dalyrimple or sorcery?" questioned Oliver.

Raffles raised an eyebrow. "Is there a difference?"

Oliver shook his head. "No, I suppose not."

"What is it, then?" questioned Raffles. "Do you mean to pursue these investigations, or do you intend to return to Company business and lead the expedition to the Westlands?"

"There's nothing left to investigate," remarked Oliver, toying with his wine glass, thinking of Sam's admonishment to live normally and keep their investigation secret. "Everyone died underneath the Dalyrimple estate. We destroyed it, you know, to ensure no hint of what was inside escaped. There's nothing left of that place but blackened earth and shattered stone."

Raffles nodded. "I heard."

"Much is unknown to me still, but I believe Isisandra Dalyrimple learned those dark arts from her parents," claimed Oliver. "Now, all of them are dead, and everything they owned has been put to torch. That's it, as best I can deduce."

Pulling on his pipe, Director Raffles studied Oliver.

"What?" asked Oliver.

"I wasn't sure you'd be willing to let it lie," admitted Raffles. "Once you've got the scent of something, you don't let go. You're like your father in that regard."

Oliver snorted. "Well, what's occupying my mind now is the Westlands. I've been eager to go there for years, and we're finally on the cusp. If your friend—"

Raffles held up a hand in protest. "He'll allocate you the shares, Oliver, do not worry. It's the only logical thing to do."

"I appreciate your help in the matter," said Oliver.

"Friends help friends." Raffles puffed contentedly on his pipe.

Eyeing him, Oliver leaned forward. "I know you well enough, old man. What is it you want help with?"

Smiling back, Raffles tried, and failed, to look innocent.

"Director of Finance, is it?" guessed Oliver.

"We both agree Pettigrew isn't right for the position," mentioned Raffles. "I hope you believe I could do a better job."

"I do," admitted Oliver, sitting back, "and a fair share of the Westlands expedition is just compensation for my support, but it's not only me you need, is it? You need to be politicking with the other directors. It's become rare for you to travel to Southundon."

"The theatre is better in Westundon this season," claimed Raffles.

Oliver rolled his eyes. "My cousin says the same."

"I wasn't lying earlier when I said the Company and Crown have always been entwined," said Raffles. "Had we any chance of independence, it vanished when the Company acquired territory and requested the Crown's aid in protecting it. We brought the Wellesleys in, and once opened, that door cannot be shut. It's as you said — we have a choice. Which royal do we want to entangle ourselves with? I suspect the board will value highly any man with a connection to the royal line. Your father and brothers are busy tending to the needs of the empire. You, my boy, are sitting in my club having a drink with me. I could go grovel at the feet of the senior directors in Southundon, but I'd rather have them come to me."

Oliver raised his glass. "I see."

Raffles set down his pipe and mimicked the gesture. "There could be many mutually beneficial opportunities in the next several years, Oliver, if we're both intent on pursuing them."

"You're worried I'll chase off on some new interest?" questioned Oliver. "That I'll be distracted with conquests of a sort?"

"Your conquests of one sort have never been a problem," remarked Raffles. "Whether it was the Dalyrimple girl or the Child twins, you have my support and envy. You're a born adventurer, Oliver, and men like you seek the next horizon. Adventures in the bedchamber, adventures exploring this world, those things do not worry me."

"Sorcery," said Oliver, studying the man across from him. "That's what worries you? No, Randolph, I am done with that darkness, and it'd please me if I never saw anything like it again. The Dalyrimples are gone, and that's enough. Let the Church sort it out if it comes up again. We certainly stuff their coffers full enough."

"Good to hear, Oliver, good to hear," said Raffles. "The Church ought to deal with these things, of course. It is not the organization it used to be, though, is it?"

"What are you getting at?" questioned Oliver. "You're thick as thieves with Bishop Yates. Can he not alleviate any anxiety you have?"

"Cardinal Langdon," answered Raffles. "The man is a true

friend of Governor de Bussy, you know? The cardinal has family in Finavia, and de Bussy married the cardinal's favorite cousin. In summers, the easiest place to find the old priest is on de Bussy's country estate in the south of Finavia. It's certainly nowhere near Enhover. The only reason that deviant hasn't been replaced as cardinal is the protection he gained from an association with the governor. Pierre de Bussy is a short step below King of Finavia, if they had one. Not to mention, your father prefers a cardinal who's never here. The Church won't cross the most powerful men in government on that continent and this one. I worry all of this has given Langdon false confidence that he has the power to manipulate the political situation."

Oliver frowned. "I did not realize how close Langdon was with the governor."

Raffles nodded and picked his pipe back up. "It's no matter, usually, but now that de Bussy has Langdon bothering your father, I don't doubt the Church will support another inquiry into sorcery both in Enhover and in the colonies. You understand, the board of directors have some legitimate concerns with any interference into our operations."

"Any inquiry won't be supported by me," remarked Oliver.

Raffles nodded. "I mean to stay on your good side, Oliver, but you know I'm a Company man. Wouldn't do, you leading our Westlands expedition and trying to investigate our activities in the tropics."

"Like I said, I'm done," responded Oliver. "The Church should handle it, if there's anything left to handle. If Langdon and his ilk think they can pressure my father, though, they're going to be surprised. There's nothing that ornery old man loves more than refusing to do what's requested of him. He thinks in terms of the Wellesleys, the Crown, and Enhover, in that order, and the list stops there. But if it sets your soul at ease, I will discuss Langdon with the old man when I bring up Crown involvement in Company business."

"I thank you for that, Oliver."

The duke finished his wine and waited for an attendant to scurry over. He requested a refill, and when the man left, he let his gaze slide across the room. Act normal, watch and listen, that was his part of the hunt now. As he looked around the Oak & Ivy's smoking room, he couldn't help but think the most powerful men in Westundon were gathered within the silk and polished wood-covered walls of the club. If a sorcerer was lurking in high society, it was no great leap to imagine him sitting in that very room, puffing on a pipe, calling the attendant for another round, and relaxing after a long night of deviant ritual and blood sacrifice.

"You said exceptions could be made to the age limit for the club?" asked Oliver, turning to Raffles.

Raffles grinned back at him. "With the right nomination, yes, I think they could be."

When the fresh glasses arrived, Raffles raised his. "To a long and prosperous friendship."

"To prosperity," agreed Oliver, raising his glass.

THE PRIESTESS III

"Welcome to the Fourth Sheet Inn," called a cheery voice from behind the bar.

Sam blinked at the woman. Bright lights from mirrored lanterns illuminated the space far more than was proper for a pub after midnight.

"Get you a drink?" asked the smiling woman.

"Ale," replied Sam. "A big one."

Nodding, the woman hurried off to pour the drink.

Sam turned to survey the room and snorted. In the far corner, she spotted a curtained alcove with a sign hanging above it offering palmistry.

When the barkeep returned, Sam asked, "Is the palm reader in?"

"She is," confirmed the woman. "When the curtain is closed, she's with a client, but it doesn't take more than a quarter turn of the clock most times. You fancy learning your future?"

Not looking back at the barkeep, Sam said, "No. I don't think there's anything there I want to know."

The curtain was pulled back, and the barkeep's voice buzzed on unheard. A middle-aged woman stepped out of the alcove, nodding thanks and then hurrying away.

Sam strode toward the curtain. She peeked inside. The woman sitting in the alcove jumped in surprise.

"I thought you could read the future," drawled Sam.

"I read possibilities," retorted the woman. "After so long, the possibility of seeing you here was slim."

Sam stepped inside and tugged the curtain closed.

"Why are you here?" questioned the woman.

"I came to get my palm read. Isn't that what you do?"

The woman tilted her head, waiting.

"Shall we go to your room?" asked Sam.

The woman's eyebrows rose. "My room, is it?"

"I want to talk, Kalbeth" claimed Sam. "I know it's been a long time, but this is important. I wouldn't have come if it wasn't."

"Yes, I'm sure you wouldn't have," said Kalbeth slowly. She waved Sam back out of the alcove and followed her into the common room.

With a nod at the barkeep, she led Sam up the stairs of the inn, climbing until they reached the top floor. Underneath low eaves, she took Sam down a hall to a locked door. Slipping an iron key from a pouch on her belt, she unlocked the door and then knelt, flicking the key underneath the door. When she opened it, she unhooked a thin wire that had been fixed to the bottom of the door and turned a small, copper disc that had been set in the center of the doorframe on the floor. From over the woman's shoulder, Sam saw she'd pushed a complex geometric pattern out of alignment by turning the disc. The woman stood and held out a hand, inviting Sam to enter.

"Paranoid?" asked Sam.

"If you can find me, then others like you can find me as well," said the woman, stepping into the room. "Did you come to kill me?"

Blinking at her, Sam stammered, "O-Of course not. Why would you think that?"

"It is your job, is it not, to kill those like me?"

"My job is eradicating sorcery in Enhover," snapped Sam. "What you do—"

"What I do is sorcery, just like what you do," challenged Kalbeth. "The only difference is that the Church condones it for you, condones it because you'll kill all of the others. What do you think they'll do when you've eradicated sorcery, Sam? You think they'll let you retire comfortably by the sea?"

"No," said Sam, thinking of her mentor. "I don't think retirement is in the cards the spirits will deal me. If you really could read palms, you'd know that."

"There's a difference between reading palms and telling the future," murmured Kalbeth. She began removing bangles and colored, glass-studded tin rings and bracelets, piling them all on a small table at the side of her room. Her boots were next, and then she discard a pattern-covered shawl.

"It's surprisingly roomy in here," said Sam, glancing back toward a dark doorway where she assumed the woman's bed was.

"I'm short, so I don't mind the eaves," claimed Kalbeth. "The room has a sitting area, a bedchamber, and a balcony. If I need anything else, I get it downstairs."

"You do enjoy being outside," said Sam, thinking of the balcony, her voice heavy with sorrow.

"It's the only place I can find quiet," remarked the woman. "Even a clean place like this has seen death. It's hard to find anywhere not haunted by the spirits. Outside, at least, the wind will carry their voices away."

"Why don't you go to the country or to the sea?" questioned Sam. "That is not the life I am destined to live, but you could find solace."

Smiling wanly, Kalbeth shook her head. "Solace... No, that is not the life I am destined to live, either, is it? You did not find me to grant me peace and quiet, Sam. Why are you here? Do you want me to read your palm, tell you what these new spirits in your shadow are saying? There are more of them than when I last saw you. You've been busy. I can see the possibilities in your future, but the only clue to your past is the stain of the souls you've sent to the other side. What have you been doing, Sam?"

"I don't need you to read those souls. I know exactly why they're haunting me," claimed Sam. She drew a deep breath and exhaled slowly. "I came for a tattoo."

Kalbeth cringed. "I don't do—"

"It's important," insisted Sam. "There's real sorcery out there, Kalbeth. I... I've seen horrible things. Death, Kalbeth, like you cannot imagine. Terrible rituals, human souls sacrificed and spent. Dozens of them at a time."

The woman grunted, looking away.

"I am not lying," said Sam. "I had to use what you inked onto my skin."

"Show me," instructed Kalbeth, taking a step toward Sam.

"I..."

"You mean to get a tattoo without taking your shirt off?" chided the woman.

"That's not why I came here," declared Sam. "It's not what I want."

"You want a tattoo," agreed Kalbeth. "You told me. Is that all you want?"

Sam shifted, meeting the other woman's eyes. Her former lover, when they had been girls, and sometimes since. It was a lifetime before, it felt like.

"That is not all that I want," stated Kalbeth.

"I need..."

"After," insisted the woman. Then, she stepped the rest of the way to Sam and grabbed her head, tilting it and kissing her.

"It had been a long time since you've been with a woman?" questioned Kalbeth.

Sam spluttered, "It's not easy to, ah, to find someone who isn't a man."

"I know," agreed Kalbeth, poking at Sam's wrist, pinching the skin and following the tattoo up her arm. "We live in their world. Any port in a storm, though, ey? You have to swim the current somehow."

Sam looked away, choosing not to mention it had only been weeks since she'd been with Isisandra. Kalbeth didn't need to know. It would only make her jealous, and if it didn't, then the explanation of the break-up was going to be rather complicated. Instead, she asked, "Have you?"

"Been with another woman since you?" Kalbeth laughed. "Of course I have, when I can find one that's interested in me and not coin or some leverage against my mother." Muttering under her breath, she added, "I've been down that path too many times."

"That's good," offered Sam. "I mean, that you've…"

"That I wasn't ruined by you?" questioned Kalbeth. "You think too highly of yourself, Sam. You always have. No, you didn't ruin me. You didn't send me crying into the arms of a man or any other nonsense, but I won't say it didn't hurt."

"It couldn't have been," murmured Sam.

"It couldn't have been as long as you worked for the Church," corrected Kalbeth. "If you'd left, we could have been together."

"I— I could not leave."

"You are not a priestess, Sam," said the woman. She sat back on her heels, gesturing to the long vein of dark tattoo that bridged Samantha's wrists, traveling over her arms, her collarbone, and meeting in the center of her chest. "Not the kind of priestess the modern Church wants."

"I agree with you there," acknowledged Sam.

Kalbeth studied her, brushing back her jet-black hair. "You understand, then? You are a tool to them, and when they are done with you, you will be discarded."

"I understand, but I will not quit," said Sam. She saw the disappointment in the other woman's face. "It is not about the

Church, Kalbeth. It is about what I have seen. I cannot turn from that darkness. Murders, sacrifices, the kind of dark ritual that you and your mother would tell me is only a flight of fancy told to scare children. It is not. I have seen it, and I know. My mentor, Thotham, you remember him?"

"Of course," replied Kalbeth.

"He was killed in a battle with a ten-yard tall monstrosity that had wings and claws the size of my arm. We faced hundreds of shades. Hundreds! Grimalkin, wolfmalkin… Those kinds of things cannot be allowed to exist, Kalbeth. I cannot quit after seeing that. There is no one else trained for dealing with this, just me."

"You could not quit before seeing those things," argued the woman.

Sam remained silent. There was no answer to give.

Kalbeth stood, her naked body gleaming in the lantern light. Like a dancer, she stepped lightly over to a cupboard and opened it. "Wine?"

"Yes," replied Sam.

Kalbeth poured them both cups and returned to sit in front of Sam, their knees touching as the woman settled down, her legs crossing beneath her, her thighs spread wide.

Sam swallowed and looked away.

Smiling over the rim of her wine cup, Kalbeth murmured, "You were not offended earlier."

Sam drank her wine.

"I can repair the damage to your current tattoos in three, maybe four turns of the clock," advised the black-haired woman. "You have some light scar tissue where the heat burned your skin. It is fixable if I work slowly. You'll regain the full function of the script."

"That is good," responded Sam.

"You understand what the cost will be?"

"There are souls within my shadow," replied Sam. "Can you use them instead?"

Kalbeth shrugged, her expression grim. "I can try, but there must be something to stitch them to. When you activate the pattern, and the souls are spent, a piece of you will be as well. The cost is unavoidable, Sam. You, what is core to you, will be tattered and torn, and part of it will be on the cold, other side. Do you understand?"

"I do," whispered Sam. "Part of me already is."

"You should know the taint on you will be obvious for a time," continued Kalbeth. "Weeks, at least. Anyone attuned will not be able to miss the darkness swirling around you. Until your skin and the shroud heals, it will not go away. There is nothing I can do to lessen the shadow. Sam, I think the price is too high. I do not think you should do this."

"I do not have a choice," responded Sam. "Without it, I'm not sure I have the skill to prevail. Kalbeth, without this, I will die."

"With it, part of you will still die," argued the woman.

Sam placed a hand on the other woman's bare leg. "I have to do this."

Kalbeth stared into her eyes. Sam guessed she was looking for hesitation, trying to find a chink in Sam's resolve, some way she could talk her out of it. Sam knew the cost, for herself and for Kalbeth. The work Sam was requesting would not come cheap. It had to be, though. It had to be.

"If you insist," said Kalbeth after a long moment. "There is something else I can do as well, something I began working on shortly after you… after you left the last time. I can shield you from a shade's notice. It is not fool-proof. If you touch them, they will become aware of you, but for a time it may give you some protection. It is a ward against the other side, in a sense."

"That sounds useful," agreed Sam.

"Do not rely on it," warned Kalbeth.

"Any little bit helps," said Sam. "You will do it, then?"

Brows furrowed in thought, Kalbeth was silent a moment. Finally, she said, "I will do this, but it will take time. Four days, I think."

"Will it?" questioned Sam dubiously.

Smirking, Kalbeth allowed, "Perhaps three if we took no breaks. I don't work for free."

"I can pay you," replied Sam.

"That's not what I meant," said the woman. "I won't take—"

"I know," said Sam. "It's just… I have access to more sterling than I need, now. I'd like you to have some of it."

"I am fine," said the girl. "What I cannot earn reading palms, my mother is happy to—"

"I have no one else to give it to," interrupted Sam. "It is not because… because I feel I must pay you. It's because I have the silver and I want to share it with you. You can do whatever you see fit with it. Give it to the orphanage if you do not want to keep it, but please, will you take it?"

"Why don't you give it to the orphanage yourself?" asked the woman. Without waiting for a response, because she knew the answer, she continued, "Where did you get access to so much sterling that you want to give it away?"

"I have a patron now," said Sam with a grin. Seeing the other woman's expression, she quickly amended, "It is not like that. Really."

"Tell me, then, what is it like?"

"After the wine," assured Sam. "After the wine and after we take a break."

Smiling back at her, Kalbeth said, "I know when the ink dries, you will leave me again. I know it, Sam, but until then, I have missed you."

"I missed you, too," replied Sam, wondering if she meant it. She leaned forward and kissed her old friend.

THE CAPTAIN I

"THIS WAITING IS A BIT SHIT, if you ask me, Captain," grumbled First Mate Pettybone. He tossed back a jigger of grog. "There's only so much time we can stall the crew with these training maneuvers. Sooner or later, the boys are gonna want to move. If we don't, we'll lose 'em."

"I did not ask you," remarked Captain Catherine Ainsley. The first mate harrumphed, and she turned to eye him. "We're not working for the Company or some minor merchant, First Mate. We're working for Duke Oliver Wellesley himself, a son of the king. It's going to be different."

"Different?" questioned the first mate. "What does that mean? This crew didn't hire on because they wanted to spend time in port with their wives. If that was the case, they woulda been coopers or butchers or some other honest trade. Naw, they signed on an airship because they want to see the world."

"It's not my concern whether the crew spends their time in port with their wives or with anyone else," responded Ainsley. "What they do in their free time is up to them. What is up to me is what they do when we're getting paid good sterling silver by the duke. While we're on his coin, we're on his time, and we'll do whatever he asks of us."

"If he wants to change the rules, he oughta change the pay, too," complained Pettybone.

"He isn't paying you more than the Company?" questioned Ainsley. "Frozen hell, man, did you even ask?"

"A-Ask?" stammered Pettybone. "You mean just ask the son of the king for more pay?"

Ainsley blinked back at her first mate. "I did."

"You asked Duke Oliver Wellesley for more pay!" cried Pettybone. "What... You can't..."

Sighing, the captain sat back in her chair. "When we return to Westundon, I'll inquire on your behalf, and I suppose the crew's as well. He's the son of the king, but he doesn't act like he knows it. This is a good posting, First Mate, the best, despite what happened up around Derbycross. We've got to adjust, but when we do, there's nowhere I'd rather be than in the duke's employ."

"That's not what you said two weeks back," argued the first mate.

"Two weeks back, we were heading to assault a spirit-forsaken sorcerer's lair," barked the captain. "Two weeks back, I thought we were going to die screaming in pain. Now, we're preparing to sail to the Westlands. Now, we're looking to embark on one of the richest commercial endeavors this world has known. If the duke was willing to increase my pay before the Westlands, just think what he'll do for us when we return, Pettybone. Just think of it."

Pettybone grunted. "In my experience, it doesn't pay to mess with royalty."

"You don't have any experience with royalty," argued Ainsley.

"I heard stories," claimed the first mate.

She snorted. "Go out on the deck, Pettybone. Make sure the new hands are tying tight knots, mending the sails soundly, and keeping my spirit-forsaken decks clean. When it's time, the duke's going to learn he bought himself the finest airship and aircrew the empire has. And when he realizes that, Pettybone, mark my words, we're going to get rich."

Mollified or not, the first mate stomped out the door, and she smiled when she heard him issuing commands and yelling at the lazy Mister Samuels. She had no doubt that with a little more time around the newer crew members, Pettybone would whip them into shape. They would be a fine group, even if they weren't truly the best the empire had to offer. They'd be close enough, she hoped.

With the first mate gone and relative quiet restored to the captain's cabin, she returned to the books in front of her. Books the duke had sent — Duvante's histories, a biography of several prominent company directors, a treatise on trading patterns with the United Territories before and after the war, and more. The duke trusted her as his captain, and he was educating her to be his agent, an opportunity that sent a shiver down her spine. An agent of the son of the king. An opportunity that never should have existed for one of her low birth, but now it did. She didn't care if the duke asked her to wait on the airship at dock for the next three months. She didn't care if he asked her to track down another sorcerer. She didn't care if he asked her to sail him into the heart of the spirit-forsaken Darklands. For the chance at a different life, a true legacy, she'd do whatever he asked.

More shouts and a high-pitched squeal drifted through the door of her cabin. Pettybone was haranguing the crew mercilessly. One thing she'd learned from the treacherous Captain Haines was that it didn't do to have others manage your work. If the crew needed discipline, it was best they saw it come from her.

She closed her books and left them on the table for another time. Now, she needed to train her men to be the best damn aircrew the empire had ever seen, or close enough.

THE CARTOGRAPHER V

"WINCHESTER," muttered Oliver. "Where did you stick my maps of the Southlands?"

"They ought to be in the drawers, m'lord," claimed the valet.

Grunting, Oliver tugged on a brass pull and hauled open a heavy drawer. Three yards long, a yard and a half deep, the thing was a huge custom job set underneath his drafting table in the center of his study. There were half a dozen such drawers spaced around the edges of the table, and they were sized for large maps to lay flat. Against the wall, he had more drawers and shelves. The drawers stuffed with original maps, the shelves with rolled copies. Those were on cheaper parchment or smaller excerpts showing just a section of a territory excised from a larger depiction.

That's what he meant to do now, sketch out a small version of the coastline around Durban in the Southlands for a new factor traveling there. He was fulfilling his role as a Company cartographer and trying to act normal. But after Derbycross and the attack against the Feet of Seheht, he hardly knew what that meant anymore.

"Can't a clerk handle this, m'lord?" complained Winchester, stooping on the other side of the table to peer into another drawer, shuffling through the maps. "These are the tropics, m'lord, so I think it must be on your side."

Oliver glared at the valet. "No, Winchester, a clerk cannot accurately copy my maps. It's more than just drawing lines on a page, you know?"

"Is it, m'lord?"

"Frozen hell, Winchester," griped Oliver. "Any fool can trace some lines, but any fool is apt to include errors. Without proper training, they wouldn't even know it. A map is more than just a line designating a coast. It has to capture the nature of that coast. It has to convey the feel of the place, the sense a traveler would need to understand a new territory as they arrive. A well-drawn map allows the user to experience a land, which is far more important than just tracing a coastline or a road. I'll give you an example. Outside of Durban, there's a narrow channel through the reefs. It was used by pirates for centuries. Discovering it, and the false maps that were displayed in the markets of that city, made the Company a small fortune. We can't trust that kind of interpretation to a clerk. They might draw the lines with accuracy, Winchester, but not with the truth."

"Are you saying your maps are inaccurate, m'lord?"

"I'm saying when you read my maps, you know where you're going," snapped Oliver.

"Understood, m'lord." Holding up a map, Winchester asked, "Is this the Southlands?"

"Those are the Darklands, Winchester," advised Oliver. "Can't you see the river down the center?"

"I saw the sea was to the north," complained the valet.

"There is sea to the north of Enhover as well," mentioned Oliver, "but you didn't think the map was of our beloved nation."

"Perhaps the map didn't quite capture the feel of the place, m'lord," piped the valet, laying the map back down in the drawer.

Oliver snorted. "Nice attempt, but it isn't my map. It's the Darklands. I've never been there. No one from Enhover has been in years, I suspect. Not even the factors in Durban will venture east to that grim place."

"Because of the sorcery, m'lord?"

"Because of the sorcery," agreed Oliver. He pulled out a map and settled it on the table. "Here it is, the Southlands. When I drafted this, there wasn't much known of the place, just the coastline, the terrain around Durban, and the steppe. See here, this is the channel we found. It allowed us to bring our freighters into the port and avoid harassment from the pirates that flit about the place like flies on a carcass."

Leaning closer, Winchester peered at the map. "The steppe. That is this blank space in the south?"

"It is," confirmed Oliver. "It's rugged, arid terrain. Nearly impossible to scout on foot. What we've learned of it, we learned from the deck of an airship. Thirty, forty leagues south of Durban, there's nothing but those rocky crags and scrub bushes. Beyond that, it's rolling hills and wild grasslands. Not so dissimilar to central Enhover, I suppose, but where we are blanketed in constant fog and misting rain, the Southlands are covered in sunshine and dust. The steppe gets hard rain, I'm told, in the form of violent storms, but those tough grasses don't seem to need much of it."

"The traders, they come from the steppe?"

"We're not really sure," admitted Oliver. "Once or twice a moon, the caravans materialize from the rocky foothills. They trade, and then they return the way they came. The Company sent men to follow them on several occasions but we lost them in the rocks or out on the plains. When I was exploring the terrain around the colony, I requested an airship to assist in mapping farther south, but the board denied my request. At the time, as now I suppose, we had more routes to run than airships to run them. Is there a city the traders head to farther south? Are they nomads? We're not sure."

Winchester frowned at the map.

"There is more to the world than even the Company and Crown know of," said Oliver. "So much more."

A gentle rap sounded on the door. Both Oliver and the valet looked up.

"Yes?"

A liveried servant ducked her head in. "A guest, m'lord."

Oliver frowned and glanced at the ticking clock on the mantle above the fireplace. "This late? I'm not expecting company. Who is it?"

"It's, ah, I don't know, m'lord," admitted the servant. "One of the Child baronesses. It could be Isabella, but I'm afraid I have trouble telling them apart."

"So late. Why—"

Oliver was cut off as Winchester squeaked. He turned to his valet and saw the man's eyes bulging, a hand pressed over his mouth as if he was trying to hold in a giggle.

Sighing, Oliver turned back to his servant and instructed, "Show her in, but first, please take my valet out with you."

THE PRIESTESS IV

"THIS IS GOING TO HURT," advised Kalbeth, dipping a thin, steel needle into a small pot of ink mixed with her blood.

"You said that yesterday," remarked Sam.

"Yesterday, I was doing touchup work across your arms and chest. Today, I'm doing intensive, detailed work on your back. Sam, this design is going to require me inking nearly a quarter of your skin over here. When I say this is going to hurt, I mean it's going to hurt a lot."

"I'm sure you'll nurse me to health when it's over," replied Sam dryly.

She didn't turn to look, but she knew her friend was smiling. Friend. Was Kalbeth a friend, something more, something less? She didn't know. She had no point of reference with something like this. She'd never been close to anyone except Thotham, but it was different with her mentor. Different because he was the one man she considered her superior, perhaps. Or maybe because they'd never slept together. The man was what she imagined a father and mother to be like— caring, demanding, and proud.

She shifted, wondering. Was Kalbeth her lover, her friend, someone she used when she needed something and left when she did not? Did it matter?

"Hold still. I don't want to hurt you," demanded Kalbeth.

"What?"

"You're not going to be facing off against deadly sorcerers and saving us all if you keep wiggling and this ends in a mess of squiggly lines instead of proper script and patterns," said Kalbeth.

"Sorry, I…"

"Can't keep still?" questioned the woman.

"Just start," instructed Sam.

She felt soft lips on her back, and when they moved, a quick prick from a needle jolted her. She clenched her hands together. Another prick, right beside the first, and Kalbeth got to work. Tiny stab after tiny stab, the artist worked the ink and her own blood into Sam's skin, fashioning intricate designs and shapes bordered in arcane script that no more than a few people in all of Enhover could read, script Kalbeth had learned from her parents over two and a half decades before when she'd lived in the Darklands.

Abandoned in Durban, Kalbeth had been pressed onto a ship bound for Enhover as a deck swab and far worse. She'd been tossed onto the docks in Southundon, diseased and on the verge of death from hunger and rough treatment. The Church had taken her in, healed her, and showed her there were more difficult fates than life aboard the ship.

When Sam had been selected and taken by Thotham from the Church's orphanage, Kalbeth had snuck out and followed. She'd followed until the old priest had spotted her and stopped her. He had sensed something about the girl standing there on the busy street, though it wasn't until years later that Sam understood what. Then, she realized the kindness the old man had shown both of them.

At the time, it seemed he'd sold Kalbeth like chattel, sold her like all that had come before in the devastated girl's life. He'd taken both girls inside of the Lusty Barnacle and declared the proprietor would watch Kalbeth. Even then, Sam had known the nature of the place. How could she not? Some of the girls working the room weren't any older than she. For years, she thought her mentor had thrown her friend and first lover into a life of prostitution. Thotham never told her it was another sort of apprenticeship that he'd placed Kalbeth in.

She had hated Thotham for what he'd done. It was only when she stumbled across Kalbeth accidentally on her own and learned what the years had contained for her old friend that Sam understood. Her friend had been given a chance, but one that carried incredible risk.

Kalbeth was attuned to the underworld and the spirits that resided there. She could sense them, sense them clinging to those who lived like shadows, sense them flitting on the other side, awaiting a bridge to come back or for the wheel to grind them down to where they could be reborn. Kalbeth sensed those straining to pass through the shroud, and she'd learned to capture them, dragging a portion of them across the barrier and tying them to the world of the living through her art.

She did not summon the shades fully into the world of the living, but she tethered them to a living soul. Was it sorcery, or was it something else? In the eyes of the Church, it was clear. Kalbeth was what Sam had been trained to hunt and kill. Yes, she had finally understood why Thotham did what he did.

Sam had met another once, with the same natural ability to hear the wails of the spirits, their constant lamentation, their endless need. He'd visited them on their farm days after Northundon had been attacked. The man had been untrained, Thotham had told her, and was unprepared for when the Church decided they no longer needed him.

Eventually, in the girl's home where the Church stabled its livestock, they would have learned what Kalbeth was capable of. She would have been broken down until nothing was left, nothing but her ability and an unassailable sense of worthlessness. Then, they would have used her until she'd been wrung dry, and then they would have killed her.

If her masters didn't do it themselves, if they'd thought

Kalbeth still had strength, then Thotham or Sam would have been asked to kill her. Instead, thanks to Thotham's snap decision, Kalbeth had been placed with Goldthwaite and trained as best the dark mistress was capable of. She'd been left there until Sam accidentally found her again.

They had used her, Sam and Thotham both. Sam had claimed she would never betray her old lover, that she would never let Kalbeth risk her own life.

She'd lied.

Every time Kalbeth trailed her fingers across the barrier, collecting the souls that lingered there, she covered herself in that cold darkness. Some of it clung to her, and some of her clung to the shroud, to the underworld. There would be a time when that darkness would catch her. When it did, it would draw her with it to the other side. Sam knew Kalbeth's life would not be a long one, and every time the woman practiced her art, it grew shorter.

"Are you feeling any of this?" wondered Kalbeth, tapping her needle confidently along Sam's flesh.

Sam grunted.

"It's been almost a turn of the clock," continued the artist. "Let's take a break."

"I can continue," said Sam.

"I can't."

Kalbeth ran a damp cloth over Sam's back, wiping up excess ink and blood. When Sam sat up, she felt her skin tingle as hundreds of tiny needle pricks protested the movement.

"That does sting a bit," she hissed.

Kalbeth smiled wanly. "I hope it is worth it."

"So do I," said Sam. "So do I."

THE CARTOGRAPHER VI

"Any word from Pettigrew?" wondered Oliver, leaning in the doorway.

Director Raffles looked up, surprised. "I didn't know you were coming down to Company House, m'lord."

"I was at the airship dock speaking with my captain," replied Oliver. "I thought I'd pass through on the way back up to the palace."

"Ah," murmured Raffles. "Director Pettigrew informed me he was meeting with the balance of the board in two days. I expect they'll ratify the change in shares as compensation for use of your airship and your work with your father. How is that progressing, by the way?"

"It's going well," said Oliver. "I've passed some messages with the old man. He has no real interest in involving himself deeply in Company affairs and he's well aware Cardinal Langdon is receiving his information from Governor de Bussy. If there is one thing my father cannot stand, it is foreign interference. No, he's merely using this recent disruption as a chance to chastise the Company's board. It's no secret he feels they've grown too confident, and this is his excuse to rattle his sword and put them back into their place. My father has no qualms about Enhover's merchants becoming very wealthy, but he is king."

"Understood," murmured Raffles.

"Perhaps if you send that bit of gossip to Southundon, you could phrase it more tactfully?" asked Oliver. "My father doesn't like merchants thinking they can encroach on Crown business, even if their charter implies they can. He'd like me putting words in his mouth even less."

"Of course," said Raffles. "I will keep the specifics between you and I, but I believe the sentiment will be understandable and reassuring to the directors. I won't go as far to say that they appreciate your father's point of view, but they understand he is the king, and there are consequences of pushing the monarchy too far. If they have not yet crossed the line with Edward, I believe the board will be happy to retreat gracefully. It's the best they can hope for, I think, given what Governor Dalyrimple was involved in. We ought to take this a stern reminder to get our house in order, and then do so!"

Oliver nodded, glancing at the papers scattered on Raffles' desk. He pushed aside a small pile and ran his fingers over the map carved into the wood. "This desk has always bothered me, you know?"

Raffles smirked. "It bothers you because you've seen it and mapped it. To me, what is a few hundred leagues? I've never been to the Westlands or the Southlands, and I never intend to go. I don't need the table to navigate by, and it supports my paperwork just fine."

Grinning, Oliver looked at the paperwork again. "Imbon?"

"What?" asked Raffles, gathering up a sheaf and tapping it on the desk to align the papers together.

"Was that a dispatch from Imbon?" questioned Oliver. "From Jain Towerson? The quarterly isn't due for another month."

"No, ah, another month sounds right," mumbled Raffles. He stood. "Care to visit the club on your way to the palace? This time of day we might find the membership manager in the office. Perhaps we can work on bending that age restriction for you."

Oliver leaned forward and pushed a paper aside, revealing a thin parchment embossed with Company letterhead.

"That's no—" blurted Raffles.

Oliver plucked the paper free and frowned as he read it. "A discovery, a trove of artifacts?"

The director shifted.

Oliver looked at him. "What is this?"

"I barely had time to peruse it myself, m'lord."

"The pool I located in Imbon," guessed Oliver. "It was not star-iron at the bottom but a hidden cache of… small figurines and stone tablets carved with symbols and indecipherable writing, this says?"

"I, ah, I believe it was something of the sort," muttered Raffles. "Perhaps some record of past kings? Likely worthless junk."

"It doesn't say that here," remarked Oliver, shaking the paper in his hand.

"It doesn't?"

"Why was I not informed about this?" questioned Oliver. "As a shareholder, I'm entitled to any news relating to the commercial prospects of the colony, and as the man who discovered this location, there may be a finder's fee involved. If nothing else, it's simple courtesy."

"I didn't send the report, m'lord. I only received it this morning and haven't had time to read it in detail," protested Raffles. "It didn't occur to me you wouldn't have gotten a copy as well. I can check into why you didn't receive it, though…"

"Pettigrew," snapped Oliver, setting the paper back down on the desk, forcing his hands back so he didn't crumple it.

Raffles' eyebrows rose. "You think the finance director intentionally did not forward the information to you, m'lord?"

"What other explanation makes sense?"

Raffles nodded slowly, a finger tapping on his chin. "Yes, yes, that does make sense. The man was distraught about the recent confrontation. He lost a great deal of prestige having to grovel and ask for more shares on your behalf. Could this be his revenge?"

Oliver stabbed a finger onto the paper. "Let's find out. Come with me, Director. We're going to Southundon."

"What?"

"I was just at the Cloud Serpent," continued Oliver. "Captain Ainsley has it provisioned for a voyage to the Westlands. It will get us to the capital easy enough. If we leave now, we should be there by sunset. I mean to settle this with Pettigrew tonight."

Swallowing, Director Raffles said, "I, ah…"

"You're coming with me, Raffles," instructed Oliver. "Send a man for whatever kit you need to spend a few days on the road. Meet me at the airship bridge in one turn of the clock."

THE PRIESTESS V

HER BOOTS HIT the stone quay. She inhaled deeply, drawing in the salty aroma of the harbor, recently caught fish, and the comfortable scent of milled oak. Barrels were stacked row after row beside warehouses, filled to the brim with dark red wine, waiting to be loaded onto shipping vessels. Ivalla's largest export, she'd been told, and certainly its most popular product back in Enhover.

"Out of the way!" cried a man laden with a flimsy wheelbarrow and a heavy stack of the iron-bound barrels.

She moved aside and watched as he trundled by her, leaning precariously to the side as he tried to peer around his barrels at what was ahead of him. Watching for the heavy carts, she made her way from the quay into the warren of stacked wine barrels, smaller casks of pressed olive oils, pallets piled with wheels of cheese, and racks hung with tubes of salted and cured meats.

Her stomach rumbled. She'd been told Ivalla offered more palatable fare than Enhover's gravy-filled pies and mashed potatoes, and she was pleased to see it was true. At the least, it smelled a great deal more enticing than the bean stews they'd served every day on the voyage over.

On her back she wore a light rucksack filled with several days of clothing and with room for a few days of food. In her hands, she held the rune-carved spear that had once been her mentor's, and on her hips hung her two kris daggers. Half a dozen more knives were secreted about her body. Down the front of her shirt, hanging in a pouch on a slender metal chain, was the bulk of the sterling she'd taken from Duke.

Borrowed, she'd claimed, but she had no intention of repaying the man. She be surprised if he noticed she didn't return the coins, and if he did, she couldn't imagine he'd ask for them back. It took a bit of the fun out of it, she thought. She'd have to get even more of the coins from him next time, see if that piqued his interest.

Hiding away the majority of her funds had been wise. Attempting to walk into a foreign nation so heavily armed was not as wise. A bored-looking guard stepped in front of her as she made her way up the wide boulevard that led from the harbor district into the city proper.

"Name and business?" he drawled. His voice was slick with the accent of Ivalla, but he spoke in the king's tongue of Enhover. It had been impressed on his people twenty years prior when they'd become tributes of the island nation, and at least in the harbor thick with Enhoverian merchants, the Ivallans spoke it fluently.

"My name is Sam, and my business is my own," she said.

The guard frowned at her.

"What?"

"Most people armed as heavily as you claim they're investigating commercial opportunities or just stepping into the city to find lower prices than the harbor rates," explained the guard. "Why aren't you giving an easy excuse, girl?"

She blinked at him.

"First time here?" he questioned.

"It is," she admitted.

"Well," he said, tucking his thumbs behind his belt, "I recommend you try to appear a bit less suspicious. A pretty thing like you, traveling alone, heavily armed, it don't look right. If the guards like me don't harass you, the thieves and rogues will. Valerno is a safe town, but… Just try to be a bit more inconspicuous, will you? Maybe find some traveling companions or carry your arms less openly?"

"Traveling alone, I might need the weapons," she said.

The guard rolled his eyes and waved her on, muttering something under his breath about those who won't help themselves.

She continued into the town. The streets were cobblestone, worn nearly smooth by long years of foot and wagon traffic. The buildings were made from thick, wooden beams interspaced with painted stucco walls. Charming, she thought, compared to Enhover's dreary stone facades. The people were dressed simply but clean, showing a comfortable lifestyle that wasn't as fashionable as those who strolled Westundon's broad avenues. King Edward collected his tribute, but he was savvy enough not to bleed the populace dry, she guessed. That's the way Duke would do it, and he'd learned it from somewhere.

As she climbed the shallow incline that led from the harbor through the city, she saw there were none of the block-long mansions of the merchant princes like she would see in Westundon, and as she passed the seat of the local government, she thought it could fit quite easily into any one of Prince Philip's multiple carriage courts.

All in all, it was a pleasant place.

She found a square lined with vendors' booths and spent half an hour browsing the goods, picking up food and a few other items she thought might be useful on her journey. She purchased a scarf which she draped over her head and a pair of locally made gloves as well, hoping the items would help her blend in. The guard had meant his advice to be friendly, and she thought it best she heed it.

It was one hundred and fifty leagues from Valerno to Romalla, the capital city of Ivalla and home of the Church, and Ivalla had none of the railways that she'd grown used to in Enhover. In

Ivalla, it would all be on foot, unless she could catch a ride on a wagon.

And that was exactly what she'd been advised to do. Once Goldthwaite had learned Sam was departing Enhover, she'd grown rather friendly and had insisted on Sam meeting some of her girls who were from Ivalla. Much of their experience was far different from what Sam hoped to find, but they did offer one valuable piece of advice. For a woman alone on the road, it was far safer to attach oneself to a merchant convoy. It should be easy enough, they crawled like caterpillars in spring along the highways. The way Goldthwaite's girls had suggested gaining passage was not something Sam was interested in doing, but she hoped with a small demonstration of her skill, she'd be taken on as a guard.

With supplies in her pack, she made her way to the edge of town near the broad river that flowed out from the center of the continent. Past the outskirts of the city, traffic from the main road, the river, and the sea all collected. Traders negotiated and passed goods on to the next legs of the journey. She'd been told it was a bit like the trading floors in Westundon, except in Ivalla, it was all open air, and there were no cohorts making markets and managing the activity.

Instead, she found a huge, open field dotted with foldable tables, small booths, and merchants scrambling between them. The noise and frenzy of the place was overwhelming. She didn't hear the man shouting at her until he roughly grabbed her arm.

With the hand that gripped her spear, she twisted and smacked the man's arm away. Her other hand whipped across her hip and rose with one of her sinuous kris daggers in her grip. She placed the point under the man's throat and growled, "Don't touch me."

"Then don't enter the market armed like that," snapped the man, his eyes angry, his nerves only betrayed when he swallowed uncomfortably.

She realized the man was not an attacker, but a guard,

stationed outside of the field to keep order. Half a dozen of his fellows were edging closer, clearly not happy about one of their brethren with a dagger against his neck, but level-headed enough to know that in such circumstances, rapid action was not always the best course.

In a flash, she sheathed her dagger and stepped back. "I apologize. It's my first time here at the market. I wasn't aware I couldn't enter armed, and I did not see you were an official. Can you tell me where I can find a position as a guard on the merchant convoys?"

The man blinked at her. "A guard?"

She nodded.

"A woman guard?"

She frowned. "The merchants won't hire a woman as a guard?"

"Well, no…" mumbled the soldier.

"I'll hire you," offered a high-pitched voice.

She turned and saw a portly man with silver-gray hair swept straight back. He was covered in a dizzying array of bright silks and had a wide mustache, curled and oiled so that the twisting tips reached past his ears. A jeweled stud was pierced through one nostril and his fingers were bedecked with sparkling gold and silver rings, most of them fixed with even bigger, brighter jewels.

"I'm carting perfumes to Romalla," declared the man. "I can always use a talented armsman to keep me entertained and safe."

"She's a woman," mentioned the soldier Sam had nearly stabbed.

"Yes, I can see that," purred the merchant, winking at Sam. "I misspoke. An armswoman who looks as though she can handle herself."

"Pay?" asked Sam.

"Six silver continentals and food and shelter while we travel."

Sam glanced at the guard to see if the man showed any reaction to the merchant's offer. She had no idea what a fair rate for guard duty was, and it seemed the soldier had no care.

"It's a competitive salary," assured the merchant. "Besides, the man was right. Most merchants will not hire a woman. At least, not to be a guard."

"A guard and that is all," stated Sam.

"A deal then?" asked the man, nodding acknowledgement, proffering one of his bejeweled hands to shake.

Sam took it.

"Come along then. We have much to do."

"IVAR VAL DRONGKO," THE MERCHANT DECLARED WHEN THEY'D made it to his tent. "I deal in perfumes for discerning men and women. I collect the finest scents from every corner of the United Territories, and then in Romalla, I sell my wares."

Half a league north of the market, the merchant's campsite was set beside the road under the broad branches of a grove of olive trees. Outside of the tent, a boy of twelve winters sat on the grass. Ivar flipped him several copper coins, and the boy scampered off without word.

"Hopefully, he did not steal too much," muttered the merchant.

She saw the man had a donkey tied behind his tent, a simple cart, and no other guards. Raising an eyebrow at the colorfully attired man, she mentioned, "I was told the roads were safest in large companies, groups great enough to scare away the bandits."

"Indeed," said Ivar, not turning to look at her as he rooted through the boxes stacked beside his tent.

She frowned at his back. "Your name, val Drongko, is that Ivallan?"

"Northwestern Rhensar," the man claimed.

She watched as he mumbled to himself and checked his goods, presumably making sure the boy who'd been watching the tent truly had only stolen a few small items.

"My name is Sam," she offered.

Ivar turned to blink at her. "Is that— Is that a woman's name in Enhover?"

"Not typically, no," she admitted. "How did you know I was from Enhover?"

"Where else would you be from?" he replied. "You stand out like a lion at the spring festival."

"A lion?"

"A big, dangerous cat," explained the merchant, finally assuring himself not too much was missing and standing to face her. "That's what you remind me of."

"Like a grimalkin?" she asked.

"Like a grimalkin," confirmed Ivar, "though those are native to the Darklands. Lions roam in what you'd call the Southlands. A lion, that's what I saw when you assaulted that hapless soldier. Just the woman, or man had you been one, that I need to escort me to Romalla."

"You believe it will be dangerous?" she wondered.

"Not if you keep me safe," he declared jovially. He waved his hands to encompass his campsite. "We'll spend the night here. Then, on the morrow, we start north."

"I'll be ready," she said.

Ivar tossed her a small glass bottle. Surprised, she snatched it out of the air.

"Good reflexes," he complimented. "Now, dab a bit of that on your neck. I can guess you disembarked from a ship just this morning, because you smell like the backside of my donkey."

THE CARTOGRAPHER VII

"I'VE BEEN CONCERNED about the Company," remarked King Edward Wellesley.

Oliver frowned at his father. "That's not what I meant."

Settling his fists on his hips, the king asked his son, "What is it you meant? Keeping you in the dark, not sharing information, those are the first steps toward sedition."

"The Company is not trying to overthrow the Crown," protested Oliver.

"What are they trying to do, then?" wondered the king.

For a moment, Oliver was silent, watching his father pace back and forth across the small dining room. The king moved in a graceful, predatory manner. Confident and quick, he hadn't lost a step in his later years. In fact, the man looked as lean and healthy as he had twenty years ago. Oliver wasn't sure what his father did to get his exercise, but there was no question it was keeping the man in shape. Briefly, the son wondered whether the father was seeing a mistress or two, but such a thing would have been nearly impossible to hide, and Oliver hadn't heard a rumor. He'd have to ask his brother John about it. John knew their father better than anyone, and if some woman was sneaking in and out of the old man's chambers, John would be aware of it.

"Well?" asked the king, stopping and staring at his youngest son.

"I don't know," admitted Oliver. "It's difficult to believe they did not send me information on the find accidentally. I'm the largest shareholder in Imbon, after the Company's own stake, and of course I'm the one who actually discovered the site."

"Star-iron, was it?"

Oliver shook his head. "Star-iron was what I thought it was. It turns out it is a trove of cultural artifacts. Evidently, no one's been able to decipher them yet, but it appears to be ancient writings from the natives. Their history and mythology."

"Histories and mythology, eh?" questioned his father. "Imbon was an undeveloped island nation when you first saw it. What history did they have before we colonized them?"

"There were people there before us," reminded Oliver. "These tablets are apparently covered with symbols and odd script. What else would it be?"

"Strange to make such an effort to hide them, then," remarked the king. He tugged at his salt-and-pepper goatee before instructing, "Bring these artifacts to me. Perhaps I can determine the nature of them."

"Bring them to you?" questioned Oliver. His father merely stood and held his gaze. Sighing, and not wanting to enter into a battle of wills with the old man, Oliver conceded, "When I get my hands on them, I'll ensure you get the first look, though I don't see why we wouldn't go straight to the royal museum with it."

"Those old scholars are drier than the bones they study," snorted the king. "After the items are recovered, what do you intend to do about the Company?"

"What do you intend?" countered Oliver.

"It depends on what my youngest son is able to achieve," said King Edward. "If it was solely up to me, I'd act aggressively, either through increasing taxes on Company imports or on their member's assets. If that did not suffice, I would move directly against the most prominent individuals on the Company's board to send a message. There are many options when one controls the ministry and the rolls of the peerage. The Congress of Lords of course would be overjoyed to slap down any merchants who have risen above their station. The trick is only targeting those who are not already peers with a seat in the congress." Tilting his head and studying his son, the king remarked, "It begs the question, do you want it to be solely my discretion? You're my son and a member of the Company. You may have your own agenda with the directors, and I don't want to interfere with your business, son, just theirs and just enough to ensure they learn the lesson."

"You will leave me freedom to act and you will not intervene in the Company's existing charters?" questioned Oliver. "You will disregard this situation with Imbon and the demands that arrived from Cardinal Langdon?"

"I care as much about the cardinal's opinion as I do the woman's who fetches me tea each morning," responded his father. "The cardinal is merely a convenient excuse to send a message, but there is a kernel of truth in what he claimed. Earl Sebastian Dalyrimple and his wife were engaged in sorcery. Their daughter and Marquess Colston were the first known practitioners of the dark art in Enhover since we pushed the Coldlands raiders back into their frozen forest. You know as well as I do, Oliver, that we must not allow sorcery a foothold on our shores. What happened before is too terrible to repeat. From where I stand, it appears a Company governor was practicing the dark art in a Company colony, and then his wife brought the terrible business back to us. If you and the Company's board of directors cannot address this matter, then I won't be in position to ignore the latest rumblings. I will not stand for sorcery in Enhover, Oliver. I will not."

Oliver nodded. "I understand. Let me deal with the situation, Father. I'm the one who dealt with the threat in Derbycross, and I will deal with anything else."

"Yes, you did deal with it before," admitted the king. "You killed the sorcerers that you knew of, but are you confident you got them all? The Dalyrimples may have passed their knowledge though the generations, but Marquess Colston learned it somewhere. Who did he learn from? Is anyone else at the Company involved?"

"Do you have anything to drink?" muttered Oliver.

"The cupboard over there," said the king.

Oliver felt his father's eyes on him as he poured them both a stiff drink. When he turned and handed a crystal glass to his father, the old man held his gaze.

"Philip asked me to drop all inquiry into sorcery," said Oliver. "He thinks it's best left to the inspectors and the Church."

"Ah, of course. I forgot that you always do as your older brother asks," chided his father.

Oliver fidgeted.

"You don't follow orders well, son," added the king.

Shrugging, uncomfortable in front of his king and father, Oliver had no reply.

A moment passed, and the king smiled. "You haven't let it drop, have you?"

"Why do you say that?" asked Oliver, sipping the gin in his glass, tasting the subtle hint of juniper and blackberry beneath the burn of the alcohol.

"You rarely do as we expect you to," remarked the older man, "but you've never been one to lie. Despite what Philip has requested, you are pursuing new leads, aren't you?"

"There isn't much left to pursue," admitted Oliver.

"You have a plan, though?"

Oliver found himself pacing, mimicking his father's motion earlier, and forced himself to still.

"You're keeping it secret. That is good," said the king. "It is a dangerous game you play, son. Sorcerers operate from within the shadows. They have powers I don't think you can yet imagine. They'll kill you if they feel you're on their scent. Son of the king is no protection against men and women like that. They have no allegiance to the Crown, no loyalty to the Company or the

Church. They seek only power at the expense of anyone who stands in the way of their dark path."

"You think I should stop and let the inspectors and the Church handle it?"

"No," replied the king, shaking his head. "If you think there are leads worth pursuing, then you should do so, but I advise you to be careful. I cannot protect you from sorcery, my boy."

"But Philip will—"

"You are not Philip, a fact which I think everyone is grateful for, including him," interjected King Edward. "If there are any more sorcerers operating in Enhover, I believe Philip really would think it is the Church's duty to deal with them. He'd step aside, letting those feckless incompetents flail around the problem, as if they do anything other than declaim from the pulpit and fritter away the Crown's sterling. The Church did not throw the Cold-lands' sorcerers back. We did, the Wellesleys! If the dark art is being practiced in Enhover again, then we cannot wait for the Church to deal with it."

"Can you... help?" asked Oliver.

The king shook his head slowly. "Everything I do is observed carefully. Everything I say is noted by spies both foreign and domestic. I have resources, but if I apply them, then your opponents will know. They know us, but we do not know them. That's a dangerous position to be in. When the time is right, perhaps I can assist openly, but do you feel you're ready to move? Surely we would not be having this discussion if you already know your target?"

"No," admitted Oliver. "I don't know who the enemy is, but I know they're out there."

His father sipped his drink, thinking. "What is it you do, then?"

"There is a woman, a priestess. She assisted me against the Dalyrimples," said Oliver. "She has been specially trained by the Church, but her mentor was killed in Derbycross, so she is the only one of her kind left in Enhover. She's left for Ivalla to meet the Church's Council of Seven. We believe she'll find people experienced at this sort of thing. The Knives of the Council, they are called."

"I know about the Council of Seven," said the king. "The Knives of the Council have been largely absent in Enhover, but perhaps it is time for them to return. Unfortunately, I'm afraid your priestess may find the Council is greatly diminished in recent years."

"Diminished?"

The king shrugged. "Let her see what she sees, find what assistance she can. What do you mean to do while she is away?"

"I mean to live life as I normally would and not raise suspicion," answered Oliver. "I will observe, look for clues, but we agreed I was too visible. As you said, the actions of our family are closely observed. It would be too obvious if I was publicly making an inquiry."

"A wise course," confirmed the king. "You should be circumspect in your investigation, but you should not stop it. While the priestess is gone, I suggest you consider why there are few Knives left in Enhover. Sorcery is alleged to be impossible here, but you've seen the lie in that myth. Who spread the lie? Who stands to gain by focusing the Knives' attention elsewhere? Who in Enhover has the power to manipulate Church policy?"

"Are you saying…"

"I'm saying that it would behoove you to understand who benefits from the type of conspiracy you are investigating," advised the king. "Who has the motive and ability to pull it off, and what would they gain? Evidence and proof are the fodder of our court system. Motivation and capability are what the Crown must consider in statecraft. Find out who, Oliver, has the motivation and capability to undermine our empire. That is the person you must investigate."

Frowning, Oliver's mind swirled. Was his father implying the Church was involved in sorcery? Thotham and Sam certainly had made steps on the dark path, but they'd been dedicated to eliminating the dark art. If they had the knowledge, then perhaps someone else did as well?

"What else can you tell me, Father?"

"I cannot tell you anything, I can only offer questions," replied the king, "questions I would be asking if I'd set about your task."

"I've much to think about, then."

"Agreed, but as a sorcerer operates in the shadow, so should you. Your plan of continuing to live normally is a good one, and you came to Southundon for a reason, yes?"

"To sort out the Company's board and figure what is happening in Imbon."

"Then you should do it," stated the king. "Confront the Company's board of directors, get what is your due from them, and always suspect that those in power are playing a deeper game than you can see. We Wellesleys are overconfident, sometimes, because we are born on the throne. But because we are born with it does not mean we will die with it. There are those in this empire who seek to unseat us, and our role is to always be a step ahead of them. Always be aware, son, of who is conspiring against you. All empires fall, Oliver, they crumble from within. The scholars wonder when, we must wonder who."

Oliver nodded.

"Go kick the hornet's nest," instructed King Edward. "Those overly pompous merchants deserve a stern reminder of who wears the crown, and don't forget to send me whatever artifacts you recover from Imbon. I'm curious what the island people have to hide."

THE MEN SAT AROUND THE EERILY QUIET ROOM LIKE GARGOYLES perched atop a cemetery wall. Their chairs rose in tiers that bracketed opposite sides of the room. The famed director's table was placed at the head of the space, the two massive double doors that allowed entry at the foot. Every man in the room was a director, and they all wielded the power that came with the title, but it was the five men at the head table who ruled the Company, the most successful commercial enterprise in the history of the world. All five of their sour faces looked like they'd just bitten into a lime.

There were no windows, which apparently had been a decision meant protect the privacy of the Company's dealings, but to Oliver, it felt foolish. Couldn't they put a bank of windows high up? No one would be able to see in, but it would allow a little sun to shine on the Company's proceedings.

A man at the center of the table cleared his throat, and Oliver decided it was time to begin.

"President Goldwater," boomed Oliver, putting more air into his words than was necessary in the quiet room. "Thank you for assembling the directors on such short notice. Earlier, while waiting for a quorum to arrive, I stopped by the clerks' offices and reviewed the paperwork there. The dispatch from Imbon had specific instructions about which Company officers should receive an update, and my name was not included."

"Yes," murmured the Company's president. His voice was velvet soft, like the inside of his mouth had been coated with the same powder he'd applied to his stark white wig. "The supervisor informed me. He was quite upset at the interruption, you know. His office has a strict procedure for conducting business and they appreciate requests in writing, I'm told."

"I don't much care what the man appreciates," remarked Oliver coldly. He was standing in the center of the room, the five senior directors seated at the table facing him, two dozen others on the thickly padded benches that rose on either side of him. Nearly thirty men in total, almost all of the active Company directors and a few inactive ones that Oliver suspected had only come to witness the show.

"We rely on our clerks, Oliver," chided President Alvin Goldwater. "Without them—"

"I'm properly addressed as Duke Wellesley, Alvin," snapped Oliver, interrupting the older man. "If you intend to sit there and lecture me about proper procedure when speaking to a clerk, then I expect you to do it with full respect for Crown authority, something that seems to be lacking around here recently."

Goldwater shifted uncomfortably. "That's not what—"

"Clarify, then. Are you concerned with propriety, or are you not?" cried Oliver, interrupting the man again.

"Of course I am, ah, Duke Wellesley. It was merely a slip of the tongue."

"A similar slip to the one where I was not informed of the details of the find in Imbon?" demanded Oliver.

"M'lord," protested Goldwater. "A simple clerical error."

"Was it?" questioned Oliver. "Which clerk, Alvin, made the error? I'd be pleased to know what the punishment is for such a mistake."

"Well, I don't think this is at all necessary," complained Goldwater. "We are all human, Oliver, and we all make mistakes. If we do not allow some leeway, we'll frighten the rank and file members into inaction. Surely you understand that?"

"Did you mean to say 'Duke Wellesley', Alvin?"

Director Goldwater winced.

"By the Company's bylaws," said Oliver, glad Raffles had taken time to show him those bylaws on the flight down, "all shareholders in an expedition are required to be updated about material changes to the value of their investment. I was not informed, which is a violation of our longest-held policies. As the man who discovered the site, I'm entitled to additional shares of the specific find, which have not been offered since I was not even aware until yesterday. That is two direct violations of the Company's bylaws, and if I'm not mistaken, it constitutes a serious breach of our operating practices. I'm fully entitled to an independent investigation of these violations."

"I, ah…"

"Director Pettigrew," said Oliver, turning to the finance director who was seated left of President Goldwater. "You are most familiar with Company policy. Who would conduct such an investigation into impropriety by Company officers?"

Pettigrew sat, pale, sweating, and silent.

Goldwater turned to his finance director. "I won't pretend I know every word of what's in that musty old document, but you do, Pettigrew. Tell us, who conducts an investigation?"

"The investigators would be assigned by the Crown, I believe," murmured Pettigrew, his eyes fixed on his hands clutched on the table in front of him.

"The Crown." Sighing, Goldwater looked back to Oliver. "What is it you want?"

"One," answered Oliver, ticking off items on his fingers, "I want our agents to follow procedure. They should have informed me, and I expect that they will in the future so we do not need to revisit this matter. Two, I want whoever was responsible for this list of names to account for why I was not included. I will be honest, Alvin. It strikes me that it had to be intentional. And third, I want details of what was found and I want to be given an opportunity to stake my claim."

"You, ah… D-Did you not inform Governor Towerson you were content with your standard share as an Imbon stakeholder?" stammered Director Pettigrew.

"Our bylaws require these decisions to be written and signed, and that discussion was informal," challenged Oliver. "Not to mention, it was based on a stockpile of star-iron, and at least so far, I'm not even sure what it is we've found. There's no way I can comment on what allocation I believe is fair until I know what prize we're splitting."

Pettigrew's pale face grew red.

"Perhaps our director of finance can comment on how the information was spread about this find?" questioned Goldwater, eyeing Pettigrew.

"What? I… no, ah…"

The man's babbling started a murmur of surprise amongst the watching ranks in the risers. Every man in the room was a battle-tested merchant, trained and experienced at reading an adversary. These men were sharks, and as one, they smelled blood in the water. Oliver glared at the finance director as Pettigrew fumbled for an explanation.

"I wasn't sure," said Goldwater, glancing back at Oliver, "but the correspondence clerks do fall under the purview of our finance director. Duke Wellesley, this is a serious and unfortunate breach, but I believe it was conducted solely by one actor."

Oliver crossed his arms over his chest.

Pettigrew groaned.

"I call for a motion to replace the finance director due to failure to follow Company bylaws," shouted a voice from the side.

Oliver turned and saw Randolph Raffles there, nodding at him. Several voices seconded with their support.

"Motion to replace the finance director by voice vote?" said Goldwater, glancing to the senior directors at the table around him.

None raised an objection. Pettigrew wouldn't even look up to meet his eyes.

"We'll vote then," announced Goldwater.

All of the present directors voted in favor and none in rejection.

"Please move from the director's table," Goldwater requested of Pettigrew.

Shame-faced, the man stood and shuffled past Oliver to the giant double doors at the opposite end of the hall.

"I will release the supervisor of the clerks from service as well," remarked Goldwater. "As to the nature of the artifacts found, frankly, I do not know. I'll send someone for a copy of Towerson's report, but there was little detail. I think the governor had become quite excited about the prospect of star-iron. Old junk may have been the phrase he used. If you want these items, Duke Wellesley, I suspect no one will object."

"When can the artifacts be brought to the capital?" questioned Oliver. "My father has a keen interest in them. Given the recent tension between the Company and Crown and given the lack of apparent commercial value, I advise we turn these objects over as soon as we can."

Another of the men at the table, the director of shipping, cleared his throat. "With the troubles in Arctan Atoll, we have no airships scheduled to depart for Imbon. We could send a message on the sea, and I'm certain Towerson would quickly pack and ship the items, but..."

"But that could be two months," observed Oliver. He frowned and then offered, "I will go retrieve the artifacts myself."

Goldwater raised an eyebrow.

"I'll take the Cloud Serpent," said Oliver. "My crew is new and many of them are untested. A trip over familiar seas will give them a bit of seasoning before we embark to the Westlands, and while we are discussing that, Alvin, I expect a thirty-percent share."

"I know Pettigrew intended to raise this matter, but a stake that large in such a unique and sizable opportunity is rather unusual," complained the director. "Now that he's removed, I think some time to consider—"

"Every man in this room knew the topic would be up for discussion," interjected Oliver. "Are you asking for time to assess the merits of my proposal or time to weasel out of providing fair consideration? Don't forget, Alvin, without my direct involvement, the Company wouldn't have an exclusive charter. We wouldn't have an escort of the royal marines, and we wouldn't even have an airship to make the journey. The truth of the matter is, without my involvement, there is no expedition to the Westlands, and I should warn you, the longer I'm asked to keep my airship in reserve, the larger the share I believe I'm entitled to."

President Goldwater worked his jaw, at a loss for words.

"I call for a motion to grant the duke the requested thirty-percent share," called Raffles from the gallery again.

Goldwater looked as if he meant to protest, but following a wave of seconds, he allowed the vote. Again, it was unanimous.

Evidently, no one wanted to anger a son of the king after it was so recently shown the Company had been acting against its own bylaws and against the Crown's interest.

When the vote was settled, Oliver suggested, "With such tumultuous times, I believe we should not go long without a finance director, Goldwater. I nominate Randolph Raffles to the position."

"That's not…" mumbled Goldwater. He trailed off, shaking his head. "Next meeting, the Company's board will return to proper etiquette and procedure."

"Fine by me," assured Oliver. "A return to procedure at the next meeting."

"Very well, then," said President Goldwater. "We all know he's been campaigning for it. Shall we vote on Randolph Raffles' appointment to finance director?"

THE PRIESTESS VI

IVAR VAL DRONGKO WAS LOQUACIOUS, flamboyant, funny, and he smelled delightful. He passed their days on the road regaling her with tales that she strongly suspected contained more fiction than fact, but they were entertaining. He'd started by spending the evenings imperiously directing her to care for his donkey, to unpack his tent, and to fix his supper. After the first few nights, they'd settled into a tentative truce, where Sam agreed to set up the tent if val Drongko dealt with the donkey and the food. Luckily, the man was fastidiously clean and washed thoroughly between the two activities.

She had no interest in the slow-plodding animal, and after her first attempt at a meal, neither one of them had an interest in her cooking. She hadn't cooked for herself regularly since she had been fifteen winters, which led to an awkward explanation of why she had cooked for herself then, which led into an even more awkward, though probably just as untruthful, discussion of val Drongko's upbringing.

After a week on the road, they'd seen nothing but fellow travelers and merchants. She'd asked Ivar about bandits, and the man had laughed, gripping his belly and shaking his head. Evidently, over the last decade and at the behest of Enhover's Crown, Ivalla had instituted harsh penalties for banditry. The first violation led to an unceremonious hanging on the roadside. Attacks were down, Ivalla saved continentals because they were able to reduce the number of patrols, and tax revenue was up. All in all, it seemed to have worked, unless you were one of the bandits.

But, Ivar had said, the other merchants had a terrible habit of sabotaging the competition. He'd claimed it would be no problem as no one could approach his cart while he slept next to it. She'd asked why he had paid to bring her along then, and he'd merely grinned and shrugged. You never know, he'd told her.

She'd thought about leaving the perfumer so she could make better time on her own, but she decided it would be imprudent for a woman alone to travel along the open highway. Ivalla seemed safe, but it wasn't that safe. Not to mention, the perfumer really could cook.

Sitting across their small fire from him, sipping on a jug of crimson Ivallan wine, Sam pondered how such a man had gotten to be where he was. He was wealthy, no question. Even if his jewelry was stained glass, his wares were worth a fortune. The small cart was filled with cupboards packed full of vial after vial of perfume. The scents were worth good sterling, more than their weight in silver, in some cases. So much of it, even if it was second quality, was more wealth than she'd ever held. But the man was alone, with no employees, and evidently not many friends.

He plucked at his colorful doublet and tsked. "It's impossible to keep silk clean on the road, don't you find?"

She shrugged. "I wouldn't know."

Glancing at her, the perfume merchant snorted. "Leather trousers, surely more practical than silk in southern Ivalla."

"I'm not the one complaining," mentioned Sam.

Ivar grunted, kicking a silk-slippered foot. "Are you going to drink all of my wine?"

"We're in Ivalla," declared Sam. "Wine is cheap. If you can afford to change into those slippers every night and stomp around camp in them, then you can afford to share a jug of wine with your only guard."

"The slippers are comfortable," grumbled Ivar. "Have you tried… No, of course you have not."

Sam glared at him. "No, Ivar, I have not tried silk slippers."

"You should," he suggested.

"Next time I stop by my tailor, I will order a pair," snapped Sam. She leaned forward and tossed another stick onto their fire.

"What are you doing, girl?" asked the perfume merchant.

"What do you mean?"

"Why are you traveling from Enhover to Romalla?" he pressed. "It is rare for a woman such as you to be alone in Romalla."

"Is it?"

Ivar val Drongko rubbed his mustache, pinching the hairs, twisting them into curls.

"My business is my business," she said.

"Of course it is," he said. "You are working for me, though, so it's not unfair to say your business is also my business. What secrets do you keep?"

Using both hands, she tilted up the wine jug. Around them, a dry breeze stirred the cypress and wild lemon trees that bordered the empty dirt highway they'd camped beside. When she lowered the jug and wiped her lips with the back of her hand, the silk-clad merchant was still watching her, waiting. Anyone clad in silk was someone she'd learned to distrust, but the man's colorful attire was as far from the black silks of Isisandra as she could imagine. Ivar val Drongko may have been many things, but he did not appear to be a sorcerer. She had no secrets from him. Not many, at least.

"I'm a priestess of a sort," she admitted. "I'm traveling to the Church in Romalla."

Ivar pursed his lips but did not comment.

"It's true," she insisted.

"I believe it," he replied. "It's still unusual to see a priestess, of a sort, traveling alone. Does the Church not provide an escort for her daughters?"

"Not in this case," remarked Sam.

"Ah, you're choosing to be alone?" wondered Ivar. "An adventure seeker, are you?"

"I will not share your bedroll," declared Sam.

"I wasn't asking," said Ivar, looking offended. "You are a beautiful girl, but I hired you because you nearly took that soldier's head off, not because I hoped to bed you."

"You prefer men?" questioned Sam.

"Why do you think that?" asked Ivar.

"The silk slippers, that ridiculous mustache, you sell perfume…" mentioned Sam.

"Fair enough," murmured Ivar.

"Am I right?"

Ivar frowned, the first time she'd seen it. "My preferences… I spend my nights alone. This world prefers tradition, and I prefer… Well, I am not sure what I prefer. I prefer the unknown."

Sam rolled her eyes and raised the jug again.

"Have I offended you?" asked Ivar.

"I prefer women," acknowledged Sam.

"A lonely life indeed," consoled Ivar.

"Not as lonely as you think," responded Sam. "I've found… I've found friends."

"You have?" questioned Ivar. "A marvelous thing, I imagine."

"Surely there are many men who'd be willing to do whatever it is that two men do together," said Sam. "In my experience, men are not choosy creatures."

"You are a stunning woman, one even I can appreciate," replied val Drongko. "Any man would choose you. I, though, am a bit overweight, a bit old, and inexperienced in the art of giving pleasure to another man. I'm afraid it's not quite as easy for a man as it is a woman."

"If you say so," allowed Sam, not believing a word of it. "At least you smell nice."

The merchant cackled with mirth, flopping onto his back and kicking his silk-slippered feet in the air.

Sam watched as he rolled in laughter. Later, she imagined, he'd be upset about the dirt clinging to the back of his silks, but now, the man was truly enjoying himself. It might have been the first time in a long time.

As he stilled and regained his breath, she asked him, "Why did you hire me?"

He sat up and blinked at her, wiping tears from his eyes. "I needed a guard."

"I don't know this land," she replied, "but I know one female guard is going to do little to dissuade any bandit gang or these rival saboteur merchants you've told me about. It's quite possible seeing me might even encourage them."

"The roads are safe enough," mumbled Ivar, looking away from her. "I'd like you to stay with me when I sell my wares in Romalla."

"What?"

"A woman like you would attract wealthy men like flies to dung," insisted Ivar.

She frowned at him.

"Sorry. That's a bad analogy," he admitted, "but you would attract them! The clean, subtle scent of my perfumes means nothing to those men, but you... for you, they will make a purchase."

"Are you attracting wealthy men or women?" questioned Sam.

"Whichever pays," declared Ivar.

"If a man purchases his woman a bottle of perfume, what is the message he is giving? He's telling her she smells bad, no? If a woman purchases a bottle of perfume, the message is that she wants to be desired. That, Ivar, is not something I can sell."

"You cannot?"

Sam brushed back a lock of jet-black hair. "I will not."

"What if... what if there was something in it for you?"

"I do not need your sterling. I only need to get to Romalla," advised Sam.

"There are many strange and rare ingredients in perfume," said Ivar, "ingredients that may be of interest to someone like you."

Sam's lips pressed together and her hand twitched.

"Specialty scents and specialty potions share many of the same characteristics," claimed Ivar. "A priestess like you, I imagine you know a little bit about potions."

"What are you saying?"

"Your daggers, your spear, I saw the runes there. This is Ivalla, girl, the seat of the Church. The moment I saw you accosting that guard, I knew you were the one I needed."

"Needed?" asked Sam, confused. "The guard… What are you talking about?"

"A guard, yes, that's what I'm talking about," said Ivar. "When we arrive in Romalla, there will be many guards there. Guards with swords. Guards with training and the senses to detect the supernatural. A woman like you, though, with the taint of the underworld on you but the blessing of the Church? They'll know you and know to avoid you. My cart full of potions will roll in unnoticed and unsearched."

"Hold on," said Sam.

Ivar val Drongko tilted his head and waited.

"You mean to use me as… as a distraction?"

"Yes, was I not clear?" wondered val Drongko. "No mundane guard will accost me if I'm accompanied by one such as yourself. Churchmen are like feral dogs. They tuck their tails when a bigger animal walks by."

Sam glared at him. "You were clear, but why do you think I will agree to such a thing? Calling me a dog is of no help, Ivar."

"You're a Knife of the Council," stated Ivar. "Don't protest. I can tell. An important role, but a thankless one in Ivalla, and I assume Enhover as well, no? The Church has made the tools necessary to do your job illegal. The supplies you need are impossible to come by, unless you happen to know someone."

"You were waiting in Valerno for a Knife to come strolling by?"

"This is not my first trip to the capital and it's not my first time to work with a Knife of the Council."

"You know other Knives?"

Ivar shifted. "I've met them."

"Can you introduce me to them?" asked Sam.

Shaking his head, Ivar replied, "It does not work like that. Don't you… You haven't met another, have you? You're from Enhover, eh? No sorcery? I can sense the cold of the underworld around you, though, so you must know something of the dark path."

"I had a mentor," she explained, deciding there was no sense in hiding that information from the merchant. "He's dead. I've never been to Romalla, but I have need now. I need help from the Council and the other Knives."

Ivar pinched his mustache. "I'm afraid it is not so easy. The Knives, the Council, they operate in secret. I can sometimes sense the taint of the underworld on them, as I can on you, but I cannot tell you where to find them. I could walk around in the city, I suppose, hoping to stumble across someone, but we don't know each other well enough for that. I'm of no use to you."

Sam frowned.

"Can you not just knock on the door of the Church?" wondered the merchant. "You are one of them, are you not?"

"It's not that simple for me, either," muttered Sam. "I am one of them, but they do not know me. Some of what you sense around me, they will sense it as well. I need to approach them in a way where I can explain myself."

"As I said," replied Ivar. "We both need to get into the city, and we both fear we will be unwelcome. Let's start from that point, and as we walk tomorrow, perhaps we can find a way to help each other out."

Sam tipped up the wine jug again and gulped. Approaching a Church that may consider the markings on her body against their laws. Traveling with an illicit potion peddler who was certainly against their laws. Trying to find a powerful sorcerer before they realized she was hunting them. No, it wasn't simple at all.

THE CARTOGRAPHER VIII

"Smoke," said Captain Ainsley.

"I know," responded Oliver.

He was leaning against the gunwale of the Cloud Serpent, watching the speck on the horizon that was Imbon. Hanging above the place was the tattered remnants of a pillar of smoke. Several days old, guessed Oliver. Several days and the column still drifted, blown by the constant tropical breeze, but not gone.

"Marauders?" wondered Ainsley.

"There's no way to know, Captain, not until we draw close," replied Oliver. "Either way, it's best if the men took stations and got ready for action."

"Understood, m'lord," replied Ainsley, steel in her voice.

"What's our complement, Captain?"

"Ten brass cannon, m'lord, with eight-inch-wide barrels," the captain informed him. "We can load them with cannon balls or scattershot. We have four three-inch deck guns that we can set on swivels. Two-dozen small arms, but while we're in the air, they'll be nearly useless. We've got cutlasses and other bladed weapons to outfit the entire crew, which is two score of us, m'lord."

"Bombs, rockets?"

"None, m'lord," replied the captain. "Our armament is

intended to be defensive, what we'd need for protection in the Westlands. We're not outfitted for a true battle, Duke Wellesley."

"Understood, Captain," replied Oliver. "Anything on the water or an emplacement on the shore, we ought to be able to wreak havoc on with our cannon, but you're right, in dynamic combat we're not much more use than a vessel on the water."

"Correct, m'lord," agreed Ainsley. "We can defend ourselves against almost any force and escape to safe skies, but…"

"But we'll see what we're up against as we draw close," responded Oliver. "I don't mean to risk the ship or crew unless we have to, but get the men prepared at stations. I want the cannon primed and the shot at hand. I want blades on hips and firearms available on deck. See to it, Captain, and let's offer a hope to the spirits it is not necessary."

Spinning on her heel, Captain Ainsley began to bark orders, and the crew began to scramble.

Two-score men, outfitted for an exploration expedition. They weren't prepared for combat, but to their credit, Oliver only heard one complaint behind him as the men readied for battle. A meaty smack and a shout from Pettybone quieted the cantankerous Mister Samuels.

They sailed closer, propelled by steady winds. Oliver collected a leather-bound brass spyglass from the first mate and peered through it, scanning over the town of Imbon where the smoke originated from.

A boiling churn rose in his stomach as they drew closer. The village had been burned. Smashed and burned. The fire had threatened the Company's compound as well. The tall bamboo barricades were charred black. He was relieved to see the gate was fastened shut and there was motion inside. Men were in the towers, on the walls, and moving about the yard in the center of the structure. He frowned. The cannon at the corners of the fort had been turned, and instead of toward the sea, they pointed down into the village below.

"Something's gone terribly wrong," he muttered.

"What do you mean?" asked Captain Ainsley.

He glanced over, surprised the captain had approached and he hadn't heard. He handed her the spyglass.

Putting it to her eye, she surveyed the destruction. "It's as if… as if they fired upon the town."

"That was my thought as well," said Oliver.

"Do you think raiders took the compound and then turned on the town to destroy any resistance, or were the raiders able to take the village but the fort was successfully defended?"

"If it was raiders, they wouldn't have holed up in the compound. They would have sacked the place and left," surmised Oliver. "Whoever barricaded themselves inside is hoping for a rescue. They must be Company men."

"Then who is outside the compound?" wondered Ainsley. "The only ships in the harbor appear to be Enhoverian. There are people in the village… You're right, m'lord. Simple corsairs would have fled. If they could not breach the compound immediately, they would not have waited patiently for someone like us to arrive."

"And if we had caught them still in the village, they'd be fleeing now," added Oliver. "No one familiar with these seas would attempt to stand against an airship. Pirates would be on their boats now, sailing in opposite directions so we couldn't sink them all."

"What does it mean?" wondered Ainsley.

Oliver didn't reply. He knew, he thought, but he couldn't bring himself to say it.

"When close, drop sail and run out the sweeps. Float us low and slow over the town," instructed Oliver. "We'll make sure everyone sees us. While we maneuver over the Company compound it will give them time to think things over."

"Them who?" questioned Ainsley. "What will they think over?"

"Surrender, I hope."

They hung one hundred yards above the Company's compound. Down below them a flag flapped in the wind signaling an alert. It was a bit unnecessary. From their position, there was no doubt a rebellion had risen in the town below and the natives had rushed the Company's fortress. Somehow, the defenders had managed to shut the gates in time. With elevation and superior weaponry, they'd fought back into an apparent stalemate. The efficacy of their defense was apparent from the scores of bodies littering the ramp up to the compound and in the streets below.

Oliver grimaced, looking away from a cluster of women and children that lay dead and defiled. Cannon shot had ripped through them, mutilating their bodies into something barely resembling humans. The size of the corpses gave away which piles of blasted meat had been something smaller than a full-grown man.

"Are you sure about this?" questioned Captain Ainsley.

Oliver shrugged. "What else are we going to do?"

"Fly back to Enhover?"

He shook his head and tugged on the thick, leather gloves he would use to hold the rope as he descended into the compound. "Can you take us a little lower?"

"We'll risk small arms fire from the village if we do," answered the captain.

Oliver grunted. "I'll be risking that anyway."

"I'm going with you," declared Ainsley suddenly.

"I need you on the ship," protested Oliver.

"Pettybone can handle the crew," replied the captain. "You need someone watching your back."

"Very well," he said. "You'd better arm yourself."

Nodding, the captain rushed off to find her weapons, and Oliver peered over the edge of the gunwale.

One hundred yards below them was the roof of the governor's mansion. They would drop down on a line and land on the sloped surface. Then, it would be a short walk to the side where they could safely climb to the adjacent barracks roof and into the governor's window. All rather easy, except the dangling from a rope one hundred yards above a fatal drop. Not to mention the small arms fire that Ainsley was so worried would pepper her airship. It would take a lucky shot to hit them, but men bet large at the tracks and won every day.

A gust of warm tropical air pressed against the airship, rocking it slightly, causing the dangling rope to dance a sinuous pattern, floating back and forth over the governor's mansion and the courtyard three stories lower.

Oliver grimaced.

Breathing deep to steady himself, he turned to Ainsley as she stomped back on deck. On her hips, she wore a brace of long-barreled pistols, and on her back, she'd strapped two cutlasses. In her knee-high boots were the wooden-handles of two daggers. She'd set a floppy black tri-cornered hat upon her head and a grim expression on her face.

"What?" she asked. "I just bought this before we left. You don't like the hat?"

Shaking his head, Oliver turned back to the rope that stretched out of sight over the edge of the airship. "No, I don't like hats."

"It keeps the sun from your eyes," she advised as she tugged on her pair of leather gloves. "It's awkward with a wig, but you don't wear those either, do you?"

"I don't like wigs," replied Oliver, reflexively running his hand over his hair, checking the knot in the back.

Ainsley put one tall boot on the gunwale and looked back at him. "You want a pistol or something? If we get into trouble, I'd want a bit more than that broadsword."

"I've got you," he said.

She grinned at him.

"You ever shoot anything with those pistols?" he wondered, taking his place beside her.

"I beat a man over the head in the port of Durban with one

once," she claimed. "I would have shot him if my powder had been dry and if I'd had time to load it."

"Your pistols are loaded now?" asked Oliver.

"That they are, m'lord."

"Then let's go."

Refusing to look down, Oliver dropped over the side of the airship, his hands clenched around the rope, his legs wrapping it tight. He hung there for a moment, bouncing off the rough, wooden sides of the airship. With his heart pounding and his breath coming fast, he loosened his grip and began to slide down the rope.

Ainsley, her floppy hat threatening to blow away in the brisk tropical breeze, descended on her own rope beside him.

"You need to pay me more for this, m'lord," she called out.

"Now is not the time, Captain."

"We might not get another chance," she quipped.

Closing his eyes, Oliver continued to slide, tilting his head as the thick hemp rope dragged along his face, rubbing him raw.

After what seemed an eternity, he risked opening his eyes and saw they were a mere dozen yards above the roof, near the edge. Overhead, the airship was drifting, taking them past the roof of the mansion and over the courtyard, where their ropes would end two stories above the hard-packed dirt. The crew was working the sweeps, but the breeze had blown the airship sideways. They couldn't simply row forward and gain Oliver and Ainsley the room they needed.

"Hurry, Captain," called Oliver, and with a lurch, he dropped faster, the rope hissing as it sped through his gloved-hands.

Two yards above the roof and one from the edge of it, he let go. He fell and hit hard, his boots sinking into the tightly woven thatch. He collapsed onto his back, forcing himself away from the edge.

He saw Ainsley hanging above him, her ridiculous hat flapping in the wind, her pistols and cutlasses swinging wildly as she tried to speed her descent, but she was too late. The airship was drifting, and the end of her rope slipped off the edge of the roof.

Cursing, Oliver scrambled off his back. On hands and toes, he bear-crawled to the edge of the roof. Gripping a handful of thatch with one hand, he reached out with the other, catching Ainsley's rope and tugging on it, pulling it toward safety. He flopped over, hauling on the rope to where she could let go and fall beside him.

"Spirit-forsaken breezes," muttered the captain after she landed, glaring at her airship above. "Ah, look. Now, they're getting her turned."

The ropes swung loosely as the airship repositioned, the ends dragging along the thatch, right between Oliver and the captain.

"Always a steady breeze in the tropics," grumbled Oliver, glaring at the tail of the rope.

"I know. I-I should have accounted for that," admitted Ainsley, sitting beside him. "This crew will be good, m'lord. Soon as we—"

"We made it, Captain," interjected Oliver, struggling to his feet on the soft surface. "It was close, but we made it. Learn from this and get better." He looked down at his boots which were sinking into the tightly bound grasses that covered the roof. "This is going to be hell to walk across."

"First time the crew has had to drop someone on a roof, I suspect," she muttered "Next time, maybe you should—"

"Captain," warned Oliver.

"Right. Well, we're here now, so nothing to do but get on with it."

Oliver glanced up where the airship was slowly moving farther away in the warm breeze. Pettybone would turn it and come back, he hoped. For the moment, they were alone in the compound.

The pair of them traversed across the treacherous roof, leaning into the slope and then finally reaching the end where they were able to climb down onto the steep roof of the adjacent barracks building. It allowed them access to a window in the governor's mansion covered by a locked shutter.

Cursing to himself and annoyed to be clambering around in the tropical heat, Oliver kicked the shutter open, only half-disappointed to find no glass behind it. They climbed inside and then exited a small room, walking into in an empty hallway. As they stalked down the corridor, Ainsley's pistols and cutlasses banged and bounced.

"Not one for sneaking, are you?" complained Oliver.

"We arrived in the middle of the day on an airship," observed the captain, "so, no, I'm not trying to be sneaky."

"Well, maybe it will help us find Towerson," grumbled Oliver, peeking into an open doorway and an empty room.

They moved along the corridor, finding nothing except bloodstains and broken doors. Ainsley's clatter led the way. They passed down a stairwell and found the second floor of the building to be just as vacant as the first.

Then finally, as they descended to the ground floor, an exhausted voice called for them. "Oliver, is that you?"

He turned and saw Senior Factor Ethan Giles lumbering down the hallway.

"It is," replied Oliver. "What happened here?"

"Sorry I didn't meet you upstairs," said the merchant. "When I saw you drop in, I rushed out to the walls to make sure the chaps were looking sharp. Hate to have to explain to the board of directors that we got Duke Wellesley shot while he was visiting the compound."

Oliver raised an eyebrow.

"Uprising," explained Giles. "Natives rebelled against us. Luckily, they hit the governor's mansion first. It gave us in Company House and the royal marines in the barracks time to arm ourselves. The marines accounted themselves well, m'lord, and within a turn of the clock they'd pushed the rebels out the gate and secured the walls of the compound, but there were too many of the bastards for a complete victory. We're stuck in here, and they're stuck out there. Been a bit of a standoff for the last week, them waiting us out, hoping we starve I guess, and us hoping an airship like yours would arrive."

"Where's the governor?" questioned Oliver.

"Ah," mumbled Giles, shifting his weight on his feet. "When I said it was lucky they struck here first, I meant for the survival of the colony, not as much for Towerson himself. I'm afraid the man was trussed up like a Newday hen and carried out of here when the rebels fled. He was alive four days ago, for what that's worth."

Oliver grimaced.

"How many men did you bring?" questioned Giles, eyeing the well-armed Ainsley out of the corner of his eye.

"Not enough to conduct a war," said Oliver. "How many men do we have here, and who's in charge?"

"Well," replied Giles, tucking his thumbs behind his belt and drawing himself upright, "I'm in charge at the moment, as everyone more senior is dead or in captivity. We've got a score-and-a-half marines who are hale enough to fight, another two-dozen men who aren't trained for battle but are steady enough to swing a blade or hold a blunderbuss. That's, what, fifty all told? The men are tired, though, Oliver. They've been on twelve turn-shifts for days now, guarding the walls constantly. At any moment, we only got about a score walking patrol. It's enough we can watch every angle and raise an alarm, but not enough we can hold much longer in this spirit-forsaken heat."

"The natives, what have they demanded?"

"Demanded?" asked the factor.

"What do they want?" pressed Oliver. "Presumably they attacked and are holding the governor for a reason. Why?"

"Hell if I know," muttered Giles. The old merchant shifted, placing a hand on the wooden handle of the blunderbuss at his hip. "We'd finally drained that pond you found and breached what appeared to be a sealed tomb. We emptied it, but it took most of the royal marines to haul the artifacts back to the compound. Bastards caught us that night while the men were worn out and resting."

Oliver blinked at the man.

"What?" questioned Giles.

"Do you think the events may be related?" asked Oliver. "You find some new wealth on the island and then they attack?"

"Wealth?" scoffed Giles. "There wasn't nothing we found in that tomb that was worth the digging, if you ask me. Some figurines — little statues, I mean — and a couple of tablets they'd done some scrawling on. Weird writing, like nothing I've ever seen. Might fetch a little sterling from a collector back in Enhover, but that's hardly worth the freight to get it there. We didn't find anything of value on a commercial scale. Towerson thought there must be something there, the way the natives were getting agitated about the project, but I went in the chamber myself and there was nothing, just old rubbish. If it was worth anything, why they'd bury it?"

"These statuettes and tablets, where are they now?" questioned Oliver.

"Company House," replied Giles. "You want to take a peek?"

"Of course I do," growled Oliver. "The relationship between Company government and the natives has always been strong here. If it changed so suddenly, there was a reason, Giles. It defies imagination to think the reason isn't what you found up in those hills."

"Not what I found," replied Giles sternly. "What you found."

"He was right," remarked Captain Ainsley.

Oliver grunted.

"It's just rubbish," she said, gesturing around the room.

He shook his head but did not respond. Holding the basket-hilt of his broadsword so it didn't inadvertently swipe any of the figurines, he moved through the room, stooping to study them, barely breathing.

There were three dozen knee-high wooden statuettes roughly

carved into the likenesses of men and women. In other circumstances, he would have guessed they were simple tropical artwork, maybe the work of a single individual who fashioned the shapes to pass the time, but after what he'd seen, and the natives' reaction to the discovery, he was certain they were more. These were totems. Totems scratched and carved with patterns and runes.

As Giles described, they looked like nothing Oliver had ever seen before, but the symbols were too uniform to be random markings. No, these totems and the shapes carved into the strange wood were for a specific purpose. Since they'd been discovered within a tomb, he shuddered to think what that purpose might be.

Finally, after examining each of the figurines, he stood and moved to the tablets. Some were fashioned from hardened clay or stone. He didn't recognize the writing, but they felt familiar, and he wondered if he'd seen the symbols before. The creeping sense of worry in his gut was turning to dread. Ash-gray clay etched and then fired... There was only one place he'd seen a similar substance. In the markets of the Southlands, stalls were filled with clay objects purported to be from the Darklands.

"Frozen hell," muttered Oliver.

"What?" questioned Ainsley.

"We've got to find out why this stuff was buried way up on the hillside and then flooded," explained Oliver. "It's... it's magical in nature."

"How are we going to figure that out?"

"We're going to ask the people who buried it," he replied. "Something Towerson should have done the moment he breached the tomb. We're going to ask the natives."

"THIS IS A BAD IDEA," WARNED GILES.

"I've had worse," claimed Oliver.

"No doubt," agreed Giles, "I still think we should float your airship over to the other side of the village and, between the shore guns and the shipboard artillery, reduce this place to nothing but broken sticks and blood."

"The governor is down there, isn't he?" inquired Oliver. "The royal marines will not fire upon a peer."

"They will if you tell them to," insisted the senior factor.

Oliver shook his head.

"There," hissed Captain Ainsley.

Below them in the village, a small group of men was slinking out of cover and walking up the hard-packed sand and soil incline that led to the compound.

From a simple bamboo walkway above the compound's gates, Oliver, Ainsley, and Giles watched the natives approach. Spread out along the top of the wall were clusters of royal marines and Company men clutching what firearms and bladed weapons they'd scrounged from the barracks. Hanging one hundred yards above was the Cloud Serpent. It was a terrible angle if they meant to use the vessel in combat, but it was impossible to miss and hopefully intimidating to anyone approaching for the parlay.

From the corner of the compound, they'd raised the royal flag signifying House Wellesley and a white one beside it, signaling they were ready to talk. Giles had mused darkly that they would either talk or face an attack.

It was a risk, Oliver had agreed, but one they had to take. He was certain there was occult significance to the objects they'd found at the bottom of the pool, and he was just as certain it was the reason the natives had revolted. What he didn't know was why. Why did they attack, were they willing to negotiate, and was there anything left worth negotiating for? Life in the colony would never be the same, and unless Governor Towerson lived, there was little the men and women below could offer to change their fate. When word of the uprising reached Southundon, the Company and Crown would have only one response. The natives had to know that.

Grim-faced, Oliver waited, watching the approach of the delegation.

"The men are ready?" he asked.

"Aye," affirmed Giles. "Every one of them lost someone they knew in the attack. They're ready."

Oliver grunted.

Below, the delegation paused within shouting distance, but out of range for an accurate shot with a blunderbuss. Of course, that wasn't saying much. The two pairs of snipers they'd placed at the corners of the compound should have a clear shot, though. Either the natives weren't aware of the Company's rifle-bored firearms, or they'd thought to risk it.

"I am Duke Oliver Wellesley," called Oliver, wondering suddenly just how far rifle bores had spread. It'd be a difficult angle, but a skilled marksman from below in the village…

The group on the ramp huddled close together, making themselves a tempting target for the cannon, but if they fired upon them, Oliver knew they'd be no closer to resolving the conflict and no closer to recovering Governor Towerson. The man was likely dead, but if they didn't find out for sure, the Congress of Lords would have a fit. Even in a Company colony in the midst of an uprising, Enhoverian peers received the treatment their station deserved.

Interrupting whatever discussion was happening below, Oliver continued, raising his voice and shouting, "You've kidnapped the rightful governor of this island. I demand you release him."

At that, a large man broke off from the group. Thick, black hair was swept away from his face and coiled into ropes. He was shirtless, displaying finger-thick scars on a prodigious torso. Oliver guessed the man's rolls of fat hid massive muscles. The man had the look of a warrior, but Imbon hadn't seen war in over a decade.

"That's a hell of a man," whispered Ainsley appreciatively.

Oliver frowned at her.

"Masuu," said Giles. "He's a chieftain of sorts."

"Of sorts?" wondered Oliver.

"The natives have no government of their own," explained Giles, "hence no chief. Masuu represents their interests when there is a conflict between one of ours and one of theirs. He's well-respected by his people."

"Where'd he get all those scars, then?" wondered Ainsley, studying the approaching man with interest.

"I don't imagine you get to be chieftain without dispatching a few rivals," guessed Giles. "First time I've ever seen the man without his shirt, actually. He's normally quite civilized."

"Too bad." Ainsley sighed.

"Captain, get a hold of yourself," said Oliver, studying the man's scars as he covered half the distance between his companions and the gate. They were painful-looking scars, twisted into symmetric patterns across the man's broad chest. Not from combat, those. It was ceremonial scaring. It could be simple tradition that had been passed down and lost its meaning years or ago, or it could be something else.

"You are Masuu?" asked Oliver when the man stopped.

"I am," rumbled the giant.

"Is Governor Jain Towerson alive?"

"Come down and find out," barked Masuu.

"Tonight, when you see the glow from our fires, know it is the figurines we found inside of the tomb," shouted Oliver back down to the man. "Which spirits are bound to those objects? Those of your own ancestors? I viewed them when we arrived here, and despite being found in a flooded pool, the wood is quite dry. I suspect it will take less than a quarter turn of the clock to turn them all to ash."

Masuu's mouth fell open and he stared at Oliver. Behind him, the party he'd arrived with shuffled agitatedly. Giles cursed under his breath.

Oliver ran a hand back over his hair, checking the knot at the back. Perhaps he'd come on a little strong. His intent had been to negotiate calmly, to try to understand the reason the natives had rebelled, but it hadn't come out like that. Well, he'd started now, nothing to do but continue.

"What will happen when those bindings are broken? Will their spirits pass to the underworld?" called Oliver. "If you have no means of contacting them, I imagine that will be like losing them all over again."

Oliver waited, watching Masuu and the other men's reactions. He regretted the missed chance at sensible conversation, but with blood spilled on the sand already, there would be no peaceful resolution. He only hoped for a chance to get Governor Towerson back alive, if that was still possible. If not, he wanted confirmation the man was dead. Whether or not the natives held a peer in captivity made all of the difference in the amount of iron and fire the Crown would unleash upon the place.

"Those are not our ancestors," cried a man who was scrambling up behind Masuu.

Oliver glanced at Giles.

The senior factor shrugged. "Never seen him."

The newcomer, white-haired and wizened, had the look of an elder or a shaman. That or the village drunk.

"Those figurines contain the spirits of our enemies, foreigner!" declared the old man. "If you destroy them, you will release their shades upon this world. They will not return to the underworld where they belong. They cannot return. If you release them from the traps we fashioned, the angry spirits will stay here. They will ravage."

"Your enemies," replied Oliver tartly. "I can guess where they will go first."

"You do not know of what you speak," wailed the old man.

"No?"

Frustrated, the man clenched his fists. Beside him, Masuu looked like he was ready to charge the gates alone.

"Yes, you are right," admitted the old man. "If released, the shades will come and rend our souls from our bodies. Our people would be slaughtered. Do not be foolish and think the shades will stop there. These shades, reavers in your tongue, they will never stop. They will kill anyone they can reach. They will inhabit the corpses and then come again. You cannot kill what is already dead, foreigner! Your wigs and scarves, your airships and your stone palaces, your technology, it will do nothing to protect you. This is old magic, magic your people have lost."

Oliver frowned and called back, "We've not lost as much as you think."

"You know nothing!" cried the old man. "Our ancestors? Why would we hide the spirits of our ancestors in an underground cavern and then flood it? The spirits trapped within those statues are ancient enemies of us all! You must not destroy the statues. You must not break the bindings."

"He seems pretty serious," whispered Ainsley under her breath.

"You are a shaman?" called Oliver.

The old man shook his head, his thick shock of white hair waving in the tropical breeze. Like Masuu, he was shirtless, dressed in traditional native garb, his skin marred with scars.

"What is it you want from us?" asked Oliver. "Why did you attack the compound? Why did you take Governor Towerson?"

"We attacked to prevent you from doing what you claim you will," growled Masuu. He pointed to Senior Factor Giles. "Tell him, Factor. Tell him he can trust my word. It is a foolish mistake to release the uvaan."

"Perhaps I would have trusted you before you attacked, killed scores of my friends, and tied up and dragged off my superior," growled Giles.

"If you want your governor back, you will have to trust us," declared Masuu. "We are willing to bargain. We will end the blood-letting, but you must be willing as well."

"What do you want in exchange for him?" asked Oliver.

"We want the uvaan back, the figurines," answered the big native. "Bring them and set them outside of the gate, every one of them, and we will release your governor."

"Let me see him first," said Oliver. "Surely you understand we need to know Jain Towerson is alive before we return the… the uvaan to you. You cannot ask for our trust without giving us that small bit of assurance."

The big man crossed his arms, but the older man tapped his shoulder. They bent close and whispered to each other for a long moment.

Finally, Masuu stood. "We ask for your trust, so I will show you trust. I will bring you your governor and release him to you, but in return, I demand the return of the uvaan. They are worthless to you, foreigner. Bring them to the wall, and we will send you your governor."

The smaller native scampered back to the delegation, and after quick words, another man split off and trotted down into the village.

"Well, that was easier than I expected," stated Giles. "Want me to send word to the Cloud Serpent to lower the figurines?"

"No," replied Oliver slowly, watching as the man below disappeared into the thatch-and-bamboo village.

Much of the place had been damaged from the cannon fire that the defenders on the walls had unleashed, but at least half the buildings still stood. Any one of them could contain the governor. Any one of them could contain scores of attackers waiting in hiding as well. After the airship had arrived, the crew of the Cloud Serpent had reported frantic activity below. Now, it was all quiet. Where had the people gone?

"No?" asked Giles. "What is all of this for if not to recover the governor? We can't all flee on your airship, Oliver, but a few of us could. We can be to the United Territory colonies in the Vendatts in two days. Governor de Bussy would assist us, for a price to be sure. We could be to Archtan Atoll and back in a little over a week. We can go get help, Oliver."

"If they wanted the figurines back, why didn't they ask for them earlier?" wondered Oliver. "If that was their purpose, what was the point of waiting until I arrived in this place? Why not ask right after the initial conflict died? Why not in the days that followed?"

"Well… I don't know," admitted Giles.

"They attacked, were repelled, and have been waiting since. What were they waiting for?" A tremor of worry crawling along his back, Oliver turned and glanced up. Hanging one hundred yards above them was his airship. He looked back over the village. "They weren't waiting for me. They couldn't have known anyone more senior than Towerson or yourself was due to arrive. They could only be waiting on something they knew would eventually come to this place. Something that wasn't already here."

"Th-They can't get up to the airship, can they?" stammered Ainsley. "Even if they took the compound, the crew isn't going to let a swarm of attackers climb the ropes. They'll simply cut them free. There's no way to board the Cloud Serpent unless you're invited up."

"No, not… Wait," said Oliver, smacking his first against the wooden palisade they stood on. "I recognize a symbol from the tablets. The last time I saw it, it was on the back of a dead man's neck. I'd just sliced it in two."

"Say that again," requested Giles, scratching the back of his own neck, looking confused.

"They can take control of a man's body," said Oliver, "and manipulate them like a puppet. With a human marionette under their sway, they could sabotage the airship and drop it within reach. There are thousands of natives left, didn't you say, Giles? If they made it within the compound, they could easily overwhelm us."

"But why the airship?" wondered Ainsley. "Things have been peaceful here for years. What has changed?"

"The tablets and figurines," said Oliver. "If that symbol is what I think it is, it's evidence of sorcery. They had to know that eventually we would recognize it, and once we did, the Crown, Company, and Church would all be united in eradicating it. It's why they risked storming the compound. They must have figured they were already dead. They were willing to risk everything to protect those artifacts, the uvaan they called them. These people have been living a hidden life, defying Church law, right under our noses! They've been practicing sorcery, and now that we've discovered the evidence, they'll do anything to escape."

"Escape where?" wondered Ainsley.

"Somewhere they can't use one of those sea-going vessels to get to," said Oliver, pointing at the harbor. "They're going to go somewhere only an airship can reach."

"There is Governor Towerson," murmured Captain Ainsley, pointing down the slope.

Oliver spun, peering down the hill where the governor was supported between the arms of two burly natives.

"He looks worse for wear," complained Giles. "They're not making much effort to care for the poor man."

"It does look like they are holding their end of the bargain, though," remarked Ainsley. "They're going to carry him up here and turn him over."

"Shoot him," instructed Oliver, watching the governor's stiff, stumbling progress up the slope.

"What!"

"The snipers," continued Oliver. "Have them shoot Governor Towerson."

"You can't be serious," declared Giles. "When I suggested we attack, I didn't think he was actually still alive. He's there, Oliver! We can't… we can't shoot the man!"

"They've taken over the body of the governor," said Oliver, certain now he recognized the symbol on the tablets. The governor's straight-legged, halting movement was identical to the footmen he'd battled in Westundon. "If they want to commandeer the airship, the easiest way would be to simply hand that man over, knowing we'll hoist him up immediately to get him out of danger and into proper care."

"If you're right!" cried Giles. "What if you're wrong?"

"Shoot the man and we'll find out," barked Oliver.

"M'lord, I don't think—"

Next to them, a pistol cracked, and a cloud of burnt gunpowder billowed around the two men. Ainsley cursed and holstered her pistol, drawing her second without pause.

"Now!" cried Masuu from below them. "Now!" The native man continued in a frantic stream of incomprehensible shouts.

"How many passengers can we hold on the Cloud Serpent, Captain?" asked Oliver, his voice taut, his gaze locked down on the village where swarms of natives were pouring out of the bamboo-and-thatch structures.

Squinting one eye and peering down the barrel of her second pistol, she said, "I—"

"You won't hit him from here, not with that weapon," chided Oliver. "We need to evacuate what we can of the compound. How many can we flee with?"

"With the crew, ah, another thirty souls somewhat comfortably. Fifty or sixty if we stuff them in the hold, m'lord," said Ainsley. "We're not provisioned for it, though. We have water to make the Vendatts with that many. We'll come short of the atoll. M'lord, getting them on board…"

"Giles," said Oliver calmly, his hand finding the basket-hilt of his broadsword. "Begin with the women and… Are there any children? Before hoisting them up, strip every one of them down and examine them. Anyone with a strange tattoo or marking stays. I don't care how long ago they say they got it. Have the crew haul them up by rope and don't let that airship drop within fifty yards of any structure within the compound. Ainsley, you ascend first and prepare the Cloud Serpent for passengers. Giles, you get… get as many as you can."

Swallowing, the senior factor nodded, his eyes fixed down below where the natives continued to bring Governor Towerson closer. More and more of them streamed out of the village behind. Ainsley held her pistol, still cocked, her arm trembling.

"Both of you go now!" snapped Oliver.

Giles bolted off. Oliver guessed he was heading to Company

House where his wife resided, and their children, if they had them.

His native wife.

Oliver opened his mouth to call out to the factor, but Ainsley interrupted, asking, "What will you do, m'lord?"

"I'll lead the defense. I'll give you as much time as I can," declared Oliver.

"The defense, the defense against... Frozen hell," breathed the captain.

A sharp, terrible cracking drew his attention, and Oliver turned to see a scaled behemoth shoving its way through the broken, ruined village. Dark green with bright orange spikes down its back, the thing stretched the length of one of the sailing vessels in the harbor.

"It looks like a monitor lizard," said Oliver, "except—"

"Except it's spirits-forsaken big!" cried Ainsley.

"Get to your airship, Captain," instructed Oliver.

Shouts of fright and surprise rose from the men on the walls. As Oliver scrambled to climb up the cannon platform at the corner of the compound, he heard a rising tide of cheers below. In the village, the natives had begun their charge. Dozens and then hundreds waved clubs and farming implements. They were racing toward the soil incline that led to the gates, and then they spread out to climb the berm that the compound sat upon.

Oliver made it to the top of the platform and began shouting instructions to the men. "Turn it, turn it! We need the cannon on that— Damn. There are three of them. Shoot those spirit-forsaken lizards!"

Behind the first of the giant monitor lizards, a second and third had emerged from the surrounding jungle.

"Frozen hell," cursed a cannoneer.

Grunting, Oliver rushed to the heavy brass cannon where a pair of men were trying to turn it. He placed his shoulder against the hot metal and shoved with them, grimacing as the weapon slowly scrapped across the wooden boards.

"Is there no swivel for this thing?" he muttered.

Beside him, one of the two royal marines offered apologetically, "Don't often have to turn it, m'lord. In this humidity, the gears rust…"

Muttering foul curses as a team, they maneuvered the heavy brass cannon to face the three giant lizards.

Oliver stepped back, wondering where the hell the creatures had been hidden. Buried artifacts, giant lizards, what else was happening in Imbon that he and the Company were not aware of?

The cannoneers scrambled to adjust the aim of the giant weapon.

A man struck a taper and glanced at Oliver. "I'd cover your ears, m'lord."

The man lit the fuse. Seconds later, the weapon thundered. Smoke and fire burst from its angry brass mouth, rolling over the platform, obscuring the field in front of them.

THE PRIESTESS VII

A GUARD EYED THEM SUSPICIOUSLY, his gaze sliding over the spear she clutched in front of her, down to the kris daggers on her hips, and then over to the cart where Ivar val Drongko and his donkey stood pretending to wait patiently.

"We're going to need to search the contents of that cart and, ah, examine some of your items..." The guard looked as if he'd say more, but he paused, like he was unsure how to address her.

"Do you stop and search everyone who enters Romalla?" wondered Sam.

"No," responded the guard, shifting uncomfortably.

"Then why us?"

"You know why," muttered the guard. He glanced over his shoulder to where a partner was in discussion with a man hauling his own radish cart. Or what looked like a radish cart. If the scrawny man had strength to pull the thing loaded with such a towering pile of radishes, Sam would be amazed.

"Unrefined poppy bulbs," said Ivar, nodding at the cart.

Their guard frowned.

"Go on then," suggested the colorful perfumer. "See what he has hidden underneath."

The guard glared at him. "That man isn't the only one attempting to sneak contraband into this city."

"I work for the Church," said Sam. "I am a priestess."

"From Enhover?"

"You can't tell from the accent?" jested Sam, attempting a smile.

"Here with Bishop Yates?" questioned the guard.

"Bishop Yates, is he... Yes, I am here with him."

"What's he look like, then?" asked the guard, his voice stern and his stance square.

"Fat," said Sam. "He's got three chins and a belly I could fit inside. It's been years since his white hair has reached the top of his head, and his nose is bright red from too much sherry. Is that a close enough description for you?"

The guard shrugged. "I have no idea what the man looks like."

"You will if you keep holding us up," said Sam. "I had an assignment that delayed me. The bishop asked me to catch up as quickly as possible. We're scheduled to meet with the Council later this evening."

"The-The Council?" stammered the guard. "You know the password, then?"

She blinked at him.

"All of the other Knives give us the password," asserted the guard. "It's the only way to know who really works for the Church."

"I'm from Enhover," she reminded him. "I was meant to be traveling with the bishop, until... The truth, this is my first time in Romalla. If I do not make it inside in time to meet with the Council, it may be my last. Whatever password, whatever protocol you have, I do not know. Please, help me. I will make it up to you after your shift is over."

The guard cringed and waved them by, but under his breath, he muttered, "Learn the password, ey?"

As the cart rolled out of earshot of the guard, Sam glanced at Ivar. "I think he was one of yours."

The man laughed. "Not one of mine, but you are right. Your attention wasn't arousing the poor man, it was scaring him. He was near shaking in his boots he was so frightened by you."

"Frightened of me?"

"Shouldn't he be?" wondered Ivar. "If you'd met that man late at night in a tavern and he'd tried to make your acquaintance, would you have given him a tumble or slit his throat? You could do either one, and if I'm not mistaken, you'd feel the same about both."

"That's not fair," argued Sam.

"Who is Bishop Yates?" asked Ivar.

Sam smiled. "He's the man I need to find."

"Care to escort me to the market first?" requested Ivar. "Once I'm there, I can obscure my wares from nosy watchmen, but if I meet one on the way…"

"I'll take you there and then I'll have a look at what you've got," stated Sam. "That's part of the arrangement, isn't it? I see you safely to the market, you give me my pick of your potions?"

"Well, I wouldn't say your pick," huffed Ivar. When he saw her raised eyebrow, he quickly added, "We'll talk. We'll talk."

Nodding, Sam turned back to study the street and wondered what other strange encounters she'd have in Romalla, home of the Church.

THE BISHOP STOPPED, AND A PAIR OF HULKING, CASSOCK-CLAD guards paused behind him. He frowned at her as if he recognized her but couldn't make the connection as to how.

She nodded in greeting and watched as his gaze traveled up and down her body. She resisted the urge to roll her shoulders back, pushing her breasts against the tight fabric of her shirt, to swing a hip out to the side in a saucy pose, and to favor him with an inviting smile. Knowing how to tug on a man's desires did not

mean one should always do it. Now was not the time for toying
with the bishop.

"Who are you?" asked Bishop Yates.

"I am— I was, Thotham's apprentice," she replied.

"Ah," said the churchman, pinching his chins and nodding.
"And what are you doing here, then?"

"I came to see the Council of Seven," she replied. "I need your
help finding them. It seems even in this place, the Church holds
her secrets closely, and I've been afraid to approach a stranger. My
mentor never brought me to Romalla, but he warned me how
they may treat, ah, those of our ability."

"He was wise, your mentor," said Bishop Yates, his jowls
shaking as he spoke.

"Wise?" she wondered.

"Keeping you from those vultures," answered Yates. "Why are
you trying to reach them, girl? The Council of Seven has little
interest in Enhover. It's best that way, I've found. Is this about the
Dalyrimple affair? It was my understanding that matter was
resolved."

Sam shifted, eyeing the men behind the bishop.

"Is my understanding incorrect?" asked Yates. "Or do you
believe there is another sorcerer operating within our borders? If
so, why have you not brought this accusation to me? I could help
you, girl."

"No, I have no proof there are any sorcerers in Enhover,"
replied Sam. "It stands to reason, though, that if there was one,
there could be another."

"Fair enough," agreed the bishop, smiling. "We have you,
though. That is your role, to monitor our people for any violation
of Church law. If and when you find some clue, you should come
directly to me, girl. I'm hurt that you did not."

"You will not help me?" asked Sam, her eyes narrowing to a
slit.

The bishop tilted his head, studying her. After a moment, he
said, "I will help you find the Council of Seven, though, there are

no longer seven of them and I believe you will be disappointed. The Council is like to be less helpful than you imagine. When you are done with them and they are done with you, come to see me. Your mentor and I were, well, not friends, but we understood each other. It would benefit us both if we shared the same relationship."

"I am no girl," she declared.

The bishop smiled. "No, not any longer, are you? I misspoke."

"The Council?" she asked, hoping to get what she needed and then end the conversation. There was a reason Thotham was so cautious, she knew.

Bishop Yates evidently wasn't bound by the same secrecy, and he waved to one of the priests behind him. "Take her to Bishop Constance."

The man nodded, and she fell in beside him as he walked through the sprawling stone corridors of the Church. It was a massive complex, three or four times the size of the Church in Westundon, larger even than Prince Philip's palace and twice as old. The Church's halls teemed with cassocked priests and armed guards. The latter carried menacing pole arms and clanked as their archaic plate armor moved beneath pure white tunics emblazoned with the golden circle of the Church. Many of the men stopped and stared at her as they passed.

"Not a lot of women in the priesthood in Ivalla, you think?" she asked.

"Not why they're looking at you," advised her guide. "Sorcery is a bigger concern here than at home. Many of these men are trained to detect it. I imagine few of them understand what they're feeling, like a proper attuned would, but even someone with no training could detect the dark presence of spirits around you."

"The presence of the spirits?" she asked.

"Surely you know they cling to you," replied the man, looking over his shoulder at her. "You're like a burning torch walking down a dark hallway. Why is that? Why do the shades cluster in your wake?"

"It will fade," she said, looking away.

"It will fade?" asked the man. "That doesn't answer my question."

Sam agreed, but she still didn't answer. She cursed to herself. Kalbeth had warned her. The tattoo across her back, even after several weeks, seemed to writhe on top of her skin. That skin had healed, but evidently, the piercing of the shroud had not. The cold taint of the underworld would follow her for a time until it did.

Her guide was studying her, waiting for an answer.

"What is that?" she asked, pointing toward a silver emblem hanging around his neck, trying to distract the man.

"It is a symbol for the Sect of Sages," replied her guide, picking up the silver pendant and showing it to her. A quill bisecting the Church's circle. "It's an order of scholars within the Church. It's how I earn my bread, you could say."

"And Bishop Yates allows you into his entourage because of that, because you're a scholar?"

"He is a Sage as well," said the priest. "The Church can be a lonely place, if you do not surround yourself with likeminded people."

"I'd rather be alone," claimed Sam.

"Your kind are strange," complained the man, shaking his head, reaching up to brush away a shock of copper-red hair. "Whether you're from Enhover or Ivalla, you're all strange and secretive. Perhaps that's why there are so few of you left."

"I'm still here," she asserted.

"Aye, and where is here?" he asked.

She paused, looking around at the blank stone walls and nondescript doors that lined the dim hallway the man had led her into. A hand dropped down to one of her daggers.

Her guide laughed. "Don't worry. I'm leading you where you want to go. My point was you don't know where that is. You are marching blindly with no clue where you're headed. You have no vision. It is a trait of the old Church, to move without thinking, to never make progress because there is no end to your path. The old guard were never going anywhere."

"What is that supposed to mean?" she asked.

The man merely shrugged in response and kept walking deeper into the labyrinthine hallways. As they went, they saw fewer and fewer people, and eventually, they were alone, only their footsteps echoing back at them.

"A last bastion of the old Church," said the man after a long stretch of silence. Then, he stopped in front of a moonlit garden. "She's likely in there somewhere. It's her haunt, I suppose you could say."

"In this garden?" questioned Sam, "And if she's not?"

"Then I don't know where to find her," claimed the man. He watched her face and added, "She should be here. She retires here every night, I believe. Bishop Yates met her in these gardens just two evenings past. This is one of the few spaces deep in the bowels of the Church where one can get fresh air and see the night sky without looking through a pane of glass or a set of iron bars. It used to be a cemetery."

Sam grunted.

"Good luck," offered the man. "Both with the bishop and…" He waved his hand at her, seeming to encompass her body and the spirits floating around her.

"What is your name?" asked Sam.

"Adriance," replied her guide. "Timothy Adriance."

"I'll remember that," said Sam, "and maybe we'll see each other again, Timothy Adriance."

The man simply smiled at her.

When he left, Sam turned to peer at the dark foliage out of a wide, arched opening. Drawing a deep breath, she stepped forward.

From a narrow alcove just inside of the garden, a hidden voice asked, "What is it?"

She jumped in surprise.

A short woman rose from a bench and stepped into the open. "That was Bishop Yates' man, Adriance? You must be from Enhover as well. Allow me to guess, Thotham's mysterious apprentice? No one else surrounded by darkness like you would be so bold to walk into the Church and seek me out. Am I right?"

Sam's throat was dry. She nodded.

"Come along then," instructed the little woman. "The others will want to see you."

THE OTHERS, IT TURNED OUT, WERE JUST THREE. THEY SAT BEHIND A semi-circular table, four seats filled, three empty. The Council of Seven, as they'd once been known.

"Your mentor could have joined us, you know," remarked Bishop Constance. "Years ago, we invited him, but he refused to return from the field. So few do, these days. Either they cannot leave behind the adventure, or they die. Unfortunate that, but none of us live forever. It's difficult, with fewer Knives, to find those with the constitution and wisdom to join us at the council table."

"I can see that," acknowledged Sam. "I've come for your help. When Thotham died, we lost so much. His knowledge, his skill, it's gone, but the threat is not."

"He was a skilled Knife," agreed Constance, bobbing her head.

"We believe there is another group of sorcerers loose in Enhover," continued Sam, her gaze flicking over the assembled council. "Ones superior to what we dealt with in Derbycross and Archtan Atoll. Sorcerers that are behind much of the recent unrest in Enhover."

"Hmm, unrest you say, another group of sorcerers?" scoffed one of the Council.

Sam hadn't caught the grouchy-looking man's name, but she decided she didn't need to.

Sitting forward, sticking his head out like a bobbing turkey, the man continued, "It is true that sorcery made a brief return after we believed it dead. We'd be fools not to acknowledge that, but I've seen the correspondence, and I spoke to Bishop Yates. Sorcery in Enhover is dead again."

"What—"

"Harwick was cleansed," declared Constance, speaking over both Sam and the man to the side of her. "Harwick, Archtan Atoll, and Derbycross. We made sure that nothing remains of those foul nests. The practitioners who once conducted the dark arts in those places are dead, and their equipment and materials are destroyed. We sent Knives behind you to clean up your mess, and they've confirmed there are no more leads to follow. Unless you have some evidence to the contrary, I'm quite confident that there is nothing required in Enhover. Since you are here, though, what is your name, girl?"

"Sam," she answered, spitting the word out quickly. Keep her secrets, Thotham had told her, but she could not expect help from these people if she would not even share her name. "And I am no longer a girl."

"Of course not. Sam… Samantha?" questioned Constance. "I ask that you remain some time in Romalla, Samantha, and then we can reassign you to a more suitable post. Perhaps paired with one of our more experienced Knives? There have been rumblings up in Rhensar, and it's imperative that we deal with them quickly. Well, as quickly as the Church does anything. It is our mission to address these things before they reach the Prelate's ear, and word travels quickly here on the continent."

Bishop Constance sat back with a pleased smile upon her face. She looked as though she believed what she'd just related would be pleasing to Sam as well.

"I… No," babbled Sam. "No, I came for help in Enhover. The threat is there, Bishop."

"Is it?" asked the woman. "Why do you think so?"

"Just before I came," explained Sam, "a secret society was

attacked in Westundon. Dozens were killed, merchants, peers, and common alike."

"Who was behind this attack?" questioned the old man to Constance's right.

"Well, I don't know," said Sam. "That's why I need your help."

The man snorted and crossed his arms over his chest.

"I read your mentor's reports... what he was able to report before he was killed," consoled Constance. "You arrived at my garden with Bishop Yates' man, so I suppose you know I met with him as well. He relayed the details of the encounter in Derbycross that had not been transmitted already. Terrible what that family did, but it's not the first time we've seen awful secrets passed down through the generations. In my experience, it would be the first time that knowledge was shared outside of the family. Those people do not maintain secrecy of their dark pursuits for centuries by speaking of it. Tell me, is there any of this Dalyrimple family left alive?"

Sam blinked. "No, I—"

"It is settled then," declared Constance.

"Marquess Colston, he was an elder in a society called the Feet of Seheht," argued Sam. "He was a sorcerer with incredible power. The Feet of Seheht was the society that was attacked. Many were killed. Whoever is left is covering their tracks. They're killing anyone who could lead us to them."

"Was any sorcery used during the purported attack?" questioned Constance, her matronly mask falling away and a hard-eyed inquisitor taking her place.

The Whitemask, Thotham had referred to her as, and Sam understood. The warm, friendly expressions, her appearance, were all a mask. Underneath lived a woman ruthless enough to lead a council of assassins.

"Bishop Yates did not mention if sorcery was used," said Constance. "If this Marquess Colston had shared what he knew, then certainly someone would have that knowledge and would use it to defend themselves. From what I was told of Derbycross, no mundane thugs would be able to burn down that man's home. If there were sorcerers within this group you speak of, then why did they not protect themselves? And if there is a powerful sorcerer snipping leads, then why have they not come after you, Samantha? Why have they not come after this Duke Wellesley who was so deeply involved in the affair? Yes, Bishop Yates told us all about that. This is not our first time following the trail of a dangerous practitioner. There are tell-tale signs that followers of the dark path leave. I see none of those in Enhover. Do you have any hard evidence, any suspects?"

"I… I-It's…" she stammered.

She thought of the Book of Law, the grimoire she'd found in Isisandra's effects. Simply owning the book was a violation of Church law. Reading it was worse. Sam's kind were dispatched to kill those who tried to decipher such forbidden knowledge. She knew, in her gut, that sorcery was still a threat, but she couldn't tell them everything that she knew or suspected. Not if she wanted to walk out of the room alive.

"You cannot show me evidence because it does not exist," asserted Constance. "If there were sorcerers operating in the way you insist they are, we'd see the signs."

"But Thotham's prophecy!" exclaimed Sam, glaring at the council members.

"Here we go," muttered one of the men who had not yet spoken. He rolled his eyes and glanced at Constance.

The bishop smiled at Sam from behind the table. "I'm familiar with your mentor's claims. A darkness, yes, rising from Enhover? We all thought it silly decades ago when he first claimed to have seen the vision. I admit I thought he was quite mad just years ago when he last tried to convince me it was a true portend. Prophecy is a rare gift, Samantha. Much throughout history that has been claimed as a true vision is merely dream and conjecture. Sometimes, due to random chance, those visions have come true. More often, they do not."

Sam frowned.

"You trusted your mentor. That is good," said Constance, the matronly tone working its way back into her voice. "Perhaps he was right, and his prophecy was one of those exceedingly rare pronouncements that had a seed of truth. However, consider this. What if his prophecy has already occurred?"

Sam gaped at the bishop.

"You did not think of that, did you?" chided Constance. "The tree of darkness and the seed or whatever it was the old man claimed. Isisandra Dalyrimple could be the seed of darkness. She gained her powers from the branch of her family tree. You prevented her from spreading that darkness, as Thotham foresaw. The prophecy, if it was ever true, seems to have already happened."

"Hold on," protested the man to the bishop's right. "I'm not ready to declare this a true—"

"It does not matter," assured Constance, turning to the man and holding up a hand to stop him. "I was merely trying to make the point that if it was true, the threat is already over. True or untrue, it does not matter except for what we want to acknowledge in the record books. For our purposes, what we must decide on today, the course is already set because it does not matter. Maybe the prophecy was merely a vivid dream that Thotham had, or it was something more and has already transpired. In both cases, sorcery is dead again in Enhover. Samantha, by order of the Council, I ask that you remain here until the shadow passes from your soul. I can feel it upon you, some residual stench of the battle in Derbycross, I imagine. When it passes, you will be reassigned."

Sam shook her head, but she found herself speechless. The Council, the group she'd sought for guidance and assistance, was turning everything on its head. Not only were they not helping her, they were instructing her to… No. She would not do it. She would not let go of the trail she and Duke had found.

"Do not argue, girl," advised Constance.

"I'm not a girl," declared Sam.

"Come with me, then, Knife of the Council."

THE CARTOGRAPHER IX

THROUGH THE ACRID haze of gunpowder, he saw splinters of bamboo and thatch flying as flashes of dark green skin crashed through the village below.

"Fire again!" he called.

"I'm trying, m'lord!" snapped a cannoneer.

The man was working frantically with the team to reposition the cumbersome weapon, but down in the village, the giant lizards moved with strength, grace, and speed. Unlike their smaller brethren who spent much of the day lounging on sun-baked rocks and branches, the giant lizards crawled closer with lithe determination, snaking between structures or smashing through the wreckage.

Down the wall, the blast of cannon erupted in violent staccato bursts. Evidently, the crews needed no instruction that they should turn the mouths of their giant brass firearms toward the approaching ship-sized lizards. Swarming at the base of the wall were hundreds of natives. Only a few were armed with modern weapons, but the rest would quickly overwhelm the defenders if they made it inside. With only moments until the lizards reached the walls, they wouldn't have long to wait.

On the scaffolding above the gate, royal marines were aiming down and firing furiously, each discharge of their blunderbusses scattering tiny shot amongst the attackers, but for every attacker who went down screaming in pain, two more emerged from the village to join the assault. Superior weapons against superior numbers. The royal marines had faced such circumstances before, and it was a core part of their training, but Oliver doubted they'd ever been coached to stand against a monstrous lizard that could swallow them whole.

"We should retreat, m'lord," suggested one of the cannon crew.

Under his breath, Oliver hissed, "To where?"

"What, m'lord?"

"We hold position," ordered Oliver loudly.

Suddenly, from above them, a salvo erupted. The men on the wall raised a cheer. The Cloud Serpent had entered the fray.

A full fusillade exploded from the starboard of the hanging airship, rocking it in place. A shrill voice screamed, and Oliver looked to see a woman dangling fifty yards above, being hauled up toward the deck of the airship. Captain Ainsley was still loading evacuees, but she was not one to turn from a fight. From above, he heard frantic commands as the arms master cajoled the shipboard cannoneers to reload faster and roll the weapons back out the portals for another volley.

Turning to see what the airship had accomplished, Oliver saw one of the three giant lizards limping, a bloody trough burrowed in its hind leg where a cannon ball had grazed it. There was another gaping wound in its front shoulder that pumped buckets of bright red blood. The things could be injured, and it looked as if one of the three may fall from the fight. It was a start.

"Center mass!" cried Oliver.

The cannon crew cursed and complained, and Oliver admitted to himself it wasn't as if they weren't trying, but the Cloud Serpent had to take time to reload, and those cannon crews had the added difficulty that the airship would be moved from the force of the discharges. They couldn't merely adjust their aim from the previous volley, they'd have to start all over again. The men on the walls in their stationary positions had to make each blast count.

Then, a hand, browned from the tropical sun, slapped down on the wall in front of Oliver. Someone was climbing up the bamboo structure.

"'Ware the walls!" he shouted, drawing his broadsword and leaping forward to slash down and remove the offending fingers from the edge of the Company's compound.

He heard a startled, pained shout from the other side of the wall, and the hand disappeared, only a bloody smear showing it'd been there. A moment later, an angry face appeared, and Oliver shoved the tip of his steel broadsword between bright white teeth, following a pink tongue down the open throat. Crimson blood gurgled up around his blade, and the dead man fell silently away.

Down the wall from him, Oliver heard the clamor of hand-to-hand combat and the discharge of small arms as the royal marines tried to maintain their hold on the walls. On the artillery platform, Oliver shouted for the cannoneers to continue firing while he protected their perch.

"We have to retreat m'lord!" yelled one of the men.

Snarling, Oliver lashed and jabbed with his broadsword, defending as half-a-dozen men clung to the sides of the wall, trying to scramble over. If they made it atop, Oliver knew he'd be quickly outnumbered and overwhelmed. And if the cannoneers stopped firing, they'd be just as quickly overrun by the menacing lizards.

Taking another man in the eye, Oliver staggered back, catching his breath and glancing around wildly at their surroundings.

A shadow fell across him, followed by a wash of heat, like he'd stepped into a steam bath. It felt comfortable, safe even, until he looked up and saw the giant, green-skinned lizard towering above, feet splayed with giant claws, a narrow tongue flicking out, tasting the air.

Screaming in panic, the cannoneers fled, jumping off the back of the platform into the courtyard of the compound. The huge lizard reared above them, snapping its jaws at the Cloud Serpent, although it was still dozens of yards below the floating airship.

Oliver scrambled to the cannon, snatching up the taper and wondering if the men had finished loading the shot. With no time to look, he set the sizzling stick against the wick and offered a hope to the spirits.

The brass cannon thundered as powder exploded and a heavy iron ball was flung from the mouth. Acrid smoke billowed over Oliver, and the cannon crashed against its wooden frame.

The giant lizard's angry cry turned into one of shock and pain. Oliver gaped in surprise as he saw blood pour from a grisly hole torn in the creature's stomach. The cannon had been loaded, and the lizard was so close that even he couldn't miss. The lizard started to topple forward, right onto cannon platform.

"Frozen hell," he muttered.

THE PRIESTESS VIII

"RAYMOND AU CLAIR," murmured the jauntily dressed man.

He had one leg draped over the arm of the stuffed chair he lounged in. In his hands, he toyed with a gleaming dirk. His vest was fine purple velvet adorned with golden buttons. A tightly woven, snow-white linen shirt was underneath it, and his trousers were snug, more like leggings. They did little to hide his well-formed calf as he aimlessly kicked his leg. Instead of boots, he wore slippers. The man made no move to rise after introducing himself, and he offered a rakish smile as she looked at him.

"Bridget Cancio," remarked the woman who stood at the edge of the room. She was slicing thin pieces off a long, red sausage. "Salami? Cheese? Stick them both between a slice of this bread and it is quite good."

"Wine," replied Sam.

Winking at her, Bridget nodded to an earthenware jug sitting at the edge of the table.

"Constance tells me you are to work with us," drawled Raymond.

Sam grunted, pouring a healthy cup of wine and then shuffling over to accept a slice of sausage from Bridget.

"I met your mentor once," continued the rake, either ignoring that she hadn't responded to him or not caring. "He was a competent Knife, if a bit misguided. You know, aside from Thotham, we haven't had a regular presence in Enhover for years."

"Do you find a lot of sorcerers here in the United Territories?" asked Sam, looking over her shoulder at him before popping the chunk of the meat into her mouth.

She blinked. The sausage was salty and fatty. Its sharp flavor seemed to meld with the cheese as she bit off a piece of that as well. Her mouth was full of the savory flavors when she took a sip of the wine. The rich, red liquid rinsed away the strong flavors of the food, and she had to stop herself from licking her lips. Ship and road rations it was not.

"We've found a few sorcerers, aye," said Raymond, still carelessly kicking his leg and fiddling with his dagger. He looked at the blade and then back to Sam.

"She's not interested in you," advised Bridget, leaning back against the stone wall of the room, folding together a bit of sausage, cheese, and bread, and then taking a bite.

"No?" asked Raymond, his gaze lazily shifting between the two women.

"No," confirmed Sam.

"That's a shame. It really is," declared Raymond, his jaunty pose unchanging, but his smile faltering. "You're missing out."

"If you used your dick as well as your dirk, perhaps she would be," cackled Bridget. "Instead, she'll just have to settle for your insufferable leering and pandering."

"You didn't mind last time we were in bed together," claimed Raymond, rolling his head to glance at his partner.

"That was two years ago," she reminded, "and I was so drunk the only thing I recall is waking up next to you."

"That's not what you said back then," he replied, "and if it was nothing, why do you keep bringing it up?"

"You brought it up," she reminded. "You bring it up constantly. If it'd been any good, I'd do it again. It wasn't."

"So you do remember. Give me another try then, darling?" cooed Raymond.

Bridget glanced at Sam. "Are the men in Enhover so difficult?"

Sam nodded. "Most of them."

Raymond twisted the dirk in his hands, showing his white teeth in a big grin. "Attitude is earned."

"Not by you. Not in the bedroom, at least," muttered Bridget under her breath.

Ignoring her, Raymond continued, "A wolf can be none other than a wolf. Why bother to fight it? I'm a wolf, but so are you two. It's in our blood. We are wolves that hunt the deadliest game. Sometimes in the streets, sometimes between the sheets, eh? They should make that into a sign and put it above the entrance to our apartments."

"That would last until the first time Constance strolled by," mentioned Bridget.

"Dangerous game, men and women," said Sam.

"Indeed," replied Raymond. "We hunt the most dangerous game alive. Sorcerers, practitioners of the dark art, the masters of the spirits of the underworld. We track them down, and we eradicate them."

"I'm aware of that." Sam took another bite of the sausage. "It's what I do as well, you know."

"Is it?" questioned Raymond.

She frowned at him.

"The stench of the underworld is all over you," he said, his foot and hands suddenly stilling. "I can feel the spirits clinging to you. You breached the shroud. That is illegal by Church law. Bishop Constance sensed it as well. Why do you think she sent you to us?"

Sam's blood ran cold. Her eyes darted between the two Knives.

"If we meant to kill you, we would have done so already," said Bridget, still leaning against the wall, but her body was tense, and it didn't take years of training to see she was ready to spring into action. "We all know that in our line of work, rules are inconvenient. There are things we do which we wish we did not have to do to complete our tasks. Raymond and I have both done things we are not proud of, but things we felt were necessary. We did it for good reason. We did it to stop the spread of sorcery, no matter the cost. Can you say the same, Sam?"

Sam scowled. "I've faced sorcery before. I thought you would have heard."

"I'm well aware of what happened in Harwick, Archtan Atoll, and Derbycross," murmured Bridget. "I know what you did there, and I know what you left behind. Take Harwick. You found a nest of sorcery in that cold little village in the north of Enhover. You even killed a man, but you didn't stomp out the nest, did you? In Archtan Atoll, you dealt with the witch, but what about those who had dealt with her? What about those who'd felt the taint of the underworld and kept coming back to the woman?"

"I don't understand," responded Sam.

"We've had to go clean up your messes," explained Raymond. "We went to Harwick. We were the ones who put down the other members of the Mouth of Set. We traveled to Archtan Atoll, a brutal slog without the ease of your airships, believe me, and we had to find and exterminate the swamp witch's contagion. It's all we've been doing these last months, following you around and cleaning up what you've left behind." Still seated, Raymond held up his dirk and pointed it at her. "I've killed dozens you left alive, dozens touched by the foul shadow of sorcery that you did nothing about."

"I killed the sorcerers," declared Sam, shifting uncomfortably.

"Our job is to ensure the taint is gone, completely gone. It's the only way we can guarantee sorcery will never rise again," said Bridget, her tone patronizing. "You only did half your job, Sam. It's time you showed us you can do the rest."

"What do you mean?" cried Sam. "I've faced sorcery like nothing you've ever—"

"Ivar val Drongko," interjected Raymond.

"Ivar?" wondered Sam.

"You've asked for help from the Council and its Knives," said Bridget, finally standing off the wall and stepping toward Sam. "It's time you proved you deserve it. It's time you show you're willing to do what it takes to end sorcery in this world."

"B-But he said…" stammered Sam. "He said that he's worked with Knives before, that there was an arrangement."

"Are you willing to do what it takes to end sorcery?" questioned Bridget. She glanced at Raymond's dirk then back to Sam. "Because if not, if a willingness to do anything does not explain the spirits we feel clinging to you, what are we to think?"

"I've proven myself," said Sam, standing tall, glaring at the pair of them.

Her hands twitched and she strained to keep them from her daggers. She was confident she could move first if it came to it, but against two opponents who must have had similar training to her own, in the heart of the Church, she had no chance. As confident as she was in her own skills, she'd be a fool to not admit the odds if there was a fight.

Again, she stated, "I've proven myself."

"Not to us, you haven't," declared Raymond.

Suddenly, he stood, his languorous mask falling away.

She saw him as the threat he was. This man was a lothario and a rake, but first and foremost, he was a killer.

"Ivar val Drongko has crafted potions, infusing them with ingredients that are illegal under Church law," stated Bridget. "He's called upon the spirits for some of his preparations. He's aided those we believe to be practicing sorcerers. By our law, the sentence is death. Take us to him, Sam, and show us you can enforce the law."

"I'M SORRY ABOUT RAYMOND," REMARKED THE WOMAN. SHE WAS seated across from Sam, her lips red from the wine, but otherwise, she looked as severe and sharp as the weapons Sam suspected were secreted about her body.

"He's a bit of an ass, but aren't they all?" replied Sam.

Bridget grinned at her.

Sam sipped her wine and glanced around the quiet tavern. It was a place the other woman had suggested. Late in the evening, it was filled with young couples and small groups of men. There were a few pairs of women as well, just like them.

Sam turned back to Bridget. "He plays the bad guy, and you're the one to make nice?"

"Something like that," acknowledged Bridget.

"Is it usual for women to be out alone in Ivalla?" wondered Sam. "Back in Enhover, I find I'm the only woman in the pub this late at night."

"Alone?" questioned Bridget.

Sam nodded.

"You have your pick, then." Bridget laughed.

"I have my pick, but it's not the selection I prefer to choose from," remarked Sam dryly.

"Ah." The other woman sipped her wine. "It's not usual in Ivalla, either. This tavern is different, though. It draws a more agreeable crowd."

"Interesting," said Sam, glancing at a pair of women who were leaning close together in the corner.

"You understand why we're asking you to do this with val Drongko?" queried Bridget. "We are not cruel people, Sam, but we enforce the law when it's needed."

"And this is needed?"

"It is," claimed Bridget. "What we do requires incredible skill. Sometimes, achieving that skill requires putting a foot on the dark path. I can sense it around you, so this is no surprise to you. It is the terrible bargain we must make. We have to immerse ourselves in the very evil we seek to eliminate. Periodically, we have to prove we haven't become that evil."

"By killing someone?" Sam smirked.

"In this case," answered Bridget, bobbing her head to concede the contradiction. "Sometimes, death is the only way to stay connected with life."

"I've found other ways," claimed Sam.

Bridget raised an eyebrow and sipped her wine.

"Life is about connection," continued Sam. "Everything is connected. Some philosophers say death is merely the severing of those connections. I've never been to the other side, and I've never given much thought to philosophy, so I cannot say if that is true. I do know that by reinforcing our connections to other lives, we strengthen our hold on our own. We cannot perform our mission without dipping into the darkness, but the tighter our grip on life, swimming fully within the current of life, we are impervious to the allure of the dark path."

"To an extent," said Bridget.

"To an extent," admitted Sam. "When it comes down to it, though, I'd rather maintain my presence in this world by experiencing life rather than causing death. I'd rather connect with someone, even if it's a transitory fling, than end someone. It's more pleasant, don't you think?"

"It is," allowed Bridget. "A brief fling is pleasant, but it is not our role. Whether we like it or not, we are here to kill. We kill so that others can live."

"Perhaps it's different in Ivalla," said Sam, leaning on the table with her elbows, pinning Bridget with her gaze. "My mentor taught me to kill, but he also encouraged me to live. He taught balance, said that you could only be so successful at one without the other. Life, death. Day, night. Our world, the underworld. Everything is balanced, and that requires two weights on either side of the fulcrum. I've experienced my share of death, but that is not all I have experienced."

"You've done your share of living, then?" asked Bridget, sitting back and grinning, breaking the tension.

Sam winked at her. "I will do what is necessary tomorrow, but that is tomorrow."

"Do you have a place to stay?" asked the other woman, her lips curling into a coy smile.

"Not yet," replied Sam.

"Come with me then," insisted Bridget before tipping up her wine and finishing it. "I've a bed you can share. Tonight, we will swim the current of life together. Tomorrow night, we will do as we must."

Sam raised her glass. "To swimming the current."

AT NIGHT, ROMALLA LOOKED MUCH THE SAME AS WESTUNDON. Except for the main thoroughfares and the pub districts, the streets had emptied. Shutters were closed, and only street corner lamps provided illumination to the blank facades of the buildings and the vacant stone-paved avenues.

The air was drier than she was used to, and sound seemed to bounce and carry over the rambling stone architecture. The city smelled of dust and spices, the sharp scents of cured meats and rich wines. The reek of waste lingering in the gutters, waiting for a storm to wash it away. Perfume and refuse.

When they had reached the central market, she'd seen it was still bustling with laborers, finally out of work for the day, scrambling to gather whatever supplies they needed before the merchants pulled the canopies down in front of their stalls and the entire city closed its doors until dawn. The narrow aisles between the stands in the market were relatively well lit and regularly patrolled. City watchmen clustered thick in the area, either to ensure the security of commerce, or to avoid the darker places farther from the main pathways. Immediately, Sam had seen it was a terrible place to kill someone.

"We'll wait outside of the market. Take him there," she advised.

"We?" questioned Raymond au Clair. "This is about you, lass."

"If we know where he is, why wait?" challenged Bridget. "Take him now. Don't let him slip from your grip."

Sam looked meaningfully between the two of them. "Is this my operation or yours?"

"Yours," conceded Bridget. "How do you know where he'll be, which way he will go?"

"Call it instinct," said Sam.

With the two Knives in tow, she slipped along the alleyways of the market, taking few pains to hide, but passing through the shadows when she could find them. She could feel the stares of her companions on her back, but she wouldn't explain herself, and they wouldn't stoop to asking.

In front of them, a party of brightly dressed men shouted and hooted, trekking from one tavern to another. In truth, Sam did not know where Ivar val Drongko was staying, but she had a good guess where he'd go after the day's business. The man had peculiar tastes, and in the Church city of Romalla, there would only be so many places he could satisfy those wants. She'd seen where he stored his goods, and she'd seen what was around it.

Three blocks outside of the market, halfway to the seedier end of the theatre district, Sam stopped at an open-fronted wine merchant's stall. She held up three fingers, and when the proprietor passed over the wine, she and her companions clustered around a tall, narrow table the merchant had set in front of his shop. They drank slowly and quietly, waiting.

"How do you know he'll come this way?" wondered Bridget, surreptitiously peering down the darkened street.

"How did you know I traveled here with him?" retorted Sam.

Raymond rapped the table with his knuckles. "That is the best question you've asked today. Perhaps the old man did impart some knowledge upon you."

"The guard at the gate?" wondered Sam.

Raymond smiled and shook his head. Sam frowned, glancing at Bridget, but the woman gave nothing away. Both of the Knives watched her silently.

Finally, Sam shook her head. "Ivar himself?"

"He wouldn't betray his relationship with us. He reported your presence as soon as he arrived," explained Raymond. "We knew you were in Romalla before you located Bishop Constance. She was waiting for you."

"If you know him, why have you not done this yourself?" complained Sam.

"Because I know I'm capable of it," answered Raymond. "I do not know if you are. If you are to be one of us, you need the instinct to kill. If you're going to be given leeway on certain matters, to bend the rules as we do, then you have to prove your heart is with the mission. The work we do is critical to the safety of the people under the Church's domain. To do that work, we must be as hard as the steel of our daggers. And like those daggers, we should do only the bidding of those who direct us. You've gotten sharp, I admit, but are you still directed by the hand of the Church?"

"You think I'm a sorceress?" scoffed Sam.

"You wouldn't be the first to have taken a step too far on the dark path and found it difficult to turn back," remarked Bridget. "Your mentor coddled you, it seems. Our line of work requires ruthlessness. We use those we must to achieve our goals, but despite the help they may have given us, they are not of the Church. They are still subject to its laws. They must face the consequences of the choices they have made."

"And when the Church decides that despite your hard work, you are also in violation of those laws?" questioned Sam.

"There's a reason there are no old Knives left to take seats at the council table," claimed Raymond.

Bridget shook her head. "What we do is sanctioned by Church leadership. We skirt the outline of the rules, that is true, but that is the core of what I'm explaining, Sam. We operate at the direction of Constance and the Council. We're a blade, sharpened by tools and tactics that may be illegal, but we always remain in our master's firm hand. That, Sam, is what we must find out tonight.

Will you be wielded by the guiding hand of the Church? Bishop Constance is not sure, and she requested we find out."

"Let Samantha decide on her own," muttered Raymond.

Sam sipped her wine and eyed the two of them. They looked calm and ready, predators comfortable on the hunt. These two could speak Church law until they were out of breath and blue in the face, but she knew why they did what they did. It wasn't because of some benevolent light shining through the Church's circle. It wasn't because as younglings they'd been inspired by a priest shouting from the pulpit. They were killers. They enjoyed it. They used those like Ivar val Drongko and then discarded him when they were done. They used each other. They would use her. They'd have no regrets if it ended in bloodshed.

Studying them, she guessed most often it did end in bloodshed. The reason there were no senior Knives to join the Council was because they turned on each other. Without active sorcerers, they found other prey. One day, Raymond and Bridget might face each other, and they knew it. They'd slide a knife between each other's ribs as casually as they had shared wine and a bed. They'd do the same to her without blinking.

She still needed them, though, a dagger in the sheath. She hid her grimace with her wine cup, her eyes seeking the dark streets that led to the square they occupied.

When he got close, Ivar would sense her. She didn't know how close it had to be, but based on her passage through the Church grounds, he would need to be within fifteen or twenty yards to feel the cold shadow of the underworld that surrounded her. That should give her enough time. She would see the man before he sensed her. Once he did, he'd turn the other way. The three Knives standing together, surely the man would realize what it meant.

When he fled, he would lead her companions away. Away from where she suspected he was going. Away from his companions there. Away from the hidden stores of his merchandise she knew he did not keep in his market stall. With luck, Raymond and

Bridget would only know of the stall, and the rest of his wares would be hers alone.

A sharpened, uncaring blade indeed.

She'd grown to like Ivar on their journey together, but her companions were right. He'd violated Church law. He facilitated sorcery and the terrible kind of violence she'd witnessed in Enhover. He'd known the risk he was taking. She was a hunter, and despite her feelings toward the perfumer, she needed help from the other Knives and she needed his potions. The game she hunted required more than she had to give.

She tapped a finger on the table, and her companions leaned close. Whispering, she said, "There he is."

"What is next?" asked Raymond, experienced enough not to turn and look for their quarry.

"When he sees us, he will flee," she explained. "He knows his potions are illegal. He has no choice but to run. He'll fly like a fat rabbit, and we will hunt him like one. We let him get a few blocks away and stay behind him until he turns down a quiet street. Then we will strike. I imagine in Romalla, even for us, it's best to conduct this business in darkness and avoid discussion with the city watch."

"It is easier to leave them out of it, to be sure," agreed Raymond, nodding in appreciation. "The watch commander loves paperwork. When you move, we'll be right behind you."

Smiling tightly, Sam waited as Ivar val Drongko walked closer, his slippered feet falling silently on the paving stones, a tune whistling through pursed lips. Then, it stopped.

She stood from the table and nodded to the perfume merchant.

He cringed and spun on his heels.

The chase was on.

THE CARTOGRAPHER X

THE PLATFORM SHATTERED UNDERNEATH HIM, and his planned graceful leap off the top into the courtyard below turned into a cartwheeling, flailing fall. He slammed against the side of the barracks and bounced off, hands clawing helplessly against the bamboo slats that made the wall of the building. Fingers slipping, toes scrabbling, he barely slowed himself as he dropped another several yards and landed hard on the sandy ground.

In front of him, the giant lizard crashed down, its carriage-sized head landing and bouncing with a thunderous boom. Its eyes, still wide-open, were glazed with shock. He breathed a sigh of relief when he saw the life had left them. He gasped in pain as the air filled his lungs, pressing against a rib that he offered a quick hope to the spirits wasn't broken.

Struggling to his feet and collecting his broadsword, he looked at the ruined wall and platform. The cannon had disappeared underneath the lizard, and at the moment, its body was blocking the gap it'd crushed in the barrier. He knew there were over a hundred native warriors on the other side of that wall, though, and within moments, they'd be scrambling over the corpse of the giant lizard and into the compound.

Wincing, he broke into a quick trot and headed toward the

back of the compound to Company House, which would offer the most defensible position. The lizard's impact had knocked down the wall of the compound and the corner of the barracks. There was no hiding behind those structures anymore.

Above him, the Cloud Serpent rumbled and shook as another salvo of cannon fire erupted from the starboard side. On deck, he could hear small arms cracking in irregular intervals, and the deck guns barked sharply, sending apple-sized balls of heavy lead screaming over the walls with enough force to rip through half-a-dozen bodies if they caught them packed tightly together.

It was an impressive display of force, but it wouldn't be enough. On the ground, individuals would be too mobile to be caught by the full brunt of the airship's artillery. They could move and scramble out of the way of the cannon quicker than the sailing master could adjust. The small arms barrage would strike some of them, but from the deck of the airship, aiming a blunder-buss was an exercise in pure chance.

Cannon was impressive and devastating against ships on the water or static structures, but against unorganized foot soldiers, they needed the royal marines. Oliver saw with dismay that they were quickly running out of those. Just thirty of the boys in blue had survived the initial uprising, and as he scanned what remained on the walls, he saw the contingent wasn't more than half of that now.

"Duke Wellesley," called a voice emerging from Company House.

Oliver looked to see Senior Factor Giles trotting out, bloody cutlass gripped in his hand. The merchant, his old friend, advised, "It's time to see you off, m'lord. You need to be on the next lift up."

Scurrying across the courtyard to meet his old friend, Oliver saw panicked women, determined men, and screaming children clustered within the entrance to Company House, all waiting their turn to evacuate on the airship.

"Not until we get the women and children out," declared Oliver, gesturing as another rope jerked tight around an evacuee.

A grim-faced woman rose into the air, a small child clutched snug in her grip.

He turned from the crowd awaiting rescue and raised his broadsword, knowing that in moments, the first wave of attackers would arrive.

"I was worried you'd say that, m'lord."

Oliver looked over his shoulder and frowned at the factor.

"What's that?" gasped Giles, pointing to the walls.

Spinning to follow his friend's finger, Oliver didn't see the butt of the cutlass that crashed against the back of his skull. The world went black.

THE PRIESTESS IX

THE COLORFULLY ATTIRED man lumbered out of view.

She scampered after him, Raymond and Bridget close on her heels.

"Don't let him get—"

"I know," hissed Sam, cutting Raymond off.

They made it to the street Ivar had disappeared down and saw a flash of color as he turned a corner ahead of them. Traveling at a loping jog, Sam pursued. She'd been worried the perfumer would bolt straight for the watch or some other official agency to seek protection, but evidently, the knowledge that he was violating Church law was enough to encourage him into a different, and more foolish, plan of flight. For crafting potions, the watch would toss the man in the gaol. She and her companions would kill him. Of course, it quickly became evident the corpulent perfume master had no intention of being caught by anyone.

"Faster than he looks, ey?" asked Bridget, breathing evenly as they chased after the man.

"Not fast enough," said Sam as they spotted him hurrying across another intersection and down a nearly black street.

They ran after him. Then, she stopped.

"What?" growled Raymond, taking steps past her toward the direction Ivar had disappeared.

"This way," declared Sam, turning the opposite direction.

"I saw him!" screeched Raymond.

"You saw someone," replied Sam, breaking back into a trot.

"If you're wrong…"

"If I'm wrong, we'll track him down," assured Sam. "The man is big, colorful, and far too full of himself to remain in hiding for long. He'll be easy enough to locate."

Silently, Raymond followed her. Either he was also certain they could find the man later, or he was cautiously avoiding a strenuous objection on the off chance he'd be wrong. Cautious. Not what she would have guessed initially, but it seemed the killer could contain himself when necessary. He could think about his next step before taking it.

Sam took them down another side street, this one narrow and grim. She could reach out and span the alley with her arms. Above them, rickety, wooden scaffolding allowed the tenants the means to ascend and descend from the higher floors. Perhaps someone had built the structures originally as a fire escape, but looking around the area they were passing through, she guessed it was an escape in case the watch ever came bashing down the front door.

"This doesn't look like the perfume purveyor's normal haunts," worried Bridget. "We all saw him. Why do you think…"

Sam touched her nose and winked.

"Ah," said Bridget, drawing a deep breath and then appearing to immediately regret it.

"I'd wait until we're away from the refuse," suggested Sam, pointing at a slimy pile on the side of the alleyway.

Twenty paces later, she paused at an intersection. The three of them turned, glancing down two dark pathways in front of them.

Cautiously, they sniffed the air, and Sam glanced down at the dry streets below their feet. "Pavers in an alley?"

"Welcome to Romalla," said Raymond. "Home of the Church."

"Pavers are unusual in the poor areas," said Bridget, glancing at the bricks beneath their feet. "I believe we've stumbled into someone else's domain."

"Someone else's..." said Raymond, trailing off in confusion.

"He went this way," said Sam, pointing down an alley to her left.

"How do you know?" wondered Bridget, sniffing quietly. "I lost his scent."

Sam smiled. "Music, laughter. Ivar's found himself a crowd."

"If he wanted a crowd, why'd he run all the way over here?" asked Raymond.

"I don't know," admitted Sam, "but his flight wasn't random. He anticipated we'd come for him and had someone waiting to lead us astray. He must have been suspicious after speaking to you and arranged the decoy. Wherever he went, he expected to find allies there."

Wordlessly, they stalked down the alley. Sam knew that Ivar himself would likely sense her approach when she got close. He'd demonstrated the ability when they'd first met, but hopefully, whoever he was around could be caught by surprise. An entire nest of potential magic users would be difficult to address, even with the other two Knives of the Council.

As they plunged deeper into the alley, she saw they'd already been spotted regardless of affinity to the spirits. Eyes reflecting the limited light in the alleyway blinked back at her. Atop the roofs of the three-story buildings, moving along the scaffolding, she heard movement. The alleyway was swept surprisingly clean, and unless Romalla was far different from Westundon, no one kept a street so clear of debris if it wasn't their front door.

They turned a corner and stopped.

Ten yards away was a tavern. Its shutters were open and the door was closed. Inside, they could hear the tinkling of some stringed instrument and the melodies of a singer. The sound of the music was almost overwhelmed by the clunk of full mugs, the shouts and jeers of drinkers, and general revelry.

"That's rather odd," remarked Bridget. "Who'd put a tavern here, so far away from the main thoroughfares?"

"Neither of you recognizes it?" asked Sam.

"There are a lot of taverns in Romalla," explained Raymond. "Can't say I've been to them all."

Nodding to herself, Sam stepped forward, her hands held clear of her body, her eyes scanning the windows and rooftops around them. There was movement, but so far, no overt threats. Watchers, likely reporting their presence, but without orders to defend the place.

"Where are you going?" hissed Raymond.

"It's a tavern," replied Sam. "I'm going to get a drink."

She pushed open the door and stomped halfway across the room before stopping. At the bar, Ivar val Drongko slowly turned around. He was attired in a simple priest's cassock, though the glittering rings on his hands and the bracelets on his wrists gave the lie to that disguise. All around them, people started to leave.

"What is this place?" wondered Bridget.

"Thieves' guild, I imagine," said Sam.

Ivar smiled. "You shouldn't have followed me in here. I'm not just a perfumer, and you are not my only friends."

"I can see that," remarked Sam.

From the corners of her eyes, she spotted a dozen men and women forming a loose circle around them. A few head-knockers, a few door-bashers, and a few who looked truly dangerous.

"Sam…" murmured Raymond under his breath. "This isn't the way we do things."

A heavy thump drew their attention to the bar where the man behind it had placed a short, two-barreled blunderbuss down on the ale-puddled surface. The barman was short like his weapon, but his arms were thick with muscle. They were as wide as her waist, and it looked like the man could punch his way through a solid stone wall. From the scars on his knuckles, she wondered if perhaps he had.

"Ivar val Drongko is under our protection," remarked the barman. "I think it best you leave."

"Do you know who we—" began Raymond.

Sam held up a hand, stopping him.

"I could ask you the same question, mate," responded the barman, a hand resting comfortably on the butt of his blunderbuss.

Sam held the burly man's gaze for a moment then, in a blink, whipped her hand down and drew the dagger from the small of her back. In the same motion, she flung it at Ivar val Drongko.

The gleaming blade shone in the lamp light for half a breath before it sank into the perfumer's neck. He gurgled, falling back against the bar. One hand grasped the hilt of her dagger, his blood bubbling around tightly clenched fingers. The other hand pawed at a pouch on his belt, but his ringed fingers were quickly losing coordination. Blood spilled down the front of his priest's cassock, and she decided the perfumer was too late. Whatever potion he kept which might have the potency to save him, he wasn't able to retrieve. Instead, he wavered, coughing crimson streamers of sticky liquid. Then, he collapsed, sliding down the front of the bar, her dagger still buried deep in his neck.

"Frozen hell," muttered Raymond.

"I'll collect my dagger, and then we'll be leaving as you asked," Sam told the barman. "I hope you were paid in advance."

The muscled man gaped at her.

Not waiting for a response, she hurried forward and knelt, yanking her weapon free with a sickening sucking noise. Trying not to show her nerves, she wiped the bloody blade on Ivar's cassock and stood, sheathing it behind her back and nodding at the barman.

"If you weren't paid in advance, the man's jewelry and the contents of his pouch should settle the bill." Unsure what else to say, she offered, "Have a good evening, then."

She turned and the skin on her back prickled as she thought about the polished brass barrels of the blunderbuss, but the room remained silent. She brushed by Raymond and Bridget and exited the open door.

The two Knives scurried after her. Once back out in the alley and a dozen steps from the tavern, Raymond hissed, "You can't do that! You just killed a spirit-forsaken thief in the middle of the spirit-forsaken thieves' guild! They will not allow that!"

She shrugged, feeling a bit of comfort as they walked farther from the open door behind them. She couldn't hear pursuit, and in another score of paces, they would enter a twisting warren of back alleys. If the thieves were going to strike, they'd do it now, on their turf.

"The thieves won't—"

"That's why I didn't ask, Raymond," she said. "Of course they weren't going to agree to us slaying one of their own. Better to ask forgiveness than permission. Is that a saying here?"

"You didn't— You can't…"

Sam stopped and spun to face the outraged man. "You asked me to kill Ivar val Drongko, so I did. Now you're upset because I offended some thieves? Stop and think. Once he knew we were coming after him and he found safety in that tavern, we never would have seen him again. Those thieves would have spirited him away, or if he could afford it, they would have come with knives out for us. Besides, what the thieves do is against the laws of Ivalla as well, no? Instead of berating me for doing exactly as you asked, perhaps you ought to run to the watch commander and let him know what you found. Or maybe you're not as serious about protecting the innocents as you claim?"

Raymond snorted.

"How many sorcerers have you killed?" questioned Sam.

"I've lost count," he snarled back at her.

"He's done his share," interjected Bridget. "It's just… we didn't expect you to be so abrupt."

"This wasn't the ending of some tragic play," replied Sam, starting to walk again. "The man was involved in sorcery, so I killed him. It's what we Knives do."

THREE DAYS LATER, SHE LEFT ROMALLA ALONE.

Bishop Constance, the Whitemask, had been enthralled with Raymond au Clair and Bridget Cancio's depiction of Sam killing Ivar val Drongko in the midst of the thieves' guild. The bishop's eyes had sparkled with glee at the thought of the stunned thieves' faces when one of their own, one expressly under their protection, collapsed dead on the floor of the tavern. Ivar's potential usefulness to the Council of Seven and the Knives' previous involvement with him were treated with a wave of the hand and assurances that there would be another potion mixer coming along if they needed one. The discovery of the thieves' guild itself was given even less attention. Evidently, the Church had no interest in enforcing the laws of the government.

Sam had spent the days worried the thieves would retaliate, but it seemed in the Church's capital, even those operating outside of the law were not foolish enough to anger those under the banner of the golden circle.

Disgusted with the complacent council and the haughty disdain the Knives had for anyone who wasn't them, Sam had quickly decided she would be leaving, with or without the Church's blessing.

There was no proscribed punishment for a Knife who refused to follow orders or acted alone. Thotham had certainly done it often enough, but that didn't mean Sam wouldn't pay for the betrayal. The Council didn't need a rule written down to decide one had been broken. Bishop Constance, underneath her matronly veneer, did not seem the type to easily forgive and forget. Sam knew when she left there was a risk the woman would send a pair of assassins after her, or the bishop might merely note it, and Sam would have a new enemy for life. Either way, it was certain she would never receive official help from Romalla.

As she scurried out under a gibbous moon that paved her path in pale white light, she thought it didn't matter. The Council was broken. It would have been nice to have the assistance of the Knives, but the two she met were only interested in bloodshed. Saving mankind from sorcery? It was an unintended consequence. Not to mention, Raymond was a bit of an ass.

The threat in Enhover was real. She was more certain of it now than when she'd arrived. Raymond and Bridget spent their days hunting down harmless potion brewers, wood witches, and others on the fringes of what the Church considered sorcery. After talking to the pair of them, she found they'd never seen a circle used like she did in Archtan Atoll. They'd never faced what she had underneath Derbycross. The Council of Seven did not believe her urgency because they'd never seen the depths the dark path could reach. In all of their years, Bishop Constance and the others had never seen true sorcery. Everyone said it was dead in Enhover, but from what she'd heard in Ivalla, it was even more dead there. The Council didn't even have the memory of Northundon to fuel their fear. The comfortable narrative they told themselves had overgrown the seeds of truth.

Ivar val Drongko had violated Church law, but the man had not been seriously moving down the dark path. He'd been a tinkerer, a man trying to make his way in the world. The fact that he was also a thief spoke volumes about how successful his potion brewing had been. He was not supplying the continent's sorcerers with nefarious brews. In fact, she'd lay the rest of Duke's money on a bet that Ivar's best customer had been the Church itself.

Killing men like him did nothing to further their mission. It did nothing for the world. Killing men like him only made it more difficult to find the true threats, the ones she alone was hunting. She knew that behind the Mouth of Set and the Feet of Seheht, there was a looming darkness. There were those intent on working with the dark trinity, with Ca-Mi-He and the like of those terrible spirits. When she'd mentioned those names to Bishop Constance, the woman had laughed. Constance had claimed that no mortal could bind such powerful spirits, that even attempting to contact them would lay the sorcerer's soul bare and would ensure an existence of servitude on the other side of the shroud.

Perhaps, but that didn't mean no sorcerer was trying. Whether he or she paid a heavy price was not Sam's worry. It was what he or she could do in the world before that price was due. Every time she'd confronted the bishop or the other Knives with her need, they brushed her off. They didn't believe her because they hadn't seen it with their own eyes.

That, and they were all old enough to recall when Ivalla had been independent. Ostensibly loyal to the Church and protective of each of her territories, they had loyalty to home as well. When Sam had raised Duke's name with Bridget and Raymond, she'd seen it in their eyes, a gleam of bitter joy that Isisandra and her ilk have given the royal line such trouble.

They wouldn't ignore a threat of sorcery if they believed it, but they wouldn't shed a single tear at the fall of Enhover. Their hatred of the empire and the Wellesleys tilted the scales to inaction, and there would be no help coming, no matter what she said to convince them. The death of sorcery was a convenient excuse to avoid Enhover, to avoid thinking of the yoke the empire had laid upon their shoulders.

In her hands, she gripped Thotham's old spear, the one imbued with his spirit. On her hips hung her two kris daggers, on her back a rucksack filled with a clattering array of Ivar val Drongko's potions. The man's death was serving some purpose, she hoped. The trip had not been a complete waste. Beneath the tightly sealed vials and bottles of Ivar's work was something else she'd been saving, something she'd meant to show the scholars in the Church's archives but knew now was her task alone.

The Book of Law, found amongst Isisandra Dalyrimple's effects.

Filled with incomprehensible symbols and writing, Sam was certain the book contained secrets which would help find the sorcerers she hunted. A true grimoire, a map of the dark path... she just had to find a way to read it.

As the rising sun bathed the tiled-rooftops of Romalla, she saw the gates stood wide open. The Church was secure in its supremacy, supported by a new empire that had conquered the old one. No one in the city, including those she'd come to find, were worried about what was outside. They should be, she knew. They definitely should be.

THE CAPTAIN II

Captain Catherine Ainsley placed the compress against the man's forehead, unsure if that was what she was supposed to be doing. Maybe it was supposed to be cold, or wet, or something else? She couldn't remember, but she decided it shouldn't be wet. What good would that do? Maybe hot?

Suddenly, he stirred, and she jumped back. A trembling hand snuck out from under the rumpled linen sheets and he clutched his head, groaning.

She waited quietly, letting him wake on his own. She twitched, wondering if she should dash outside and find… someone. But there was no one else. She was the captain. This was her duty. Well, a physician's duty, but she'd sacked the one they'd had. Arguably, that made it her obligation. Not to mention, if her patron died, it was likely she would no longer be a captain or even allowed within sight of an airship ever again. In short, if putting the dry rag on the man's forehead was going to help keep her position, she would sit there all evening until he recovered.

Finally, the duke's eyes blinked and managed to stay open. He licked dry lips, and she reached to the side to get one of the three copper cups she owned. She uncorked a sloshing glass bottle and was about to tip it up when he croaked, "Water."

"What?"

"Do you have any water?" asked Duke Oliver Wellesley.

"I-I suppose I could find some," she said. "This is grog. I didn't think…"

He grunted. "Water first. Then the grog."

She stood and turned, glancing over the array of items Mister Samuels had dumped on her table— a washbasin, a few rags, the grog, and another stoppered glass bottle. She opened that one and sniffed it suspiciously, given that it came from Samuels. It had the musty scent all the water on the ship acquired when they'd been aloft for some time. Had Samuels filled a grog bottle with barrel water? She wanted to castigate the man, but she supposed the bottle must have been easier to carry into her quarters. Then, she began to wonder what happened to the grog that had been in there?

Resolving to track down Mister Samuels later, she splashed a measure of water into the cup, glad that even Samuels wasn't thick enough to bring a washbasin with no water. A washbasin. Perhaps that compress should have been wet? Would Samuels know such a thing?

Duke Wellesley sipped at the water, working the moisture back into his mouth. "Have you been caring for me?"

"I've been trying." She admitted, "It's not my strong suit."

"What happened to the ship physician?" he questioned. "I seem to recall signing off on hiring one."

"He was a drunk," she murmured, looking away, "more so than usual. I was in the process of finding another when we left. The second mate had some skill in that regard, but, ah, we lost him back in Imbon. He'd gone down to assist the evacuation, and we had to leave, you understand? We could only hoist so many people up before those giant lizards and the natives overran the place. We'd started with women and the children, and…"

Duke Wellesley tensed. "The colony was overrun?"

"A total loss, m'lord," she admitted.

"But… I… what happened?"

"I was told that Senior Factor Giles decided you were trying to be heroic and would hold until the end," she said. "He took matters into his own hands."

"He hit me," guessed the duke, a hand reaching back behind his head.

"I saw the lump," replied Ainsley. "He hit you rather hard."

"Where is he?" demanded Duke Wellesley.

She didn't answer, but she could see in his eyes that he understood.

"How many?"

"We left behind half-a-dozen crew members but hauled up a score-and-a-half from the compound, mostly women and children," she replied. "Giles demanded you were next. You were unconscious…"

"I know."

"We only got three more after that, m'lord," she said. "Those lizards smashed through the compound's walls, and a flood of blade-wielding men came after. We blasted two of the monsters from up here, and someone on the ground got a third, but more of them were crawling out of the jungle. Between the lizards and the native horde, m'lord, I decided there was no purpose in continuing the fight. The compound was overrun, and anyone else we hauled up was as like to be an enemy. Retribution is due, but not by us. We're outfitted for exploration, not war. I-I made the decision as captain to return to Enhover. May the spirits watch over those we had to leave behind."

Duke Wellesley breathed deeply for several long moments, the fingers on one hand probing the back of his head. The other hand held his half-empty water cup. He finished the rest of the water and said, "You made the right choice, Captain. Pour me a bit of that grog?"

SHE WATCHED THE DUKE AND HER FIRST MATE STANDING TOGETHER ON the forecastle. Pettybone was loyal to her, and while the duke was clearly upset at the situation, he didn't appear to be lying the blame at her feet. Still, the spirits only knew what men spoke about out of earshot of a woman. Smirking, she thought, the spirits and her.

She sidled up to the base of the stairwell that led to the raised forecastle of the ship and was bent, pretending to sort through a locker filled with spare supplies. Just a captain taking inventory, nothing to pay attention to.

"Pettybone, is it?" asked the duke.

"Aye," responded her first mate.

"You're a well-traveled chap," said the peer. "What did you think of those lizards? Have you ever seen the like?"

"The like of that, no," remarked Pettybone, scratching his head underneath his woolen cap. "I believe it was magic, m'lord. Something akin to the grimalkins that the Darklanders keep."

"Grimalkins are not magic, are they?" questioned Duke Wellesley. "They are natural beasts, trained by sorcerers for protection."

Pettybone shrugged. "Perhaps. They seem magical to me, though. There are many such tales of strange or wonderful creatures over the horizon. They all sounded fanciful when I was a boy, and of course everyone knows sailors have big imaginations, but now I've seen enough to know some of it is true. Grimalkin, fae, glae worms, those monsters that lurk beyond the walls of the Company compound in the Westlands... I wouldn't have believed any of it until good men I trust swore it was true or I saw it with my own eyes. Who knows what lays beyond the lines of your maps, ey? Grimalkin yesterday, giant lizards today."

"Who knows," agreed Duke Wellesley. "Apparently, we don't even know what lies within the bounds of a small colony. Maybe you're right, first mate, and there was magic afoot. I wonder, though, was it sorcery, or the magic of the druids? Those lizards, they felt... warm, to me. Not cold, like the bitter clutch of a shade. They were... vibrant."

"I'm a simple sailor, m'lord," replied Pettybone. "I couldn't tell you the difference between magic and sorcery. Far as I know, both are dead in Enhover, and in truth, with my own eyes, I've never witnessed anything I'd ascribe to either one. Not until Imbon, that is."

"You know what we faced in Derbycross," said the duke. "Sorcery is not dead, but perhaps it was in hibernation. What other wonders have been lost, just waiting to return?"

Pettybone shrugged and scratched his head again.

"Tell me," instructed the duke. "What are you thinking?"

"The world is full of strange things, m'lord. Some were beyond belief when I was a lad, but we take them for granted now." Pettybone rapped his knuckles on the gunwale. "We're standing on the deck of an airship that's supported only by floating rocks. The fae we import from the Southlands can't even survive in our air, but contained within glass globes, they provide a light that's safer than fire and never dies. You ever see a glae worm pod explode, m'lord?"

Duke Wellesley's shrugged, as if he wondered whether Pettybone was saying anything other than nonsense.

Ainsley, still pretending to sort through the storage locker, shook her head. What was the man talking about? Magic?

Pettybone held up two fingers, pinching them close together. Then, he clapped his hands and spread his arms. "Glae worms are harvested in tiny pods. They may be no bigger than my fingernail, and the biggest are no larger than my fist. When the pod breaks open, their invisible, sticky bodies are flung everywhere. Outside of the pod long enough, they're no longer sticky, and they can be stretched for leagues. I couldn't tell you the science behind it, but some wit figured out how to vibrate those bodies and interpret it into words. It's common now, but can you imagine what it was like for the first man to crack open one of those pods? That was a surprise, ey? Bastard probably got tangled up for half the day until the worms dried a little and someone could pull 'em off. At the time, that man must'a thought those sticky little worms was magic."

"I know how glae worms work," muttered Duke Wellesley. "My family is the one who applied the technology and used them to build the transmission network, after all. Technology, first mate, not magic."

"Is there a difference?" questioned the sailor. "We call it magic when we don't understand it and technology when we do. It's all one and the same, ain't it?"

Duke Wellesley frowned at the first mate.

"I told ya, m'lord, I'm a simple sailor," said Pettybone. "If there's a difference between sorcery and druid magic, I don't know it. I can tell you this, though, what we saw back in Imbon was unlike anything I've ever witnessed with my own eyes."

"It seemed magic to us, but maybe it was common to the natives," speculated the duke. "We think of the natives as primitives with no understanding of the modern world, of technology, but what if that misunderstanding goes both ways, Pettybone?"

The first mate gaped at the duke.

"Those lizards, whatever they were," continued Duke Wellesley, "the tablets and figurines we have down in the hold... I don't understand any of it, just like they wouldn't understand a mechanical carriage or how use of red saltpetre speeds travel along the rail. We think we are smarter, wiser, but I'm not so sure. Our airships have allowed us the superior might to build an empire. We conquered Imbon with little difficulty, but in part it was because they didn't unleash those monsters on us! What if they had?"

"Then I'm not sure Imbon would'a been a colony, m'lord," speculated Pettybone. "I can't imagine even the most dedicated Company factor would'a bedded down with those things crawling through the jungle."

"I think you're right, first mate," said the duke. "The natives in Imbon let us take over their island, let us rule them, but why?"

"Maybe we didn't have as much control as we thought,"

replied Pettybone. "Seems they was up to some things the Company didn't know a stitch about."

"We put ourselves in charge," said Duke Wellesley. "We thought we were bringing order, modernity to the place, but what if we weren't? We think we're advanced, but what if we're down a trail that others have decided to forgo?"

"Aye, like the druids did," agreed Pettybone.

"The druids?"

"Those old fortresses they built, you've seen 'em, haven't you?" asked the first mate. "They was building those buildings long before our people had the technology to match 'em. Far as I know, there was never a war, never any reason the druids disappeared. They left, but their fortresses remain."

"I used to live in one," admitted Duke Wellesley. "The Crown's keep in Northundon was built by the druids. We still rule from the bones of their throne. It's been two hundred years since the last one of those magicians was on our shores. It's a good question, Pettybone. Why? Why did they disappear? Why did the natives in Imbon hide their capabilities?"

"Your father holds the reigns of the empire," murmured Pettybone, his voice barely carrying above the rushing wind, "but there's more he doesn't know than what he does. No offense, m'lord."

The duke grunted and stared down at the sea passing below them. After a long break, he said, "I know a peer named Pettigrew. You have a bit of his look, though clearly you're a man who has spent his years adventuring. This other man spends his time shuttling between his favorite pastry shops. Still, the similarity… Such an odd coincidence."

"Aye, the Pettigrews," boomed her first mate, regaining his bluster and drawing himself up. "No coincidence, m'lord. I would call them distant relatives. Cousins, you might say."

"Alexander Pettigrew was the finance director for the Company," remarked the duke skeptically.

"That branch of the family has done rather well," expounded Pettybone. "We're right proud of how they turned out."

"I'm sure you are," said the duke as Pettybone begged off to hurry the men and prepare to lower the sails. They were approaching port.

Ainsley sniggered to herself and looked away while her mate scurried down the stairwell and began haranguing the men. She climbed up beside the duke and looked out below them to the bustling city of Southundon.

"Your first mate is an interesting man," remarked Duke Wellesley.

"He's an old sailor, m'lord," she replied. "Men like him have been at sea or in the air more than they've had their boots on the ground. They travel to strange places, get odd ideas."

"How long has he been in service to the Company?" asked the duke.

She shrugged.

He frowned at her.

"It's his tale to tell, but he's had a colorful past, m'lord." She assured him, "It's all behind him now. He's a good sailor and as loyal as a pup raised from birth."

"A privateer?" guessed Duke Wellesley.

She shifted, regretting getting herself into the conversation. He kept looking at her, waiting for more. Finally she said, "It's not unusual. It's why some of them get nervous when in Enhover's ports. They're worried the inspectors will come knocking."

"Really?" wondered the peer, turning to her in surprise.

"What do you think makes a man go to sea?" she asked. "That's where we do all of our recruiting, you know? We hire men and women who've got experience on the water. Makes it a bit easier to teach them the ropes up here. We can't take 'em all from the Company's freighters. That'd mean the sea captains would always be losing their best hands. It isn't good for the overall business, ey. So, we get 'em where we can. Before they got straightened out, most of our hands have either fled trouble with the law or trouble with a woman. And Pettybone's experience with women is about as extensive as his experience with that peer you think he's related to."

Duke Wellesley snorted. "You were listening in, then?"

She flushed.

"Don't worry," he assured her. "I won't say I appreciate it, and I won't say I'll act as kindly the next time you're caught, but I understand. This is your airship, and you're nervous about whether or not I'll take it from you when we tie up to the bridge."

"I—"

"If a man goes to sea to avoid legal trouble or because of a woman, what drives a woman offshore into the wild unknown?" he asked her. "Is she running from trouble as well?"

"More like looking for trouble," declared Ainsley. "In my experience, at least."

Duke Wellesley laughed.

"Do you intend to replace me as captain, m'lord?" she asked, forcing herself to keep her voice calm and steady.

"No," he replied. "If I'd been in your boots, floating above Imbon while it was overrun, I don't know what I would do. I don't know if I would have lashed out and blasted the place with shot until the cannons were baking hot. I don't know if I would have chosen to fly home as you did. Even now, I'm not sure what the right decision was. The Crown and Company cannot stand for such affronts, but we're not outfitted for that type of action. We have women and children evacuees aboard. And there were more of those giant lizards? We would spend every ounce of our shot just taking care of them. So, Captain, I can't tell you if you made the right decision. What is important is that you made one. A captain must master her ship and her crew, and even in the face of uncertainty, she's still the master. Sometimes, it's more important that something was decided rather than what was decided."

Ainsley drew herself up.

"You know you're the first woman airship captain?" he asked.

"Neither the Company nor the royal marines have had a female captain in their fleets."

"I'm aware," she responded.

"You'll always have to keep earning that role, Captain," he advised. "Others will try to undermine you, to jostle for your position. There are men out there who won't be able to stand seeing a woman at the helm. I can promise you, though, as long as you do continue to earn it, you'll have a place as captain of my airship."

"Thank you, m'lord."

"Now," he said, "it looks like there's a wait to tie to the airship bridges. Spice season in the tropics and everyone's coming back at once, I suppose. Take us around them, and tie us to the first open bridge."

"The other airship captains won't like that, m'lord," worried Ainsley.

"They're not going to like you no matter what you do," claimed the duke. "Run up my colors, get around them, and if they have a problem, they can come tell it to my face."

"Understood, m'lord," she said, fighting to control a growing smile.

She turned to shout instructions to the men on the decks below. Swing around the other airships and take the first place in line, no matter what anyone says about it.

THE DIRECTOR I

HE DREW on his carved ebony pipe and slowly exhaled the blue smoke out his nostrils. Across from him, the bishop clutched a crystal glass of sherry in his hands like he was protecting the last of a mythical dragon's hoard. He asked the churchman, "The girl is not giving up?"

"She is not," confirmed Bishop Yates. "I'd thought… Well, I'd thought Bishop Constance would reassign her, send her somewhere else. We were close to being completely free of the Knives of the Council in Enhover."

"We still could be," suggested Director Raffles. "It wouldn't take much to eliminate a young woman who no longer has backing of the Church."

"And what would Duke Wellesley do?" questioned Yates. "The two of them continue to work together. If she goes mysteriously missing, it will only encourage him. Unless he also—"

"No," said Raffles. "No."

"Why not?" hissed Yates. "If you're in favor of killing the girl, then the duke…"

"We've risked too much in a short time," interjected Raffles. "We had to do it, to snuff out any line of inquiry into the Feet of Seheht, but it's raised the suspicions of Prince Philip. You know whatever he is pursuing is shared with King Edward. I spent days chasing the boy between here and Southundon, trying to appear normal, making sure they had no reason to look at me. If suddenly Oliver is murdered, how do you think the king and prince will react? We cannot battle the Crown, Yates, not yet. We can't touch Oliver, and you were right, we should keep our hands off the girl, for now."

"We speak often of what we cannot do," responded the churchman.

"At the summer solstice, we will be ready," stated Raffles, gesturing with his pipe. "Then, we'll call upon the dark trinity and bind them to our will. Then, we'll control the second most powerful creature of the underworld, and then, not even the Crown can stand in our way."

Bishop Yates didn't object, but it didn't look as though he agreed.

"We've succeeded so long because we operated in silence, Gabriel," insisted Raffles. "Neither the Church nor the Crown know of our pursuit. It should remain that way until we're ready to declare ourselves publicly."

"And how do you envision we do that?" questioned Yates.

Director Raffles smiled. "In the days after the solstice, we bring down the Wellesleys — the dukes, the prince, and their father. We destroy them all. We crush your Church. We send all who oppose us fleeing. Blood will flow in the streets. The women's lamentations will be heard from shore to shore. All of that, Yates, and whatever else the poets think of to ascribe to our reign. That's not really the point, though, is it? Whether there is bloodshed when we assume control, whether there is not, does not really concern me. My only concern — my only one — is that we have the power to do it. Success is the only thing that matters to me."

The bishop grunted.

"Revenge, that is all the matters to you?" asked Raffles.

Yates scowled.

"You will get your revenge. I'll have my power, and our partner…" said Raffles, trailing off.

Yates sipped his sherry then asked, "What is it that our partner wants?"

Raffles shrugged. "I do not know. To be king?"

"The throne would be a crowded place with three of us upon it, don't you think?" asked Yates. "And we are equal partners, are we not?"

"As far as I'm concerned, we are," assured Raffles.

"Do you think our partner shares your democratic ideals?" pressed the churchman.

"We will find out when we unveil our new powers, I suspect," said Raffles. "A wise man would be prepared for any eventuality."

"You think we'll turn on each other, then, and tear our pact apart? Without the three of us working in harmony, the dark trinity will find a way to throw off the cords we aim to bind them with. Without a united front, we'll be in terrible danger. A danger far more permanent than either the Church or Crown presents."

"I agree," said Raffles. "I do not plan a betrayal, Yates. Surely you don't think I'd be so foolish to mention this to you if I did? I'm simply saying that precaution is a means to ensure our alliance remains strong. We must trust each other and distrust each other."

The bishop nodded slowly, his jowls jiggling with the motion.

"Besides, it is not our partner I am worried about. It is not our errant priestess or even the duke," continued Raffles. "I am worried about who else travels the dark path alongside us."

"That has always been a concern," agreed the bishop.

"Of course," continued Raffles, "but I have been thinking about it a lot recently. Hathia Dalyrimple contacted Ca-Mi-He, yes?"

The churchman glanced nervously around the nearly empty smoking room of the Oak & Ivy.

"Hathia, who fell to your agents in Harwick," continued the

merchant. "I've come to doubt her power. If she could command Ca-Mi-He, then certainly nothing your assassin was capable of would have damaged her. If she taught her husband and her daughter what she knew, then Oliver and the girl would not have been sufficient to defeat them either. Even with the help of the old man, they would not have prevailed against the strength of Ca-Mi-He."

The bishop finished his sherry, letting the director continue.

"Somehow, that connection was facilitated for the Dalyrimple woman," guessed Raffles. "Somehow, someone opened the way for her pathetic sorcery to reach far deeper into the underworld than she was capable of venturing on her own. Did the spirit himself reach out to her? Is there another sorcerer in league with the great darkness?" Raffles set down his pipe and leaned forward. "If there is another sorcerer and this person facilitated a connection with Dalyrimple and Ca-Mi-He, what was the purpose?"

"To give the woman a weapon against us?" guessed Yates.

"If the sorcerer has bound Ca-Mi-He, he has all he needs to crush us now, at least until we control our own powerful ally," challenged Raffles. "No, I've mulled it over and I believe they have a different purpose. What if they've somehow become aware of our activities? That either by the great spirit or through other means they've found us preparing the bindings. They could know what we do, but they may not know who we are."

"And Hathia's attempts with the blessed dagger were merely a ruse to draw us out?" wondered the bishop, his eyes growing wide.

Raffles collected his pipe and drew on it again, settling back in the chair.

"What… what did they learn, then? Do you think they know us now?"

"If they did, I suspect we'd be dead," remarked Raffles stiffly.

The bishop's fingers drummed a nervous pattern on his empty sherry glass.

"Oliver and his companion seek us still. I think we can be sure of that after the girl's appearance in Romalla," mused Raffles. "Without realizing it, they are doing the work of this other traveler on the dark path. The narrative fits, Gabriel, and I can think of no other explanation for the way the events have unfolded."

"If they are agents of the other, even if they do not realize it, then why should we not kill them?" questioned Yates.

"We should kill them at the appropriate time," suggested Raffles, "when the loss of the agents strikes a crippling blow to our opponent. Until then, we wait, and we watch. We prepare as we have always done. When it will cause maximum harm, we will strike. In the meantime, there is an advantage knowing the two of them operate on behalf of the other. Perhaps our opponent will reveal himself inadvertently when trying to steer his agents? Perhaps they can be encouraged to turn on their hidden master?"

Yates nodded sagely. "I will reach out to the woman, Samantha, and inquire how her meeting went. I will endeavor to keep her within the folds of the Church so that when that time comes, she's at hand. I believe you are right. She may be doing our opponent's work, but I don't think she knows it. We can use that."

Raffles smiled at Yates.

"Shall we tell our partner?" asked the churchman.

"No, I think not," murmured the director. "I think it best he remains focused on completing his role in the pattern. Besides, there may be some use to him staying ignorant of what we suspect."

THE CARTOGRAPHER XI

"I ESTIMATE at least a thousand have died already!" cried Oliver, pacing the room while his father and the Company's president, Alvin Goldwater, looked on. "It's a tragic loss of life, for what?"

"For what indeed," murmured the king.

"I'm afraid I do not understand, m'lord," murmured the president. "Imbon can be reestablished. We can draw labor from our other colonies and the debtors' prison here. A terrible setback, to be sure, but from what you describe, I do not believe the situation is unsalvageable. To be frank, the Company's financial position is as strong as it's ever been. Not that we ever want to weather a crisis of this sort, but those natives couldn't have picked a better time to revolt."

"The Crown will assist, of course," added King Edward. "The royal marines are on regular patrol now between Enhover and Archtan Atoll. It will only be a few days out of their path to fly over Imbon. In fact, perhaps we'll dispatch two airships directly from here," mused Edward, tugging on his salt-and-pepper goatee. "We'll outfit them with holds full of munitions and marines. If they eliminate these giant lizards that you described, they'll have only a few thousand poorly armed natives to contend with. It should be quick work."

"Ah, m'lord," said Goldwater. "We do request that care be taken around the spice groves. The Company has spent a decade growing them, and our productivity will collapse if we're forced back into the jungle to harvest. We'll lose half the debtors within months to tropical diseases if they must work in the bush."

The king waved a hand dismissively. "Of course. I'll instruct Admiral Brach to conduct that piece of the campaign on foot. You understand, though, that the village and the Company's compound are unlikely to survive? If the natives take shelter in the buildings, I will not risk the lives of my men to root them out when we can simply reduce the structures to smoking ruin from above."

"Yes, yes, the Company understands that the marines will not take undue risk," said Goldwater, nodding his white-haired head. "We appreciate your assistance in this matter, m'lord."

"And I'll appreciate the tax levies when the colony is up and running again," acknowledged King Edward. "How long do you think before the full revenue stream returns?"

"The full stream?" replied Goldwater, tapping a finger on his chin. "I'm afraid a year or more. Much of Imbon's success was the wharfage fees and tariffs we charged United Territory vessels in our harbor. That will take time to recover. The spice trade itself should be back in short order, though. While your marines prepare for action, I'll see about gathering sufficient labor to work the plantations. We will need quality intelligence, though, both for the campaign in the air and on the ground. Maps, of course, and the man who knows the most about them."

Oliver spun, glaring at Goldwater. "Is this your payback for being embarrassed at Company House?"

Goldwater held up his hands, palms out. "I would never retaliate against the Crown, m'lord. It simply makes sense that you are the one to lead the resettlement of Imbon."

"He's not wrong, son," remarked King Edward.

"I want no part of this!" shouted Oliver. "The blood of those natives will not be on my hands."

"Will not?" snapped Goldwater. "You discovered Imbon. You identified the island held commercial value. You were there when we raised the first wall of the compound. You were the largest individual shareholder in the colony, and you were the one who discovered the pond which evidently led to this conflict. No blood on your hands? I've never even seen one of these natives, much less killed one with my own steel. Can you say the same, Duke Wellesley?"

Oliver stood, his hands convulsing into claws, rage surging through him, but he did not voice a reply. Instead, he thought of the face that had popped up on the other side of the wall in Imbon, the one he'd slid his sword into, the point of the blade punching down the poor man's gullet like he'd swallowed death itself.

"It's unfortunate so many died, Oliver," consoled the king, "but such is the stuff of empire building. When I was born, Enhover was a nation besieged. What are now the United Territories and the Coldlands meant to march over us. Today, they are our tributes or dead. We've established toeholds in the tropics, in the south, and even in the Westlands. Enhover, and our influence, is spreading outward. These people paid the cost. Unfortunate, but someone has to pay."

"They paid the cost. That is true," growled Oliver. "I don't think they would have agreed to the exchange."

"That's why we don't ask," responded King Edward with a wry smile on his face.

"Empire," snarled Oliver, stalking back and forth across the room. "Blood staining our hands, our souls, for what? All so we can draw new lines on the map? Thousands will die because of this. A culture will vanish. Father, the wisdom these people held will be gone. Do you not wonder what they could have taught us? We'll learn nothing now. That is the price of our empire."

His father tilted his head curiously. "I could make the argument, son, that there's not a man in Enhover who benefits more from the Company's adventures abroad than you do."

Oliver stopped walking, staring at the king.

President Goldwater, to his credit, stayed wisely silent.

King Edward gestured around him, seeming to encompass the room, the palace, the city, and the nation around it. "Everything we stand upon, everything we have, was bought in one way or another. Sometimes, it's the shrewd trading of the Company's factors. Sometimes, it's the bravery of this nation's explorers and their bold forays into the unknown. Sometimes, it's the concessions we wring through diplomacy. But sometimes, Oliver, what we have is purchased in blood. It's the way it has always been for our family, the way it has been for every empire since the beginning of time. That blood buys us new lines on the map, Oliver, but it also bought your lifestyle, your opportunities. We bought that for every citizen of this great nation, for every child that has a chance at a better life than their parents. That's what it is for, and yes, someone has to pay. It's better them than us."

"Imbon was different," argued Oliver. "We could have worked together with the natives. We didn't have to just take."

"Different in what way?" questioned his father. "It's ending as it always does."

Oliver stormed to the side of the room and jerked the stopper out of a crystal decanter of wine.

"Pour one for each of us," instructed his father.

Not trusting himself to respond, he poured, sloshing wine over the rim of one of the delicate glasses but not caring, hardly even noticing.

"I do not mean to interrupt," ventured President Goldwater, clearly intending just that, "but, Oliver, what is it that you would have us do?"

Oliver handed the older men the wine glasses and resumed pacing. His father and the Company president drank quietly, letting him think the matter through. As he did, he found no easy solutions. The bloodshed, the horror he'd witnessed during those moments in Imbon, who else was it for if not him? A son of the king, a shareholder of the company. His father was right. He benefited more from the colony than anyone. He'd been there at nearly every important stage of development of the place. From its rise to its fall, his hand had been there, steering the course, drawing the map that had led to annihilation.

"It could have been different," he said finally. "The relationship with the natives was strong. Until this, they benefited from our presence. That's the way it should be."

"How do you think the natives benefitted from our occupation?" asked King Edward.

Oliver blinked at him.

"We took control of their island. We put them to work on our plantations. We taxed them. We forced them to adhere to our laws, and I don't doubt our men took their share of joy from the native women," said the king. "We brought them our medicines, true, along with diseases that they had no tolerance for. We brought sterling, which they give back to us for goods only we can provide. Which part of that, Oliver, do you think the natives enjoy the most? Don't lie to yourself and say that Imbon was different. It wasn't. It just took longer for the blood to spill."

"It doesn't have to be that way." Oliver drank down his wine. "It doesn't—"

"It's the way it has always been," interrupted the king, "the way it always will be."

Snarling, Oliver spun and stomped back to refill his wine.

"What happened?" asked the king. "Why did they rebel?"

"We— I, found a cache of artifacts," answered Oliver, pouring his wine and not looking back at his father. "The natives ascribed some importance to them. They claimed the spirits of their enemies were captured within wooden figurines. There were tablets as well, ones with…"

"With what?" asked the king quietly.

"I could not read the script, but I recognized a symbol," explained Oliver "In Westundon, before the events at Derbycross, I was attacked in the courtyard of Philip's palace. Three footmen had somehow been, ah, taken. They were like puppets, controlled by Isisandra Dalyrimple or Marquess Colston, I'm not sure which. The footmen had tattoos drawn on the backs of their necks, identical to a symbol I spotted on one of the tablets. I don't know what else is on there, but…"

"Sorcery?" wondered the king. "That explains the reckless behavior of the natives. To protect knowledge like that, men have done awful things. Who would have thought, in Imbon?"

"The Church," said President Goldwater, looking from the duke to the king. "Shall we call for their opinion?"

"I'd like to see the tablets first," stated the king. "The last time sorcery was a threat to Enhover, it was Oliver who faced the danger. The time before, it was me. The Church declaims loudly from the pulpit, but it has been a long time since I've heard of their actions on the field of battle. In time, we will turn these tablets over to them, but first, I want to see the objects that caused a bloody revolt."

Goldwater shifted, as if he wanted to speak up, but between the duke and the king, he evidently decided there was little room for commercial interest. Not when he was relying on that same king's marines to return his colony back to him.

"They're still on my airship," said Oliver. "I'll have the captain transport them to you."

"I'll send a delegation of marines to fetch them so they'll be in my study later this evening," offered his father. "Perhaps a note from you to your captain? I'm told she's rather feisty, and I'd hate for her to think we're robbing her hold."

Oliver snorted. "Feisty. That she is."

"Do you understand, son, what we have to do now?" asked the king.

Oliver paused a long moment. "It did not have to be this way. It didn't. But now, I understand what must be done."

The king nodded, evidently satisfied, and Oliver heard Goldwater letting out a slow wheeze where he'd been holding his breath. Bloodshed. It had been unnecessary, Oliver knew that, but what was the alternative? What could he do about it now?

Oliver wrote the note his father had requested and retired quietly to the room that he'd grown up in, the one his father kept vacant for when his son returned to the capital. In that room, Oliver sat and held his head in his hands.

THE SPECTATOR I

"I'M DEVASTATED Oliver couldn't join us," Lannia Wellesley pouted, adjusting her shawl so it revealed a bit of her bare shoulders. "I haven't seen him since I was in Westundon some months ago, and he doesn't make time to visit me in Southundon like he used to. He seems preoccupied in recent days, does he not?"

"You're not wrong," agreed King Edward, shifting forward in his seat to peer over the balustrade at the slowly filling theatre floor below.

Peers and merchants were trickling in. Only a few members of the orchestra had reached their chairs in the pit below the stage. Unorganized twangs and whistles rose as the musicians checked their instruments and arranged their spaces. The murmur of quiet conversation filled the rest of the theatre floor. She smiled, seeing some of that crowd looking up toward them.

"A quarter turn of the clock before it begins," she advised.

The king glanced at her before pulling out a small circular pocket clock and frowning at it. "The program said it was to begin now, did it not?"

"It did, but the theatre always starts late," she said loftily.

King Edward grunted and settled back in his chair.

Briefly, she wondered if she should have arranged for them to arrive later. When Oliver used to attend the shows with her, he would always insist on arriving the moment before the curtain parted. Efficient, but it would spoil the effect of Southundon society filling the chairs and glancing up to see her seated beside the king. No, if they'd arrived after the lights dimmed, most of those sniveling snakes wouldn't notice, or at least would pretend that they had not.

Smiling at him, she put a gloved-hand on Edward's arm. "Do not fret, uncle. This will give us a moment to talk. I've been feeling quite abandoned, you know? With my father racing between Westundon and here, you so busy with your studies, and Oliver off doing whatever it is that he does, no one has been around to squire me about town. Why, not even John has had time to escort me."

"John has a young family and responsibilities as Duke of Southundon," reminded the king. "Besides, what good is hanging your arm on that of your cousin's? A girl your age ought to be out with suitors! I know what happened with Viscount Brighton, but your father told me you barely even glanced at the man when he attempted to court you. He wasn't a bad sort, was he? Adequate income from, ah, what was it? Whale oil or steel manufacture? Timber?"

"Viscount Ethan Brighton's death was no severe loss to Enhover or to me," declared Lannia, pointing her nose in the air.

"That's unfair," chided Edward.

"You weren't being asked to marry the man," she stated, "or, worse, to move to that… that village he ruled. I can't recall the name of it. Where are the Brighton family lands?"

Edward tugged on his goatee.

"You don't know either!" she squealed.

"I'm not saying you should have accepted a proposal from Viscount Brighton, or even spent more than a few turns of the clock with the man before you sent him on his way, I'm suggesting that you should consider a suitor, any suitor. It would be good for you, Lannia, to have someone in your life."

"Is that the same advice you give Oliver?" she questioned.

King Edward smirked. "My youngest would benefit from a lasting union, yes, but he heeds little of my counsel."

"Well, when you, my father, or any of your sons can find a match who can afford theatre seats this grand, I'll be happy to accompany them to any show they invite me to."

The king rolled his eyes. "No one can afford seats like these, not as often as you want to attend. You grew up with Enhover's treasury at your disposal, Lannia. You cannot expect a suitor to have access to the same funds. The only men of your age with that sort of income are your cousins. Will you marry one of them?"

She smiled at the king. "No, of course not, but that does not mean I shall lower my standards. The man I marry must have standing amongst the peers, and he must have the financial resources to take care of me. Perhaps someone with shares in Company stock and a barony. That would be a good start. As well as solid income and a title, he must be interesting and interested. He must be handsome, of course. Well read, versed in sport—"

"You forget that he must exist!" The king laughed. "I'm not sure there's a man in Enhover who meets those criteria, my girl. Perhaps a compromise? You can find a man with standing amongst the peers, and your father's estate will provide the financing for your lifestyle, or you can find a solid Company man, and we'll look at granting him a title. A good woman molds the man to the form she desires, but you've got to start with the man!"

"And the theatre seats?" jested Lannia.

"Find the man, and I'll share my seats," claimed Edward. "I'm too old for going out and taking in these shows anyway. At my age, I'd much rather be sitting in my study in front of the fire sipping a glass of mulled wine."

"You don't drink mulled wine," said Lannia. Her lips curled into a smile. "Besides, uncle, your books and scrolls are not going anywhere. They'll be the same they were the year before and the year before that. The theatre is changing. The theatre is dynamic.

Every season there is something new. You should be out while you're young and spry. Save the books for when you're old and decrepit."

King Edward snorted. "I am old and decrepit."

Lannia shook her head, grinning at her uncle. "You're in better shape than men half your age. I don't think you've aged a day since I was a girl, uncle. We should go out tonight, after the performance. Let's have drinks and go dancing!"

"Dancing?" cried Edward. "You want me to go dancing? I'm the king, niece. I do not go dancing."

"Perhaps not dancing," she admitted. "Maybe Oliver will go with me. Is he still at the palace?"

"He is," confirmed the king. "The boy's growing up, though, Lannia. He has a lot on his mind this evening. You heard about Imbon and the uprising?"

"What does that have to do with Oliver?" she demanded.

The king stared back at her.

"I know. I know," she groused. She glanced down at the orchestra pit and judged a few more minutes before the lights would be dimmed. Turning back to her uncle, she asked, "Grown up. You don't mean he won't go dancing or give a girl a tumble. What is it, then, uncle? What do you mean Oliver is growing up?"

"I mean Oliver is at a point where he must decide what is important to him," explained the king, "his own flights of fancy or the Crown? He was quite upset about all of this mess with the Dalyrimples. What he saw in Imbon only exacerbated what he's going through."

"What he's going through? I don't understand," said Lannia. She felt a flicker of annoyance skirt across her consciousness and roughly shoved it down. "It's terrible we lost the colony, but you'll be able to get it back, won't you?"

"Of course. That's not what the boy is upset about. It's not so different from what your own father struggled with," continued Edward. "Both he and Oliver have personal ambition along with intelligence and skills. That's taken them far. Both had to decide, though, where their loyalty lies. They have to choose a path. Is it in their own ambition, or is it with the Crown? Oliver had a difficult awakening in Imbon, and he's facing the reality that despite his talent and resources, there are some things he cannot change. The world is a harsh place, yes? Sometimes representing the Crown, we have to act in ways that seem harsh as well. It's what we must do, for Enhover. Our ancestors formed this nation from the four distinct regions of the continent. They consolidated it and held it. They built a strong core. It is on our shoulders to continue expanding their work. The colonies, the United Territories, the land beyond the horizon, those are the blank pages we can write upon. The reach of our empire goes where we carry it."

"And Oliver is no longer interested in carrying that weight?" wondered Lannia.

"Every generation must become accustomed to the heft of their responsibilities," said the king. "Oliver, our cartographer, has drawn his lines with ink. He's learning that sometimes those lines are drawn in blood."

Below them, the discordant plucking of the instruments silenced. The lights in the theatre dimmed, and the drums began to boom a commanding beat. The show was beginning.

THE PRIESTESS X

"THEY HAD me kill the man in cold blood," she said. "A knife in the neck and that was that. He dabbled a bit in potions, maybe some other things he should have left alone, but he wasn't a bad sort. He helped me get from Valerno to Romalla, for one. He didn't have to do that. Didn't have to take the risk that he did."

"Ruthless killers," agreed Duke. He drank deeply of his ale and then wiped his lips.

"The worst was that they'd known the man. Known him for years!" exclaimed Sam. She snapped her fingers. "They made the decision to kill him just like that. For what? To prove a point?"

"A pointless point," muttered Duke darkly.

"Are you drunk?" she wondered, glancing at him out of the corner of her eye.

"Nah." He sipped his ale again and set it down. "I had a little wine earlier's'all. What I meant was that they had you prove yourself, and then you left. You didn't get their help, and they didn't get yours. The man's death was for nothing."

"Nothing," agreed Sam, nodding slowly. "I did collect some of his potions, at least. Better in my hands than theirs."

"Aye, we might need the stuff," responded Duke. "Assuming we ever find out who is behind all of this."

"Right, if we ever do."

Duke drank down the rest of his ale and circled his finger in the air to the barman for another round.

"The uprising, I saw it in the papers," mentioned Sam. "Was it as bad as it sounded?"

"It was worse," replied Duke, his speech thick and slow. "I didn't read about it. I saw it." He shuddered, toying with his empty ale mug. "There will be thousands dead by the time all is said and done. My father and the Company are assembling a retaliatory force now. They'll bomb any two sticks they find leaning against each other and send the marines trooping through the jungle to slaughter anyone who doesn't know the difference between Middlebury and Swinpool. There won't be a native left alive when they've finished. For what? Another warehouse filled to the rafters with spices? Another storeroom shelf stacked with pounds sterling?"

"They will kill everyone?" questioned Sam.

Duke snorted. "Everyone. They wanted me to do it, to lead the forces myself. I told them no. They don't need me. Every living soul on that island will be dead in the next two weeks with or without my involvement. Spirits, my involvement... It's what started this, isn't it? Without me, none of this would have happened."

"Someone would have found that island," consoled Sam. "With or without you, the rail was laid. Conflict was inevitable. It's the way of the world."

Duke shook his head.

She thought he looked like he could use a hug. Instead, she asked, "Can they escape?"

"On the way out, Ainsley blasted holes in every sailing ship of decent size," answered Duke. "They could fashion rafts, I suppose, but with the currents in those seas, I don't think they stand much of a chance of making shore anywhere. Unless the United Territories or some other unwitting visitor arrives with a seaworthy vessel and a captain who doesn't survey the port before dropping anchor, there's nothing they can do."

"Terrible," said Sam. "Just awful."

The barman Andrew dropped off two more mugs of ale, his eyes darting between the pair of them. Then, he moved away without speaking.

Duke returned to his ale with determination.

She gave him a moment before asking, "Is it true there were lizards longer than an airship?"

"Depends if you count the tail," answered Duke, not bothering to look up.

She gaped at him.

"I killed one of them," he slurred. "Shot it in the belly with a cannon. Tore a hole straight through the thing. It fell down next to me. Head was the size of this bar counter, teeth the size of you."

"That wasn't in the papers," she mumbled. "What... what was it?"

"The natives have some knowledge of the supernatural," answered Duke. "The artifacts we collected were related to sorcery. I turned those over to my father for further examination. The lizards, though... it didn't feel the same. I don't think sorcery is the explanation. In Derbycross, Archtan Atoll, it was cold. Does that make sense? I could feel the bitter chill seeping from Isisandra and Colston. In Imbon, it was warm."

"Imbon is rather warm," reminded Sam, wondering just how drunk the man was.

Duke shook his head. "Not like that, it was... a sense, I guess. I could sense a warmth that was outside of the ambient air, outside of anything I can describe. Like a warm pitcher of water pouring over my skin, but... but not like that, really. Is druid magic like that? Warm?"

"Druid magic wasn't part of my training," said Sam. "I haven't heard of anything or felt anything like what you describe. It makes me curious, though. If that kind of thing is possible in Imbon, then it could be possible anywhere. Armies of giant beasts strolling across the countryside, sacking cities, wrecking armies. Some of the lizards are still there in Imbon?"

"Not for long," remarked Duke. "My father and the Company are going to kill every man, woman, lizard, and child on that island. They're not going to pause and figure out how it was done. I'm sure Admiral Brach would love the secret, but my father will be happy as long as no one else has it. Someone directed the creatures, so someone knows, but that knowledge is going to be lost forever."

"Such a waste," replied Sam.

"Such a waste," agreed Duke.

"I need something stronger than this ale," declared Sam. She looked up to the barman Andrew. "What do you suggest?"

"Well," said the bartender, studying them, "if you want to get proper twisted…" He reached behind and opened the narrow cupboard where he kept the wormwood liquor. "This is a new batch from Rhensar. It packs a punch."

"Sounds good," declared Duke, banging his empty mug on the counter.

"I don't know," worried Sam. "That stuff'll grab you different than ale or wine."

"What do you mean?" wondered Duke. "You said you needed something strong, no?"

"They call it blood of the fae," offered Andrew. "It used to be popular with some of the society sets. You know the ones I mean. Tipplers claimed it helped to see the world like one of the fae. Others say it just gets you drunk. In my opinion, a good drunk can help you sort things out, sometimes. And you two, as usual, have got a bit to sort out."

"I don't think—" she began.

"Pour it," instructed Duke. "I want to wake up when all of this is over."

Sam met Andrew's eyes. The barman must have seen her concern, but without comment, he began preparing the glasses for them. Sugar, water, and the blood of the fae. There was art and pleasure in the preparation, she knew, but all she could think of was that they were walking down another unknown path, and this one would be lit by a strange, green glow.

"See you two on the other side," said Andrew, setting down the bottle in between the pair of glasses.

THE CARTOGRAPHER XII

BITTER COLD ENCOMPASSED HIM. His breath billowed in front of him like angry fire disgorged from the maw of a mighty dragon. Turning, he looked back to see if he had a long green tail like those creatures of story, but there was nothing there. Nothing at all. He was incorporeal, insubstantial, less than the mist he breathed out. He looked down at himself and saw nothing.

He could see around himself, though. Spread before him were high, knife-edged mountains. White like bone, rimmed in frost. Mountains he recognized from long ago. Cold surrounding him, he felt a flutter of trepidation and a creeping understanding that he knew this place. He'd seen it long ago and not so long ago. He turned, and through the shroud of his breath and the shroud of other, he saw the billowing, cold fire. White flames reached to the sky in a raging, frigid, slow-moving inferno. The flame shed no light on him or on the mountains, no light on anything, but from a distance, he could feel the cold of the fire creeping through his nonexistent flesh.

Northundon, the source of the flame. Unending fuel for the fire.

No, he realized, the city was not the source of the fuel. Below him, in a long, single, sinuous line, marched the dead. Souls headed toward the inferno where they'd be consumed in its cold, white flame. Souls that had once been citizens of Northundon, he knew. His people now marched across the underworld in an unending sacrificial parade. Why were they marching to destruction? What would happen to them, he wondered, if they died in the underworld?

"Have you come to join us, Oliver Wellesley?" they asked him. Their voices, like dry bone rubbing against another, came from ahead of him, behind, and under. Each soul in the line, speaking as one, they asked him, "Is it your time?"

He didn't answer. He couldn't answer. He had no body in this strange place. Though he breathed and had breath, he had no mouth and no words. The world spun as he considered that. He had no answer, no understanding of what he was seeing and feeling, but it was not his time, he knew that. Not yet.

"Do you seek her still?" asked the souls. "You were told once before she is not here. She never was. Why do you come again, Oliver Wellesley, if not to join us?"

He strived to ask the souls what they spoke of, but he could not.

"She was part of the bargain, Oliver Wellesley," intoned the souls. "She was once there, in that place, as were we. She was part of the bargain, part of the sacrifice. Where is she, Oliver Wellesley?"

His mother. They spoke of his mother.

"Will you take her place so that the bargain can be completed, Oliver Wellesley? We have waited so long, suffered so long. End our torment, Oliver Wellesley. You can take her place. You can join our sacrifice, fulfill the bargain. Your blood, Oliver Wellesley, will suffice."

His mother was not here, not in the underworld, not part of… of what?

He shifted, turning his insubstantial body to face the fire, to feel the blistering chill, the horrible menace radiating from its white flame. Towering far above what he could see, the flame stretched beyond the sky, certainly beyond what Northundon looked like following the attack.

She was not here, but she had been there. What did the shades at his feet mean?

"You see her. Do you see her?" questioned the march of souls. "Find her. Send her soul to finish the bargain or take her place. We suffer, Oliver Wellesley. Complete the sacrifice. Free us."

She was not here, but she had been there. Where was she?

"Find her, Oliver Wellesley. Look for her there. We invite you. We welcome you. Find her and find your answers. Free us. Understand. Go there."

———

TERRIBLE, THROBBING PAIN ASSAILED HIM. IT FELT LIKE A STRONG MAN with a hammer was bashing his skull over and over again. He only wished the man would finish the job and finally crush the mess of bone and flesh. Spill his brains and end it. He raised his arms, gripping his skull, keeping his eyes squeezed tightly shut.

"Frozen hell, I'm hung over," complained a voice next to him, the sound rough and painful, not unlike the bone-dry rasp of the marching souls. "Spirits, why are you so cold?"

Beside him, warm flesh shifted, and he felt a wave of air slide down his side. Cold air, but it warmed him. He was cold, but the tight agony in his head forced out all other discomforts.

"Frozen hell, I've got to start the fire… Make some tea or something," complained the brittle, scratching voice.

He curled tight into a ball, the pounding in his head continuing, the cool air not bothering him. The voice was right. He was cold. He wanted to be cold.

Clatter and curses intruded on his pain, but he refused to open his eyes. The relentless throb in his skull beat in time with grim flashes of vivid memory. Not of the night before, he couldn't recall any of that, but of the horrific dream he'd had. The underworld, his mother, Northundon…

"I have sugar now," called a voice from somewhere distant. "We got it from that apothecary along with the... Ah, why am I talking about that..."

Something smelled awful and his stomach churned.

Hungover. He'd felt worse, he thought, or maybe not. Probably not, he decided.

Struggling, he forced himself to sit, half-slumped over, but better than lying flat. A scalding hot bath, coffee, some powder to relieve the pain, and gentle fingers to massage his head and neck. Definitely some water. Dry toast and a nap once the powder went to work. Sleep and give time for the drink to bleed from his system. One of his servants could rub his neck and shoulders until he sank into unconsciousness. That was what he needed.

"Well, this isn't as hot as it probably should be, but I think it's hot enough to steep the leaves. I put sugar in yours. Do you take it? If it's not hot enough, ah, I suppose we could make more. Last time, I burned it rather badly, which I don't quite understand. It's just water and leaves. Took me a full turn of the clock to scrape the damn things off the bottom of the kettle. I tried the leaves in the mugs this time. I don't have a lot of sugar. If you want some, this is the cup."

He risked opening his eye, grateful that the room was dim. No windows. No lights, either, except what spilled around a form standing in the doorway. A naked form silhouetted by the light from another room. He tried to blink the sleep from his eyes, staring at the shape of the woman, wondering where he was.

Sam. It had to be Sam, and they were in her apartment. That made sense.

"Why are you naked?" he asked, scratching his bare stomach. A flash of panic bit through the throbbing pain in his head. "Why am I... Did we?"

She laughed, and his panic steadied. They had, they must have, in their drunken stupor. Not the first time for either of them, and she didn't seem upset at the—

"No," replied Sam. "I'm naked because I always sleep naked. I just woke up. I needed tea more than I did clothing."

She set a lukewarm mug of water and tea leaves on a small table beside her bed and then stooped to gather her leather trousers from the floor. He felt himself stir at the sight of her backside, blood thankfully draining from his aching, swimming head.

"You don't always sleep naked," he claimed, remembering sharing a room on the airship. It was about all he could work out in his pathetic state.

"I do," she said, speaking over her shoulder and tugging her trousers on. "Ah, you're thinking on the Cloud Serpent? I slept naked there as well, but I fell asleep after you and woke before. I don't sleep much. A relic of my time on the farm, I guess."

"Farm? When were you on a farm... Is that a new tattoo? What is that?"

"It is," she said, bending again and collecting a linen shirt which she slipped on.

"What is it?"

"It's ink embedded in my skin," she replied, not answering what he was asking. "Are you going to drink your tea?"

He did, his mind struggling to return to productive thought.

But he was awake enough to tell that her tea was shit.

Though, as she'd claimed, it did have sugar. Finally, after several sips and grimaces at what was slightly warm sugar water with tea leaves floating in it, he asked, "If we didn't... If we didn't... why am I naked?"

"You got sick all over yourself," she explained. "We might have... well, not after that. I stripped you down, with little help from you I should say, poured a couple of buckets of water over your head, and we both passed out. You twisted and squirmed half the night. I'll be honest, Duke, if you aim to be a serious drinker, you ought to learn how to do it proper."

"We might have?"

She smirked at him. "Come on. Let's get you something to eat. Maybe some dry toast?"

"Yes, ah, I'm rather naked," he said after throwing off the sheets and then quickly pulling them back over himself.

"You saw me," she reminded, nodding at his midsection, "and it seems you enjoyed the show. It's my turn now."

"I thought you preferred girls," he complained.

"You also thought we had sex last night," she said. She sipped her tea and made a face. "This is awful."

"I know," he agreed.

"Well, get up and make some, then," she requested. "I'll work on the toast."

"Can I... can I borrow some clothing?" he asked.

"Sure," she replied, slapping a hand on her thigh. "I have a couple more pairs of these leather trousers. Check the wardrobe. I think you'll fit into them nicely."

She turned and disappeared into the other room.

He looked around helplessly. On the floor, wadded in the corner, was his clothing. As she'd claimed, it was damp and filthy with what appeared to be sickly green stains. Her wardrobe was in the corner, but he didn't bother. Even the shirts and vests she wore were tailored. None had a hope of fitting him. Instead, he stood, drawing her sheets around him in a sort of wrap, and shuffled out into her sitting room.

"We ought to burn your clothing," she advised, "and probably that sheet. You're going to have to buy me a new one."

He waved a hand dismissively and then cursed and caught the sheet before it slid all the way to the floor.

She gave an appreciative nod at the flesh that had been displayed. "For a coddled peer, it sure appears as if you stay active."

"For a woman who prefers women, it sure appears that you keep looking at me."

"I prefer ale to wine," she said. "That doesn't mean I never enjoy a glass of wine."

He snorted and shuffled closer to her fire, peering down at a kettle set on the hearth. "I prefer coffee to tea. I don't suppose you have any?"

"No," she replied.

"We have to do something about my clothing," he said. "I cannot walk back to my brother's palace like this."

"I offered a pair of my trousers," she reminded, grinning at her own jest.

He shook his head. "Can you find a for-hire-carriage? We'll send a note to my man Winchester. He'll come fetch me and bring fresh attire when he does."

She shrugged. "Do you care to discuss what was keeping you awake last night?"

He shot her a hard glance.

"You were mumbling in your sleep," she explained. "I couldn't pick up much of it, but enough to know you were seeing something."

"I don't want to talk about it now," he said. "Come with me to the palace. We'll get cleaned up and then talk."

"I've enjoyed a glass of wine in the past. I didn't say I was looking to enjoy one now."

He rolled his eyes at her. "If I wanted to… Well, I suppose taking a woman back to the palace is exactly what I'd do. Not this time, though. This time, I need time to think, and then we need to talk."

She nodded.

He sipped the lukewarm liquid in his mug. "And we need to find something potable to drink."

She simply shrugged and then cursed, scrambling to a griddle suspended over the fire. Muttering to herself, she flipped two pieces of bread. They'd acquired a thick black crust on the bottom and the stench of burnt toast filled the small room.

"Ah, that's not so bad," she claimed. "Last time I tried to cook bread, it caught fire."

WINCHESTER STOOD IN THE CENTER OF THE SITTING ROOM, HIS GAZE disdainfully moving around the space. "Mistress Sam, your maids are doing a terrible job."

Oliver laughed, and Sam hissed.

"She doesn't have maids, Winchester," he advised, rubbing his head.

"Well, someone is doing a terrible job," huffed the valet. "I'll send some women down from the palace. Because it's such a small place, they'll have it straightened in no time."

"Excuse me," snapped Sam. "It's not… Did you say you'll have some women sent down?"

"Cleaning women," said Oliver with a wink.

"Of course," answered Winchester primly. "Sweeping, straightening, perhaps a little polish. I think the place will look, ah, like less of a dump, I hope."

"Speaking of clean," said Oliver, still wrapped in Sam's sheet. "I have some clothes in the bedroom. Can you take a look?"

The valet nodded and set a small trunk at Oliver's feet. "I took the liberty of a selecting an outfit, m'lord."

"You always do," acknowledged Oliver.

While the valet cautiously entered the bedchamber, Oliver flipped back the lid of the trunk and saw simple trousers, a shirt, and a woolen coat. Adequate for the trip up to the palace. He glanced at Sam.

She leaned back in her chair, balancing it on two legs, and propped her feet on her breakfast table. "I'll wait."

Grunting, he shimmied out of the sheet and quickly yanked on his small clothes and trousers.

By then, Winchester returned with the clothing from the day before, one hand pinching the clothes out in front of him, the other hand pinching his nose. "This is awful, m'lord, even by your standards."

"You don't think—" Oliver cut himself off as his valet tossed the damp items into Sam's fire.

"That is going to smell even worse," she complained.

"Let's depart until this place can be sterilized and freshened," remarked the valet.

"Sounds good to me," muttered Oliver, pulling on his shirt and shaking out his coat.

"M'lord, if you mean to be a frequent guest of Mistress Sam, may I suggest securing an apartment that has a closet for the necessaries, indoor plumbing, a gas line, and a proper kitchen? A private carriage court wouldn't be remiss, but that might be impossible in this neighborhood."

"It's not like that, Winchester," said Oliver. "We are not having a tryst."

"Then why were you naked?" questioned the valet, clearly not believing it.

Oliver shrugged.

"Are there are a lot of women you pay apartments for?" wondered Sam.

"I wouldn't say a lot," grumbled Oliver, glaring at his valet as the man dramatically mouthed a number. "Let's go to the palace."

LATER THAT EVENING, HYDRATED BUT STILL FEELING LIKE THE BOTTOM of a boot, Oliver sat in front of a crackling fire in a giant stuffed chair. Sam, sitting in an identical chair, had her feet propped up on an embroidered and tasseled ottoman.

"I could get used to living like this," she mentioned.

He swirled his glass, dark amber liquor coating the sides of the crystal and then slowly running back to the base. His eyes were locked on the fire, hot and orange-red, but it flickered and leapt just like the cold white fire from his dream.

"You're not getting drunk again, are you?" she questioned.

"No, not for a long time," he replied. "At least, not that drunk."

"What is it, then?"

"I had a dream," he told her. "It was… vivid. Exceptionally

vivid. It was like what I saw when we fought Isisandra and Colston beneath Derbycross. I think… I think maybe some of that powder is still in my body. Is that possible? Could the drink have, I don't know, triggered it somehow?"

Sam shrugged. "Maybe."

"I thought you were an expert on these things," he complained.

"There is far more to sorcery than anyone can be an expert on," she claimed, "or would want to be an expert on. The dark path is a twisted and evil one. A vision, you said?"

"A dream, I said."

"As drunk as we were, I'm surprised you recall anything. It's certainly a little fuzzy to me. What was this dream about?"

He sipped his whiskey, letting the liquor warm his throat and his stomach, hoping it would ease the dull pressure in his head. "It was the underworld, I think, or Northundon. Maybe my imagination of what the city looks like on the other side? I don't know, but I recognized it clearly. I knew with certainty that was what I was looking at. It was cold, and the city was on fire. There were tens of thousands of souls marching into the city, into the fire. I don't know what happened to them there, but they spoke of sacrifice and a bargain. They just kept marching. They… they said my mother was not there. That's the same thing they said when Colston threw the powder into my face."

"It was cold?" asked Sam, toying with her own glass, the rest of her body stone still. "What color was the fire?"

"Bone white," replied Oliver. "It was dark, though, all over. Somehow, I could still see. It was as if shadows were moving on a mime's screen, but opposite, white on black. Despite the dark, I knew what was happening. That's the way it is in dreams, isn't it? And I had no body, but I could still feel."

"The underworld is a hard place to describe," said Sam. "Descriptions vary, as some observers are more articulate than others, but they match what you're telling me, Duke. What you're saying you saw could be the real underworld, the actual other side of the shroud, a mirrored reflection of our own reality."

He frowned at her.

"You said the souls spoke to you. What did they say?"

"They told me to go there," he murmured, staring into the crackling fire. "Northundon, I think they meant."

"Your dream may have been a vision." She drew a deep breath. "A prophecy, some would call it."

"A prophecy!" he said incredulously, staring at her. "I don't think it was that. I didn't see the future."

"Maybe you saw the present?" she suggested.

He quieted, uncomfortable with the idea.

"What else did the spirits tell you?"

"They told me my mother wasn't there," he answered. "That's the same thing they'd said before, that she wasn't there but that she had been. They wanted me to find her, to complete some bargain or a sacrifice. I don't know what they were talking about, just that they wanted her and claimed she was not there, not in the underworld."

"That's a prophecy, Duke," said Sam. "That's just like what my mentor said he saw, a vision that was startlingly clear. It stayed with him his entire life, every detail. In it, the message was of a darkness spreading from Enhover. He thought I was to be involved in stopping it, along with you."

"Me?" snorted Oliver.

"Duke," chided Sam, "you did help stop Isisandra Dalyrimple, did you not? In Romalla, a member of the Council, Bishop Constance, claimed that my mentor's prophecy had already come true. She said we had already stopped the tree of darkness that Thotham claimed would grow out of Enhover. He didn't think it was over, but... I don't know. It could be. It could not be. You were involved, though, just as Thotham predicted."

"Can we ask him?" wondered Oliver. "He's in the spear, isn't he?"

"Do you know how to speak to an incorporeal spirit that's imbued into an inanimate object?" asked Sam. "Because I do not."

"Well, how do I know if it's... if it's real? A prophecy, I mean."

"There's only one way to tell," answered Sam. "You wait to see if it comes true."

"What, wait and see if my mother is alive?" scoffed Oliver. "It's been twenty years. She's—"

"The spirits said she was in Northundon," interjected Sam, "but she's not now?"

"I don't know," he admitted. "They weren't very clear. I couldn't speak back to them. I could only listen to what they told me."

"That's prophecy for you," she replied sardonically. "We could scry for her, I suppose."

He blinked at her.

"Do you have anything that belonged to her that could help fashion the bridge?"

His hand drifted up to his head, back over his hair, to the leather thong that kept it tied back. "I do."

"It's risky," she admitted, "but what else can we do? We both agree there are sorcerers out there, more powerful ones than even Isisandra Dalyrimple. They've cleaned house and severed the threads that may lead us to them. We don't have any other leads. After the fiasco in Romalla, we don't have any assistance on the way. It's just us, and we have nowhere to go."

He frowned. "I'm not saying I agree to this, but if I did, where would we start?"

"Just like I did when searching for Thotham, except this time, you'll be the one directing the spirit. I can help you with that. First, though, we need to get the supplies."

"Back to the apothecary, then?"

"Back to the apothecary," agreed Sam. "First thing in the morning, we can—"

"Let's go now," suggested Oliver. "If I recall, the man lived upstairs of his shop. He should be around. A brisk walk in the weather may do us some good. Get the blood flowing and help us wake up, and if not, perhaps the man will have something that can help with my head. The pressure inside of my skull has been beating like a drum since we woke."

"Didn't Winchester give you something?" she asked.

Oliver grunted. "It could have been wig powder for all the good it's done, and I wouldn't put that past him. He gets sullen, sometimes."

She smiled. "Well, as I'm no longer in the employ of the Church, I don't have much else to be doing. Let's go."

THE PRIESTESS XI

A MONTH after the winter solstice, the nighttime streets of West-undon were vacant and frozen. Proper folk had long since retired in front of their fires or darted quickly to where they needed to be. In the heart of winter, late at night, there was no lingering out on the streets. Even the pubs they passed in their rumbling mechanical carriage looked half-empty. Thick, wet sleet pattered against the glass window, threatening to melt and freeze as the night wore on. Already, Sam saw the streets had gained a slick, reflective sheen.

"I'm not sure this was a good idea," she said.

Across from her, his long coat pulled tight around him, a thick wool scarf wrapped around his neck, Duke admitted, "It probably wasn't, but we're almost there."

She grunted and looked back out the window. On the street corners, big gas-lit lamps spilled a glow that barely cut through the precipitation. Dark stone buildings twinkled with lantern light around their doorsteps, but the windows were shuttered and dark to stop the chill from seeping inside. The mien of the city, closed and crouching, fit her mood.

Sitting back, she rubbed gloved hands together. "I wish I'd brought the rest of my drink."

"Maybe the apothecary will serve us something," offered Duke.

"They're known for that, aren't they?"

"Surely there's a pub nearby we can stop in on the way back," suggested Duke, taking her place at the carriage window and frowning. "Assuming we can find one open."

Moments later, the carriage slowed to a skidding stop.

Duke tugged his scarf tight. "Ladies first?"

She snorted.

Sighing, the nobleman opened the door and stepped down into the cold, night air. Digging through his purse, he flipped their driver a shining silver coin and waved as the man professed extreme gratitude.

"He deserved it, out in this," claimed Duke, swatting ineffectively at the sleet that plonked down on his head.

"We'll need good luck to find another ride," said Sam as the carriage rumbled away. "Maybe another one of those silver coins and he would have waited?"

"Frozen hell," muttered the peer. Frustrated, he turned to the apothecary's shop and stomped toward it, nearly losing his footing on the slick cobblestones. "Watch that. They'll be covered in ice in a turn of the clock."

She stepped carefully past him and moved quickly, hoping to get out of the frigid air. Then, she paused, staring aghast at the door of the shopfront.

"What's wrong?" groused Duke, catching up. "Hammer the door. Let's see if we can... Oh."

On the door was a small parchment slip, the sort the watchmen left. It was legible, but globs of sleet were accumulating on it and melting, causing the script to run. Sam peered close, squinting in the darkness,

"Attention to the family of the apothecary known as Rian. Please visit the judiciary at Garden Street for information on the disposition of the body and assets."

"Frozen hell!" she cried. "The man is dead!"

Hands stuffed into his long coat, Duke leaned around her, reading the note as if he couldn't believe it.

She stalked away from the door, looking up and down the dark street. Houses, bakeries, a grocer, not even one proper pub or anywhere else that had a welcoming light on late in the evening. At a far corner, she saw a bundled figure disappear into a stair-well, but otherwise, the street was dead quiet, not another soul moving about on the awful, dreary night.

"I knew I should have brought that drink," she muttered to herself.

Then, she jumped, nearly flopping down on the slick cobble-stones when a sharp crack split the air. It was far too loud in the silence. Turning, she saw a gaping hole where the door to the apothecary once stood. Duke was disappearing inside.

"Did you just break that door!" she called. "You can't do that. The watch has sealed the building!"

"Well, when they come to arrest me, I hope they bring a proper hot toddy," he called from inside.

Cursing, she hurried after him. As she passed the threshold, a pale blue glow bathed the room. Duke was shaking a glass globe of fae light. He held it high, the swirling fae sparks gleaming with anger at their disturbed slumber.

"Damn things hate the cold even more than we do," complained Duke. "This room looks just like I remember it. Want to collect the jar of those... What did you say they were? Lizard penises? You know, the ones that look like pickles?"

"If you like," she said. "From what I saw this morning, you need all the help you can get."

"From what you... spirits forsake it! It was cold, and I was still drunk!"

"Yes, I'm sure you were," she said, passing around him, ignoring his blustering protests, and walking to the back of the room. "Come on. I want to see what's behind the curtain."

They passed into a small, dark room, the apothecary's inner

sanctum. They found row after row of obscurely labeled cabinets. The containers were stacked floor-to-ceiling with a simple ladder propped against the wall to reach the ones on top. She opened one and smelled it. Nutmeg. Nothing suspicious, but if each cabinet was as full as the first, it was a veritable fortune in spices, herbs, tinctures, mixtures, and minerals.

"It appears the man was doing quite well," she remarked.

"You don't remember what that bandit charged us?" groused Duke. "Look. Another door at the back."

She led the way into a narrow, cabinet-lined hallway.

"Just more storage," muttered Duke, holding up the light behind her.

At the end of the hall was another door. She tried the latch and found it was unlocked, so she pushed it wide. As she stepped into the room, an ice-cold chill swept over her body which had nothing to do with the weather outside.

"Frozen hell," muttered Duke from behind.

On the floor, a chalk-drawn pentagram spread six yards across. The five points of the star were marked with small, black candles. Duke lowered the glass globe of light, and she saw the interior of the pentagram reflected with tacky blood colored purple in the blue light of the fae.

"It's the same spirit-forsaken scene we saw in Harwick," muttered Duke.

Not moving farther inside, she glanced at the walls, back at the floor, and rubbed her face with both of her hands.

"H-How… What does this mean?" stammered Duke.

"It's a message," she said. "A message to us."

"That can't be…" he trailed off. "No, you're right. Who else would recognize this? But the man who did the one in Harwick is dead, isn't he?"

"The hound is dead, but the master is not," she said. "Is the message a warning, do you think, telling us to stop our investigation?"

"We practically have," argued Oliver. "We have no leads and no clue as to who could be behind all of this. Frankly, if someone was following our progress, they could easily see we don't know where to look."

"This blood is fresh," mentioned Sam. "It was spilled today, just a few turns ago."

"It's certainly an odd coincidence," he admitted, his hands still shoved deep in his coat pockets.

"Duke, your vision," she said. "What if it's not a coincidence? What if those we pursue sensed what happened and are now acting to thwart us? What if they knew, or at least suspected, we might come here? They killed the apothecary to prevent us scrying for your mother. They want to show us they have control, that they know us, and that we know nothing."

Beside her, Duke ran his hand back over his hair, checking the leather tie. "If that was the message, I can't say they're wrong, but why would they not just kill us instead? It'd draw attention, I know, but if they believe we have some lead on them, I get the impression these people would not hesitate. There's nothing they will stop at, Sam, so why a message and not a direct attack?"

"You weren't in the palace," reminded Sam. "You were at my flat during the vision. They could sense what was happening in the underworld, but they didn't know where you were in our world. If they could tell you were looking for your mother and learned she was not dead, it's logical that we would come here next. It's the only apothecary I know in Westundon that sells the supplies we need."

"The blood is a few turns old," mused Duke. "That means the apothecary was killed shortly after we returned to the palace, a place anyone would be certain to watch if they were trying to find me."

"You'd be easy to find there but are well protected by your brother's men," remarked Sam. "They wouldn't… Oh."

"Frozen hell," growled Duke.

He turned and drew his basket-hilted broadsword. She

unsheathed her two kris daggers, cursing herself for not bringing Thotham's spear. It had seemed a bit much to visit an apothecary, but now, she wished she had every weapon she could get her hands on.

They waited a long silent moment. Beside her, Duke shifted uncomfortably. Like her, she guessed he could hear the slow trod of heavy feet in the front room. Like her, she imagined he didn't enjoy being in the small, cramped, windowless stock room while unknown enemies assembled outside and pinned them in.

She leaned close to him and whispered, "Should we charge out?"

Duke looked sick. He whispered back, "Is that panting?"

Grimacing, she realized it was. "Wolfmalkin."

"Like in Derbycross?"

She waved for him to shush. With an unknown number of wolfmalkin lurking outside, it wasn't the appropriate time for a long, involved discussion on the things. At least his broadsword would do some good against them.

Duke opened his mouth to ask another, likely foolish, question, and she shook her head sharply. It wasn't the right time to do anything but attack. Wolfmalkin in the tight confines of the storeroom would be nearly impossible to avoid, and once the ferocious creatures got a hold of them, they'd be finished.

Without waiting for input, she stalked to the doorway and peered out into the cabinet-lined corridor, seeing nothing. She heard a snort, and a shiver went down her spine. It wasn't just one or two of the wolfmalkin moving outside in the front room. There were several of them.

Behind her, she heard a pained gasp.

She spun, seeing Duke struggling with an insubstantial shadow that appeared fuzzy in the waving light of the fae. He stabbed hopelessly behind himself with his broadsword, catching nothing but air.

She knew his steel would be worthless against the shade that was throttling him. Shades, she amended, as she saw more shadows emerging from the broken pentagram deeper in the room.

The broken pentagram.

It wasn't a message.

It was a trap.

"Frozen hell," she groaned.

THE CARTOGRAPHER XIII

BITTER COLD WRAPPED around his neck and his head was jerked back. It felt like an iron bar, left out in the winter chill, was pressing against his throat, sealing it, slowly crushing it. He whipped his broadsword around and stabbed back, striking nothing. He stomped a foot down on the wooden floor and then back kicked at nothing.

He dropped the globe of fae light, and it bounced on the floor. He kicked it with his flailing feet, and the lights swirled as the globe rolled into the corner.

"Frozen hell," Sam cursed.

She then sprang at him, thrusting over his shoulder with one of her sinuous kris daggers. The sharp steel plunged past him, and the constricting pressure on his neck vanished.

"See to the wolfmalkin," she hissed between gritted teeth. "I'll try to close the portal."

"T-The what?" he stammered, glancing back and seeing wild shadowy forms spilling into the room from… from nowhere.

She didn't answer, but she didn't need to. Within the blood-soaked area of the pentagram, shadows were blooming with alarming speed.

Out in the hallway, a board creaked under a heavy foot, and he heard a snarl, as if an animal was alerting its pack it'd found their prey. Adjusting his grip on his basket-hilted broadsword, he hoped Sam knew what she was doing. He stepped out of the doorway into the narrow corridor. Flat, wooden walls lined one side, and row after row of the apothecary's storage cabinets lined the other.

In front of him, illuminated only by the faint glow of the fae light from the room behind, loomed a giant shape. At least a yard taller than himself, it stooped as it entered the hallway. In its hands, he could see a massive battle axe, similar to what he recalled in the sorcerous chamber beneath Dalyrimple Manor.

"Where do they get those things made?" he whispered under his breath.

The creature in front of him growled low in its throat, its breath coming fast through its large nostrils, its teeth clacking as he imagined the shadowy shape's mouth opening in hunger. The wolfmalkin blocked the entire opposite end of the corridor. In the storeroom behind, he heard Sam's curses and scrambling as she was locked in a battle with the silent shades pouring through the pentagram.

"Good luck swinging that axe in here," Oliver told the creature in front of him. Then, he lunged forward, thrusting his broadsword.

The wolfmalkin, surprised at the direct attack, barely moved to parry with its battle axe. Oliver's broadsword pierced its torso, sinking deep into the muscled flesh, bouncing off a rib, and sliding into the thing's heart. It uttered a helpless whimper, whining like a kicked dog, and slumped to the side, its battle axe falling heavily on the wooden floor.

Oliver smiled, smoothly sliding his weapon free.

In the doorway to the main room, he heard a growl and looked up to see three pairs of glowing yellow eyes all clustered together, crouched to look into the hallway at him. He knew that the light coming from behind him defined his silhouette perfectly, and his shadow bounced in front of him as he scrambled back, watching the dark shape of a second wolfmalkin duck into the corridor and step over the corpse of the first.

This one held up its axe, ready to fight.

THE PRIESTESS XII

POURING like water from a burst dam, shades spilled into the room, appearing within the circle of the pentagram and stepping out where the barrier was broken. She had to repair it, to seal the circle to trap the shades inside and then figure out a way to deactivate it. To complicate matters, she had to get through half-a-dozen shades with more appearing every breath.

Spinning her twin kris daggers in her hands, she advanced slowly, lashing out at the chimerical shapes dancing in the low light radiating from the fae globe. The shadows dissipated as she struck them, only cool patches of air giving evidence that they ever existed. For each one she banished back to the underworld with her inscribed daggers, another appeared, and while she could barely sense the shapes as she slayed them, she could definitely feel it when they struck her.

A solid blow to her shoulder sent her reeling to the side. She scrambled to stay on her feet and kicked back instinctively, her foot catching nothing. A shade grasped her leg and jerked it up, knocking her off balance. She tumbled across the floor and sprang back to her feet, slashing her daggers wildly, not taking time to even look for what she was attacking, trusting that if she moved fast enough over a wide enough area, she'd hit something.

A glancing blow struck her back, and she dropped, spinning on one heel with her kris held out straight. Cool air kissed her face as the shadow evaporated. She lurched back up, arms windmilling, fighting closer to the edge of the pentagram.

Chalk outlined the pattern filled with blood.

She had no chalk on her, but she did have some of the other ingredient — blood. If she could spill her blood within the design of the pentagram, she could sever the bridge to the underworld and have a chance to seal the circle.

"Duke!" she shouted. "I need chalk. Look in the cabinets!"

"What?" he cried back incredulously.

"Get me chalk!" she barked.

Then, in the corner of the room where Duke had dropped the globe of fae light, one by one, the fae began to extinguish. A shade crouched over the globe, reaching an insubstantial hand through the glass, feeling blindly as the life and death spirits could not see each other. But the shade could feel the fae, and when it did, it pinched them, killing them. She gaped at the vanishing light until solid knuckles from an invisible fist socked her in the jaw.

THE CARTOGRAPHER XIV

"DUKE, I need chalk. Look in the cabinets!"

"What?" he shouted back, biting off a curse as the second wolfmalkin stepped over the body of the first and thrust down the hallway with the head of its giant battle axe. The corridor wasn't wide enough for a proper swing, but the sharp hook of the axe blade, pushed by the massively strong creature, was certain to make a far larger hole in his body than Oliver was interested in having.

"Get me chalk!" screamed Sam.

Then, the lights began to go out.

The wolfmalkin, in a rush of creaking floorboards and hungry grunts, charged.

Oliver crouched to the side, and the huge battle axe smashed into a cabinet above him. Debris rained down — bits of wood, glass, and dried herbs. Ignoring it, Oliver stabbed into the blackness, trusting to luck and grinning maniacally when he felt his blade impact flesh.

He lurched to the other side of the corridor just in time to avoid the heavy battle axe crashing down onto the floor, splintering the boards but missing his body. He stabbed again into the darkness and then jumped back, this time feeling the air as the battle axe smashed against the wall.

Thrusting and retreating, Oliver waged blind war on the giant creature in front of him. To his advantage, he could hardly attack without hitting the huge monster. To his disadvantage, if the wolf-malkin caught him with the axe, he was probably dead.

Whimpering and snarling, the wolfmalkin fell back after Oliver landed another thrust. He couldn't tell where he'd struck it, but each blow drew blood and caused pain. Like the wolf it was bastardized from, it had reacted by lashing out, and when that didn't work, it retreated in fear.

Behind it, he heard a roar and knew the third creature had entered the narrow corridor.

Lurching forward, he tried to race ahead and drive the wolf-malkin farther back, but he tripped on broken floorboards and pitched head first into the fur-covered legs of the thing.

Cursing, he scrambled away, dodging to the side, thinking the axe would could down on him. He felt the beast's thick, muscle-bound arm against his face as he shimmied along the exterior wall of the corridor. When that arm lifted away, he dropped onto his bottom.

Above him, there was a huge crack and the sounds of shattering brick.

The wolfmalkin had swung with the spiked butt-end of its battle axe, punching through the wooden interior and brick exterior walls of the building. A slender finger of silver light poked in from outside, illuminating the shape of the wolfmalkin.

Snarling in rage, it tugged on the axe, the haft stuck through the broken wall.

Jumping up, Oliver slammed his broadsword into the unprotected stomach of the creature and twisted it as he yanked it out, a torrent of blood gushing from the wounded beast.

It raised its head, it howled in anger, finally freeing its battle axe, but it fell back, and Oliver blinked. A hole the size of two fists was left in the wall. The dim light from outside spilled into the corridor. The wounded wolfmalkin stumbled away, the shapes of others clustered in the hall behind it.

One of them reached around its companion's neck and tore its claws across the injured pack mate's throat, ripping the flesh wide open. Gurgling helplessly, its yellow eyes reflecting panic and pain, the wolfmalkin collapsed.

The two behind it shoved the body aside and squeezed past, their massive shapes crunching the cabinets beside them as they forced their way around their dead peers.

The cabinets. He needed to find some chalk. Some chalk or… ash? They'd used ash before in the scrying ritual and the traps the Knives had fashioned at his estate. Would it work? Chalk or ash, he needed to buy time.

The cabinets, leaning precipitously from the battering the wolfmalkin had given them, were tilting alarmingly away from the wall as the next creature clung to them, shoving by its fallen brethren.

Oliver dropped his broadsword and ran forward, jumping and grasping the top of one of the cabinet units. He scrambled higher with his feet on the one next to where he was hanging. He shoved hard, pushing with his legs, rocking the heavy piece of furniture.

A clawed hand smacked against the wood, inches from his face, but he pulled harder, and to his relief, the cabinet toppled over, falling on the wolfmalkin and him.

He let go and fell to the floor as the giant storage unit collapsed over him, the top crashing against the opposite wall of the corridor, all of the individual cabinets sliding open and showering him with their contents.

Enraged howls erupted from where the wolfmalkin had been trapped, but the thing wasn't stuck long. The cabinet unit flew back, bashing against the wall, smashing to kindling as the angry beast pounded it with arms and axe, shattered debris filling the hallway.

Stunned, Oliver crab-walked back, finding his broadsword as he moved along the floor, not seeing any chalk in the wreckage.

He did notice Sam's rucksack that she'd dropped by the doorway before entering the storeroom with the pentagram. She had to have something in there worth trying, he hoped. He snatched his broadsword and the pack, moving quickly. The two surviving wolfmalkin were forcing their way through the broken cabinetry.

The storeroom was near black, the tiny sliver of light punched through the exterior wall in the corridor doing little to illuminate the frightful battle that was taking place inside. Sam, grunting, cursing, and thrashing around, sounded like she was fighting frantically against herself. The shades made no sound at all.

Dropping the pack and falling to a knee, Oliver dug his hand inside, hoping to find something he could use. His hand closed on a cool, glass vial. Not the healing salves he'd seen her use. Those were stone. This was something else. He pulled it out and smashed it down on the floor, halfway between him and where he thought the pentagram might be.

The scent of lavender and sandalwood filled the room, doing nothing to stop the terrifying sounds of Sam's battle with shadow or the wolfmalkin making their way through the corridor behind him. The little light he had faded, and he knew one of the creatures had passed the broken hole in the wall. Luckily, they probably couldn't see him and wouldn't know the layout of the storage room, but unluckily, he was out of ideas.

"Did you just break a bottle of perfume?" screeched Sam before making a sound like a raw slab of meat slapping down onto a granite table. She groaned and shrieked, "Stop messing with my perfumes and do something. Duke, we're going to die in here!"

"Can't you activate your tattoos?" he cried, rifling through her pack, finding more of the smooth glass bottles of perfume, yanking them out, and smashing them on the floor. "Why do you have so many of these?"

"Frozen—" snarled Sam, breaking her curse off as an explosive blast of air whooshed out of her stomach. Gasping, she called, "I can pay the price and gain strength, but I can't see or feel these damned things! Swinging harder is not going to do any good if I don't know what I'm swinging at. Take my kris, do something!"

He heard the skittering of sharp metal across wood. She'd slid one of her daggers to him. He couldn't see where she was, but as the wolfmalkin behind lumbered into the storage room, a pale sliver of light appeared from the corridor, putting a faint gleam on the steel of Sam's dagger.

He reached for it, picked it up, and stood. As hard as he could, he crashed her dagger against the edge of his broadsword, knocking several sparks free. He struck again and again, dashing sparks from the steel until one of them landed in the puddle of perfume at his feet and ignited it. The liquid burst into flame, casting the shades on top of Sam into stark relief.

She whipped through them with her remaining kris dagger, and Oliver pitched forward, stabbing through another, feeling motion behind him.

The heavy edge of a battle axe caught his shoulder, gouging a shallow but painful cut through his flesh and sending an arc of his blood flying across the room. Oliver fell into a roll, losing his broadsword, awkwardly trying to come to his feet but flopping on his side instead.

The wolfmalkin was joined by its peer, and the two of them stood their full height, the fire on the floor casting their features in terrible relief.

Lying on his back, only Sam's dagger in hand, he was all out of ideas. He admitted, "I couldn't find any chalk."

THE PRIESTESS XIII

"IT'S NOT THE CHALK," she growled through gritted teeth. "It's the properties of— We'll talk later."

The first wolfmalkin advanced on Duke, who was lying prone on the floor completely defenseless. She jumped on its back and dragged the edge of her dagger across its throat. The creature, surprised at an attack from behind, stumbled.

Slipping off the massive beast, she shoved it, and the dying wolfmalkin fell onto the border of the pentagram, half in, half out. A soft thump emanated from the pentagram as the monster died, passing the barrier between life and death, reversing the flow of the pattern, sealing the edge of the design with its body. Sam turned to face the remaining wolfmalkin.

"Who sent you?"

The creature blinked at her.

Still lying on the floor, Duke asked curiously, "Can they understand the king's tongue?"

"I have no idea. It was worth a try," she muttered. Then, she attacked.

The monster, stunned by the death of its peers, wasn't going to wait long before coming after them, so she didn't give it time. She launched at it, swinging with her kris.

The wolfmalkin lurched to the side and then lashed out with the butt of its giant battle axe.

She dodged away, quickly realizing the wolfmalkin was twice her size, the axe ten times the size of her dagger. Not ideal conditions in the small storeroom.

Duke was still flopping around on the floor, trying to stand up like he was a boneless, dying fish.

In a flash of inspiration, or perhaps desperation, she tossed her dagger at the wolfmalkin's face. The creature brushed her weapon aside. Yellow eyes glowing eagerly, it advanced on her, raising its axe, prepared to bring it down and chop her in two.

The moment the massive beast raised its weapon, she darted forward, trusting to speed instead of strength. She reached behind her back and swept out the knife she kept secreted there, whipping the blade around and burying it in the wolfmalkin's knee, twisting the steel.

The wolfmalkin stumbled, whimpering in pain. Then, it crashed the haft of its axe against her.

She'd expected the attack and had stepped into it to avoid the sharp point of the weapon, absorbing the blow from the wooden shaft and flinging her body as she was struck, hoping to prevent what would otherwise be a bone-shattering blow. She was flung across the room, only her jump saving her. She tumbled across the floor before thudding into the wall. Pain radiated from her side and arm where she'd taken the strike, but she thought nothing was broken.

The wolfmalkin growled and stepped after her. It wavered and whimpered. It collapsed, falling onto the knee where she'd injured it.

Smiling, she stood.

"Take off its head!" she cried.

Duke, having just stood, blinked at her dumbly. He glanced down at her kris dagger, the only weapon he held.

The wolfmalkin didn't know that, though, and tried to spin, anticipating an attack from behind.

She pulled her two poignards from her boots and darted forward, jabbing them into opposite sides of the wolfmalkin's neck. The narrow spikes of steel drove deep. When she pulled them out and jumped back, twin spurts of blood followed her.

The creature fell down dead.

"I guess they can understand the king's tongue," she remarked.

"What?" asked Duke.

"Never mind," she replied, eyeing the dying fire Duke had set on the floor. "We have to burn this entire structure."

"We're in the middle of the city!" cried Duke. "The damage would be—"

"Run and find the fire brigade," she instructed. "I'll start dousing the place with fuel."

"But—" he started and then looked down at the bodies of the dead wolfmalkin, at the pentagram, at her.

"No one can see this stuff," she insisted. "Sorcery is a scourge, a disease. We have to quarantine it. We have to destroy all of this. Think what sorts of secret knowledge the apothecary may have hidden in this place. We cannot risk someone finding it, Duke."

For a long moment, he stared at her. Finally, he admitted, "You're right."

"Half a turn of the clock, then I'll start the fire," she said. "Keep them from fighting the blaze until we can be certain the inside of this building is good and charred."

"You don't want to brave that cold outside to make it to the fire brigade?" he questioned.

"You're the duke," reminded Sam. "They'll listen to you."

Grunting, he turned and left, cursing as he shoved his way through and climbed over the debris and dead bodies in the hallway outside.

As soon as he'd made it into the front room, she removed a small vial of fae light from her rucksack and shook it, bathing the room in a low, green glow. Then, she started to search. She yanked drawers out of their cabinets and tossed the contents on the floor.

She rapped on the walls, listening for the hollow thumps of hidden compartments. She rifled through goods stored in the room. Finally, she stepped on a floorboard that creaked differently from the others.

Grinning, she knelt down and pried the board up with one of her daggers. Inside was an iron case. Muttering under her breath, she hauled the heavy container up and flipped the lid open. It was empty. Whoever had killed the apothecary had taken the time to ransack his secret storage. Whatever knowledge the man had hidden was gone now, but someone had known it was there.

She threw the container back into the hole and dashed to the front room. There, by the light of her vial of fae light, she sorted through the former apothecary's desk, looking for his record book, the tome every shopkeeper kept, accounting each purchase. When she found it, she flipped it open and saw that dozens of pages had been ripped out.

Cursing, she slammed it shut, glancing around the room. She stood a moment, realizing that there had been clues they could have collected, but now it was too late. There had been an avenue for investigation that they'd completely ignored.

Finally, she opened the book again, tearing out more sheets of paper, wadding them up, preparing to start a fire. She didn't have time to continue searching the place. Duke would return with the fire brigade soon enough. Given the empty secret compartment and missing pages in the ledger, it was likely there was nothing dangerous left in the building, but just in case, she'd still burn it down. Better safe than sorry.

She was standing outside watching the flames lick at the doorframe at the front of the building when Duke arrived back.

"Where's the fire brigade?" she asked him.

"Coming, I hope," he said. "I realized when I got there I had no reasonable explanation for how I knew this building would be on fire. How was I going to explain why I was lurking around a place that had just recently been the site of a murder and now was the site of an arson? I found a drunk outside of the nearest pub and paid him to go inside and alert the brigade. I waited until they were gathering their supplies, and then I left. We'd better hide or get out of here soon, because I have no intention of relating all of this to my brother."

She nodded. "That's smart. I didn't think of that."

They stood there for a moment, watching the fire grow, waiting for the clanging bell of the fire brigade.

"I suppose we won't be able to scry for my mother, then," he said after a long moment, pain and frustration tightening his voice.

"It's probably for the best," she replied. "Duke, if they were able sense your vision and set a trap for us here, then they may be able to do the same if we scry. We wouldn't be able to defend ourselves, then. It's too dangerous. There are too many things that could go wrong."

Grimacing, he asked, "Back to the palace, then?"

"No, I don't think so," she replied, thinking quickly. "Someone may have spied us there, right? If we return to the palace, they will not hesitate to try again. If they're willing to unleash wolf-malkin within Westundon, what else will they do? It's best if we stay hidden and find a place no one will think to look."

"Not your apartment, then, or any of my estates."

"I have an idea," she said.

THE CARTOGRAPHER XV

"So this is your patron?" asked the odd woman, eyeing him up and down.

"He is," acknowledged Sam.

"And you haven't slept with him, yet?"

"No," answered Sam, frowning at the other woman. "We're working together. He was the one in Derbycross, remember? I told you about that."

"I remember," said the woman, still eyeing Oliver. "Of course I remember. How could I forget?"

Sam grunted.

"Nice place you have here," said Oliver. "It's, ah, cozy."

Crouched down under a low rafter, he looked around at the tattered couch, a single iron pot by the fireplace, a narrow cupboard, a table piled with cheap jewelry, a thin carpet spread across the floor, and not much else.

"I've grown to like it," said the woman. She turned to Sam. "Come with me."

Without responding, the priestess followed the strange woman into another room, and they shut the door. Oliver stood in the center of the sitting room, staring in confusion. Then, as noises of passion began to seep out from behind the barrier, he frowned and looked around the room again. He didn't see a drop of ale. There was a half-empty bottle of wine, but that would not get him far. Thank the spirits, the girl lived on the top floor of an inn with a well-stocked pub below.

As the noises behind the door grew louder, he decided he was going to need it. He unhooked an iron key from beside the door, stepped into the hall, locked the door, and tucked the key into his coat pocket. The woman, Sam's old friend, didn't seem like she'd be needing it anytime soon. Stomping down the hall and down four flights of narrow stairs, he found the pub and ordered an ale.

Someone had tried to kill them. Their enemies had set a trap in the apothecary's building, knowing Oliver and Sam might go there. He needed time to think. He sipped his drink and did just that.

The wolfmalkin and the shades made it obvious they were facing another skilled sorcerer, and it was clear that whoever it was, they were no longer content to remain in the shadows. Their opponent could call upon untold horrors, perhaps even worse than they'd faced in Derbycross. Then, they had been prepared. They had Thotham. Now, they were alone, and anytime they made themselves known in polite society, he'd have to be looking over his shoulder. Even a trip to warn his brother of what was happening would be fraught with danger, for both them and Philip. If the sorcerer they sought was willing to kill a duke, Oliver doubted they would hesitate to kill a prince. King Edward could only get so outraged, after all.

No, thought Oliver. Running to his family, requesting their help, might make the situation worse. The royal marines, the airships, they could only act on available intelligence. They could only confront enemies they knew. The Crown's resources be worthless against an unknown sorcerer, and while they flailed, people would die.

He and Sam needed information. They needed to find out who

their adversary was. There was only one lead he could think of, one avenue they hadn't yet fully explored. He ran his hand over his hair, feeling the knotted leather cord at the back.

Had it been a dream or something more? He didn't know, but they had to find out. They had to go to Northundon.

THE PRIESTESS XIV

KALBETH'S HEAD was cradled in Sam's lap. They were naked in the women's bed, and Kalbeth was looking up at her. Sam wondered if she'd made a terrible mistake, coming back to the Four Sheets Inn.

"I didn't think you'd come back," said Kalbeth, as if reading her mind.

"I didn't plan to," admitted Sam.

"The man out there, he's the Duke of Northundon, a son of the king?"

Sam shifted and felt Kalbeth's long black hair slide across her bare skin. "He is."

"I did my research after you left," remarked her friend. "I looked into the competition, you could say."

"I'm not sleeping with him," assured Sam.

"I believe you," replied Kalbeth, offering a bitter smile, "but you are spending time with him, more time than you ever spent with me."

"It's not like that," insisted Sam.

Kalbeth sat up. "I know it's not sexual, Sam. Maybe it never will be. That doesn't mean the man isn't taking you away from here… from me. He can give you things I cannot. He can show you places I'll never see. He can—"

"We're hunting sorcerers together," snapped Sam, catching Kalbeth's chin in her hands and stopping her. "Last I was here, I told you what they'd done. I told you the horrors I'd seen. What would you have us do, ignore it? He's the Duke of Northundon, as you said, the son of the king. He has a responsibility to the empire. I'm the only surviving Knife in Enhover. I'm the only one trained to do what is necessary. Kalbeth, we're the only two capable of facing this threat. We have a responsibility!"

"What about the royal marines, the king's army?" argued the woman, pushing Sam's hand from her face.

"They cannot fight what they do not know," responded Sam. "There are things we can do that no one else can. There are things we know that no one else does. We have to try, do we not?"

"Things you know," retorted the other woman. "What do you know? You know nothing of what you face. Last time I saw you, you were begging my help to translate your grimoire. You can't read more than one in ten words in that text. Do not claim you know what it is you are stepping into. You have no idea."

"I may not know ancient Darklands script, but I know what I must do," declared Sam. "I know where we have to go. We have to keep fighting, Kalbeth. We have to."

"Fight who? Go where? You don't even know who your enemy is, Sam," argued Kalbeth. "What do you and Duke Wellesley mean to do? Where do you mean to… Oh. I see. Duke Wellesley. The Duke of Northundon."

"It's the only lead we have," said Sam, "I have reason to believe the spirits haunting the place will not oppose Duke. With the tattoo you inked on my back, I think we have a chance. We have to do it, Kalbeth. There is no other choice."

"You've spoken to the man, already planned this out?" questioned the black-haired woman. "Why are you here then? I will not help you with another tattoo. I cannot."

"We haven't spoken about it," replied Sam, looking up to meet her lover's eyes. "Do not worry. I did not come here to ask any more of you, but it is obvious what I must do, is it not? If you have another idea, please tell me."

Kalbeth was silent.

"That is why I must go," said Sam.

"You could stay here. Forget it all," replied Kalbeth.

"You could come with us," offered Sam.

Kalbeth looked away, her black hair falling across her face.

Sam stood abruptly from the bed. "We'll stay here tonight, but we must go soon."

The other woman did not respond, so Sam dressed quickly. Without speaking, she walked into the sitting room and saw both Duke and the key were missing. She knew where he would be.

THE CARTOGRAPHER XVI

OLIVER SAW SAM slinking through the busy common room of the Four Sheets and waved for the barman to bring another mug. He'd already ordered a pitcher of ale and was halfway through it.

"Good night?" he asked her.

"You mean aside from… from what we did earlier?" she asked.

"Well, I don't know what you did earlier," he huffed. "I've been minding my own business, drinking ale."

"Are you jealous?" asked Sam.

"No, I…" he trailed off, certain he wanted to say no, but not certain it was true. "I'm just worried, is all."

"Worried about Kalbeth?" questioned Sam. "That sounds like you're jealous."

"Is that her name?" he wondered. "I'm worried but not because I'm jealous. She's rather a lot like Isisandra Dalyrimple, is she not?"

Sam blinked at him. "No, she's no sorceress. Her magic is small, just an affinity. She can't do any… Is that what you meant? That you think she is a sorceress?"

"I meant she has black hair, is quite petite, and prefers

women," he mentioned. "She is a sorceress as well? That gives me real concern, Sam. You can have a type, but I'm not sure that type should be those on the dark path. Those you're tasked with hunting."

Sam grabbed her ale and drank. "She's no more a sorceress than I am."

He grunted. Jet-black hair, slender figures, preferences for the same sex, and an affinity for the dark path. Isisandra, Kalbeth, and Sam. If she didn't see it already, he wouldn't point it out to her. Not yet, at least. Not until he learned more about this new woman. Not until he could say it without an uncomfortable twinge of jealousy worming its way into his voice.

"I was thinking," Sam said, ignoring his expression. "We only have one lead, one way to turn, even though it's a rather dangerous line to pursue."

"Northundon," he said, smiling at her shock. "I've been thinking too. We can't show ourselves anywhere I would be recognized. We can't solicit help from anyone with the strength to actually help us. If we did find help, we still don't know who we're up against. That leaves only one trail we can follow, as far as I can deduce."

"Northundon," agreed Sam. "If we go, though, we must be prepared. Prepared for what's ahead and prepared for those who will seek to stop us before we get there. We need a plan, and we need supplies."

"Well, the only apothecary I know has recently closed shop," remarked Oliver, "or were you thinking of mundane supplies?"

"Those too, but I think that's easily handled," she said. "I meant, ah, something a bit more esoteric."

"Is there another vendor for that type of material?" he asked her.

"None that I know of, but…" Sam's eyes darted toward the stairwell.

"But your friend upstairs might be able to help?" questioned

Oliver. "This friend who has nothing at all to do with sorcery, huh?"

Scowling at him, Sam said, "We'll have to talk fast to convince her."

"Don't worry," he assured her. "I have a way with women."

THE DIRECTOR II

THE FORMER SOLDIER slammed his fist on the table, smashing the solid wood like he meant to snap the boards in two.

Cringing, Raffles shot a glance at Bishop Yates, who was cowering in a corner and looking like he may soon wet his priest's robes.

Shaking himself and resolving to not appear such a coward as the churchman, the director held up a hand. "Hold, William. We missed them, but you must understand. We were not prepared. This was an emergency situation. The wolfmalkin failed, but we will not."

"Will not?" snapped Enhover's prime minister. "You already have. I'd be outraged that you killed my nephew without talking to me first, but trying and failing to do so? That is even worse. It's appalling."

"He visited the underworld!" cried the director. "He saw a true vision! What would you have us do?"

"The girl was in Romalla, soliciting assistance from the Council of Seven," added Bishop Yates. "They did not agree to help her due to my persuasion, but we are being hunted, William! Your nephew, the girl, they may not know who they are seeking yet, but they are seeking us. How confident are we that we've snipped every thread, closed every avenue to our identity? I am almost certain there is nothing in this world that can lead to me except the two of you, but shall we risk the last twenty years of labor, our stations, everything we've done and hope to accomplish? Are we that certain, after so long, we've left no trace?"

"If there was a trace, the other would have found it," snapped William, stalking back and forth across the room.

"The other?" wondered Raffles, sharing a look with Yates.

"Don't be coy with me," growled the prime minister. "There is another who works against us. One who has been subtly foiling our maneuvers for years. I don't know who it is, but I'm confident they do not know who we are, either. If they did, I can only imagine the three of us would have our throats slit by now, if we were lucky. No, there is another walking this path with us. The signs are obvious. If we'd left clues, the other would have followed them."

Randolph Raffles snorted and pointed a finger at William. "Your nephew is as persistent and as dangerous as only a Wellesley can be. You think the other would have found any trace that was left? What about Standish Taft? The man lived in Swinpool for years, and if someone had found him, he could have spilled secrets about what you discovered in the Coldlands. Any time, the other could have unmasked our identities, but it was your nephew and the girl who found Taft."

"They don't have to operate within the shadows," remarked Yates. "Moving in the open, unafraid to ask questions, unaware of whose notice they might draw... They moved faster and more thoroughly than any of us could have imagined, and they aren't stopping. They've already gotten too close, too close by far."

William clenched his fists on the table, but he didn't respond.

Raffles took the opening. "We acted because your nephew had a true vision. In it, Oliver spoke to spirits of the underworld. They interacted and communicated with him. I do not know what they told him, but I was able to confirm the contact. Those spirits still speak the boy's name."

"Let us call to them, then, and bind them to our design," suggested William. "We'll find out what they told him and use that to help find the boy."

Raffles shook his head. "The spirits are in the thrall of Ca-Mi-He. They are sacrifices to him. Hearing Oliver's name, sensing their recent knowledge of him in the underworld, that was all I could determine before I had to flee. If they'd found I was observing them, if they'd felt the blessing of the dark trinity upon me... Ca-Mi-He could learn of our ambition."

William grimaced but nodded. "More and more often, it seems we stumble across spirits in the thrall of that one. His power... Even with the strength of the dark trinity, I worry—"

"It will be enough," counseled Bishop Yates. "Three are stronger than one as has always been the case. It is why only the trinity has a chance against the great spirit. It is why when we bind them to us, we'll be unstoppable."

"You are sure?" asked William.

"I am," answered Yates. "You brought me into this group because of my research, because of my access to the Church's archives. Everything there reaffirms that one can never stand against three, not when those three are formed as one, at least."

William grunted at the obvious barb.

"Oliver had a true vision of the underworld," said Raffles, drawing the two other men's attention back to him. "We don't know what he learned, but does it matter? If he pierced the barrier and survived, he could do it again. He has an affinity, it seems, and it will only become stronger as he develops his talents. But even if he does not, can we risk it? Is there any other option — was there any option other than his death? I am sorry, William. I know you have feelings for the boy, but will you gamble every-thing we've worked for?"

The former soldier's jaw bunched and he squeezed his eyes shut. A vein beat furiously in his forehead. His breathing was quick and violent. When he finally responded, his voice was tight with strain. "You are right. We've sacrificed much, and we've always known we may need to sacrifice more. I do not like it, but... If he had a true vision, we cannot allow him to continue freely. Oliver must die, and we must immediately bind his spirit. The girl as well, of course."

"Of course." Raffles nodded.

The three men sat silent for a moment.

The director, ever practical, finally mentioned what they were all thinking. "We have to find him first. He hasn't been back to the palace. He hasn't been to his home in the city or that ridiculous estate of his in the middle of the park. I've put watchers around his valet, and the man has had no contact. Neither of them has visited the girl's apartment, and they haven't been seen near the Church. I've sent people to inquire discreetly at all of the reputable inns in the city, and of course we'll monitor the boy's usual haunts."

"The Child twins?" asked William.

Raffles smirked. "That's where I would go if I was him, but he hasn't seen or even written either one. Once we've checked the reputable establishments in the city, we'll begin checking the disreputable ones. There are hundreds, though, and I only have so many people I can trust with this. It will be a week before we can inquire at every ale sink, inn, and hostel."

William nodded, rubbing his temples with his fingers.

"They could have left Westundon," offered Yates. When the other two men turned to glare at him, he said, "We have to face reality. It's possible he's already gone from Westundon, maybe even Enhover."

"We've been watching the main highways and rail lines," reminded Raffles.

"What about his airship?" asked William. "If he boards it, he could be leagues from here before we'd even know he was going. If it was me, that's the way I would flee. Does the Company have vessels nearby that can match the speed of his?"

Raffles shook his head. "We have one in Westundon, the sister ship of Oliver's. It's an identical vessel. Could our captain overtake his in a chase? I would not bet on it. What about the Crown? Surely the royal marines have something that could pile on the sail and pursue him?"

"The Crown's attention is on the tropics at the moment. Trying to convince Admiral Brach to divert resources to Westundon is a fool's errand, and the admiral will be up my brother's ass in a quarter turn of the clock if he hears of me commandeering one of his airships," said William. "The marines claim allegiance directly to the king and his line, not the ministry. If it came between Oliver and I, they'd support the boy. There are those in the service I have turned, of course, but I cannot man an entire airship with them on such short notice without raising suspicion."

"Disable Oliver's airship," suggested Yates. "Break the bindings on the levitating stones or kill the crew. Whatever is necessary to prevent travel. If he leaves on the rail or the road, we have a chance of catching him. In the air..."

Raffles glanced at William and said, "It makes sense."

William shook his head. "If we disable the airship we force him to be creative. If he's creative, it will be more difficult to guess his next course of action. Instead of disabling it, I suggest we lay another trap. Summon shades, hundreds of them, post them around his airship, and when he boards, direct them to attack. If we're lucky, he'll walk into our snare, and we don't have to worry about finding him."

"I like it," admitted the director. "It's simple, a small burden on our resources, and it might be our best bet. I'll arrange something. In the meantime, any additional resources we can gather should be devoted to finding the boy and the girl in case they do not try to flee on the airship. Stopping them must be our highest priority. If he touches the underworld again, has another true vision..."

"I will take over monitoring the shroud," stated William. "The boy and I share blood. I will be able to sense if his presence breaches the barrier again."

Raffles nodded, glad the prime minister had suggested it

himself. "Good. I'll lead the search here. You cover the underworld. Yates, I think it is time to approach the Council. Inform them that the girl has delved too far into true sorcery and we require the assistance of the Knives."

Gabriel Yates swallowed nervously. "You want to invite more Knives of the Council into Enhover? Are you sure?"

"I don't have the first clue on where we could find that girl unless she turns up with Oliver," said Raffles. "Do you?"

Yates shook his head.

"Do it, Gabriel," instructed William. "If the Church sends her Knives at your behest, at least we'll know who they are. We can hide from them as we always have. Either they'll find our missing prey, or we will. Whoever does, we can be assured both of us will quickly kill them, and I'll be standing ready to take their spirits at the shroud. We've come close to disaster, but we can still rescue this situation, and it's possible we can turn it to our advantage."

Raffles raised an eyebrow at the prime minister.

"Oliver doesn't know who he is hunting," explained William. "It could be the other just as easily as it is us. When he is at the barrier, when I take control of his soul, he will not stop his hunt. Except this time, he'll be working on our behalf."

THE CAPTAIN III

"ARE you sure this is wise, Captain?" asked Pettybone.

"Of course so," she chided her first mate. "What would be unwise about it?"

"Sorcerers, spirits, violent death…" muttered the man, peering anxiously over the gunwale into the fog. "An attack we only suspect may be coming but we don't know when. It all seems rather, well, insane I suppose is the word I'm looking for."

"The spirits favor the bold," insisted Captain Ainsley. She propped a tall boot on the gunwale in front of her and rested a hand on one of her two long-barreled pistols. "All of those giant palaces we see in the city below us when we lift off, all of the estates out in the countryside, how do you think those people made their wealth? It wasn't by sitting at home and taking no chances."

Pettybone snorted. "A lot of people have ended up dead, too, by taking chances."

"If you don't fancy dying a rich man, then you're on the wrong airship," declared Ainsley.

"I fancy being rich. I don't fancy dying," complained the first mate.

"What was that?" asked Ainsley, suddenly leaning forward

and peering into the fog. She pushed up the brim of her giant, tri-cornered hat with one finger, wondering if the disturbance she'd seen below was a quiet gust of air, a laborer moving quickly through the night, or something else.

"Nothing, Captain," said the first mate, joining her in peering into the darkness below them.

Suddenly speaking behind them though she'd made no sound on the approach, the odd priestess who traveled with the duke whispered, "Is the cannon ready?"

Ainsley nodded.

"Winchester spread word two turns ago that Duke was departing on the airship. That's enough time for our enemies to assemble their attack. They won't wait long. It should be any moment now," advised the woman, crouching down and looking directly into the fog across from them.

There, thirty yards away, docked the Cloud Wolf, their sister airship. It occupied the berth they were assigned to, according to the bridge master's logs. At night, the two ships looked identical. If anyone came sniffing around for them, they hoped their deception would lead their pursuers to the Wolf.

Through billowing tendrils of fog, the vessel passed in and out of view, sometimes only the globes of fae light set on its deck providing any certainty it was still there. Then, the fog drifted away for a moment, and a shadow passed distinctly in front of one of the lights.

"Now," hissed the priestess.

Ainsley called loudly, mimicking a tropical bird from Imbon, which she suddenly realized was a rather grim choice, but her men below heard it and understood. The bank of cannon under the deck exploded, sending a blistering volley of scattershot into the flank of the ship just thirty yards away.

Splintering wood and falling sail could barely be heard above the echoing boom from the big guns. A second volley followed heartbeats later, the aft guns run out on the starboard side where the sweeps normally emerged. It gave them two bites at the apple, so to speak.

As soon as the second fusillade was unleashed, Ainsley called to fly. The lines were cut, and the Cloud Serpent rose into the sky. The captain drew her pistol and seized the deck gun beside her, aiming it down. She pulled the trigger on her empty pistol, striking a shower of sparks which caught the deck gun's fuse. The three-incher barked, blasting an apple-sized ball of iron into the ruined ship below them.

They rose quickly as the lines had been the only thing holding down the bone-dry levitating stones in their ballast. Westundon, dark and foggy on the cold winter night, faded away, only surprised shouts and rising alarm bells chasing them into the sky.

"You know that shot wasn't blessed," said the strange priestess, nodding at the deck gun Ainsley had fired. "It didn't do anything expect smash a little timber."

Grinning, Ainsley claimed, "Sometimes smashing a little timber is what is called for."

Blinking at her, the priestess shook her head.

"Three days if the weather holds," said Ainsley. "We'll approach from the sea, staying out of sight of Glanhow and then coming to land north of the Sheetsand Mountains. There might be a few stray shepherds or hermits, but I can't avoid all eyes. Anyone who sees us ought to be several days from a glae worm station, if they can be bothered to make the trip."

"I'll tell the duke," offered the priestess.

As she walked way, Ainsley called, "Are you sure those… those things cannot follow us?"

"No," said Sam. "I don't even know what it was we just fired on. Shades, wolfmalkin, something worse? But I've never heard of any of them flying. While it's my fervent hope that blessing the iron did the trick and banished whatever it was they sent, there's no certainty in this, Captain."

The priestess disappeared into the captain's cabin to speak to the duke, and Ainsley turned to look at the vanishing lights of Westundon.

"The Cloud Wolf was the only ship within fifty leagues of here that could keep up with us," said Pettybone. "We've got a head start, if nothing else."

"We've got the time we need," assured the captain. "We'll set the duke and the priestess on the slopes of the Sheetsands and then find ourselves somewhere to lay low. It will be a week before anyone even knows where we went, if they ever do."

"They'll know we're the ones who fired on a Company airship," remarked Pettybone. "We were the only other vessel tied to the bridge. By morning, they'll find out we switched the paperwork, and it was the Wolf and not the Serpent that took the beating. Once they know that…"

"The duke'll protect us," claimed the captain.

"You're making a rather large assumption that the man lives through the next few days," complained Pettybone. "What's your plan if he doesn't? You think the king is going to listen to some wild tale that his son told us to fire on a Company airship, which would personally cost Duke Wellesley a fortune, and then he told us to deposit him at the most dangerous location in all of Enhover? We won't get half the words out of our mouths before they string us up."

Ainsley glanced around the deck, ensuring the crew was hard at work and out of earshot. Then, she leaned close to Pettybone. "If the duke and his priestess do not survive, then we do not return to Westundon. If they die, we'll have to leave Enhover."

"What?"

"You're right, Pettybone," she said. "The Crown, the Company, either one of them would have us hanging from a yardarm the moment they captured us. If the duke dies, we can't go back. There's nothing we could say that would explain what just happened. The duke himself is our only ticket home. But if he dies, well, at least we'll have our own airship. There are worse things, Mate Pettybone, than having your own airship."

"You aim to turn pirate," accused the first mate.

Ainsley winked at him.

Her first mate crossed his arms and opened his mouth to protest.

"I know about your time in the Vendatts, Pettybone," she advised.

His mouth snapped shut.

"The spirits have put us in the service of the duke," she said. "I aim to serve him faithfully as long as I can. And when I can't, well, there ain't never been a pirate airship before, has there? Our dreams of dying rich don't end with the duke."

"Rich," huffed Pettybone. "I want to be rich, not dead."

"We all die, First Mate. We all die sometime."

THE PRIESTESS XV

THE PALE LIGHT of morning shouldered its way through clouds, hard and gray. In the far north, the sea, the light, the clouds, and the raw stone underfoot melded into a bleak tableau. It reminded Sam of a short stint she'd spent in Glanhow's gaol some years ago, but at least then there'd been other inmates to speak to.

Now, it was just Duke and Captain Ainsley, and Ainsley looked like she'd rather be anywhere but the slopes of the Sheet-sand Mountains, peering down over the ruins of Northundon.

"There," said the captain, pointing to a sharp outcropping half a league to the east of them. "We'll have good visibility there and can easily swoop down and drop a line."

"It looks like a bit of a climb," remarked Duke.

Ainsley shrugged.

"There," said Duke, pointing far below them at the grim city. "The peaked tower. That is Northundon's Church. Several blocks north of that structure is a flat-topped tower. It's half the size, but it still rises above the buildings around it. That's Northundon's keep. You can drop a line and pick us up from there."

"You want me to fly above the city?" questioned Ainsley.

"The shades can't reach you," assured Duke. "Remember, my father spent days floating above this place dropping bombs down into it. From a height, you're as safe over the city as you are on these slopes."

"What if the keep is damaged?" wondered Sam.

"I don't think it will be so damaged we can't make the top," replied Duke. "It was built by the druids long before the Wellesleys arrived in Northundon. It's been through a lot and has always stood strong. Red saltpetre bombs may have damaged it, but you can see from here, they didn't knock it down. The interior should be intact."

"Druids lived in the heart of Northundon?" wondered Sam.

"Aye, Northundon and near some of the other cities as well," replied Duke. "There is a massive keep just across the river from Southundon."

"I always thought druids lived out in the forest and talked to squirrels," said Ainsley.

Duke shrugged. "Maybe they did. They were gone long before we walked this land, long before our grandparents did. From what I understand, though, they were interested in all life. Life in the forests, but life in the cities as well."

"Interesting," said Sam, which she supposed maybe it would have been in other circumstances. Now, standing above Northundon, a city turned graveyard, it wasn't.

"It's grim to think of now," said Duke, "but back when I was a young boy, the rumor was the keep was haunted."

"Haunted?" questioned Sam.

Duke waved a hand dismissively. "It's an old druid fortress, and there are always rumors about those places. I spent several summers in the keep here. It wasn't haunted, not like the rest of the city is now."

"If you make it to the top, light the flare. We'll see it and be on down," said Ainsley, peering at the ruins, absentmindedly toying with the trigger of one of her paired pistols. "I'll have a man watch the roof constantly with the spyglass."

"If you're not careful, you'll set that thing off," remarked Duke, eyeing her pistol.

The captain smirked. "You're one to lecture about being careful."

Together, the three of them turned and looked down the harsh slope of the mountain. Three leagues away, shattered stone and tumbled walls marked the outskirts of Northundon.

"Do you think the spirits can see us?" wondered Duke.

"No, not yet," assured Sam. "They can't see at all, really. They'll sense us, though, when we draw close."

"If I don't see you again…" murmured Ainsley. "Well, good luck, I suppose. If you don't return, I'll take care of the Cloud Serpent for you."

Duke snorted.

"I wanted it said," declared Ainsley.

Without word, Duke clasped the captain's arm. Sam gave her a quick embrace, and they both started down the slope. They stepped carefully from rock to rock, making sure not to slip on the lichen, the only life growing on the barren terrain. Below lay the city of the dead.

THEY CROUCHED IN A CULVERT THAT FOLLOWED THE LINE OF Northundon's main highway. Peering over the road, they studied the city in front of them. She glanced to the left nervously, seeing the pale, yellow sun hanging disturbingly close to the horizon.

"Are we really going in there at sunset?" asked Duke.

"Do you want to camp out here overnight, two hundred yards from a haunted graveyard the size of a city?" wondered Sam. "I'm not sure sleeping nearby is any better than walking through those ruins. Could you even sleep? I couldn't."

"We should have timed this differently," worried Duke, glancing back behind them and grimacing.

They both knew they couldn't have safely made it down the steep slope at night. They would have tumbled to the bottom and been lucky to only break one or two bones each. Besides, Ainsley had timed the approach to shore so that the Cloud Serpent passed Glanhow's fishing fleet in the night. They were counting on no one knowing where they'd gone after the little incident back in Westundon, and the fleet had a history of reporting what it saw.

When they did return to civilization, even Duke would face some tough questions about why his airship opened fire in the middle of the city on her sister ship. He rightfully didn't relish the idea of explaining that they'd tricked a gang of sorcerers into thinking they were aboard, hoping to destroy the spirits the group sent after them, to destroy any chance of pursuit, and to get away cleanly. They'd thought there might be a chance the sorcerers would reveal themselves, but the only thing they'd seen were shadows.

The timing of their arrival outside of Northundon's broken walls was unfortunate but inevitable. Still, it didn't mean the thought of proceeding into the spirit-infested ruins at night was pleasant.

"You're sure they won't, ah, come after me?" asked Duke.

She shrugged. "Kalbeth seemed reasonably certain."

He frowned at her. "Kalbeth also seemed like she wouldn't mind sticking one of her tattoo needles into my eye."

"She didn't, though," retorted Sam, and he shifted. "If she wanted to kill you, she would have, and if she wasn't confident that we could survive this, she wouldn't have let me come with you."

"That's fair," he murmured, looking ahead at the darkening city in front of them.

"It's only logical the spirits haunting Northundon are the shadows of what you saw in your vision," she said, trying to convince herself as much as the peer. "They did not attack you there, so it stands to reason they will not attack you here."

He grunted.

"They tried to help you," she reminded. "That's what you said, right?"

"They invited me to come to Northundon," he said, his voice

tight with tension. "Can shades from the underworld be friendly? Can they make a choice not to attack someone? This might be another trap, you know."

"They do what they are bound to do," explained Sam. "If they were loose, they would attack us. If their summoner set them to another purpose…"

"They attacked the citizens of Northundon," reminded Duke. "They overran the city and killed everyone in sight. Then, we suspect, those killed rose again and continued the carnage."

"They were bound to a task," insisted Sam, shifting in the culvert, eyes on the ruins in front of them. "They're still here. That means their task is not complete. If they were set to merely kill everyone inside of the city, they achieved that decades ago. We have to risk it."

Grim-faced, Duke agreed. "We have to risk it."

"Come on," she said.

She climbed out of the culvert. Ducking low, she scampered across the highway, dropping to the other side, and then in a crouch, hurrying toward the abandoned city.

The black ink injected into her skin, formed into swirling patterns that covered half of her back, should offer her some protection. If the spirits were not specifically directed against her, they'd have a natural aversion. She'd be invisible, in a sense. Duke, however, they hoped would find allies amongst the shades. In his vision, they'd invited him to Northundon. They'd promised answers.

It had seemed a better idea when they were back in Kalbeth's apartment.

Sam clutched Thotham's spear in her hands, feeling the sweat on her palms rapidly cool in the bitter chill of the northern winter. Duke held a spirit-blessed obsidian dagger. It was a small weapon, tiny even. He'd asked for something bigger, and she told him it wasn't the size of the blade but how you used it that mattered. That wasn't entirely true, and she certainly wouldn't want to rely on such a small weapon, but it was what they had.

The peer had been kind enough not to ask for one of her kris daggers. That, or he hadn't thought about it. Either way, the weapons were special to her, one more link to Thotham. She wanted to keep them herself.

Hand brushing his basket-hilted broadsword, a weapon sure to be useless against the shades, the little dagger clutched in his other fist, Duke trotted ahead toward the weather-beaten ruins. She would be most effective if the shades turned on them, but he knew the way through the city.

"Do we wait for one to appear?" he asked, glancing back at her.

She shrugged. "The ruins should be thick with them. Some may have been ground by the wheel over the last two decades and returned to new life, but I suspect many remain. It shouldn't be long before we see them."

He nodded and stepped over a pace-long block of stone that had fallen from Northundon's broken wall. The wall, as far as she could see on either side of them, had tumbled out, collapsing in a scattered heap, only tall towers still standing. Half a dozen, maybe more, she'd seen as they approached. Evidently, someone had constructed the towers of sterner stuff than the walls. More influence of the druids, she wondered? Duke didn't have an explanation when she mentioned it, and now, she pushed it from her mind. There were more immediate concerns.

Entering the city, they hoped to find a shade on the outskirts and see if it attacked them. If it did, they'd have no hope of fighting their way through the legion and searching the Welles-ley's old palace. If attacked, their only hope would be to turn and run. If they could test their theory, that the shades would not assault them, then they'd have some meager comfort before surrounding themselves with thousands of the spectres.

By unspoken agreement, they fell silent as the granite walls of Northundon rose above them. Duke, still holding his tiny obsidian dagger in one hand, clambered over the head-high remains of Northundon's outer wall and then jumped down inside to land on a stone street. She followed him and quietly dropped into a crouch.

Inside the city, old snow drifted in the corners and between the buildings. Outside, a constant breeze off the sea prevented accumulation, but here, it was as still as the grave. She shivered, wishing a different comparison had occurred to her.

Duke hesitantly moved forward, his feet crunching softly on the thin layer of snow, his eyes scanning windows and doorways already darkened an hour before sunset. The buildings were ruins, destroyed in the initial attack by the Coldlands, further wracked by Enhover's own bombing campaign. And the structures that survived were still subject to the deadliest enemy of all — time.

But the northern city had been built tough, built to stand against the brutal winters and violent summer storms. The granite blocks had survived generations of harsh weather, and a little war wasn't enough to knock them all down.

They passed a block in peace, the street clear of both debris and the spirits of the dead. Then, Duke froze. She stopped behind him, looking over his shoulder at a ghastly shadow that drifted across the open avenue in front of them.

It slowed and turned.

She tensed. In the fading daylight, the shade was barely discernible, just a darker patch in front of gray stone. It was still for a moment and then drifted away, evidently losing interest in them.

She released an explosive breath. Her heart was hammering. She adjusted her sweaty palms again on Thotham's spear. The shaft was warm, comforting, and she hoped it signaled they were making the right decision. If they weren't, she supposed they'd be joining her mentor soon enough.

Duke started moving again, climbing over rubble when they could, routing around spots where they could not. It seemed half the buildings had been destroyed, but the damage was sporadic and random. Sometimes, an entire block had collapsed into the street. Other times, it looked as if people could return at any moment.

In addition to the destruction to the buildings, they saw evidence of the old violence that had washed over the place. Bodies, desiccated after two decades in the open, littered the streets. More of them were piled in the buildings, where she guessed citizens had attempted to hide from the unnatural marauders. Occasionally, some bit of steel or clothing survived, but the corpses themselves were bare bone or covered in dry, jerky-like skin. Her stomach roiled in protest at the thought. She shook herself. The bodies were of no concern, now. The souls that had departed those physical forms were what she was worried about. Those souls still lurked in the streets, still stirred restlessly. Why? Why did they not pass to the other side?

As they walked deeper into the empty city, she was surprised to see no overgrowth of plant life. The city, abandoned for two decades, was entirely dead. No people, no plants. The taint from the underworld wrapped firmly around the place. It made her shudder, seeing the results of long-term exposure to the other side. If the sorcerers they hunted breached the barrier in a similar way, this would happen elsewhere. The taint would seep through, and death would spread over the lands.

They kept going and found more bodies and more shades drifting through silent streets or peering out of vacant buildings. Some of the shades seemed to trail them, following Duke as he strode through the domain of the dead. Once, when he climbed ahead to scout, the spectres began to close on her, and she could feel the angry cold of their intention.

The tattoos that Kalbeth had so carefully inked on her skin seemed to slow the spirit's notice of her, but they were drawn to Duke, and beside him, she was drawing their attention. It wasn't the ink on her back that kept her safe. It was the shades' connection to Duke that held the spirits at bay. The shades' purpose somehow aligned with Duke's. If she fell away from him, they'd close on her, and she would have no chance against so many of them.

She stayed on his heels, following never more than two or three paces away. They didn't speak, but she could see in his eyes that he understood.

When he wasn't climbing, one hand clutched his dagger and the other unconsciously rose to touch the back of his head, where the simple leather thong kept his hair tied back. His mother's old tie, she knew. Somehow, the purpose of the shades was aligned with this man.

How? She wondered and worried.

THE CARTOGRAPHER XVII

"THERE," he said, eyeing the hulking stone building that stood at the end of a broad boulevard.

Past it, he could see open sky. The structure sat atop a ridge, and below it, the city fell away to Northundon's harbor. Perched as it was, it had a commanding view of the commercial district and was within easy walking distance of the Church and Northundon's other important institutions. Spreading out along the ridge to the sides were the residences of Northundon's peers. Former peers, he amended.

He wondered if the shades of those peers haunted their own homes or if they drifted through the city like all the others. Were the shades even former citizens of Northundon? He realized he wasn't sure. No one who'd been in the city when the Coldlands attacked had escaped. There was no news of what had happened, nothing to go on except for what the royal marines had found when they'd flown over the city. As far as he knew, the shades could be the result of the destruction or the cause of it.

He shivered from the cold and the prevailing sense of dread that suffused the ruins. The skin on his back crawled. Behind him, scores of shades drifted in his wake, lurking nearby as he and Sam traversed the city, but why?

He forced himself to look ahead to the broad avenue they were walking along. It was lined with giant mansions, but the building at the end was different. It had been built in an earlier age. Before Enhover was a global empire, before Northundon was even part of the nation. This structure, unlike Philip's palace in Westundon, unlike their father's seat in Southundon, represented a time when the druids ruled, when those ancient magicians walked the cold, northern shore.

In Northundon, the Wellesleys were interlopers. Officially, they had ruled the northern quartile of the continent for centuries, but in practice, the northerners looked after themselves. They paid their taxes to the Crown as the price of being ignored.

It had never felt like that to Oliver when he'd visited, though. Northundon was his mother's home. She was of the place, and despite being married to his father and taking residence in Southundon, she never lost the ice in her veins. That same ice ran through his own body, he felt. Northundon was his place, and he wondered if the spirits sensed that or if they had some other plan for his presence.

"You're sure this is it?" whispered Sam, glancing at the other grand buildings that lined the boulevard.

"That's where I would have ruled from had all of this not happened," he mumbled. "Yes, I am sure. If there is some clue to where my mother is, to what happened here, it will be inside that building."

She nodded. "Shall we?"

He started forward again, wincing every time he felt a passing chill, knowing it meant a shade had come close or had touched them. The apparitions seemed interested in him and what he was doing. As they neared the palace, hundreds of the spectres clustered around them, but so far, none had interfered.

That was the worst, knowing that these creatures summoned to destroy his home were now letting him pass. They thought his purpose was their own, and it was the most terrifying thought he could have.

Northundon's ancient keep sat in front of them, only damage to the west wing hinting at the violence that had happened around it. It seemed even his father and the royal marines had qualms about bombing this place. His and his mother's place, he thought grimly. It had been, once, but it was dead and empty now. Shaking himself, stealing a glance over his shoulder at the lurking shades, he led them toward the front of the building.

The door, once proud steel embossed with the Wellesley sigil, was a rusted ruin, hanging ajar, resting on the marble steps that led to the huge portal. He didn't think he could move it alone if he tried. Fortunately, two decades prior, it'd been left wide open by either the invaders on the way in or the defenders on the way out.

Through the front door, the keep appeared sturdily constructed but bland. It was like that on all of the floors above the surface. Underneath was where the druids' odd construction stood out. There, twisting, snaking tunnels burrowed deep into the ridge that the keep sat upon. There were rumors of something strange down there, in the earth, but he'd never seen anything. No one had. He wondered if the tunnels were unchanged as they'd always been. They didn't have time to look, and with the crowd of shades trailing behind, a dark, windowless tunnel wasn't where he wanted to be.

He stepped inside, trying to shove down the wave of feelings that cascaded over him. In the foyer there were more bodies. Some of them were wearing tattered, time-faded livery. He'd spent most of his days in Southundon with his tutors and brothers, but he knew he would have met some of these people. They would have served his dinner, drawn his bath, and jested with the young duke.

But the uniformed dead were the easiest. His mother wouldn't be wearing livery. The skeletal remains of women in disintegrating dresses made his blood run cold.

He couldn't recall when the attack had occurred or if anyone had known. Morning, evening? Would his mother have been wearing jewelry? Would she have been armed? He didn't know, couldn't know. Her skeletal remains may be unidentifiable, even by him. All the dead looked the same. They could be stepping over her body, and he would never know it.

"Are you all right?" whispered Sam.

He shook his head but continued on. They were there, and there was nothing to do but continue on.

He led Sam to his family's personal quarters, not knowing if his mother would have fled, if there had been time. Would she have been on the walls, leading the defense?

Somehow, he knew that wasn't the case. Not that Lilibet hadn't been brave, but he felt a tug, a pull, toward where he'd seen her most. Her place within the old building called to him like a warm embrace.

The shades, hanging behind them, seemed to be waiting, watching as they walked through the dead hallways. Would they interfere if he went the wrong way?

It didn't matter. Not knowing why, he knew exactly where to go.

He walked unerringly to his mother's garden. In the winter, it'd been dormant, but during summers in the north, it bloomed with an exhilarating explosion of color and scent. The garden seemed all the more vibrant in the warm months because of the contrast with its lifeless, skeletal appearance in the winter.

Now, as they approached the towering glass doors that led back outside, he could see the garden was as dead as everything else in Northundon. Not surprising. He'd known to expect that. He'd known they would be looking down over the empty city through the bare branches of trees. Dead from the cold of winter or the life-stealing presence of the shades, it didn't matter. It looked the same.

He frowned, peering through the glass doors, stained and cloudy from decades of salt air and weather. The dirty windows obscured parts of the empty garden, but other parts were visible through broken panes.

Oliver clenched the obsidian dagger in his fist. Some sort of structure had been erected in the center of the lawn. He didn't recall seeing it before. He glanced behind them and saw the shades had stopped and were waiting.

Grimly, he tried the door handle. Ravaged by weather and disuse, it broke off in his hand. With a sigh, he reared back and smashed the iron-and-glass frame with a boot, bursting the old barrier open with a crack. A rainfall of glass clattered to the ground as the door swung open and slammed against the wall. The noise was shocking after the quiet hours spent stalking through empty streets.

Behind them, the shades remained motionless.

"Well, I think it's all right to talk now," said Sam. "If anything was going to hear us, it has."

He nodded, still not speaking, his eyes focused ahead on the bizarre arrangement in the center of the lawn. A dozen posts, twice his height, had been set into the ground. Cables connected them in an intricate pattern, but it was broken. Several of the ropes had crumbled and fallen in decaying heaps. A circular block of stone, three yards across, sat in the center, and as they walked closer, he saw a skeleton was stretched across the stone. It was bare bone, worn down from the weather, no sign of clothing or debris around it. A two yard-long lance of jet-black obsidian had been stabbed through the skeleton's chest. It pierced the block of stone and pinned the bones in place.

He glanced at the small blade in his hand and swallowed.

They walked closer, and he saw skeletons hanging from each of the posts, a dozen of them, all with their arms chained above their heads, all facing the one spread-eagle on the circular stone block.

Ropes were strung through the skeletons' ribs, but then, he uncomfortably decided they weren't ropes at all, but twenty-year-old entrails tied to the structure, woven around it like some mad-weaver's fever dream.

"Ah, Duke…" murmured Sam.

"What in the frozen hell is this?" he gasped. "I-I've never seen anything… This looks like what we found in Farawk, off Archtan Atoll. This wasn't here when I was last in Northundon."

"Yes, I imagined that," replied Sam dryly, stepping carefully around the structure, peering at it and the earth beneath the construction.

He glanced behind them and saw the shades clustered on the other side of the glass doors. None of them ventured into the garden. They were thick, there, on the other side of the barrier. Hundreds of them, he guessed, though it was difficult to tell because their incorporeal forms blended together. In the bright light of the moon, it was impossible to distinguish the individual shapes. The garden was completely clear of them, though, the only space that had been so since they'd made it through the first block of the city.

He turned to Sam and saw her still carefully circling the structure, eyes darting between it and the dead garden around them. The silver light of the moon cast the scene in stark black and white. He blinked. The vials of fae light they'd looped around their necks had gone dark. When had that happened?

He shook his, but the creatures inside the vial refused to flare alight. He glanced at Sam. "What is this?"

She stopped on the opposite side of the structure from him and turned toward the sea.

He waited while she stood, stone still.

"I suspected… I suspected, but I could not know. No one could," she murmured, her voice barely audible over the cold wind and the rush of waves far below them. "This is an altar, an altar specially built for a sacrifice."

He ran his hand over his hair, looking at the heavy, circular stone block. "Obviously…"

She shook her head, turning from the sea to face him. "Not this. Not just this, I mean. I'm talking about Northundon, Duke. Northundon is the altar. The people trapped inside the city walls were the sacrifice. All of them. The entire city, Duke. That's what the shades were talking about in your vision. Northundon is what they meant when they spoke of the sacrifice. Every man, woman, and child who died here was sacrificed on an altar of dark, foul sorcery. This is… This is unlike anything we've seen before. This isn't Archtan Atoll again. It is far, far worse. Northundon, the entire city, was the altar. The white fire you saw, Duke, that was why the shades were marching into it. They were going into the inferno of sacrifice over and over again until the bargain can be completed."

His mouth fell open.

"Tens of thousands of people…" She gagged. She looked away and softly repeated, "Northundon was sacrificed. They… they are still being sacrificed on the other side."

"But…" He clenched his fists, looking at the shades clustered inside of the building then back to Sam and the structure.

"What did the shades in the underworld tell you, Duke?" she asked suddenly. "In your vision, what did they tell you?"

He closed his eyes, forcing himself to breathe deeply, to remember. The vision came to him clearly, as if he'd just witnessed it moments before. A true vision, he knew that now.

"They told me she was part of the bargain, part of the sacrifice," he said. "I didn't know what it meant. How could I know what that meant?"

"You couldn't. No one could," assured Sam, walking around the structure to stand beside him. "Your mother was part of the bargain, but they said she was not there, not in the underworld. Your mother escaped, Duke. What else could it mean? That's what the shades were telling you. Your mother escaped, so the bargain has not been completed. They want her soul to finish the sacrifice, and only then can these shades return fully to the underworld, reclaim their rest while they wait upon the wheel."

Emotions rushed over him like a summer storm. He staggered beneath their onslaught. His mother was not in Northundon, but where was she? Why had she not come to his father and brothers in Southundon? Why had she disappeared?

"This structure," said Sam, waving at the macabre scene in

front of them. "I don't think it was built by the same sorcerer who unleashed the shades on Northundon. This pattern is an anchor, a binding designed to ensnare anything that crossed the barrier from the other side. I think this design is meant to hold the shades here, in the city."

"I don't understand..." muttered Oliver, falling to his knees.

"The entrails from the bodies, the obsidian lance," she said, frantically moving around to the other side of the structure, "the twelve points, symbolizing entirety, completion, mimicking the full-moon cycle, a year... How many towers are there surrounding Northundon, the ones we saw still standing along the exterior wall? I'd gamble all of my sterling there are twelve of them. That pattern was set long before, though. This design mirrors that of the city. See, twelve posts, twelve towers. The stone that skeleton is lying on is the same material as the keep, is it not? Druid stone, I suppose. I've never seen the like. That block represents the palace, I think, and the lance is this garden. The design is similar to a bridge to the other side, but there's no opening. No part of this pattern breaches the shroud. This is a trap but not for us."

"H-How... For who?" stammered Oliver.

"For the dead," she said. "If the shades were locked here, within the circle of Northundon's old walls, then they could not fulfill their purpose. They could not pursue the one they needed to complete the bargain. They could not finish the sacrifice. Duke, I think this pattern was meant to hold the shades in Northundon while their target escaped."

THE PRIESTESS XVI

SHE LET him mull that over, not wanting to say it. He had to see it himself, to understand the awful knowledge. In his vision, the shades had spoken true. There was one element of the sacrifice missing. There was one person who was meant to die in Northundon but had not. There was one person who would benefit from crafting the pattern in front of them.

His mother was a sorceress. She'd fled while Northundon was consumed by an army of the dead. She'd trapped them there, the souls of every man, woman, and child who had lived within the city walls, trapped them there for decades so that the city remained nothing more than a war-ravaged necropolis. She'd made her home inhabitable, filled it with the spirits of its former residents. Had she done it to save herself, or was there some other purpose?

Sam didn't know.

Perhaps there was an explanation. Perhaps someone else had built the construct to protect her. Maybe something other than callous self-preservation was at play. The pattern in front of them was beyond anything Sam knew. The sacrifice of the city... It was beyond anything she could fathom. All she knew was that Duke's mother, Lilibet Wellesley, had survived but had not fled to

Southundon. Lilibet had not sought out her husband, her children. She hadn't even written a letter. Were those the actions of a guiltless victim?

"My mother's alive," Duke whispered, staring at the grim tableau in front of them.

Again, Sam waited, hugging herself tightly in the cold night air.

"How?" he asked. "How could she be alive? She was here when the attack happened. When... Who could have done this?"

His face was twisted in confusion, and as he looked around the garden, seeing the banks of windows that flanked it, she saw the terrible light of understanding dawning on him. Hundreds of people likely worked in the palace. Who could have done such a thing right in the center of the structure and gone unmolested? Crafting the pattern would have taken a full day, if not longer. Who else could have been responsible? How could his mother have fled and survived when so many others died?

Duke fell to his knees, rocking back and forth.

Sam suspected he'd need comforting soon, but first she'd give him time for understanding to truly sink in. She left him for the moment, eyeing the shades still crowding within the building. She began to walk the grounds of the garden.

It was situated at the back of the palace, placed in the center, overlooking the city and the harbor below. From that garden, the arrival of the Coldlands raiders would have been obvious. For half a day, maybe a day if it was clear, their sails would have been visible. Was that enough time to craft the pattern? Maybe if the city had been able to defend itself, to hold off the attackers for a long enough period. Had Lilibet Wellesley been frantically building her sorcerous construct in the gardens while the battle raged below?

As Sam walked, studying the terrain below, she realized something was not fitting. The harbor, protected by seawalls studded with cannon emplacements, was undamaged. Neither the Coldlands raiders nor Enhover's bombardment had touched the frost-encrusted jetty that sheltered the anchorage. She could still see frozen brass barrels pointing out to sea, undisturbed after two decades. There was no sign of war, no sign of anything down at the mouth of the harbor. According to the common narrative, the fighting should have been hottest down there. How could the Coldlands overrun Northundon without fighting through those first barricades?

The only news Enhover had of the attack was a report from Glanhow's fishing fleet that Coldlands longboats were headed directly for the city. Had they beached east or west and attacked on land, avoiding the fortifications around the harbor? If so, wouldn't the defenders in Northundon have known? Wouldn't they have sent a transmission along the glae worm filament? Even if it was cut, a messenger by carriage or even on foot?

The city had been surprised. The lack of warning spoke the truth of that part of the story, at least, but how?

The common belief was that the Coldlands raiders had called the spirits which assailed Northundon. Could they have done so from the deck of a moving ship? She'd always imagined the spirits were called when the raiders had made landfall, that their ranks had been swelled by Northundon's own dead. The pristine harbor below did not tell of battle, though, and she had difficulty imaging how the shamans would conduct such a powerful ritual at sea. Each rocking wave was an opportunity to make an error in the pattern. If they'd made landfall and prepared their designs and rituals there, Northundon would have had plenty of time to alert the rest of Enhover that an attack was underway. It didn't add up.

The Coldlands had been known to practice small sorceries for centuries. Even in the face of the Church's rise and her push to eliminate the practice, the Coldlands and their shamans continued their rites. There'd been no reports she'd ever heard, though, of anything like this. From what Thotham had taught her, from what she'd learned on her own, from the stories in countless pubs and taverns, there had never been anything like this. Not in the Coldlands, not anywhere.

Could they have done it? Why would they have done it?

Why did the Coldlands suddenly and unexpectedly attack a single city in the north of Enhover? They must have known that by doing so they'd force a war between the nations, one that even with sorcery on their side, they could not win. Even if Enhover had not vanquished them, the nations that eventually formed the United Territories would have marched north. They would not allow such powerful magics to exist a border away, would they?

It was a risk the elders in the Coldlands would be aware of. They had to know the armies of the world would ally against them after they perpetrated such a heinous act. Why did they do it?

She glanced back at Duke. He was still kneeling, his head in his hands, sobs wracking his body. She walked to him and knelt beside him, placing a hand on his shoulder. He looked up, his eyes rimmed with red, his lips pressed tightly together.

"Duke," she asked, "why did the Coldlands attack Northundon?"

"I... W-What are you talking about?" he stammered, clearly struggling to reconcile the pain of his mother's disappearance with the unexpected question.

"What did they have to gain from unleashing all of this?" she asked, waving her hand around them. "If they meant to cripple Enhover, then why Northundon? Why not release the shades in Southundon where the bulk of the government and military reside? Had they been successful here, what would they have gained? War with Enhover, surely to be engaged by Rhensar, Ivalla, and Finavia as well? The Coldlands were raiders. They'd never shown acquisitive tendencies or held onto territory. If I recall my history, they were not ruled by a king but by a council of village elders. It was a loose federation rather than a proper nation. Why come together and begin a campaign they must have known they would lose?"

"I-I have no idea," mumbled Duke. "They're sorcerers. Maybe..."

"What if they didn't do it?"

He stared at her, confused.

"What if the Coldlands did not release the spirits that attacked Northundon?" she pressed. "That sorcery is advanced beyond anything they've been known to achieve. It's beyond anything anyone has been known to achieve. Finding a bridge and crossing it with so many souls? It doesn't seem possible from such a distance or from the deck of a ship. The raid seems to serve no purpose that the Coldlands would benefit from. What if... What if the Coldlands was not attacking but responding to an attack?"

Duke shook his head, speechless.

"Duke, I don't think they did it," she declared. "I think someone else unleashed the shades which haunt these ruins. I think someone else made a bargain with the spirits of the under-world, and that bargain has not been completed. Your mother was meant to die here, but she escaped. While she lives, the bargain is not sealed. That is why the spirits continue to haunt this place. Their purpose is not finished."

"What... What was the bargain?" asked Duke.

She shrugged. "I do not know."

"But, my mother... Do you think she..."

"I don't know," said Sam. She stood, looking at the shades lurking inside the building. After a long moment, she asked, "Who benefited from the destruction of Northundon?"

"No one," said Duke, standing, brushing his knees off. "No one did."

She crossed her arms under her breasts. "The war with the Coldlands, the push into the United Territories forcing them to be tributes to Enhover, the expansion of the Company's global reach..."

"The Church's monopoly on religion," he snapped.

She shrugged. He wasn't wrong.

"What are you saying?" he demanded.

"I don't know who could have done such a terrible thing as to sacrifice this city," she said, "but I know the Coldlands did not gain from the tragedy. If they were capable of such awful sorcery, why did they set it to this purpose? It was assumed they had no time to prepare a defense when Enhover fought back, but surely, they would have anticipated retaliation? How could they not? If they were so powerful, why do their actions make no sense? If they could simply perform a ritual and destroy a city of this size, how did they lose the war? They didn't do it, Duke. The more I think about it, the more I am sure the Coldlands did not release the shades against Northundon!"

Frowning at her, he asked, "Then who did?"

She admitted, "I don't know. I think… I think the shades called us here to show us this. They wanted us to understand that what we think is true is not. What we think happened did not." She stabbed a finger back toward the glass doorway that overlooked the garden. Surging against the barrier like the sea against a harbor wall, shades clustered and watched them. "They're not attacking us, Duke, because the Coldlands did not bind them to do so. They were forced to another purpose, one that is not finished. They brought us here so we could understand that, so we could know that there is more to it than some pampered peer leveraging family secrets to gain a little power. There is so much more. Duke, they didn't bring us here for answers, they meant to give you questions. We have to keep going. We have to keep asking the questions."

"I have plenty," he remarked grimly. "You're right. The Coldlands did not benefit, but no one else did either. If there are no answers here, then… Wait, no. You don't mean… That's crazy!"

"As crazy at venturing into Northundon, the city of the dead?" she questioned.

"We don't even have… Ah, frozen hell," he muttered. "Ainsley."

Sam's lips formed a humorless smile. "Coming to Northundon was the only thread we had to follow, the only way to find out who is behind all of this. We still have that thread, Duke, but it doesn't end in this garden. We have to see where it leads."

Silently, he looked at the terrible apparatus in the center of his mother's place. He studied the symbols inscribed on the posts, the cords — entrails they could plainly see now — that were strung between the posts, and at the skeletons that had been sacrificed in a terrible, arcane ritual.

"This was your home, once," she continued. "Twenty years ago, it was destroyed. We all thought sorcery was dead, gone from Enhover, but it's not. If you have any other idea, tell me, but we both know we cannot quit. Whether this could happen again, whether the perpetrators are even still alive, I don't know, but I know we cannot quit."

Rubbing his hand over his hair, touching the leather thong that tied it back, he said, "All right, then. Let's go to the Coldlands."

THE DIRECTOR III

"FROZEN HELL," muttered the former soldier.

Director Randolph Raffles grimaced, watching Prime Minister William Wellesley's face contort in barely controlled rage. The man's neck and cheeks were turning a terrible shade of crimson. His jaw was locked like he might never open it again, and his breaths were coming in quick snorts, like that of a bull preparing to charge. He wouldn't, though, not here.

The director was no fool. He'd requested they meet in the prime minister's club so the man would have to contain his rage. At least for a bit. As long as they were in the comfortable alcove off the Hunt Club's bar area, William wouldn't risk making a scene and telling Raffles exactly what he thought.

Instead, with torturous restraint, the prime minister asked, "No clue, you said?"

Raffles nodded. "We have no clue where they flew off to, m'lord. The Cloud Wolf was disabled in the volley, and there were no other airships within fifty leagues of Westundon to give chase. It was a cloudy night, both the stars and moon obscured, and once they passed out over the sea, there was no way to track which direction they went. Obviously, they circled either north or south staying out over the water, but we don't know which way. We don't know if once they were clear they departed Enhover or found some safe haven above our shores. They couldn't have planned their escape at a better time, m'lord."

"You mean, you couldn't have planned a worse time to attack their airship," accused William.

"We all agreed, the three of us, just four days ago," reminded Raffles. "You voiced no objections then. We heard Oliver was on the airship and preparing to depart in the morning, so we sent the shades. What would you have done differently? It's simple, your nephew outsmarted us, m'lord. All three of us."

William snatched a glass of whiskey and quaffed it in one gulp. He sat it back down and waved toward the corner of the room where a uniformed attendant was loitering. The two men sat silently while the attendant refilled their drinks. When the attendant departed, Raffles sipped his, waiting for William to speak again.

"Could he have had help?" asked the prime minister.

Raffles could only shrug. "The wolfmalkin in the apothecary, the surprise against our shades as they attempted to ambush the ship… If they do not have help, he and the girl are proving shockingly resilient."

"The other," remarked William. "Our fellow traveler on the dark path, what is his plan? Does he think my nephew and the priestess will uncover who we are? Does he plan for them to do his work for him?"

"That's what I believe," agreed Raffles. "The other does not know who we are but knows we exist. Like a hunter after a fox, he's following the braying hounds. Your nephew and the girl are meant to catch our scent and send us running."

"We've cut all ties and obscured all trails that may lead to us, no?" questioned William.

"The boy is more capable than I would have expected," admitted Raffles, staring down into the dark amber liquid in his glass. "I don't know of any clues that will tie to you, me, or the churchman, but I wouldn't have expected him to survive our attacks and vanish so easily, either."

"He's no mere spoiled peer." William sighed heavily and sipped his drink.

"Gabriel left two days ago on one of the Company's airships for Ivalla," said Raffles. "He anticipates no problem convincing his colleagues to loan him the use of the Council's Knives. He's going to tell them that one of their own betrayed them and is outright practicing sorcery. From what I understand about the way the priestess left Romalla, I imagine they'll be easily persuaded. The Knives could be in Enhover in a week."

"A week," muttered William. "Oliver has an airship and a skilled crew at his disposal. He has financial resources like no one else. He's more knowledgeable about the terrain around Enhover and the surrounding world than any man living. For years, he's explored and traveled, facing challenges that required resourcefulness and quick thinking. Prior to that, he was trained by the best tutors the king's sterling could buy. A week is too long, Randolph."

"What do you suggest?"

Grimacing, William pounded his fist on his leg. "I don't know."

"Perhaps it's time we considered the end of this path," suggested the director.

"The bridge to the underworld will be strongest during the solstice," reminded William. "We all agreed that timing will give us the highest probability of success."

"The summer solstice is five moons away," retorted Raffles. "Five moons! We cannot wait that long."

"If we attempt the binding and fail…" murmured William, shaking his head.

"If we do not attempt it and your nephew disrupts our plans, or worse, unmasks us to the other, it will be just as bad of an outcome," challenged Raffles. "There are steps we can take to ensure the ceremony progresses smoothly."

"More blood," said William heavily.

"More blood," agreed the director. "I do not like it, William, but we're left with a risk we cannot control. You are right. A week is too long to leave Oliver untethered, but we don't know where he is or what he is doing! Either we offer a hope to the spirits your nephew foolishly stumbles into our clutches, or we escalate the timeline. The only way we can take this matter back into hand is by fashioning a conduit deep enough into the underworld to reach the dark trinity."

"How many?" wondered the prime minister, toying with his glass.

"Yates is best suited to handle the calculations, but it will be a lot," speculated the director. "Glanhow is tied too closely to Northundon. We cannot risk Ca-Mi-He's taint of that place interfering with our ritual. Eiremouth, Swinpool… there could be difficulties forming the patterns with so much water nearby. We need open space, leagues of it. Derbycross is too small, but Middlebury is not."

William gaped at him. "Middlebury?"

Raffles met the other man's eyes. "Do you have a better suggestion?"

"That's… There are sixty- to seventy-thousand people living in Middlebury, Raffles. Surely you can't mean…"

"We've killed hundreds over the last two decades," remarked Raffles, "thousands between the three of us. If you consider what you did in the war against the Coldlands and the United Territories, I won't even bother to speculate."

"That was different," insisted William. "This is… this is just murder."

"Incredible power requires incredible sacrifice," murmured Raffles. "Balance, William, in all things. When we aimed for incredible heights, the price was always going to be high."

"This high?" questioned the prime minster. "The stain of this will never wash off of our souls."

"No, I expect it will not," acknowledged the director. "We will have time, though, to try and forget."

"We will have all time," said William, nodding solemnly.

"With the strength we'll have after binding the dark trinity, we'll be able to control the barrier between our world and the underworld. The three of us need not cross that barrier, William, but others will have to do it in our place. We've known this since you uncovered the secrets of the trinity in that frozen forest. We've known since you shared your finding with Gabriel and I. We've already paid so much, William. There is no turning back. We are already too far down the dark path, and now the only way is forward."

"There is no other way, is there?" asked William rhetorically, his shoulders slumped. "We cannot turn back, but I wish there was another way."

"As do I," agreed Raffles.

He was surprised to realize that he meant it. Twenty years ago, he'd known his soul would be steeped in blood, that the depths they would have to sink to would be unforgivable. He'd decided he was willing to do anything, though, to live forever. It was unfortunate that so many innocents would have to die, and he truly wished it could be another way, but such was the dark path. Such was the wicked way to immortality.

"What do we need to do, then?" asked William.

"We relocate your resources from Southwatch to Middlebury," advised Raffles. "We need Yates to return from Ivalla and lay out the design. He's done the research, and he knows the patterns better than us. Without the solstice, the design will have to be perfect. The moment he returns, I'll discuss it with him. I'm certain he'll see things the same way we do. How long will it take him to craft the arrangement? A week? During that time, I will assemble the required material—"

"The souls," interjected William.

"I will assemble the required souls," amended Raffles, "to initiate the ceremony and begin the ritual. It shouldn't be difficult.

Because of the situation in Imbon, Edward has already agreed to open the debtors' prisons to the Company. He couldn't make it any easier for us. By the time they find out my allocation isn't going to the tropics, it will be too late."

"For Yates to return to Enhover, travel to Middlebury, and lay out the pattern... just under two weeks?" wondered the prime minister. "It seems so fast."

"Not fast," disagreed Raffles. "We've been working toward this for twenty years. It won't interrupt anything you have planned, will it?" he asked with a smirk.

William snorted. "It will interrupt everything. There is much you and I will need to do to prepare. I'll need to marshal the forces from Southwatch to Middlebury. You need to assemble the Company's airships and have them ready to defend against the royal marines in case it comes to that. If we're interrupted halfway through..."

"It cannot come to that," insisted Raffles, leaning forward and speaking quickly. "The Company's airships are outfitted to face pirates or the United Territories. They don't have the armament to win against your brother's marines."

"If I can slip my men from Southwatch to Middlebury in secrecy, we'll have strength from the army, but don't be foolish and think it will be sufficient," warned William. "I will do my best to encourage Admiral Brach to deploy his forces to the tropics and whatever other far-flung place I can imagine, but he will not send everything. My brother promoted the man because of his paranoia. The admiral will never leave Enhover unguarded. My men can dig in and hold on the ground for a time against my brother's troops, but we'll need your airships to prevent attack from above. If Brach is able to fly over my men, the battle will be a short one. Not to mention, the other is out there and will certainly feel what we attempt. Airships, armies, legions of shades... we have to be ready for anything."

Frowning, Raffles nodded. "I'll arrange what I can. I only have so many loyalists, you know. No matter what I tell them, regular

Company men will not fire on the royal marines. Crewing a few airships with men in my thrall will take all of the resources I have."

William glared at him sharply.

"It will be enough," the director claimed. "If the royal marines fly north, they'll be looking for what is on the ground. They won't expect us to strike first from the air."

"Two weeks then," the prime minster said, sitting back in his chair, cradling his whiskey. "Two weeks and we either achieve the ultimate, or we suffer for eternity."

Raffles nodded. "Two decades of study and hidden machinations all for this."

William raised his glass. "A toast, then, to the ritual."

Raffles raised his as well and nodded before sipping along with the prime minster. He was pleased. After the man's initial objection, he'd come along quickly. A tremor of uncertainty assailed the director, though, as he considered that. William was as strong willed as any Wellesley. Had he already considered progressing with the ritual? The director decided it didn't matter. He was getting what he needed from William. The man had agreed to conduct the ritual, and that was what mattered.

They'd been preparing the ritual since William Wellesley had returned from campaign in the Coldlands. They'd infiltrated the nation's secret societies, its government, its economy, and its religion. They'd accomplished incredible things by working together. It was all a lead up, though. There was only one worthwhile goal, as far as Raffles was concerned, and they had not yet reached it. There was still one rank left to obtain, one achievement that would set them above all men.

Tilting back his whiskey, Raffles finished it, letting the harsh liquor burn down his throat.

Immortality.

Once it was his, then he would worry about the blood he'd spilled to get it.

THE CARTOGRAPHER XVIII

THE ICE-CLAD coastline emerged from the sea mist like the bottom of a raised mug of ale. Foam from crashing waves spilled off the rocky shore, leaving gleaming ice in its wake, only to smash again on the uncaring land. Beyond the violent confrontation of sea and shore, a solemn forest covered the soil. Towering pines, untouched in a generation by man or woman, stood sentinel over the forgotten territory.

The Coldlands, harsh and unwelcoming, had been decimated when his family had sailed against them two decades before. Every building they'd found had been razed, every person killed. The land had recovered, it seemed, but no other settlers had found reason to venture into the forbidding forest and make it home. There was open land farther south, fertile land where one could fly above it on the deck of a speeding airship without one's balls freezing off, imagined Oliver.

He tugged his long coat tighter and briefly considered taking one of Captain Ainsley's ridiculous hats. Sam, standing beside him, had doffed one of First Mate Pettybone's ratty knit caps, which might be warmer than Ainsley's offering, but the high possibility of head lice had convinced Oliver to pass. He didn't care how often the man denied it, Pettybone looked like the kind of person who would have head lice.

Sam scratched absentmindedly at the back of her head, murmuring something about itchy wool, and Oliver nodded to himself. Just as he'd suspected.

"Well, I don't think we're going to find you a clear spot in the forest we can settle down over," said Captain Ainsley, "and to be honest, I wouldn't want to if we could."

"The men having trouble keeping the stones clear?" asked Oliver.

"We pulled up most of the planking in the cargo hold, and I've got them scrubbing away any ice that forms, but the air spirits are always sluggish in the cold, and it doesn't much help that it's ice forming and not water," remarked Ainsley. "Normally, as the ship moves, the stones shift with the tilt of the deck and whatever condensation has formed rolls off. But at such a low temperature it freezes almost immediately. There's not much we can do to keep the frost off except removing it manually. The water tanks above are an even worse mess. Every quarter turn of the clock, I've got the men tossing fire-hot stones into the tank to keep it from freezing, but m'lord, there's only so long we can keep this up. I understand now why so much of the Coldlands campaign was conducted on the ground."

"Set us down on the shoreline, then, Captain," instructed Oliver. "Near the river. We'll use that as our egress into the forest. When we're clear, head north for a bit to reconnoiter the coastline. I don't think you'll find anything, but it's worth the effort. A day up, a day back, then you can travel south and let the Cloud Serpent thaw until our meeting time."

The captain looked ahead at the unbroken forest. "A lot can change in twenty years."

Oliver grunted. He knew. He'd left the faded, two-decades' old maps of the region stashed in the captain's cabin. They had the charts that were part of every airship's library, but those hadn't been updated since the campaign. They depicted the coast-line and the mountains dozens of leagues inland, but everything else the cartographers had noted had likely changed. The villages of the Coldlands folk were all gone, for one. If they were to find something, they'd have to do it in the trackless expanse of the frozen forest.

"There," said Sam. "Is that the river?"

Oliver nodded to Ainsley. The captain relayed instructions to the first mate, who informed the crew, and the Cloud Serpent began a slow descent toward the break in the forest where a narrow band of white split the wall of gray tree trunks and frost-covered nettles.

Checking his kit one last time, Oliver sifted through the tightly packed rucksack and then strapped it shut. His satchel, a constant companion on expeditions all over the world, was back in the cabin with the maps. He wouldn't be charting this journey. If they found what they were looking for, he suspected it was better left secret.

Sam, standing at his side, hitched her own pack onto her back and gathered Thotham's spear. The intricate runes remained free of the relentless sheen of frost that covered every other surface left exposed to the elements. He knew the weapon was warm to the touch, but that was all he knew. Whatever strange powers the priest had imbued in it, they'd yet to see them displayed.

Frowning, he realized he'd rather not see it used. If Sam was forced to use the weapon, then something had gone wrong.

Oliver checked his basket-hilted broadsword at his hip, noting the steel had already frozen in the sheath. He rattled it, breaking it loose in case he needed it when they disembarked. He slung his own pack and moved to stand beside the thick hemp lines Ains-ley's crew would drop overboard so they could shimmy down to the rocky shore, just a couple of dozen paces from the thick forest and frozen river.

"Nervous?" asked Sam.

"Not even a little," he said.

He gathered the rope and clambered onto the ice-slick gunwale before he could see her expression.

No, not a little nervous. A lot.

HIS FEET CRUNCHED ON THE HARD COATING OF OLD SNOW THAT covered the frozen river. A steady breeze, channeled down the opening in the trees, blew a calf-high blizzard around their feet. The snow was shallow because of the constant wind, and they'd found walking on the river was far easier than braving the thick drifts that accumulated underneath the trees.

Marching for three days now, they'd made relatively good time, and he estimated they'd traveled twenty leagues inland. It was slower than he could have traveled across the rolling turf of central Enhover, but in the forest, it was the best they could do.

Each night, they'd made rough camp underneath the trees, digging through the snow until they'd found drier branches they could light for a little bit of heat. They carried a weather-treated canvass from the ship that they fashioned into a makeshift tent, and each night, they'd slept back-to-back for the shared warmth. They ate salted meat and hard biscuits they'd taken from the ship's larder. Oliver tried not to think that fresh meat would have kept just as well in the bitter cold. They had a few wizened pieces of fruit and no vegetables. Water wasn't a problem, at least. They filled canteens with snow and stuffed them inside of their garments. Within an hour, it was water.

He never thought he would have craved something green so badly, but after three days of salted meat and biscuit, he would have paid a fortune for a pile of buttered peas or a handful of roasted sticks of asparagus. He would have killed a man for a proper drink.

Sighing, he pressed forward, leaning into the steady wind,

blinking constantly to keep his eyes from accumulating ice. Three days of frozen trekking, three days of seeing nothing but the slender ice-bound river, its tall banks, and the unbroken forest around them. His face was chapped, his fingers numb, and he couldn't feel his toes. He could only hope to the spirits that they weren't frost-bitten. If they were, there was nothing to be done about it.

Worse than the current discomfort, though, was that with each plodding step, he knew they'd have to return the same way to meet Ainsley and the Cloud Serpent.

They only had food for seven more days, which gave them two more to hike inland then five to return. Neither one of them had any experience with foraging, and in the frozen northlands, Oliver thought their chances would have been grim regardless. No, in the next two days, they needed to find what they sought, or the journey would be wasted.

"It was a good idea," said Sam through chattering teeth.

He grunted.

"If someone still lives in this place, they'd settle near fresh water. Your maps only indicated a few sources that are more than seasonal streams. Water, fish, the animals that would come for both... It made sense that this would be the place, Duke."

"If we can't find someone," he said, turning his head so the blowing snow wouldn't pelt into his open mouth, "we have no hope. There's no way we can locate and search the old villages underneath this snow. That's assuming something would even be left after my uncle's best efforts to destroy evidence and twenty long years of weather to finish the job."

It was Sam's turn to grunt.

A long shot, they'd both known, but they had no other ideas. Back in Enhover, they would be hunted by the unknown sorcerers behind all of this mess and likely by his father's government as well, now that they'd fired on an airship tied to the bridge in Westundon. If they returned, he knew it was only a matter of time before their hidden opponent caught them unawares. How can one protect against shades from the underworld, wolfmalkin, and whatever the frozen hell it was that Marquess Colston had turned into? Moving forward was the only way to find an end to the trail, but in two days, they would reach their limit. They'd have to turn around.

"I wonder if Ainsley's found anything along the coast?" asked Sam after a long pause.

Oliver shook his head. "Harwick's whaling fleet sometimes passes within sight of the shore. If there was a settlement along the sea, they would have seen it. It was worth having her check, but I'm certain there will be nothing there."

"Maybe a few passes over the forest, then?" suggested Sam. "If there's smoke from a substantial fire, we could see it from a distance. We can find a way down into the forest once we have a location."

"If anyone survives in this land, it's because they've learned to avoid detection from the air," said Oliver, "first, twenty years ago when my uncle led the royal marines here, and then from the periodic patrols my family has sent since that time. If people still live here, we won't spot them from above. We'll have to find them on foot. We'll have to find them on this river in the next two days."

They kept on trudging along the snow-covered frozen river. There was nothing else to say.

THAT NIGHT, THEY HUDDLED CLOSE TOGETHER. DARKNESS FELL EARLY beneath the trees, but they'd pushed hard to try and cover as much ground as they could before having to go back. By the light of half-a-dozen stubborn, cold-slowed faes, they dug under the snow, struggling to find branches dry enough to start a fire with.

The pathetic result in front of them was barely providing enough warmth to thaw his toes and nothing to warm the rest of his body. Oliver knew that if he tossed the remaining wood on it, the fire wouldn't last half the night. They'd have to take what little heat they could, stretch it out, and make it last.

He sat next to Sam, their sides and legs pressed tight together to share the heat of their bodies and limit the amount of space the bitter, cold wind could slice across them.

"I've been on worse trips," said Sam, her voice muffled in the scarf she'd wrapped around her head.

"Really?" he asked.

"No," she admitted, "though I have been almost as cold."

Rubbing his hands together then holding them toward the tiny pile of crackling branches, Oliver asked, "When was that?"

"I spent a few months in Glanhow's gaol," she explained. "I was younger then and didn't have any meat on my bones. The stoves didn't do much to keep the girl's dormitory warm, and it wasn't uncommon for the guards to get lazy and let it go cold. The other girls would all huddle together for warmth when it was really cold, but back then, I was a bit of a loner."

Slowly, Oliver turned to her. "As a young girl, you spent several months in Glanhow's gaol?"

She blinked at him. "I hadn't told you that?"

"You've told me nothing about how you grew up," he said.

"I guess I didn't think it was that unusual," she claimed. "Kalbeth and a lot of the girls I got to know, they'd been in the same circumstances or worse."

"Worse?"

"There are worse things than a few months in gaol, m'lord," she muttered into her scarf.

"I saw a gaol, once," he said, studying her out of the corner of his eye. When she didn't respond, he asked, "What did you do?"

"I killed and ate a man," she claimed. "We were trapped together in a frozen forest, and I only had a few days of salted meat left in my rucksack."

He snorted. "Keep your secrets, then."

"A girl needs a few of them, don't you think?"

He picked up a handful of slender twigs and set them on the

fire, watching as the fresh wood popped and hissed. Dry, frozen snow melted and boiled up in a thick cloud of smoke.

"Do you smell that? Is that smoke?" she asked suddenly.

"Yes…" he said, frowning at her, his hands still held out to the fire. He wondered if she'd gone snow-mad. Was that a thing?

"Smoke and… and meat, I think," she said, standing quickly, a shower of frost falling from her long coat and dusting Oliver.

Muttering under his breath, he stood as well and looked around the forest, hugging himself tightly now that her warm body had moved. After staring into their fire for the last hour, all he could see was black under the trees. All he could hear was the whistle of the wind through the tree branches.

"I can't smell anything," he complained. He inhaled deeply, catching the smoke from their fire along with the clean scent of ice. He coughed, hacking up the smoke, and scowled at Sam.

"There's something…" she murmured, quickly packing up her rucksack. "Let's explore."

Sighing, not wanting to venture into the cold but not wanting to sit at the tiny fire alone, Oliver packed his gear. He shook a treated canvass tarp over the fire and let the puff of snow settle on it before kicking several more piles to extinguish the dancing flames.

He complained, "At night, it's going to take us half a turn of the clock to get that going again."

"It would go out anyway if we leave it untended," said Sam. "It's better to conserve the fuel. I think there's something out there, Duke, but if not, I will apologize profusely and make it up any way you'd like. There's no point being out in these woods if we don't investigate potential activity."

He hitched his pack, checked his broadsword, and thought about what he could get away with requesting if she was wrong.

Ignoring her knowing look, he gestured for her to lead them. She started off into the dark, promptly tripping over a hidden branch and falling to her knees.

Wordlessly, he helped her to her feet and was relieved when

she started down the trampled trail they'd taken from the frozen river. Out on the river at night, the wind cut like a knife, but it was better than braving the knee-high snow drifts beneath the trees in utter darkness.

"Which way?" he asked, his breath billowing out in front of him, blending into the moonlit white landscape. He tried not to think how familiar it felt to his vision of the underworld.

"Inland, I guess," she said, raising a hand above her head, apparently trying to feel the wind.

Silently, they marched into the dark, trusting the moon to show the path. If anyone actually was cooking meat, they didn't want the fae light to give them away. Their boots crunched like fireworks on the frozen snow, but there was nothing they could do about that.

After several hundred paces, Oliver paused, sniffing. Sam stopped beside him and nodded. Wood smoke, definitely, and they'd been traveling away from their own fire. Perhaps a bit of burning fat? His stomach clenched in hunger, and he looked at Sam tight-lipped. She'd been right. Someone else was in the woods with them. Trying unsuccessfully to walk quietly, they continued on until several hundred paces later, they stopped again.

Small sounds echoed through the trees on the frozen night. Nothing identifiable, but along with the smoke, Oliver was certain it was man-made. They looked around, peering between dark tree trunks. Oliver pointed her to the right bank and then he climbed the left. He peered into the forest, seeing nothing but white snow and black bark. Across the frozen river, he could see Sam waving him over. He crossed and climbed up beside her. He saw a telling glow deeper in the forest. A fire, a big one, was burning merrily.

"What do we do?" whispered Sam, pointing at the snow around their feet. "Sneaking will be almost impossible in this stuff."

He nodded. She was right. "We don't sneak, then. Remember, we came all of this way to talk to someone."

Resigned, she nodded and then started into the dark woods, feeling her way carefully forward through the knee-high drifts.

He followed behind, one hand on his broadsword, the other hand steadying himself against trees as they passed. Certain they were making enough noise to alert anyone of their approach, he wasn't surprised when they finally entered a clear space and found a roaring fire and nothing else.

"Well, that's rather strange," remarked Sam, edging closer to the blaze, he guessed to warm herself, but she pointedly sniffed like she was trying to find the cooking meat she'd claimed was nearby.

"They must have fled," he surmised, glancing around the empty clearing.

"I did not flee," said a voice from the opposite side of the fire.

Oliver jumped, uncomfortably aware he'd just looked in the space that a small man was now occupying. Had the man been in hiding, or had he simply appeared?

The old man smiled at Oliver as if he could read his thoughts and said, "Follow me."

Oliver shared a look with Sam and then shrugged. They'd come looking for someone, and they'd found him. On the positive side, the man did look rather old. Hopefully, he could answer why the Coldlands had sailed to war twenty years earlier.

The old man led them down a path in the snow worn clear by frequent travel. He moved with a spry dexterity that reminded Oliver of Thotham. The man seemed at home in the woods, lit only by the burning fire behind them. It cast tall, menacing shadows from the three of them on the trees ahead before they lost the light behind the thick trunks.

Shortly, they saw a black mound of rock rising out of the forest. It was near a height with the trees and likely would have been invisible from the river. From above, it would have looked like any of the other giant boulders that lay scattered throughout the forest. As they approached, Oliver saw the front of it was bracketed by two pinpoints of light. They braced a dim glow, which he guessed was the mouth of a cave.

"I apologize for the odd invitation," said the old man over his shoulder. "Some discussions are best conducted in mystery and at night."

"What is this place?" asked Oliver as they reached the mouth of the cave. He peered inside the dark maw and saw a tunnel that opened into a larger room that was lit by torches.

"My home, among other things," explained the old man. "Come along."

He took them inside, and Oliver was stunned to see the room was expansive, as wide across as the Cloud Serpent was long. It was partitioned by rough branch and hide screens. It seemed a comfortable, if primitive, living space.

"Food, drink?" asked the old man, pointing toward a table where a platter of steaming hunks of meat sat beside a kettle containing a savory-smelling broth. "It is custom in the Coldlands to serve fresh meat, which we can hunt for even in the depth of winter, along with stored vegetables stewed in the animal's juices. I'm afraid there's no bread or other delicacies that you may be used to, but I do have some beer. It's brewed with tubers and only approximately similar to what you drink in Enhover. It is quite cold, though, which I believe is how you like it."

"I-I do…" stammered Oliver.

"Instead of poisoning you, I could have simply left you alone, Oliver Wellesley," said the old man. "I am quite sure that you would manage to get yourself killed soon enough."

"How do you know my name?" asked Oliver, his eyes darting around.

Sam growled, raising her spear.

"You trod across the skin of the underworld like a giant, young lord," stated the old man. He glanced at Sam. "You will not need that weapon here, Knife of the Council. I mean you no harm."

"Pardon me if I do not immediately trust you," she said.

"The spirit in the weapon, was that your mentor?" asked the

old man. "I sense no animosity from him. Do you? You trusted his judgement, once. I hope that did not change with his passing."

She frowned.

"Come, eat and drink, and we will talk," said the old man. "Elk, taken just this morning. Onions, potatoes, and carrots in the stew. Familiar fare, is it not?"

Embarrassingly, Oliver's stomach rumbled.

LOOKING DOWN AT THE PILE OF ROASTED MEAT, JUICES STILL LEAKING from the warm slices, Oliver sat back. The way his stomach felt, stuffed with the vegetable stew and mostly the meat, even the little old man might be able to thrash him. He worried briefly that was the ancient man's plan, but he decided it was unlikely, so he leaned forward and used his belt-knife to spear another delectable cut of elk.

Beside him, Sam had eaten but not relaxed. He wondered what she sensed about the old man, whether she could tell if he was one of the Coldlands' vaunted shamans or just an odd fellow who practiced on the fringes as she did. Not that she would admit to that.

"So," said Oliver, tucking his thumbs behind his belt and stretching his back, "we've waited as you asked. Please tell me why you brought us here."

The little man, his face as browned and wrinkled as a chestnut, grinned. "I did not bring you here. You brought yourselves. I only invited you into my home as I thought it possible you'd see it tomorrow when you continued your journey upriver."

Oliver blinked. "You sought us... The fire, it was meant to draw us in, was it not?"

The old man nodded. "It was. I did not draw you into the Coldlands, though. You came here on your own. I am curious. What is it you seek?"

"We're the ones asking the questions," growled Sam.

"You're the ones visiting my home," pointed out the old man.

"Perhaps we can tell you some things and then you will answer our questions?" asked Oliver.

"Perhaps," said the old man. "I am not a mind reader, you know. I do not know why you are here. I was only able to identify you because of the impression you've made on the other side. My ancestors saw you there, striding through the underworld like you were its king. They called to you, along with the others. They told me about it, and then they saw you in Northundon, where they remain trapped by your nation's awful sorceries. When a young man and a young woman arrived on our shores and hiked up the river, it was no great leap to guess who you might be."

"Our sorceries!" snapped Oliver. "You are the one talking to the spirits!"

"I speak to the same spirits that led you here," remarked the old man. He glanced pointedly at Sam and then back to Oliver. "Let us not pretend I am the only one who knows anything about them."

Oliver frowned. "Those spirits spoke to me. I did not speak to them."

"Ah, a vast distinction, is it?" questioned the old man.

"Do not seek to turn my words," warned Oliver.

The old man held up his hands and waited.

"We came here," said Oliver, "because of what we found in Northundon. We want to understand why the Coldlands sailed to Enhover, why you attacked. What did your people hope to gain from war with Enhover? Surely you understood what would happen. Surely your people knew they could not win a war against ours."

The old man, his eyes glistening, brought his hands together and bowed his head. "For twenty years, I wondered if anyone would ask those questions."

Oliver gaped at him.

"Of course we knew we could not win a war," stated the old man, his face rising to meet Oliver's gaze. "We were few, and you were many. We had our spirits, but you had cannon, firearms, bombs, and airships. We had to sail, though, to try and stop what was happening."

"The destruction of Northundon," breathed Oliver.

"No," said the old man. "We sailed to stop a bridge forming to a collection of spirits known as the dark trinity. A connection, penetrating deep into the underworld, fully formed…" The old man shivered and lifted a mug of the bitter beer he'd served them. "The connection would have granted incredible, terrible power to the sorcerers who formed it. They must have thought they could live forever, ruling this world with that power, but if the binding failed, the spirits would have had a foot in this world and their own. They could have wedged the breach in the shroud between our worlds wide open. The dark trinity, as close to the lords of the underworld as there is, could have slipped onto our side. The devastation would be unthinkable. Not just to Enhover but to us all."

"W-Who…" stammered Sam. "Who would do such a thing?"

"Oh, I'm sure the sorcerers believed they could control the spirits through their binding ritual," continued the old man. "Sorcerers are rarely humble men or women. They must have thought they'd gain complete control of the dark trinity. Maybe they could have, for a time, but eternity is a long time to trust the works of men, don't you think? Eventually, the dark trinity would have found a break in the pattern, or the binding would have failed for some other reason. Time erodes all of our creations, even that of arrogant sorcerers. Would it be a year, a thousand years? We did not know, but with the world at stake, did it matter? Any risk was too great, so we sailed to Enhover and we foiled the ritual. The full binding was not completed, and the dark trinity did not walk the bridge to our world, but the taint of the spirits was sunk deep in your land. We fought against it, tried to free the bound shades, but we could not win, so we fled."

"But why didn't you… why didn't you tell anyone?" cried Oliver.

The old man offered a wrinkled smile. "We tried to explain what was happening, but your lands are in the thrall of the Church. We found no ears willing to listen to us. I don't know if our envoys ever made it to your grandfather, the king at the time. The Knives of the Council were a more formidable organization than they are today, and they hunted our messengers like diseased rats. Our elders had known sailing to Northundon was a risk. We are isolated but not foolish. We knew that we might pay the ultimate price, but our elders had communicated with the spirits of our ancestors and knew we had no choice."

"Thotham's prophecy," murmured the priestess, glancing at Oliver. "A darkness spreading from Enhover to cover the world."

"I do not know this prophecy," responded the man, a Cold-lands' shaman, Oliver was certain, "but yes, I believe that is what could have happened. We are not entirely altruistic, I admit. We sailed in an attempt to preserve our own people. Sailing to Northundon was the only way we could do it. Our elders hoped that we would prevail, or that your leaders would come to under-stand. Despite the risk that would not happen, they decided falling in battle was still better than becoming slaves of the dark trinity. We could die and allow our spirits to be ground by the wheel until rebirth, or we could suffer eternal. Given two unat-tractive choices, we did what we had to. Those of us who survived have tried to preserve our culture, but I'm afraid we've failed."

"The sorcerer..." wondered Oliver. "Did you kill him?"

"Or her," remarked Sam. "A woman is just as capable of... Ah, you're right. It was probably a man."

The Coldlands sorcerer's lips curled into a thin, bitter smile, and he shook his head. "I do not know who offered the horrific sacrifice. A trinity, our elders suspected, but we never identified the members of the cabal."

"They're still out there!" exclaimed Sam, sitting forward, grip-ping her fork. "You have to do something!"

"It is not my task to murder sorcerers," said the man, a steely glint entering his eyes. "That is what you do, is it not?"

Sam sat back.

"W-Well, surely… What…" stammered Oliver.

"My people expended ourselves stopping the full ritual from coming to fruition," stated the old man. "We tried to do more but we failed. We ran out of time. Your airships appeared above and rained fire on us. We fled, and your people pursued us, intending to decimate every trace of the Coldlands tribes. Some few of us were able to hide, to avoid your bombs and your swords, but we are no longer a people. Our young, those few that there are, have migrated south into Rhensar. They're assimilating into the culture there, and within a generation, there will be no more of what you would recognize as Coldlands folk. We are finished in this world, and it is only a handful like myself who are able to keep the connection to the other side. When we join our ancestors, we will be forgotten. The only evidence of our existence will be in history books written by your empire."

Oliver winced.

"My people are finished," continued the old man. "I continue our ways out of habit more than anything, but perhaps there is a way I can help you. It would give me some pleasure if you were able to put a knife into the ones responsible for my people's downfall. I am an old man, but not so old that I've lost all of my petty notions of revenge."

"Help us," said Oliver. "How?"

The old man stood. "Come with me."

He led them to the back of the large, stone chamber, and Oliver saw what was clearly a sorcerous altar. Patterns were inscribed on the wall behind it, and the altar itself was comprised of piece upon piece of yellowed bone. Oliver shuddered, refusing to look close enough to see whether they were animal or… Grimacing, he saw a handful of scrolls, a knife, bowls, and other implements he'd come to associate with the dark arts, but what the man held up and showed them didn't look like it had anything to do with sorcery at all.

"Is that a chicken bone?" wondered Oliver.

"Yes," confirmed the old man. "A furcula."

"We call them wishbones," muttered Oliver, glancing at Sam out of the corner of his eye. She did not return the look. She wasn't looking at the old man either. She was studying the altar instead. "Ah, what are we supposed to do with the wish… the furcula?"

"The taint of the dark trinity is still upon this world," remarked the old man. "This bone will help you sense it. It is attuned to those spirits. With this, I believe you can find their presence on this side of the shroud. See here, see the runes inscribed on the different forks? You will feel a slight tug which will pull you to the presence that fouls our world."

"Why do you not use it?" wondered Sam.

"I am too far away," answered the old man. "Here in the forests, the furcula pulls me toward Enhover. From this distance, that is all I can tell. Is there one source of the taint, several, I do not know. I wish I could find out, but I cannot unless I traveled to your shores."

"If you seek revenge, then why have you not done so?" questioned Oliver.

"The sorcerers and your family destroyed my people," reminded the old man. "What can I do against such a power?"

"What can we do, then?" snapped Oliver.

The old man shrugged. "Do as you wish. I do not care if you die, but unless the murderers of my people return to these lands, this device is of no use to me, so I give it to you freely. I know of you, Oliver Wellesley, and I know you were only a boy when my people were killed. I hate your people, but I've gained enough wisdom in my years to understand it was not you who rolled the bombs or held the blades. There are others behind this evil, and I hope to the spirits that you kill them."

"It was his family who bombed this land," reminded Sam, eyeing the old man suspiciously. "That does not bother you?"

"I play no trick on you," assured the old man. "This device will lead you to the taint of the underworld. What you do with what you find is up to you."

Frowning, Oliver reached for the wishbone, and as he held it, he felt it tug slightly in his hand. He jumped, nearly dropping it. Gathering himself, he turned, following the pull of the small, forked bone until he was facing away from the old man. He was facing west, toward home.

"I suggest you travel to the center of Enhover," said the old man. "From there, the furcula will pull you toward the taint of the underworld. Find it, and you will find those responsible for the destruction of your home and mine."

"We'll try," said Oliver, glancing at Sam. She still looked suspicious, but she did not comment.

She was right to not trust the little man, but could he be telling the truth? If the Coldlands shaman thought a cabal of sorcerers in Enhover was responsible for Northundon, ones too powerful for him to confront alone, did it not make sense he would try to use Oliver and Sam to exact his revenge? However it turned out, whichever side died in the conflict, the old man won.

"One more piece of advice, Oliver Wellesley," said the old man. "Your family has built an incredible empire. Your power has spread across the shores of many lands. You are not the first, though, to claim foreign lands, to build such an empire. Others have gone before you, fashioning their own legacies. They are all gone now, like my people. Most are not even memories. It is the fate of all empires to fall. Even mighty Enhover will fall, when it is time. Who will be the cause?"

Oliver stared at the man, not responding.

The old man smirked. "You do not think it will happen? There are no threats you perceive that can topple you? What other nations have the strength to face Enhover's might, you think? You are right. No other nations can match Enhover, but it is always the fate of empire to fall. It is the fate of empire to crumble from within. Do not ask when, Oliver Wellesley, because it is soon. Instead, ask who. Ask who within your empire will be the seed of its demise."

"You are crazy, old man," snapped Sam.

Toying with the furcula, feeling it pull gently in his hands, Oliver turned to Sam. "It's time to go home."

THE PRIESTESS XVII

Above her, the branches creaked, rubbing against each other and showering a trickle of snow. Already, a light coating was accumulating on the tarp she and Duke had strung to provide them shelter. Their fire, rebuilt after visiting the old man, hissed as the frozen water fell into it. Beside her, the peer's breathing came in long, deep intervals.

It was time.

Moving slowly and wincing at the crunch of frozen snow, she rolled out from under the tarp and stood. Duke mumbled in his sleep. She crouched down, tucking her blanket, still warm from her body, tight around the man. She put a few more sticks from their pile onto the fire and waited. He settled down, and she stood back up.

She buckled on her knife belt, checking the kris daggers to make sure they hadn't frozen in the sheath. Cold-numbed fingers darted around her body, touching the poignards in her boots, the knife at her back, and then, she collected her spear, Thotham's old weapon. She hoped it would keep her fingers warm, and when she needed to act, they wouldn't be stiff from the cold.

Stalking carefully, she made her way out of camp, following the same trail they'd broken earlier in the evening. She arrived at the frozen river and hurried, glancing up and seeing it was two hours after midnight. Still time until dawn, she thought, to do what was needed and then return to camp. When sun broke, she hoped to be asleep at Duke's side.

The moon gave enough illumination that she was able to follow their tracks, moving silently along the frozen river then louder but slower along the path through the trees to the fire that had first attracted them. It was black and dead now, burnt out. Even the embers had been killed by the cold air and falling snow.

She walked the well-worn path the old man had led them down. His stone home rose before her, the black silhouette standing out even in the dark forest. The torches that bracketed the entrance had been extinguished. Only a dim glow gave away the opening to the cave mouth.

Sam stepped inside, gratefully leaving the crunching snow behind. She waited a moment, standing on the stone path that tunneled into the massive rock. Then, her spear held before her, she slunk along the edge of the wall, hoping the low light coming from the man's glowing hearth wasn't enough to cast her shadow.

She saw the fire first, only orange-red coals radiating heat but barely illuminating the kitchen and sitting area around it, failing to reach the ceiling of the domed space or the back corner. Stepping into the open area, she paused, looking away from the hearth, letting her eyes adjust to the dark room. The fire popped, and she bit down on her tongue, nearly squeaking in surprise. She waited, but there were no other sounds. Absolute silence. She couldn't hear the breath of the old man, which made her nervous. No snores, no shifting in a rickety cot, nothing.

Taking steps slowly, she forced herself to remember the lessons her mentor had taught her. Placing her heel carefully and then rolling the rest of the foot down, she walked across the room. Each step took her half-a-dozen breaths to complete, but she moved across the stone floor in total silence. As long as she wasn't spotted, only her own soft breathing could give her away, and she wasn't going to stop breathing.

The lessons Totham had taught her years ago were like half-forgotten muscle memories, skills she hadn't practiced in ages but had once practiced daily. The gift her mentor had left her, the knowledge of how to kill a man.

She'd been eager, at first, learning how to lash out against those who'd hurt her, learning how to get vengeance. And she'd done that, but it wasn't why he'd taught her those skills. Even then, she'd known. She'd paid for her revenge by truly becoming the man's pupil. She'd absorbed what he'd taught, learned it well, better even than the old man himself, she sometimes believed, but it had seemed for naught. For years, for a decade, they'd never found a trace of sorcery. They'd never sniffed a hint of that foul taint which he'd raised her to fight. It seemed it was already gone. Everyone said so. But now, she knew they were wrong. Now, she knew that awful stench was just as powerful as it had been back then, when Northundon had fallen. Now, finally, her purpose made sense. Now, finally, she could do what she'd been raised to do.

Sorcery was alive and well, and she was there to kill it.

Except, splayed out on the altar, his blood leaking down the front of the yellowed bones, was the old man, already dead. His bald head shone in the subtle light from the embers in the fireplace. His blood was like a black stain.

Cursing silently, she looked around. She saw no one, so she stalked closer, her spear held ready.

The man did not move and would not move. Drawing out her vial of fae light, she shook it and leaned closer. The old man's throat had been slashed wide open, showing glistening, ruby-red flesh. A clean cut, no hesitation. There were no signs of struggle. There was no weapon, either, so someone else had committed the act, but as she looked around the area, touching nothing, she saw no obvious evidence.

Someone had slashed the old man's throat to the bone, spraying his blood across the altar before he collapsed on it. There was no blank space in the pattern of spray, so they must have stood behind him. Behind, where there was no entry or exit. She surmised the old man must have known what was happening. How else could someone have snuck in while he stood there? Besides, the old man had sensed Sam and Duke. He would likely sense the approach of any others. The old man had acquiesced to this sacrifice.

But why, and who had done it?

The scrolls and several of the implements she'd observed behind the man when he'd handed Duke the furcula were missing. In the light of the fae, she could see faint outlines in the dust where some of them must have sat a long time before being taken. There was nothing of value left that she could see, except maybe...

She turned back to the altar and unceremoniously tugged the dead man off of it. He flopped onto the floor.

Tacky blood painted the bone altar where it had not spilled down the front. There were no pools of the sanguine liquid, though, which she would have suspected given how much must have pumped out of the gaping laceration in the man's neck. It had dripped through the spaces between the bones. As she suspected, it was not only an altar but a reliquary. It was hollow inside.

Bending close, she saw the reliquary was held together by slender leather thongs, tight from the cold and age. She couldn't see anything on them, but when she touched one, she felt tiny intricate marks. Runes. Someone had stenciled runes on the thongs and bound hundreds of bones together with them. It was intricate, time-consuming work.

Setting her spear aside, she drew one of her kris daggers. With the razor-sharp tip, she snicked one of the leather thongs. She moved across, slicing open a line of them, circling the entire reliquary. After sheathing her dagger, she gripped the top, carefully avoiding spots of the old man's blood, and lifted it.

She looked in and saw a note written on paper. The rest of the space was empty, though it was clear that had been a recent change. Indiscernible shapes were outlined in dust. Blood speckled the paper, so she inferred it had been laid there before the old man's throat was cut, but after everything stored inside had been removed. There was no doubt the old man had known what was coming. Why? Who? And how had they opened and shut the reliquary without disturbing the ties?

Cursing under her breath, she picked up the page, pinching it carefully to avoid the spots of blood that had soaked into the parchment. It was thick, fine quality, and in elegant, delicately formed script, she read:

"The path you walk is a dark one. Those who walk it rarely turn. Decide if you will continue the walk or if you will stay in the light of the world. The time to decide is nigh. If you continue, answers lie in the blood of the three. If you continue, know others walk the path ahead of you."

Snorting, she crumpled the paper and stalked to the fireplace. She tossed the wadded ball of parchment onto the embers then knelt, blowing on them until the paper caught. Scowling, she watched it burn. Walk the dark path? She wasn't walking the dark path, and who had written such a thing? Who even could out in the wilderness? The blood of the three. Was it a false lead or something else? Someone had placed the parchment in the reliquary and killed the old man, ensuring he could tell her nothing more. They'd known he would talk, and somehow, they'd known she would return. How had they known? Who else could be out there in the uncharted wilderness with them? Had everything the man said been a false lead? Had everything he'd said been true?

She grimaced. She needed a proper drink and a tumble. Maybe then it would all make sense.

THE DIRECTOR IV

RANDOLPH RAFFLES SHIFTED the blade with his finger, moving it a few inches over so the tip of the gleaming dagger lay directly atop the city of Middlebury. He thought about snatching it up and slamming the blessed blade directly into the location on the carved map, but it seemed dramatic, like something some foul villain on the stage would do. Not that he didn't acknowledge he was playing the role of the villain, but he was not a product of the feverish imagination of some poppy-dreaming stage-writer. Instead, he centered the tip of the knife directly above the city, hiding it from his view.

Carved with a map of the world, the dark wooden table had sat in his office in Company House for years. He'd rarely thought about it until Duke Wellesley commented on how inaccurate the depiction was. Now, he thought about it all of the time. So close to when he would achieve power to dominate all of those far-flung lands, he had a constant reminder of how little he knew of them, how unfathomable the scale of the world was, how unfathomable his power would be. The not knowing excited him, spoke to him of the possibilities. It also, in his most honest moments, scared him.

He flicked the dagger with his finger, this time spinning it, watching as the flashing steel swept over Enhover, turning for several long breaths. The blade stopped spinning, pointing to the coastal city of Swinpool.

Frowning, he flicked it spinning again. He had rather hoped it would stop and point to a more meaningful location, like Southundon, a portend of what was to come. As it came to rest the second time, the tip hanging well off the east coast where there was nothing but empty sea, he growled and picked up the weapon.

A tingle of discomfort started down his wrist and arm, like his blood was slowly beginning to boil inside of his skin. It wasn't, it was a manifestation of the blessing the great spirit had placed upon the dagger. His body was reacting violently as the touch of Ca-Mi-He was anathema to the living. He placed the dagger in the plain wooden box he'd prepared for it, and the sensation immediately began to fade.

The dagger was the one Hathia Dalyrimple had somehow managed to get blessed by Ca-Mi-He in Archtan Atoll. There was no doubt the spirit had invested it. A simple touch was enough to determine that, but after pressuring Yates to turn the thing over, Raffles had spent fruitless weeks trying to determine the nature of the blessing. Did it impart something to the one who held it? Did it cause some reaction in those who were attacked by it? He didn't know. None of his experiments had shown anything of the nature of the blessing. He'd felled two dozen subjects trying to find an answer, their corpses dumped into the harbor by the remaining acolytes of the Feet of Seheht. If the dagger had properties other than a sharp edge, he hadn't found them.

Now, William Wellesley wanted it, and Raffles was happy to pass the blade over. With everything they had to do to prepare for the ritual, he had no time for such foolishness. Whatever powers the infuriating dagger held, he was certain they would be nothing compared to what they would obtain by binding the dark trinity. The dagger held a tenuous connection to Ca-Mi-He at best. They would have direct contact with spirits nearly as powerful. They would gain control of an entity that would make them almost invincible. Soon, the dagger would be a worthless trinket. Let William waste his time with the thing.

His hand hovered above the weapon one more time, feeling the reaction within his body and nothing else. He grunted and slammed the lid of the box closed. He locked it with a small key, slipped the key into a plan paper envelope, sealed it with wax, and rang the bell on his desk. He would send the weapon to William, but he and his followers did not have time to deliver it themselves.

In a moment, a man opened the door. "Sir?"

"Writer... ah, what is your name?" he asked the man.

"Factor Quimby, sir," replied the man, a wince twisting his face.

"Right, Factor Quimby," he said, wondering if he'd ever seen the plain-faced man around Company House before. "You are the man selected for the special dispatch?"

"Yes, sir, I, ah, I'm eager for the opportunity, sir. I've been employed by the Company for over ten years now, sir, and I want to prove myself. I—"

Director Raffles waved his hand dismissively. "Ten years, Factor? Any field work?"

"In the Southlands, sir, but things went sour. Not my fault, you understand, sir, but at the time, the directors felt—"

"I understand, Quimby," interrupted Raffles. "You want another opportunity, yes, another chance to prove your worth and achieve some real wealth out in the colonies? Perform this dispatch for me, exactly as instructed, and you'll get your chance. You have my word."

"Thank you, sir. I—"

"Enough, Quimby," growled Raffles. "This requires utter secrecy, you understand? The other trading houses must not know. Even our own members must not know of your mission. It's imperative, Quimby. Take this box and this envelope to Southundon and hand them personally to Prime Minister William

Wellesley. Personally, Quimby! I would do it myself, but I was just in Southundon and have matters to attend to here. I will ask the prime minster about this, Quimby, and he'd better tell me he saw your face."

"T-The prime... the prime minister, sir?" stammered Quimby, his eyes wide.

"Insist on a personal audience, but do not inform his staff you are coming on my behalf or for the Company. Tell them it is a personal matter," instructed Raffles. "It's best they don't know who you are, if you can manage that. Make up a story if you have to. Once he knows I sent you, William will back your tale, whatever it is. Secrecy, Quimby, is why I am tasking you with this. Take the rail so no one suspects it is Company business, and, Quimby, do not delay."

"Tonight, s-sir, this evening, I mean," stammered the factor. "I will be on the way. Directly into the hands of the prime minister, sir... That you'd do this yourself if you had the time... I understand the importance, and I will not fail you, Director."

Raffles nodded and smiled. He flicked his gaze to the box and back up. "Now, Quimby."

The nervous man scurried forward, collected the items, and bowed on his way out.

Bowing, certainly not something the board of directors encouraged Company officers to do, but Raffles found he rather liked it.

His fingers drummed on the table, restless. The ritual...

He noticed Quimby had left the door open and cursed. Standing, he began around his desk to shut the door when his secretary appeared. Adjusting his powered wig, the man looked as if he'd just come running from the harbor.

"What is it, Charles?" he asked.

"He's here, sir," said the man, drawing heavy breaths. "I came to inform you immediately."

"Bishop Yates? Yes, can you—"

Interrupting him, the secretary blurted, "Duke Oliver Wellesley."

Randolph Raffles' mouth fell open.

"He's in Westundon, sir. Just arrived on the Cloud Serpent and tied up to the bridge. I'm told he was headed for the palace, which I suppose should have been expected. He's likely meeting with his brother now, sir. Do you want me to—"

"No," snapped Raffles, snatching his own wig off the rack, tugging it on, and then shrugging into his formal coat. He glanced in his looking glass, adjusted the wig, and then turned to his secretary. "Run to the carriage yard. Arrange a ride for me to the palace. I'll leave immediately."

Nodding and wide-eyed, his secretary Charles hurried off.

Oliver, back in Westundon. What was the boy playing at?

Raffles smiled at his reflection in the looking glass. Bishop Yates and the Church's Knives would arrive soon. If the spirits deigned to share any fortune, within a day or two, Oliver Wellesley would be dead.

"MY BROTHER?" ASKED PRINCE PHILIP. "NO, HE'S NOT BACK THAT I — Let's save the time, Raffles. Tell me what you know. Why do you think he's back in Westundon?"

"The Cloud Serpent is docked at the airship bridges, m'lord," said Director Raffles. "I thought Oliver would come straight here."

Standing up and striding to the double-height glass doors that led to his patio, Prince Philip charged outside, not bothering with his coat in the bitter-cold winter weather. Raffles, following him, looked out over the rooftops with the prince to the airship bridges in the distance. There, half a league from the palace, they could see two airships on dock. One, flying the Crown's colors, had been stationed in Westundon since the incident with the Cloud Wolf. The other was Oliver's.

"What in the frozen hell is he up to?" barked Prince Philip.

"I was wondering the same, m'lord," replied Raffles.

They stood there for a long moment, their breath billowing in the chill air until the prince hugged himself tight and turned from the airships. "He'll be by soon enough. He wouldn't come back to Westundon without seeing me."

"Will you send the marines after him, m'lord?" wondered the director.

"Why?" asked Philip as they strode back inside, a quizzical look on his face.

"Well, he opened fire with cannon on a friendly airship, m'lord," Raffles answered. "He-he fired cannon within the city limits. There's no telling how many people could have been killed if that airship had been occupied. It'd be murder, m'lord... I don't want to... I'm not saying..."

"No one was on the other airship, Randolph," reminded Prince Philip. "No one was killed or even hurt, so I caution you about using the word murder when it pertains to the actions of a royal. I don't know why Oliver did what he did, but he deserves the benefit of the doubt. He'll have a chance to explain himself, and if it seems a crime was committed, well, we shall deal with it then. As it stands, all we know is he destroyed Company property. A serious concern but one I'm sure we both understand he has ample resources to make restitution for. If it turns out he cannot explain his actions, Randolph, I'll ensure he pays for a new airship or hands over the one he has docked out there. It's a twin to the one that was destroyed?"

"It... Ah, yes, m'lord," mumbled Raffles.

"I know you are as concerned about him as I, Director," continued the prince, "but we must be careful about how we speak of the matter. Oliver, though he rarely acknowledges it, is a royal. How you handle your commercial affairs with him is up to you and the Company, but when it comes to the business of the Crown, I will treat him with the respect he is due. If you and he cannot work out this commercial issue, perhaps I will intercede, but do not overstep your role and begin to think Company matters and Crown matters are the same, particularly when a man of the royal line is involved."

"Understood, m'lord," said Raffles, offering a shallow bow, seething inside.

If Bishop Yates and his Knives did not arrive soon, Raffles decided he would not wait. He would kill Oliver Wellesley himself, and then the prince. The ritual was nigh, and his time of groveling for the Wellesleys was at an end.

"Go on now," suggested Philip. "I have much to do. When Oliver stops in, I will send a runner to Company House. If he appears there first, do the same courtesy, will you?"

"Of course, m'lord."

THE CARTOGRAPHER XIX

THE DOOR OPENED BEHIND HIM, and he glanced back to see Sam returning.

"Anything?" she asked.

"Yes, I think so," he answered.

She set down the heavy pitcher she was carrying and two mugs, quickly filling them both with ale.

"You have lip paint on your neck," he mentioned.

Scowling, she rubbed at her neck and then checked her fingers. "There's nothing… Spirits forsake it."

"No one goes for a full turn of the clock to buy a pitcher of ale," he commented. "I know you well enough by now. You wouldn't wait in a line that long."

"I needed to…" she trailed off, gave up explaining herself, and instead asked, "What did you find?"

Sipping his ale, he nodded out the window where they could see the ornate facade of Company House.

"It was definitely in there," he said. "The furcula held steady, pointing right at it, but half a turn ago, it started to move. A man I've worked with before, Quimby, departed and the furcula followed after him."

"We should—" began Sam, but she stopped at Oliver's raised

hand.

"A moment later, Director Randolph Raffles appeared and leapt into a mechanical carriage," he continued. "I'd bet my estate he was headed toward the palace."

"That makes some sense," replied Sam. "We did destroy his airship after all. By now, he's likely received a report that you returned. Anyone in the city paying attention is going to see the Cloud Serpent docked at the bridge."

Oliver nodded. "Quimby is a minor factor with the Company and an even more minor peer. He's never done well with the Company, always finding some way to stumble into trouble. He hasn't been able to expand on the land holding his parents bought some years back, and it's not substantial enough he can rest his heels and take his leisure as a country gentleman. His would be a falling house if it had ever achieved a height to fall from. I don't care what the furcula is telling us, I cannot fathom that man is the sorcerer we seek. He's too young, for one, and someone with that sort of power would surely not debase themselves trading with disgruntled shepherds for their spring wool. He's not the one. He was, though, carrying a large box beneath his arm. A Company factor carrying a package, it appeared rather unusual to me. Could the taint be on something inside of a box?"

"It could be," confirmed Sam. "I don't know exactly how this wish— this furcula works, but it's feasible the taint of the underworld could be transferred to someone or something. Are you thinking... You're thinking Raffles, aren't you?"

"Maybe," replied Oliver. "I've known the man for years and I wouldn't have thought he'd be capable. I've been thinking about it since I saw him, though. What makes more sense, a sorcerer toiling in obscurity handling entry-level work on behalf of the Company, or a sorcerer with a senior position, living in luxury?"

Sam grunted.

"The director is old enough," mused Oliver, continuing between sips of his ale. "He was a factor on the Company airships that supplied my uncle's war against the Coldlands, so we know he had some involvement with the place. He's not a peer, but his rise within the Company has been meteoric. Just a few short years ago, he was given a seat at the director's table and named the representative in Westundon. Through my own nomination, he was granted the position of finance director. In short time, he'll become one of the wealthiest men in Enhover."

"The power we seek is not concerned with commercial rewards," argued Sam.

"I don't care how powerful you are. You always want more sterling," challenged Oliver. "Believe me. For a man like him, whether or not he's a sorcerer, it's not about what he can purchase with that hoard of silver, it's a way of keeping score. It's how he knows he's better than everyone else. You can't tell me sorcerers have no interest in that, can you?"

Frowning, Sam looked out the window of the boarding house they'd secured a room in and peered at the frescos lining the top third of Company House.

"The furcula led us here," said Oliver. "I don't know of anyone else in that building who would be a more likely suspect than Randolph Raffles. I've spent countless turns of the clock talking with the man, and I never detected a hint of evil, but he meets all of the criteria. I think we have to investigate him further."

"You're right. He meets the criteria, and he's worth our investigation," agreed the priestess. "I worry we're being tricked into believing it is him, though."

"A trick?" questioned Oliver.

"We have to consider the possibility that the old man in the woods lied to us," replied Sam.

Oliver nodded, frowning. "We can follow the furcula's lead later, whether it leads to Quimby or another. I think for now we should stick with Raffles. Maybe the old man lied. Maybe he didn't. The director is as likely as anyone else we could investigate. I've been inside his office on several occasions and I've never noticed anything that hints of a sorcerous lair. His home is quite large, though, and there is ample space to hide whatever activities a sorcerer engages in."

"Breaking into a Company director's home. I like—" began Sam, grinning. Then, she stopped and blinked. "Duke, do you remember when we realized Isisandra Dalyrimple was a sorceress? We rushed to the palace to find her. We didn't catch her, but we were directed down to the carriage yard where those three footmen attacked us. Someone had placed those men there as a trap for us, in that specific spot."

"We were directed by Randolph Raffles," said Oliver, pounding a fist into his hand. "I never... I never made the connection. If he wanted to kill us, he had so many other opportunities. Why take a risk like that in the palace?"

"What if he didn't want to kill us?" wondered Sam. "He could have been delaying us instead, giving Isisandra time to escape. Duke, what if he knew we'd go after her, but it was Isisandra and Colston he hoped would fall in the encounter? It's brilliant when you think about it. We tracked them down and killed them, ensuring they'd tell no one about what they knew. If we hadn't found the Book of Law, if you hadn't infiltrated the Feet of Seheht's meeting because of it, the trail may have ended in Derbycross. What else would we have investigated after Isisandra died? Frozen hell, Duke, he's been playing us this entire time."

Grimacing, Oliver nodded. "You could be right. It's not enough to convict the man, but the coincidences are piling up. Somehow, he's involved in all of this. We've got to find out how."

"Director Raffles could have been the man who sacrificed Northundon," said Sam. "This is not a tribunal, Duke. We don't need to convict him in front of a magistrate. I agree we should investigate further to be sure, but let's keep in mind—"

"Raffles was a young man twenty years ago," interrupted Oliver, shaking his head. "Could he have done such an incredible feat of sorcery alone? And, Sam, if he could, why hasn't he risen further than he already has? If the man is capable of something like that, what else could he accomplish? I think he could very well be involved, but I don't think he could have done it alone. We need to learn more before we... before we do what you're wanting to do."

It was Sam's turn to frown, and she glanced back out at Company House. "The furcula..."

"Quimby isn't our target," insisted Oliver. "He's younger than I am. He couldn't have been more than ten winters when Northundon fell. If someone in that building is our target, it makes sense it would be Director Raffles. I've known the man most of my life, and I don't want to believe it, but it does fit. My question, do you think he could have done it alone?"

"I don't know," she said, still staring outside at the building. "Maybe not. The old man speculated there could be a cabal. That could be the truth. It makes sense. We should search the director's house, see what we can find there."

"Raffles knows we're here in Westundon," responded Oliver. "Whoever our opponent is, they sent wolfmalkin and shades after us, but only because they knew where we were. I think we slipped them when we landed and snuck in with the cargo. So what does Raffles do, knowing we are in Westundon but he cannot find us? He might confer with a compatriot or panic and tip his hand another way. Let's follow him, track his movements, see who he talks to, see what he does that is out of the ordinary. If Raffles is the sorcerer, we'll learn it from his actions. If not, then we'll think about breaking into his home."

"If he's the sorcerer and we act too late..." warned Sam.

"If he's not and we kill him, we'll have no way of knowing until it's too late," challenged Oliver.

Sam crossed her arms, evidently uninterested in arguing the last point.

"If he went to the palace, I can't track him in there. It's well-patrolled, and everyone would recognize me," said Oliver. "We can pick him up outside the south carriage court, though. Hopefully, if he's meeting with a fellow conspirator, it isn't in the palace."

"Everywhere we go people will know you," suggested Sam. She reached out and touched his hair. "I have an idea."

HE SNEEZED, THE MOTION CAUSING THE WIG ON HIS HEAD TO EXPLODE with another cloud of the awful powder that had made him sneeze in the first place. Eyes closed, mouth shut, nose pinched, he waited for the powder to dissipate in the gentle breeze.

Cold, annoyed at the foppish headwear, and uncomfortable on the hard wooden bench, he shifted, regretting the disguise and worrying they'd already missed Director Raffles. It'd been close to four hours since he'd spotted the man leaving Company House, and they had no assurance he was even inside the palace, though Sam had reported seeing one of the Company's mechanical carriages idling in the courtyard.

Oliver sighed.

Sitting atop an illegally commandeered carriage, a curled and powdered wig atop his head, rogue reddening his cheeks as if the cold wouldn't have done that soon enough, and a black suit of driver's guild livery. He couldn't decide if he was more worried he'd be found and arrested for carriage theft, or recognized and laughed out of Westundon by a gang of snickering peers.

But it was an effective disguise, he had to admit, as passersby streamed around his carriage in a constant flow. Parked a block outside of the palace, near the ballet, and two blocks from Congress House, his was one of many of the contraptions awaiting their cargo. No one looked at carriage drivers, and no one would expect Duke Oliver Wellesley to be so attired. And the moment Raffles' carriage rolled past him, he'd be in position to follow it with the means to do so.

Suddenly, Sam appeared on the walk beside the avenue.

"Someone's getting in the carriage," she said. "It could be him. They're wigged and portly."

"Could be him," agreed Oliver.

Sam, in the guise of a homemaker, wrapped her shawl more tightly around her shoulders and hissed, "It's freezing out here."

He stared down at her, looking at the warm, wool wrap she was clutching.

The foot traffic around them ebbed, and Sam slipped inside the carriage.

Oliver waited, watching the entrance to the palace's carriage court. He lowered his head as a black Company rig crunched over the gravel of the court and then rumbled down the cobblestone street. With a kick to the brakes and a tug on the gear lever, their carriage lurched into motion. Manipulating the steering T and the gear lever, Oliver ungracefully maneuvered the carriage into the throng of traffic.

Ahead of them, the Company carriage bounced along the predictable path that Oliver himself had taken hundreds of times between the palace and Company House. He let his vehicle fall back, allowing four more of the popping and creaking contraptions to move in between himself and what he hoped was Raffles.

Oliver was so focused on not crashing into the vehicle in front of him, he missed the Company carriage turning. It wasn't until he was passing the quieter street their quarry turned onto that he saw his error. Cursing, he stood and peered in the direction the Company vehicle had gone before it vanished around the corner of a building.

Frand Street.

He sat down, smiling. Frand Street. He knew where the director was going. The Oak & Ivy sat on Frand Street, and after four hours in the palace, it was exactly where Raffles would go.

Oliver shifted gears, twisted the steering T, and ignored the shouted complaints that followed him as he cut across traffic and took the next turn. He drove the puttering vehicle four more blocks and then stopped it, throwing on the brakes and wincing at the squeal of metal on metal as the momentum of the carriage was painfully arrested by pads pressing against the axles.

The door to the passenger compartment slammed open, and

Sam leaned out. "Frozen hell, he turned down that other street. You lost him!"

Oliver hopped down from the driver's bench and shook his head. "He's going to his club. I'm sure of it. I took this route so he'd have no chance of seeing us."

"Did you?" asked Sam suspiciously.

She stepped out of the carriage onto the stone street, still with the shawl wrapped around her shoulders, but underneath, he could see she'd changed into her leather trousers and vest. Her daggers stuck out oddly beneath the wool of the shawl, but it was possible someone might see them and not know what they were. It'd taken all of his persuasion to convince her that on the reconnaissance mission, she had to leave Thotham's spear behind.

She tossed him his sword belt, and he quickly buckled it on. He reached up to tug his wig off, but she caught his wrist.

"You're too well known, Duke," she hissed. "Keep it on."

Frowning, he pointedly eyed her changed attire. She winked and offered him a saucy roll of her hips, then started off in the wrong direction.

"This way," he whispered, pointing toward an alley between the buildings.

"You've tried that..." she began but trailed off and hurried after him as he walked into the shadowed passageway.

"It's not always a trick," he said, stepping cautiously over debris littering the narrow alley.

Sam followed close behind. When they reached the end of the alley, he leaned out to peer down Frand Street. She caught the collar of his driver's suit and yanked him back into the alley.

"What was— Oh," he said, watching another carriage roll by in front of them.

"There's only one churchman in Westundon who rates a mechanical carriage," said Sam, her gaze fixed on the brilliant golden circle emblem embossed on the door of the lacquered black vehicle.

Cautiously, they peeked back down the street and saw the

carriage stop in front of a gray, granite building. Above a set of stairs and a pair of impressive mahogany doors hung a bronze oak tree wreathed in ivy.

"Is Bishop Yates a member of the Oak & Ivy?" wondered Oliver. "It seems a rather extravagant expense for a churchman, and I've never seen him inside of the place."

"He likes his sherry, but I can't imagine the common parishioners or other priests would appreciate him being a regular member," said Sam. "Perhaps he's a guest?"

"You don't think…" mumbled Oliver, reaching up to touch his hair, then jerking his hand away when he felt the wig instead.

"I don't… Wait, you think he's meeting Raffles?"

Oliver shrugged. "I've seen them together before. They were both in Philip's study when I was assigned to investigate the Dalyrimple murder in Harwick. They both had legitimate reasons to be there, but…"

"But the coincidences are piling up," finished Sam.

"They are, aren't they," muttered Oliver, looking back to catch a glimpse of a rotund man in priest's robes waddling up the stairs to the club and disappearing inside. "They're arriving at the same club within minutes of each other shortly after we reappeared in Westundon. We don't have much on Raffles other than suspicion, and until this moment, we didn't even have that of the bishop. They both fit the profile, though, powerful men who are old enough to have been involved twenty years ago. Neither one came from the peerage, but they've somehow risen to impressive heights. They know each other and have been known to act together."

"It's enough," declared Sam, clenching her fist. "What other reason would Raffles have to meet with Yates right now unless they're both involved?"

Oliver shook his head. "It's not enough. There are a thousand innocent explanations why these men might be together and only one sinister one. We have to learn more."

Sam remained silent. He could tell she didn't agree. Suspicion alone was enough for her, but it wasn't for him. They had to know before they did anything rash.

"I don't imagine we'll have much luck sneaking into the Oak & Ivy and getting close enough to eavesdrop on the two of them, assuming they're even sitting together," said Oliver. "When they leave, they're almost certain to take different directions. Raffles may go to Company House or his townhome. I imagine the bishop will go to the Church. At any of those destinations, we're going to have a hell of a time sneaking in and spying on them. You have any thoughts?"

"What if we don't sneak?" asked Sam.

"Sam," chided Oliver. "I mean it when I say we need more information. We won't move against either of these men until we're sure they're guilty of something. That's an order."

She rolled her eyes but clarified, "I mean, what if you walk in and surprise them? Look them in the eyes, accuse them, and see how they react. Sorcery requires preparation and secrecy, so there's little they can do to you if ambush them in a public space. We'll have to scramble to get away without them following you, and it's quite possible they could scry for us, but they could do that anyway if they had the right materials and were willing to risk it. If they are the culprits, you'll see evidence of it in their faces. No one is that good of an actor."

Oliver frowned.

"I'll go with you," offered Sam. "If there's nothing you see, perhaps I can sense something."

Oliver glanced back at the Oak & Ivy, noticing that the Company and Church carriages were still there, idling. "Why does it seem we always jump into these things solely because of lack of a better plan?"

"Let's get you cleaned up," said Sam, snatching the ridiculous powdered wig off his head. "For this to work, they have to know it's you."

WIG GONE, ROGUE WIPED OFF, MOST OF THE POWDER BRUSHED AWAY, he still felt out of sorts in the ill-fitting driver's suit, but it was better than what it had been. He had his sword at his hip and Sam at his side, and that gave him some measure of confidence. Oliver strode up the stairs to the towering mahogany double doors of the Oak & Ivy. They didn't open. He frowned, knowing there was an attendant on the other side.

"They don't know who you are," whispered Sam. "It's the clothes."

Oliver slammed a fist against the door, smashing the heavy wood, hoping to hear it rattle in the frame, but his battering landed quietly on the thick, wooden surface. It was enough, though, to draw the attention of the attendant.

A neatly groomed man in the crimson vest of the Oak & Ivy staff swung open the portal and whined, "This is a private club. No public entry is allowed."

"I'm here as a guest of Randolph Raffles," asserted Oliver.

"Our membership is private as well," snapped the officious attendant, "but I can assure you, no one of that name left instructions for another guest to be allowed in."

"Yates has arrived already, then?" asked Oliver, watching the attendant's eyes widen in surprise. "That is wonderful. Pease run and tell them that Duke Oliver Wellesley is here and ready for their audience. I hope you don't mind bringing them out so we can speak here on the stairs? I'm loath to violate the sanctity of your private club."

"I, ah, I... M'lord, I didn't... Your jacket..."

Oliver smiled and brushed the black driver's guild coat, cringing as a small puff of wig powder billowed up. "I'm afraid it is only sometimes that my fashion choices result in the season's hottest trend. Do you think this outfit is better left in my closet?"

"No, m'lord, I would never presume to—"

"Go fetch Raffles and Yates, will you?" requested Oliver. "And, if it's not too much of a bother, may I wait in the foyer?"

"No, of course, m'lord. Come inside," babbled the attendant. "I did not recognize you. Come in. Come in."

Oliver strode into the grand entryway, trying to walk like he owned it, and then spun to the attendant.

"Wait, ah…" stammered the thin-faced man, glancing around nervously for support.

"You're intent on seeing me wait, eh?" asked Oliver. "Another protester of the king's taxes? Is my family too much of a burden on the gentlemen of this club?"

The man flushed, his face matching the red of his vest. He began insisting that they follow him, and in his rush to avoid offense with the duke, he didn't ask about Sam or mention that the two of them were heavily armed. Oliver suspected that was also a rather large violation of club policy.

The sweating attendant led them unerringly to the club's smoking room. It was filled with luxuriously stuffed red leather chairs that matched the shade of the attendant's vests. Comfortable booths were spaced along the walls for quiet conversation, and a vast array of clear crystal bottles of liquor were displayed behind a polished brass bar. The room was only a quarter full, and Oliver saw Raffles and Yates before the two men saw him. They were situated at the far side of the room, facing the entrance. Leaning close together, locked in a heated discussion, they were oblivious to the rest of the room.

Oliver smiled to himself, thinking their suspicions might be right, until he remembered what that meant. If Sam's and his instincts were right, these two men were exceptionally powerful sorcerers who'd sacrificed every man, woman, and child in Northundon. When considered in those terms, there was no joy at unmasking them, but it did steel his resolve. He was striding quickly toward the men when suddenly Raffles saw him from the corner of his eye and jerked back, his hand clutching Bishop Yates' wrist. The bishop's jaw fell open, all three of his chins wobbling as they landed on his chest.

"O-Oliver…" spluttered Raffles.

"I heard you were looking for me?" inquired Oliver.

"I-I was," acknowledged the director. "Surely, ah, we have to discuss what happened when... when you left. I admit I don't know all of the facts, but, Oliver, it appeared on the ground that the Cloud Serpent fired upon the Cloud Wolf as you departed. Is that... is that the case?"

Oliver frowned, his hand inadvertently rubbing over his hair, touching the knot at the back.

"I just spoke to Philip, and he requested we work this out amongst ourselves," continued Raffles. "You are aware as I am of the commercial impact of something like this. Tell me, Oliver, why did you do it?"

"You know why," snapped Oliver.

"I'm afraid, my boy, that I do not," declared Raffles, the trembling in his arms slowing, the tone of his voice dropping into his normal octave.

He was recovering from the initial shock of seeing Oliver and falling into his regular, patronizing pattern of communication. Seeing it now, Oliver realized that for years, the old man had been manipulating him, acting as a friendly uncle while he was anything but. The act was so practiced and polished that even suspecting him of one of the most heinous acts in history, Oliver felt a worm of doubt crawl across his mind.

"Shades, Raffles," hissed Oliver, his voice lowered to below the thrum of conversation in the room. "Shades called by you. We were peppering them with blessed scattershot. Can you tell me if we got them all?"

"Shades?" wondered Raffles, glancing at Yates. "I've never heard of such a thing. Perhaps the bishop can comment? Gabriel, isn't sorcery dead in Enhover?"

"We'd assumed so," said Yates, his demeanor calm now as well. "Of course, there was the Dalyrimple affair. Terrible business, that. You say you saw shadows on the airship, Oliver? I'm afraid there were no other reports. Can you describe these shadows? I assure you the Church will look into it, but unfortunately, a bit of darkness seen at a distance on a foggy night is not much to go on."

"Will you look into the wolfmalkin you sent against us in the apothecary as well?" demanded Sam, taking Oliver's side and glaring at the two seated men.

"Wolf… what?" asked Yates. "I'm not familiar with those, my girl. When did you come back from Ivalla? I was told you would be stationed there under Bishop Constance. She's more of an expert on these matters than I. Perhaps you should go see her about your inquires?"

Oliver's fists clenched. The two men were practiced liars, whether or not they were sorcerers. Without the element of surprise, they weren't going to give anything away. He had to shock them.

"Do you know how we found you here? We followed the taint of the dark trinity right to you."

Both men jumped at that.

"You're wondering where I was," he continued, leaning close. "I was in Northundon, visiting my mother's garden. I know about the sacrifice that took place there. We went to the Coldlands, too, and we spoke to one of their surviving elders. We know you sacrificed Northundon in a failed attempt to bind the dark trinity. We even know why you failed, the missing piece. We know it all, gentlemen."

He stared down at the seated men, satisfied at the stunned faces looking back at him.

"What, you thought killing a few people in the Feet of Seheht and Mouth of Set would cover your tracks?" questioned Sam. "You were too late, and you didn't get them all. We'd already infiltrated your meetings. The survivors have been talking to us, telling us everything. They even gave us a copy of the Book of Law. I've been reading your grimoire. I know what you know." She traced a quick symbol in the air in front of the men.

Oliver felt an uncomfortable thrumming in his arms.

Director Raffles' eyes bulged.

Oliver decided he'd seen what he needed to. The director and the bishop weren't just stunned. They recognized the terminology he and Sam were using. They recognized the symbol she'd made. These men knew sorcery. They were the ones behind everything. He knew it, and he could see in their expressions that they realized the masks were off. The four of them all had their cards on the table, and now, it was time to play the game.

"We'll be seeing you around," said Oliver. He turned, trying to ignore the creeping, cold sensation crawling along his spine.

"Yes, boy, we will be," called Raffles, speaking to Oliver's back. "I'm looking forward to it."

Oliver strode to the exit, Sam beside him.

When they made it through the doorway, she let out an explosive breath. "I was nervous they were going to do something, even in such a public place."

"They didn't," said Oliver, stomping down the stairwell, not pausing to speak to any of the attendants, not taking a chance that the two men would come racing after them. "They will, though, the moment they can find privacy. There is no more hiding, for us or for them. Let's get in position and see what they do next. Maybe in their panic, we'll have our opportunity."

"They'll protect themselves now," warned Sam. "They might flee. Let's not give them the chance."

Oliver shook his head. "These are men who slaughtered tens of thousands in the pursuit of power. Their souls are steeped in murder. They'll be strong, Sam, capable of far more than Isisandra was able to throw at us. They won't hide, and they won't avoid the fight. They want it just as much as you do. Did you see Raffles right when we turned? He's done hiding. They'll open a way for us to come at them. We just have to figure out how to do it without walking into a trap."

Sam grunted, and he nodded. These men were everything he'd said and maybe more. The sorcerers would be stronger than he and Sam. The two of them had to be smarter.

THE DIRECTOR V

"WELL, that was rather stupid of them," breathed Director Raffles. "We are sitting here trying to figure out how to hunt them down, and they walk right in the door."

"And right back out of it," muttered Yates. "They know about us, Randolph. They know everything!"

The director rubbed his chin. "I am not so sure."

Yates raised an eyebrow. "Did you hear something I did not?"

"They claimed they knew we were here because of…" Raffles leaned in close, "because of the taint from the dark trinity. You and I both know there is no taint on us. We've taken every precaution. But this morning, I shipped the dagger to William."

"They followed the dagger," said Yates, blinking rapidly.

"I don't know how, but they must have figured out a way to do it," said Raffles, striking a match and relighting his pipe.

"Shouldn't we be leaving?" worried the bishop.

"I don't think that will be necessary," replied the director. "For one, I can only assume the pair of them will be lurking outside waiting for us. And two, if they had additional resources, they would have already brought them. There is no squadron of royal marines coming to arrest us, Bishop. The Knives of the Council are working for us, not them. They cannot get help from the Church."

"They didn't have a squadron of royal marines, yet," argued Yates. "Oliver could be running to his brother at this moment to get assistance."

"He won't do that," said Raffles. "Think about it, man. If he had any proof we are what he accuses us of being, he would have come with an army of marines at his back in the first place. He has no proof. They were just testing their suspicions. What would he do, haul us in front of a magistrate? With what evidence? Do you think his family would take his side after he fired upon the Cloud Wolf, aiming at shadows no one else saw? If he goes to his brother or father and tells them we are sorcerers, it will only make him seem crazy. Think of the scandal."

The director sat back and drew on his pipe, his mind working furiously.

"Testing their suspicions..." muttered Yates. "I'm afraid we may have failed, my friend."

"I believe you are right about that," acknowledged Raffles. "I was stunned, and that may have been enough for them to confirm their wild guesses. Us stammering a response to such an accusation, though, is not enough for Philip. The prince would want to see hard proof, something indisputable that ties us to the dark path. I'm confident there is nothing in my residence that would incriminate me. And despite what the girl said, I've personally accounted for everyone within the Feet of Seheht who might suspect who Redmask really is. I killed the last pair of them yesterday."

"I cleansed my haunts as well," said Yates, picking up his sherry and taking a long, steadying sip. "If there are any clues remaining, I overlooked them. I cannot imagine anyone else would be able to piece together what they might be." Yates laughed, his mood visibly lightening. "I just returned from meeting with the Council of Seven in Romalla. I brought two

Knives with me to Enhover on an airship that I chartered. If I were innocent, I couldn't be doing more to hunt down sorcery."

Grinning, Raffles nodded. "There's nothing that leads to us, nothing that should spoil our plans, except… the tainted dagger, and that is out of our hands now."

Bishop Yates frowned. "We must get word to William."

"We must," agreed Raffles. "More immediate, though, we have to decide what to do about Oliver and the priestess. They may not be able to prove to Philip that we are what we are, but coming here, accusing us, they couldn't be clearer about their intentions. The girl is a Knife. She's trained to assassinate men like us."

"She is," said Yates. "Just like the two Knives I brought with me. She and Oliver admitted to traveling to Northundon and the Coldlands. They told us they spoke to a shaman there in the frozen forest. I daresay the first thing I should do is inform Raymond au Clair and Bridget Cancio of this terrible turn of events. I'm certain they'll be eager to hear."

"Let the Church do her job," said Raffles, puffing on his pipe, trying to keep a smile off his face.

"The Knives are capable sorts, but let us not underestimate Oliver and the girl again," warned Yates. "They figured us out, somehow, and they survived the encounter below Derbycross. They avoided our trap on the Cloud Wolf, and if what they said is true, they somehow survived the legion of shades that still haunts Northundon. Between them and the Knives, it could go either way."

Raffles nodded. "Perhaps it is safer to assume the Knives will only buy us some time, and then it will be on us to finish the task."

Yates finished his sherry and waved impatiently at the attendant for more. "I do dislike getting my hands dirty, but I suppose exceptions must be made. No one ever said it was an easy path, did they?"

When the attendant deposited a fresh round of drinks, Yates

requested a message be sent to his secretary, and Raffles informed the crimson-vested man that they'd be expecting two more guests in the next hour. Then, they settled back to wait.

THE CARTOGRAPHER XX

STEAM BILLOWED as he poured another cup of water on the hot stones suspended above the tiny, iron stove. Sweat poured down his face, dripping from his nose and chin. His shoulders and chest where slick with it, and the towel wrapped around his waist was going to be sodden if he sat in the moisture-filled sauna much longer, but he didn't want to go out. He didn't want to exit and face what they would have to face.

The day before, crouched in hiding outside of the Oak & Ivy, Sam had tensed beside him. She'd uttered a string of the vilest curses he'd ever heard pass her lips or any others. Two people that she recognized as Knives of the Council had entered. It took no great leap in intuition to guess they'd been called there by Yates. They could only assume the two Knives had been directed to hunt down and kill them.

They'd planned to lurk outside of the club and look for an opportunity to ambush Raffles and Yates, but after seeing the Knives go inside, they'd decided to retreat, to regroup and plan. They had discussed running to Philip, requesting the assistance of the Crown, but that would only alert Raffles and Yates to their location. There was little Philip could do about sorcery, and Oliver thought it possible his brother might not believe them. At the least, he'd want proof, and they didn't have the sort that a magistrate would accept.

Sam had surmised that if the sorcerers were going to scry for them, they already would have. It was possible the men didn't have the necessary materials, and she speculated they might also be worried her training included defense against scrying, so they had time, but the difficulty was, the longer they waited, it gave their enemies more time as well.

Their enemies, the two men who might be the only ones in the world who knew what had happened to his mother. He knew she wasn't dead, but there were no clues to her location. He'd considered requesting Sam scry for her, but what if they were wrong and she was dead? What if she was captive to some sorcerer who could ensnare them? If she were captive, it would explain why she'd never contacted his father or brothers, and it made scrying for her incredibly risky. No matter how badly he wanted to know, he couldn't gamble that. There had to be another way they could pry the information out of Raffles and Yates before… before they had to end things.

Another drop of sweat dripped off his chin, falling silently on his chest. His hair, unbound, hung around his face, damp with the moisture boiling off the heated rocks. The leather thong, the one he wore to remember his mother by, was in his hands, his fingers working tirelessly, moving the thin leather in a circle. It was worn smooth from his countless fiddling, and he knew there'd be a day when the thong broke. He wouldn't retie it when it happened. When the strip of leather snapped in two, it would be over, he told himself. Before then, he promised he would know what happened to her.

Sighing, he stood, tugging the towel tight and trudging out of the steam room at the bath house adjacent to the Four Sheets Inn. He would plunge into one of the pools there, confident that no one at the darkly lit, irreputable bath house traveled in any of the same circles he did, then return to the Four Sheets, to the attic room occupied by Sam's friend. Friend, Sam had said, though the other woman didn't seem to see it that way.

As he cleaned himself and dressed, Oliver's thoughts bounced between how to find his mother and how to kill the men responsible for her disappearance. He would have killed the two men for that alone, but images of Northundon's destruction, the tens of thousands of shades that had dogged their steps inside those ruins... Raffles and Yates had to die. If he could learn a clue to his mother's disappearance, he would take it, but no matter what, those two men had to face justice for their crimes.

Afterward... No, there was no afterward. Not yet.

THE PRIESTESS XVIII

SHE GRIPPED the other woman's hair, clutching the silken, black locks like they were a rope thrown over the side of an airship. Mouth open, she felt Kalbeth's soft lips on hers, the other woman's tongue questing, tangling.

Kalbeth rolled her over, hovering above her. She grabbed Sam's arm from behind her head, loosening the priestess' grip on her hair, and pushed it down on the bed. She caught Sam's other arm and held it down as well.

Sam, stronger, only resisted lightly, letting Kalbeth put her moist lips first on her neck, her shoulders, and then farther down. Sam stared at the exposed rafters above her, orange light dancing on them from the lone candle in the room. She writhed while Kalbeth continued the journey south. Her mind was churning, unfocused, frantic, until Kalbeth got where she was going, and all other thoughts fled. Sam's thighs closed around Kalbeth's head, and she reached down and gripped her friend's silky hair again.

A fleeting awareness, the knowledge of what was coming, that death was coming, was furiously pushed away. Death was coming, yes, but now, she needed to live. She needed to live within the full current of life, to flow on the stream of light that Kalbeth offered, that others had offered before. She needed it. She needed life so that soon, when she was steeped in death, she could turn back from the dark path. She could come back to life as long as she maintained her grip upon it.

Her mentor had taught her that, demanded that. She had to stay within the current of life. She squirmed, her back arching. She was in the current. She had to stay in the current, or else there was only the dark path.

HALF AN HOUR LATER, SHE WAS LYING NAKED IN THE BED. KALBETH was in the other room rustling about, hopefully fetching some wine. Sam's eyes were open, still staring at the flicking shadows and light that danced along the rafters above.

"After that, I'm going to have to find the bathhouse you sent Duke to," she said, calling out to the room.

Kalbeth did not respond.

Sam let her head fall to the side to see what her friend was doing. She was standing beside her small cupboard in her living room, making tea. Unfortunate.

"Why do you do it?" asked Kalbeth, turning to face her. Her pale skin gleamed in the low light, the dark tattoos that swirled on her skin crawling with the dance of the candlelight.

Sam sat up. "Do you have any wine?"

"I do," replied Kalbeth.

When the girl turned back to the cupboard, Sam answered, "I do it because no one else can. Northundon, Kalbeth, if you'd seen it! They sacrificed the entire city for what? Power? If I were to sit by idly while that happened, I would be no better than they. I did not ask for it, but Thotham gave me the ability to act. It's all I have from him or from anyone else. It is who I am. These are evil men, Kalbeth, and if I spend every breath for the rest of my life opposing them, then my life would be well spent."

"I did not mean that," said the girl, turning with one cup

trailing steam and one sloshing with wine. "I meant, why do you do it with me?"

Sam blinked at her. "I-I prefer—"

"Why me, Sam?" insisted Kalbeth, stopping at the edge of the bed and handing her the wine. "For two-thirds of my existence, we've been flitting in and out of each other's lives. I help you with what you need, and then you are off. We are sometimes lovers, friends maybe, but why me?"

Sam offered the woman a sly smile and a wink. "Because you're beautiful, Kalbeth."

Kalbeth snorted. "I met you over twenty-five years ago, Sam. Before Thotham, before Northundon, before your duke. We were girls, awkward, gangly girls. Skin and bone, not a sliver of meat on either of us. You did not pursue me because I was beautiful, and I will not ask if you love me. I know that you do not, but do you even care for me? If I were not here the next time you drop in unannounced, would it be more than an inconvenience?"

"Of course, I—"

The door rattled as someone tried to open it. Then, there were three sharp raps.

"That's Duke," said Sam. "Anyone else would knock first."

Without a word, Kalbeth turned and walked to the door. When she opened it, Duke stood in the doorway, a key in his hand and a frown on his face. He saw Kalbeth and his jaw dropped to his chest.

"Come in," offered Kalbeth. "How was the bathhouse?"

"It was…" he mumbled, unable to take his eyes off of her. "The what?"

Kalbeth walked back into the room, and Duke followed before cursing and turning back to close the door behind him. Shaking his head and muttering under his breath, he came to the bedroom door and jumped again, seeing Sam naked on the bed.

"Ah…" he said, reaching up and checking the knot at the back of his hair. "I'm back."

"I can see that," responded Sam. She slipped out of bed and

brushed by him in the doorway, looking for where she'd torn off her clothes two hours earlier. "Don't get excited, Duke. It's not for you."

She could feel his eyes on her and she took her time bending over to collect her trousers, which had somehow gotten thrown underneath Kalbeth's tiny table. Knowing Duke was watching, she wiggled her bare bottom. Living in the full current of life as it were. She had to stay in that current if they were to succeed at what was next, though, she had to admit, teasing the poor man had nothing to do with that. She just enjoyed making his head spin.

Sliding her legs into the tight leather trousers, Sam turned and saw Kalbeth, still naked, stand on her tiptoes and peck Duke on the check. The tattooed beauty let her lips linger, her nipples brushing against the peer's shirt before she stepped away.

Kalbeth told him, "Sam infuriates me, too, Duke. Maybe we'll have to talk privately about that, sometime."

Sam waited for the hot flash of jealousy she knew should come. She watched Kalbeth's eyes turn to her, knowing the other woman was looking for it as well.

"You know my name is not Duke, right?" asked Duke.

Kalbeth shrugged, her eyes still on Sam. "You two should talk. I will get dressed."

"Get us more wine when you're decent?" Sam called to Kalbeth, peering at the cupboard. "You're almost out."

"SOUTH, SOUTHEAST," SAID KALBETH, FIDDLING WITH THE FURCULA. "Southundon, you think?"

Sam nodded. "That's logical."

"I don't understand," said Duke. "If Raffles and Yates are the sorcerers, why is the device leading us south? Why is it not pointing directly to them?"

"There are three," guessed Kalbeth, "a trinity. It is the

strongest geometric structure and useful in sorcery. It stands to reason that whoever enacted the betrayal of Northundon used triangles in the formation in their ritual. You said the shaman in the Coldlands claimed the conspirators were attempting to bind the dark trinity, yes? Mirroring is powerful, and if these men knew what they were doing, they would attempt to use that as well in their pattern. If you think you've identified two of the conspirators, you should follow the tug of the device and find the third point of the triangle. It could be the taint follows control of the entity, or as you'd speculated, it might be associated with an object that man was carrying. It's not unusual for objects to acquire the aura of the underworld."

Sam took the furcula from her friend and felt the gentle tug. She moved it about, but it always led the same direction.

"There's a missing piece here," warned Kalbeth. "You told me this all started with Ca-Mi-He, that the other sorcerers you've confronted had contact with that spirit. If so, how is it that their superiors are associated with the dark trinity? Those entities oppose each other. Their animosity predates us and Enhover. No sorcerer who knows their craft would involve themselves with both of those spirits. It'd be too dangerous. I think it best you follow the furcula and find out who else is in the cabal, find the missing piece, understand their relationship to these spirits. You must know your foes before you move against them."

Duke shook his head. "No. The Knives of the Council are in the city, and we can only assume they're hunting us. Raffles and Yates are loose, and there's no telling what they are plotting. We cannot go to Southundon and delay. We've done too much of that already. Harwick, Archtan Atoll, Derbycross... every time we do not finish the job, more people die."

Kalbeth shook her head. "If you charge in blindly, it may be you who dies this time."

"It's just the three of us," said Sam, rubbing her chin.

"Two," responded Kalbeth. "There are two of you."

Sam stared at the other woman in surprise. "What do you..."

"Your fight is not my fight, though it could have been," remarked the woman, her fingers tracing the inked lines on her forearm. "You're opposed to what I am, and I see now that will not change. I will not stand in your way, not ever, but we are not in this together." The black-haired woman's hard stare spoke volumes. "I will not help you further except for this advice. If these sorcerers are in contact with the dark trinity, they will be far more powerful than you. Your only hope is surprising them."

"They know we'll come for them," reminded Duke. "Not much chance for a surprise."

Kalbeth nodded. "They will be waiting. You must do the unexpected. You must go where they think you are unwilling to go."

THE PRINCE II

"WHERE DO YOU THINK HE IS?" he asked his wife.

"I haven't the faintest, Philip," said Lucinda with a sigh. "Why don't you come to bed?"

"Soon," he murmured. "As soon as I finish these letters and ring the boy to run them down to the glae worm operator. I want these dispatches out tonight."

"Writing your father again?" wondered the princess. "He won't intercede between you and Oliver. He never has."

"You're right. He's always taken that scamp's side," complained Philip.

"That isn't true," chided Lucinda.

"It's true enough," argued Philip. "The old man has always given Oliver more leeway than the rest of us. Whether it's drunken escapades in Finavia or blasting cannon into a Company airship for no apparent reason, Father has always shrugged it off. The folly of youth, the old man would claim. Oliver is no youth! He's a grown man, thirty… thirty-four winters, I think. By his age, we were married, we had two children, and I was ruling Westundon. He's busy gallivanting about, getting drunk, seducing nubile peers, and then dashing off over the next horizon. He's no longer a boy, Lucinda, and it's time Father had that discussion with him."

"Did King Edward ever have that discussion with you?" asked his wife.

"He didn't need to," declared Philip.

"Write all you want," advised Lucinda, "but your father won't step between you and your brother. If you want to chastise Oliver, you'll need to do it yourself."

"I may," muttered the prince, turning back to the slips of parchment he'd been scrawling on.

"You said letters," mentioned Lucinda. "Your father and who else?"

"Admiral Brach and Uncle William," answered Philip, not looking up from his writing.

"Brach and William?" said Lucinda, sitting up. "Why are you writing your uncle and the admiral so late in the evening? Surely, it can wait until morning."

"You and I both know what my brother is up to," said Philip. "He thinks he's hunting sorcerers. Whatever reason he thought he had to open fire on the Cloud Wolf, whatever reason he came back to Westundon, it has to do with that."

"And…"

"And my brother is a flighty fool," said Philip, "more interested in seeing the bottom of a tankard or that of a pretty woman than reading to the bottom of correspondence from the Congress of Lords, but…"

"But he did find sorcerers that no one else believed were there," said Lucinda, finishing her husband's thoughts.

"He did," replied Philip, setting down his quill and turning to face his wife. "My brother thinks of his own ambition before the imperatives of the Crown, and that needs to change. If I could, I'd wrestle him down and force him into the administration to teach him some discipline. But as undisciplined and unprincipled as he is, he did Enhover a great service. I don't know what would have happened had the sorcerers been allowed to operate with impunity, but I know we're better off with them dead. My brother, my rakish, lothario of a brother, is the one who did it. Where were Brach's royal marines? Where were my uncle's inspectors? We employ these people for a reason, and they failed us. My father is not keen to press the matter, but I will. Admiral Brach and my uncle must answer for why their organizations failed."

"And you want assurances they are not failing again," guessed Lucinda.

"My father believes the threat is over. Bishop Yates claims that sorcery is again dead," said Philip. "They've said that before, though, haven't they? Brach and William both assured me that we had no worries during the Dalyrimple affair, but they were wrong. Now, I am guessing that my brother is racing in pursuit of what he thinks is another lead. What if, despite everything my intuition tells me, he is right, and they are all wrong again?"

"What would you have them do?" wondered Lucinda. "Oliver is in hiding, just as likely on the floor of some ale sink as in wait for a clue. If he knows something, he is not sharing his suspicions. The admiral and your uncle have no information to go on. Perhaps they should, but until you know what your brother does, what will you tell them? Nothing that will result in any firm action on their part, I assure you, my husband. You are the prince. You can harangue them, and they'll fall over themselves to appease you, but you cannot send them marching without telling them where to go. If there are sorcerers still active in Enhover, where is the evidence?"

Philip grunted. "When my brother surfaces, I will ask him. Until then, how is it that he has suspicions and our military and ministers do not? Despite my reservations about whatever it is he's up to, I cannot ignore the simple fact that last time, Oliver was right. And I agree. I do not have the evidence, but that is not my responsibility to the Crown, is it? That is why we have Brach and William. They should be pursuing this. They should have the evidence, and if they do not, I want to know why. Is it simple laziness, incompetence, or something else?"

"Something else?" asked his wife.

"Admiral Brach would like to see the royal marines rise in prominence," declared Philip. "He views their contribution to the empire as on par with, well, I suspect he views it as bounds ahead of any other organization. He's smart enough to understand his airships and swords are paid for by taxes on the Company's exploits, so he avoids angering them. He knows the Church's soft whispers fall on my father's deaf ears, so he doesn't bother with them. That leaves my uncle's ministry. Admiral Brach is trying to achieve equal footing for the military and the ministry. He and William have been squabbling about it for years now. My father seems uninterested. I worry it is on my shoulders to ensure those men's conflict doesn't rip Enhover apart. Take the Dalyrimple affair. Did the Crown miss a clue because Brach and William won't speak to each other? Does that explain why Oliver was able to ferret out leads that no one else suspected?"

"Do not be hard on yourself," pleaded Lucinda. "You couldn't have known. And besides, while Oliver prevented some amount of murder and chaos, Enhover was never truly under threat. Not by the Dalyrimples, not by anyone since the Coldlands, and we know how effectively your family dealt with that. The empire is strong, Philip. It is not falling apart, not tonight, at least. Come to bed, my love."

Standing and stretching his aching back, Philip looked at his wife. A true beauty, just as she had been over a decade before when he'd first seduced her. Or perhaps she had seduced him, he admitted. He smiled. Either way, she'd become his — his motivation and his reason. She was a good wife, a good mother, and she would make an excellent queen, but she was too trusting.

The empire was only as strong as the hands that held it together, and he was becoming worried those hands were not as sturdy as he'd once thought. Not tonight, she was right about that, but she was wrong that there was no threat to Enhover. There was. Not from outside but from within. If the organizations that supported Enhover could not be trusted, it would fall. His tutors had been too embarrassed to say it to the young prince, but it was one lesson his father had emphasized. All empires fall, they crumble from within.

Lucinda scooted over on the bed, welcoming him to join her, offering her comfort.

"Not tonight, my love, but I will come to bed," he told her. "You're right, there is nothing I can do that will make any difference this evening, but we must worry. We must always worry. All empires fall, my sweet. Decay is inevitable. Empires fall because they rot from within. Not tonight, but some day. Enhover will collapse in on itself. That is what keeps me awake."

"Some day, of course. But with you on the throne, Enhover will not fall," she assured him.

He smiled at her but did not reply.

THE CARTOGRAPHER XXI

HE SLOSHED THROUGH FOUL SMELLING, knee-high water. It stunk of refuse from the kitchens, refuse from… He chose not to think about where else. He'd been assured that the narrow waterway ran below the palace's kitchens and carried waste away from only there. The palace's water closets supposedly had separate sewers. Grimacing, he wondered why that would be, and whether Sam and the contacts she'd met with in the Four Sheets had lied to him.

She wouldn't, would she?

"Frozen hell, that spirit-forsaken woman lied to me," he growled, his voice echoing down the stone tunnel in front of him, the sound joining the gurgle of water as the stream bubbled merrily along the narrow channel, carrying a palace's worth of waste around and between his knees.

Grunting, he tugged on the rope tied around his chest, hauling the heavy, canvas-wrapped package along behind him. Floating clumsily in the foul water, it bumped and caught on every protrusion and corner of the tunnel, but it was better than trying to carry the monstrous package on his back.

Several hundred more yards if his estimate was right. Forcing his thoughts down, ignoring what he was wading through, he pressed on until finally, he saw a shaft of light ahead and redoubled his efforts, yanking the obstinate package behind him, swishing through waist-deep waste. When he walked below the opening, hauling the package closer, he saw a face peering down at him.

"Winchester," he said.

"M'lord," acknowledged the valet.

"Drop in and give me a hand?" he asked.

"I think, ah, I think I'll have better leverage from up here, m'lord."

He glared at the man, dressed in his spotless Wellesley House livery. Winchester, a man who claimed he'd give his life for his liege, evidently had his limits.

"Very well, Winchester," he said. "Drop me something to climb up. I'm ready to get out of here."

The valet disappeared for a moment and then returned with a high-backed chair. "If you lean this against the wall, m'lord, I believe you'll be able to climb it like a ladder."

Filling the air with curses nearly as vile as the muck he was climbing out of, Oliver managed to maneuver the heavy package and himself up through the grate that Winchester had opened. He found himself in a dark room that had only one exit. The stone floor was slick with slime from years of kitchen waste being dragged and kicked down into the hole to the sewers. Oliver held up a hand, looking in the light at the grimy brown and green smears on his palm. For a moment, he was certain he would be sick.

"We're down a hall from the bakery, m'lord," said Winchester. "In three turns of the clock, this area will be thick with staff up early and baking the day's bread. Now, it's deserted. I advise you to change, m'lord. I'll carry the package upstairs and… and prepare it as you instructed. I took the liberty of collecting some of your brother's garments from the laundry. I used his clothing in case anyone was watching my activities, m'lord. I gathered them from a rather lonely seamstress I've become acquainted with. If anyone was following me, they'll think I'm ensconced in her chambers, doing—"

"Understood, Winchester. I don't need the details," said Oliver, nodding his appreciation to the valet. For a moment, he was glad he hadn't made the man climb down into the sewers with him, but he was sure that feeling would fade.

"I also suggest some water and some soap, m'lord," advised Winchester, keeping his distance from Oliver. "I placed some in the washroom off the bakery along with the clothes. I recommend tossing this set back down into the sewer. Otherwise, he'll smell you half a hallway off."

"He's coming, then?" asked Oliver.

"He should be here in two turns of the clock, m'lord."

Shaking his head and stripping out of his befouled clothing, Oliver resolved to give the valet a raise, assuming he survived long enough to do so.

HE SIPPED FROM THE GOBLET, SWISHING THE WINE IN HIS MOUTH before swallowing. The light of the fire reflected on the cut crystal of the glass, making shards of red and orange, but the wine itself was nearly black. It was the best wine he'd had in what seemed ages, the best wine to be found in Westundon, perhaps all of Enhover, he imagined. His family enjoyed the finer things, and they had access to a nearly limitless supply of sterling with which to purchase it.

His brother Philip only occasionally enjoyed wine, but when he did, it would be the best available. That was Oliver's life, or had been. He wondered if it would be so again. Once Director Raffles, Bishop Yates, and their unknown counterpart were dealt with, what would happen? How would he explain to his brothers and their father what he had done?

Crown, Company, and Church. Or perhaps Crown, Church, and Company, depending on which family member you asked.

Crown, though, was always first, and it was synonymous with the Wellesley name. That mentality had been embedded in his thinking since birth, and while he had rebelled against the notion as a younger man, he kept coming back to it. Whether it was appearing at official functions beside his father, helping his brother host his galas, or meekly heading off to a tiny whaling village to assist in an investigation he didn't understand, he always kept coming back. It was in his blood. Would his family understand what he was doing now, how this was for them and the Crown?

Sipping his brother's wine, he thought they would. They'd all lost much in Northundon. They would thirst for vengeance just as strongly as he did. Sometimes, it made sense to him. Service to the Crown and his own personal objectives could be one and the same.

A door slammed shut, and he set down the wine glass, hurrying to the side of the room, out of the light of the fire. He gripped the basket-hilt of his broadsword and then released it, flexing his hands and glancing at the double-height door to his brother's patio.

Do it quickly, Sam had instructed him. That was sensible. They had some idea of what this man was capable of, if not the full scope. No sense giving him the opportunity to react. Quick and lethal. It was eminently sensible. But instead of drawing the blade, he unbuckled his belt and set the broadsword in the corner. He crouched and waited until the door opened.

"M'lord?" called a voice.

He coughed and rattled, "Come in."

"Oliver," said Director Randolph Raffles with a snort.

Steps and then door swung shut.

Standing behind it, Oliver launched himself at the back of the older man. Fingers curled like talons, he reached for the director's neck, intending to throttle him, choke any sorcerous utterances from his throat. He would throw Raffles down onto the carpeted floor and fall on him, raining blow after blow. He thought of his mother, and he thought of his fists pounding that soft, pampered flesh of her betrayer. He would beat the man into submission, and then he would question him. He would hear it from the director's own mouth.

Director Raffles spun, a forearm brushing aside Oliver's extended hand, his other arm sweeping up and pounding Oliver in the side of the head with pointed elbow. The director punched him in the gut, clutched Oliver behind the neck, and brought the duke's face down to meet a knee that shot up, catching Oliver in the chin and stunning him.

Oliver blinked, stumbling, trying to maintain consciousness and stand upright. Raffles threw another blow, this one a haymaker that connected on the side of Oliver's head, toppling him to the carpet. Unable to process what was going on, Oliver rolled away, his arms up trying to protect his face.

"What was your plan, Oliver?" asked Raffles, his tone seeming as if he was honestly curious. "You thought I'd have no suspicion this was a trap and that I wouldn't be prepared for your treachery? We spoke face-to-face in the club, boy. For the last half turn of the clock, I've had spirits watching you, flitting in and out of this room. I'd sent them to lurk outside in the halls, and they've been tracking you as soon as you came near. I know you're in here alone. I know you spent the entire time walking over to the cupboard and refilling glasses of your brother's wine. I knew the second you stood and went to hide behind the door, and the spirits told me when you unfastened your sword belt. Do you have so little respect for me that you thought this foolish plan might work, that you could surprise and strangle me?"

On the carpet, looking up at the director, Oliver breathed for a moment, letting the flashing colors fade from his vision, hoping the ringing in his head would stop long enough he could stand and face his enemy. Shades, lurking outside in the halls, tracking him from the moment he'd gotten close to the office. Shaking his head, he rolled onto his side.

"As soon as I saw you in the Oak & Ivy, I knew you'd come

after me," continued Raffles. "I knew you'd do it yourself. It's your way, isn't it, Oliver?"

Struggling onto his knees, then his feet, Oliver admitted, "You're right. How, ah, how did you do that?"

Raffles smirked, holding up his forearms toward Oliver. "You don't believe the old boxing lessons at university kept me this sharp? I bound the spirits of two pit fighters. What remains of their strength is mine. What remains of their knowledge is mine. It's a simple binding, Oliver, a sliver of what I'm capable of. Evidently, it's all I need to deal with you."

Oliver, standing now on the carpet, wobbling slightly, glared at the director.

"Was that it?" wondered Raffles after a moment. "Please tell me you didn't expect to take down a sorcerer of my caliber with your fists alone? I thought better of you, Oliver."

"A sorcerer, you admit it," growled Oliver.

The director blinked at him. "You already know, so why not admit it? It is what I am. There was a period I thought you might join me on this path. You worked with that sorcerer Thotham, and he and his apprentice shared what little knowledge they had with you. I thought your curiosity might be piqued, that you had potential to become one of us. You always had potential, boy. Everyone saw it. It's too bad it will end this way."

Oliver launched himself at Raffles, coming low, trying to drive his head into the man's gut before Raffles could get his arms up to protect himself.

The director sidestepped, and when Oliver's shoulder slammed into Raffles, the director wrapped an arm around Oliver's neck and pounded a fist into Oliver's ribcage. Oliver jerked, trying to pull away, but the man's hold on his neck was too tight. Half-a-dozen quick punches fell on protesting ribs then a hammer blow to the kidney.

Oliver collapsed onto his knees, struggling for air with Raffles' arm still wrapped tightly around his throat, holding him in a headlock.

"This is foolish," complained Raffles, pounding a knee into Oliver's defenseless torso. "I have spilled my share of blood, but I will not enjoy beating you to death. This is not my style. Tell me what I want to know, and I will make it quick. It's a true trait of mine, Oliver, I am nothing if not efficient. This is a waste of both of our time. Tell me where the girl is and who else knows."

The director squeezed hard on Oliver's neck and then shoved him away.

Oliver staggered back and stood, pain radiating down his side. He probed where Raffles had punched and kneed him, and while his side throbbed in agony, it wasn't the sharp pain of a broken rib. He could still fight. His neck felt bruised, and he coughed roughly, but he could draw ragged gasps of air. Grimacing, he danced forward, fists raised.

He slipped a jab he'd anticipated would be coming. It was the type of blow he'd seen from Baron Child's body man, the old pit fighter Jack.

Raffles' knuckles breezed by a hand in front of his face, and Oliver hooked a right into the director's body and then struck with his own jab at the older man's face, finding the soft flesh of the director's cheek. Oliver swung an uppercut, trying to finish the old man, but Raffles stepped back and then lunged forward as Oliver's swing missed.

Raffles laid three blows in quick succession to Oliver's face, the first a jab splitting the skin of his cheek, a hook that caught him above the ear, and another from the opposite side that crushed his lip. Gasping, Oliver blinked, trying to get his bearings, and then another barrage of fists fell on him. He collapsed, unable to get his hands up in time, the director pounding his head like a baker kneading a loaf of dough.

Oliver fell to the plush carpet, his head throbbing, warm blood leaking from half-a-dozen cuts. He could already feel his skin starting to swell where the older man had battered him. A copper taste filled his mouth and he spit, his tongue stinging where one of Raffles' blows had clacked his jaw shut on it.

The director had stepped back and was peering at his knuckles. Flecks of blood covered both of them. "I think some of this is mine," mused the old merchant. "Is that common in fisticuffs to split your own skin on the face of the other man? I confess I'm always more interested in the gambling that occurs at the pit fights rather than the damage the men do to each other. I've spilled as much blood as anyone, but I take no particular pleasure in causing or witnessing pain. Funny how one views the world, isn't it? I have done awful things, Oliver, but I do not think I am an unnecessarily cruel man. Do not make me do this."

He took a few steps closer then suddenly lashed out, kicking Oliver squarely in the gut.

Oliver reeled back and flopped onto his back, rolling over, struggling and failing to stand. Gasping for breath, fighting the urge to be sick, face pressed against the floor, Oliver looked up at the director. Well-fed with the body of a wealthy merchant who had little reason to leave his counting rooms, Director Randolph Raffles had never seemed an intimidating presence, but now, from that angle, Oliver suppressed a shudder of revulsion.

The man had the same doughy body that he'd always had, and he had the same mildly interested expression he wore anytime he was in the presence of royalty. Randolph Raffles' face was a mask, and it betrayed nothing of what it hid. Oliver wondered if there was anything beneath the mask. Raffles was driven by greed and a thirst for power. The old merchant had never bothered to hide it. Oliver had always known it about him. Everyone had. It was why he'd succeeded with the Company. Randolph Raffles would do anything to win, and he had. Oliver, the board of directors, they just hadn't known what was possible. They hadn't known the director's dark path even existed.

"Tell me, Oliver," said Raffles, assuming the same friendly tone he always did, only the quick breaths in between words showing any effect of the beating he'd just given Oliver. "Where is the girl, and what does she know? Tell me who else you've told, and we can end this quickly. I have no personal vendetta against you, boy. Don't drag it out."

Oliver spit another mouthful of blood and growled, "You want to know what we know? We know everything, Raffles. We know about your dark betrayal. We know about the sacrifice, the terrible bargain you and your partners agreed to. Thousands of souls, Randolph. An entire city! Sacrificed for nothing more than power?"

"Power?" scoffed the director. "There is nothing more— How did you know about our sacrifice, Oliver? How did you learn about Middlebury?"

Oliver gapped at the larger man. Middlebury. What was he talking about, sacrificing Middlebury?

Raffles reached out and clutched the back of Oliver's hair, tugging his head up. "How did you find out about Middlebury? We just made those plans, boy. The material isn't even in place yet. Did one of those two… No, no, that could not have been it. How do you know, Oliver? Are you working directly with the other?"

Oliver blinked at the director. The man looked fuzzy through vision already clouded by a swelling right eye. Middlebury? The other? What the frozen hell was Raffles talking about?

Studying Oliver's expression, Raffles shook his head and let go of Oliver's. "You don't know what that means, do you? You don't know anything about the other, but you know of our plan to sacrifice Middlebury. How do you know that, boy?"

Oliver clambered to his feet, his head reeling with dizziness and pulsing with waves of dull pain.

"How do you know about Middlebury, Oliver?" asked Raffles, his voice quiet with menace. "We'll find the girl, eventually. I do not need to torture you for that information, but Middlebury… I'm afraid I have to know. How did you find out about the sacrifice?"

A cold chill passed through Oliver's body. Middlebury, why was Raffles speaking of a sacrifice in Middlebury? Oliver had meant Northundon, but… but that wasn't what Raffles had thought. Raffles, his associates, they had something planned for Middlebury. Another sacrifice. They were going to sacrifice Middlebury!

"Normally in a situation like this," pondered the director, looking at Oliver, "I would push your face through the shroud to the underworld. I would show you a vision of that cold and terrible place, but you've already seen it, haven't you? You visited Northundon on the other side. You're not affrighted of that place, though you should be. What then? Pain, suffering, threats against your family? I can cause unceasing agony. I could send a shade after your beloved brother and kill him in his bed right now. I will do it, Oliver. You know that about me, that I'll do what I have to. You may not know that I've been responsible for the deaths of hundreds, so many I don't bother to count any longer. Do you understand, I no longer count how many people I've killed? It does not keep me up at night thinking about the souls in Middlebury who will pay my passage to breach the barrier. There is nothing I will not do to you, boy, and it is just a matter of time before you break under my ministrations. Save me and yourself. Tell me how you found out about the sacrifice, and I will kill you quickly. I will send your soul safely to the other side."

"The taint of the dark trinity isn't on you," muttered Oliver, shaking his head to clear it. "He lied to us. The old man… we followed the taint to you, but…"

Raffles laughed. "The dagger, of course. You followed the blessing on the dagger to us. We had it the entire time, you fool. Yates has been holding it in Westundon right under your nose. How did you find it, was it the priestess?"

Oliver grimaced, ready for the director to pounce, but the man did not. Raffles stood there calmly, waiting for an answer.

"Yates. That's where the girl is?" guessed Raffles. "You came looking for the blessing and saw I had the dagger. You followed me to the meeting with the churchman. That's why you surprised us in the Oak & Ivy, to confirm your hunch. Let me guess, the girl is going after Bishop Yates tonight? You thought to ambush us both?"

Oliver wiped a streamer of blood from his chin and did not respond.

"She is." Raffles nodded. "You'd want to surprise us, take us both down at the same time. What is her plan, sneak up on the churchman and put a knife in his back? Well, Oliver, he has a surprise for her. Your girl will die just as you will. She's not coming to your aid, but that still does not explain how you knew of our plans in Middlebury. Tell me, boy, before I have to get nasty. Did you overhear us speaking, somehow? Did the shades in your vision of Northundon tell you something? I must know."

"Your guesses and conjecture are nowhere near the mark," muttered Oliver.

Raffles sneered. "They're right on the mark."

"What will you gain from the sacrifice?" demanded Oliver, attempting to draw himself up, but the pain in his mid-section where Raffles kicked him left him hunched over, grasping his stomach.

"I am the one asking the questions," scoffed Raffles. He paused. "That sounds like it is out of some trashy pulp novel, does it not? You want to know what I hope to achieve, what this is all for? Immortality, my boy. Immortality and power you cannot imagine. I will bind the dark trinity, and with its might, nothing can stand in my way, not even death. If it had been you instead of us who'd stumbled across the trove that we did, would you have turned away, or would you have pursued it as avidly as I? I think you would have walked the path, Oliver. You've never been one to turn from a challenge."

Oliver looked up at the director and met his gaze. "Rot in hell."

He flung himself at the other man.

The director, assisted by his sorcerous bindings, ducked, caught Oliver in the midsection with his shoulder, and pitched the duke over his head.

Crashing to the floor, Oliver groaned. Then, he was hauled up again and tossed across the room, landing on his brother's giant desk, sliding across it, bouncing off his brother's chair, and thumping to the floor beyond. Scrambling, he tried to get up, but Raffles was there, grabbing him, slamming him against the wall, and then slinging him again into the air where he smashed into his brother's hutch, crushing decanters half-full of wine and scattering a dozen broken wine glasses, the crystal shards embedding painfully into his arm.

He snatched up an unbroken one and hurled it at Raffles, who was quickly advancing on him. The director fended it off, but Oliver threw two more decanters behind the first. The heavy, liquid-filled crystal thudded against Raffles' body.

The old man was aided in speed and strength by his sorcery, but Oliver saw he could be damaged. Raffles was touching a bleeding cut on his forehead from where one of the decanters had struck him. He looked at Oliver with murder in his eyes.

Oliver grabbed the broken neck of a bottle. Raffles rushed him, and Oliver swung the broken bottle at the older man's head. The director blocked the blow and chopped down on Oliver's arm, numbing the hand. Dead fingers let the broken crystal slip to the carpet. Raffles punched Oliver in the stomach again and hurled him across the room.

Oliver, tumbling across the floor, knew he couldn't last much longer. None of the blows he sustained were crippling individually, but the director was too strong and too fast. Raffles was losing his temper, and there was no certainty he would be able to control his rage. The moment he wanted to, the director could end the fight. Fist to fist, Oliver knew he was no match for the other man's unnatural prowess. If the director bothered to use more of the tricks he certainly had up his sleeve, then it would only get worse. The questions Oliver wanted to ask the man, the plan to goad Raffles into revealing what he knew of Lilibet, was falling apart. But Middlebury…

He shook his head, Middlebury… It wasn't what he'd tried to

learn, but now that he knew, he had to tell Sam. They had to stop it. It was time to end the fight. Oliver stood and raised his fists.

"You're a fool, boy," said Raffles.

Then, he charged, raining a flurry of blows on Oliver, backing him up toward the double doors that led to the veranda.

Between panting breaths, Raffles insisted, "You cannot fight me, Oliver. Tell me how you know our plans!"

"You told me, Randolph," cried Oliver, shouting between forearms that he'd raised to absorb the older man's strikes. "You told me everything."

Snarling, Raffles reared and kicked Oliver in the chest, propelling him back, smashing through the doors to the patio in a hail of glass and broken wood.

Oliver skidded across the tiles outside, his body sliding across the cold stone and broken glass. He looked up and saw Raffles standing in the doorway.

"Forget it. Tell me, or don't tell me. I've lost my patience," muttered Raffles. The director stepped forward but stopped, his foot hanging mid-air. He extended the foot and tried to force his body forward but could not. "What is this?"

"I wasn't sure that would work," said Oliver, flopping onto his side and forcing himself up. His body ached, and his head felt like it had been rolled over by a mechanical carriage, but he was alive.

Raffles glared at him, confused, trying to raise an arm but finding it stuck.

"I appreciate your help, kicking me through that doorway," continued Oliver. "I was worried I was going to have to figure a way to knock through it myself and have you chase after me."

Tugging at his left arm with his right hand, Raffles tried to move it away but found it stuck. The director began to panic. He strained forward and fell, his arms glued together, his legs tangled with invisible threads.

"Glae worm filament," explained Oliver, taking a step forward to look at the director's predicament. "My man Winchester placed glae worm pods around the door frame a turn of the clock before

I came in with your shades on my heels. When I crashed through the door, they exploded, shooting a web across this space. You walked right into it. The fresh filament is invisible and sticky as anything. It's nearly unbreakable. In a turn of the clock, it will dry, and you would be able to wiggle your way out without it clinging to you, but I'm afraid you won't have that much time, Director."

"Let me go!" snapped Raffles, thrashing with his arms, straining with his fingers. Each movement only caused more of the fresh filament to stick to him, and in seconds, he was completely immobilized. Helplessly, he tried to stretch his hands down his body, but he couldn't move them. He was completely stuck. "I-I…"

"Can't reach your sorcerous triggers? Can't direct your shades to attack?" asked Oliver mockingly. "Now is the time when you offer me the keys to your storeroom, an airship, or some other ludicrous bribe, but you know that won't work on me." His split lips curled into a painful smile. "No, Director, there is only one thing you can offer that might change what is to happen next."

Speechless, Raffles stared at him, tugging futilely against the invisible strands of sticky filament that held him in place.

"Where is my mother?" asked Oliver.

"You're… what?" replied Raffles. "She's dead. You want me to find her on the other side? I—"

Oliver interrupted, "It was not you, then. Another hand was responsible for the sacrifice of Northundon? The shaman lied. Did he do it for revenge or because he somehow knew what you were planning? Was it your partners?"

Raffles gaped at him.

"Immortal, you said you would become?" questioned Oliver. "The spirits able to stop you from aging, preventing even the blood from leaving your body? We weren't sure how far you'd progressed, weren't sure if you'd already achieved some level of indestructibility. I wonder, could this dark trinity of yours stop red saltpetre munitions from incinerating you?"

"No!" shrieked Raffles. "You don't understand. We're so close! If you kill me, the spirits—"

"I do understand," replied Oliver, moving to the edge of the patio where he recovered a canvass bag. He pulled out a paper-wrapped tube and a striker. "I understand, and that's why I'm doing this."

He lit the striker, showering sparks onto the paper tube. It caught, flaring a three-yard long blast of bright white sparks and billowing smoke. Holding the flare, Oliver glanced at Raffles. The director was thrashing angrily, his portly filament-wrapped body doing an uncanny impression of a struggling worm.

"Sorcery is an art of preparation, is it not?" asked Oliver. "Well, I came prepared."

Above him, he heard the creak of rope on wood and the swish of giant canvass sweeps clawing at the air.

He asked Raffles, "Any last words?"

The old man, prone on the stone floor, laughed bitterly. "I tried and failed. I have no regrets about that. Remember this, and know your own regrets. I will see you again in hell. I have friends there, and I can't wait to introduce you to them."

A rope net thumped onto the tiles behind Oliver, and a voice called out, "Hurry up, m'lord! It ain't easy to hold an airship steady in these winds."

Oliver held the flare low, looking for a long cord on the tiles. When he saw the cord, he held the flare to it, and it ignited. The cord had been soaked in lamp oil, and it burned bright and fast, illuminating the struggling director as the sizzling flame passed beside him, his face lit by the fire, angry and awful.

Oliver dropped the flare and spun, running to catch the hanging rope net, lifting away as the Cloud Serpent rose above him. He was a dozen yards above the patio when the flame on the wick vanished inside his brother's study, finding the casks of red saltpetre munitions that Winchester had hidden there.

They exploded violently.

Fire burst out of the doorway, taking a storm of debris and

broken stone with it. Every window in the room shattered and a stout section of stone wall blasted away, mortar and rocks scattering across the patio, smashing into the balustrade and raining down below.

Oliver grimaced, hoping no one in the courtyard at the base of the palace was hit. And he tried not to think how much his brother was going to charge him to fix the mess.

Raffles, or what had once been the director, was lost in the fire and the smoke. It was, perhaps, a bit overkill, but they hadn't known if the man had some sort of sorcerous connection which could preserve him. Oliver and Sam had both figured the best bet was to make sure there was nothing left to preserve. Watching the billow of flame below, Oliver was certain they'd done the job. Director Randolph Raffles was dead.

He wondered if they would be able to recover the body or if there even was a body left. It would be unrecognizable, after such a blast, but he and Sam would know who it had been. It would give them some comfort, seeing the charred remains.

Sam. He hoped her role in the evening was going as smoothly as his. Wiping a sticky trail of blood from his chin with one hand, the other hand wrapped secure in the rope net, he thought that maybe it could have gone a little bit smoother.

Below him, the city of Westundon sparkled like moonlight on the sea. All of his thoughts turned to the priestess who was down there, somewhere.

THE PRIESTESS XIX

FEET STOMPED up the solid wooden stairs. The scent of rosemary and lemon proceeded the man as he stood outside of the door, testing it then opening it. Light spilled into the room, a wedge of yellow widening as the door swung, illuminating a wardrobe, a bed, a pair of knee-high boots, and then Sam, sitting in a chair, her feet up on the bed.

"Hello, Raymond."

The man in the doorway put his hand on his dagger, his eyes darting from Sam to the long, narrow lump in the center of the bed.

"It is what you think it is," confirmed Sam.

"Your work?" he asked coldly.

"No," responded Sam. "Bishop Yates."

"Bridget and I came here to kill you," said Raymond, still in the doorway. "Bishop Yates is the one who brought us. If he wanted Bridget or I dead, he could have done it on the airship over here. Nice try, Samantha."

Sam let her boots fall to the floor. "I thought you came to West-undon because of the letter I sent to Bishop Constance. Did she get it?"

Raymond frowned at her.

"I've identified the sorcerer Duke Wellesley and I were looking for," she continued. "Remember, the one I'd asked for your help with? Bishop Constance did not believe me, but now, I have proof. The sorcerer is Bishop Yates."

"That's a rather bold accusation, don't you think?" said Raymond, his eyes darting about nervously. "You want me to believe the man who brought us to Westundon to stamp out sorcery is, himself, a sorcerer? A bishop of all people? Come, now, Samantha. That is too convenient. I'm a fop, not a fool."

She saw his gaze settling on the long, sheet-covered lump on the bed. "Do you want to see her? I'll take the sheet off myself so you do not think I am staging a trap."

"A trap," he muttered suspiciously.

"If I meant to ambush you," she said, "I would have done it the moment you opened the door. You would have caught shot from both barrels of a twin blunderbuss. You're experienced enough at this game, Raymond. Killing you isn't my goal."

He grunted. "I know you don't want to kill me, yet. What is it you do want?"

Ignoring the question, she stood slowly, keeping her hands up. Carefully, she reached down and grabbed the corner of the blankets. She peeled them back, tugging to rip the linens from Bridget's face where they'd gotten stuck from the drying blood.

Lying on her back, the dead Knife was naked. Her body was unmarked, except for her face where the skin had been delicately removed. Red flesh and white bone shone in the light from the open door.

Raymond au Clair looked like he might become sick. "Why would…"

"Why would I do this?" Sam finished for him. "I wouldn't, Raymond. I know you two were set on my trail by the bishop, but what purpose would this mutilation serve? If I thought I needed to kill you, I would, but I would do it efficiently. If that's what I wanted, I wouldn't be sitting here talking to you."

The Knife swallowed and stepped forward, looking closer at

his former partner. "Why would the bishop do it, then? He is the one who brought us here. This was no ritual, Samantha, despite what it looks like. The other materials, the patterns, are not present. This was a simple murder."

"Perhaps," vacillated Sam. "This killing is nearly identical to Hathia Dalyrimple's. At the time, we assumed it was a ritual performed by members of the Mouth of Set. We never found what the ritual was meant to accomplish, though, but I did find out who the leader of the Mouth of Set is."

"You're implying it was the bishop," said Raymond. He moved across the bed from her, Bridget's body in between them. "Why would he do this?"

"I could tell you my suspicions," Sam said, "but you won't believe anything I say, will you? You're a trained investigator. Search for yourself. See what you find."

"And if it appears that you were responsible for this?" he asked.

"I'm not going to let you kill me, if that's what you're getting at," she replied dryly. "I want to talk, not fight, but if it comes to that…"

Frowning, Raymond au Clair glanced around the room.

"I'll be down at the pub across the street," offered Sam. "That way you can do a proper investigation without worrying about what I'm doing."

"I'll see you in a little bit, then," responded Raymond.

SHE SAT AT THE BACK TABLE, TOYING WITH THE HALF-FULL MUG OF ale in front of her. Only her second, which was unusual, but the night was young, and she had work to do. It took longer than she expected, and she began to worry that Raymond had gone running to Bishop Yates to request assistance, but eventually, the foppish Knife appeared in the doorway of the pub.

His oiled ringlets were gone, and his damp hair was tied back behind his head. He no longer wore the intricately embroidered doublet she'd seen him in earlier. His dagger, the one with the jewel hilt, had been replaced with a simple steel weapon. As he approached her table, she smelled that the heady perfumes he'd worn earlier had been washed away.

"I wondered why you took so long," she remarked.

"I thought it might be time to work." He sat across from her and placed a rucksack in the middle of the table. "Have any more of that ale?"

"I saved you a bit," she said, nodding to the pitcher and an empty mug. "What's in the bag?"

"What do you think is in the bag?" he replied, reaching forward and pouring himself an ale.

She shrugged. He sipped from his mug and sat back, shifting nervously. She smiled, knowing that he was feeling anxious with his back exposed to the room behind him.

"I did not find any evidence that he committed the murder," he mumbled, his eyes darting to those around them, as if any of the drunks at the nearby tables cared what he was saying. "I didn't find any evidence that you did, either. You were in the room, though, and that's difficult to explain if you were not involved."

"I've been trailing the bishop," said Sam. "I saw you two were here, and it was no great leap to infer why you were in Westundon. I came to find Bridget and meant to discuss it with her, to convince her I was not the target you should be seeking. When I found her, she was already dead. I sent the messenger so you could view her body and investigate it. If I wasn't there, I knew you'd jump to the conclusion that I was involved anyway, so I waited for you, hoping we'd get a chance to talk."

He frowned. "That's true. I would have suspected you. I still do. Why did you try to approach her and not me?"

"She seemed reasonable. I believed I could convince her I was no sorceress," answered Sam. "You seem like an ass."

Raymond shook his head. "You're not making this any easier on yourself."

Sam shrugged. "Did Bridget tell you about us in Romalla?"

Grunting, the Knife sipped his ale.

"She told me about you when she and I were together," said Sam. "She was a talker. Surely, you know why I approached her first?"

"What do you know about the Mouth of Set?" asked Raymond, changing the subject.

"Set..." murmured Sam. "An aspect of the dark trinity, is it not? Along with Seheht and, ah, a third one."

"Seshim," supplied Raymond. "The third aspect of the trinity is Seshim, which you know. You brought it up earlier."

"Gabriel Yates leads the Mouth of Set," declared Sam, a fierce grin on her lips. "Is that what you wanted me to say?"

"He sent you to investigate a murder they were involved in," replied Raymond, "and then he requested Bridget and I to clean up the mess when you failed to snip all of the threads. If he was involved, why would he do that?"

"The same reason he'd invite you to Enhover," said Sam. "What better way to cover his involvement? What better way to allay suspicion?"

"What better way to actually deal with sorcerers?" countered Raymond.

"Bishop Yates requested your presence in Enhover twice now," said Sam. "Cardinal Langdon is uninterested, summering in the south of Finavia. Bishop Constance is denying what is plainly apparent, that sorcery is thriving in Enhover. Who do you think will get credit for stopping sorcery in Enhover? Who do you think King Edward Wellesley will thank for protecting the realm? We like to think the prelate is the most powerful man in the world, but let us be honest, it is King Edward. Attached to the king's side, what heights could Bishop Yates achieve? A place at the head of the Council of Seven, a position as cardinal in Enhover? Even prelate?"

Raymond frowned at her. "King Edward has no interest in—"

"He does," insisted Sam, leaning forward and pinning Raymond with her gaze. "Whatever you think about me, whatever suspicions cloud your mind, do not let them obscure what you know. When I say I know what House Wellesley is thinking, you know I speak the truth. Harwick, Archtan Atoll, Derbycross, you know who was with me at each of those locations. You say the king has no interest in sorcery, then please tell me why he sent his son to ferret it out?"

"But," complained Raymond, "sorcery was dead in Enhover. Everyone knows…"

"The king knew that it was not," insisted Sam. "He's been one step ahead of the Church, the Council of Seven, and her Knives this entire time. Ever since Northundon, he's held a dismissive attitude toward the Church, toward everyone in it, except for one man, who might be able to get close enough to whisper in the king's ear."

Raymond picked up his ale and drank deeply.

"You know the facts, Raymond," declared Sam. "Discount the seriousness of it if you like, but you know there was sorcery in Harwick, Archtan Atoll, and Derbycross. Each time, I was there. Each time, the Crown's representative was there. Each time, the Church has turned a blind eye. Tell me, Raymond, who would gain from such an attitude?"

"What's your assertion, Sam, that he's climbing the ranks of the Church or that he's a sorcerer?" demanded Raymond.

"Both," she said then pressed her lips together in a tight smile.

She picked up her own ale and sat back to let the man think. She'd only been able to draw tenuous connections, threads of truth woven through threads of pure speculation. The more she'd spoken of it, though, the more certain she'd grown. Yates was one of the sorcerers she and Duke sought. He'd been involved since Harwick, long before, though he and his cohort had managed to keep it secret for years. It wasn't until Harwick that they'd stumbled and left clues in the open.

Raymond busied himself drinking, thinking. When she'd started speaking, she wasn't sure he would believe her, but now, she thought he might. Some of it was the truth, after all.

He looked up at her. "You mean for us to hunt down Yates tonight and kill him?"

"That's what we do," said Sam. "He's a sorcerer. I hoped Bridget might... Well, I hoped she would see reason and come with me to confront the man. Risky, showing our faces, but between the two of us, I thought we would shock him into tipping his hand, confirming it for her. With two of us there, I thought we'd be sufficient."

"Evidently not," remarked Raymond, cringing. She guessed he thought of his dead partner. "Do you read ancient Darklands script?"

"Some," acknowledged Sam. "My mentor taught me what he could, but we rarely had the opportunity to study authentic texts. All legitimate documents in that tongue are immediately shipped to the Church's archives in Romalla. When I have seen something in ancient Darklands, it's been difficult to decipher. The old language and the new are similar but not the same."

"Few people know the old Darklands script these days," agreed Raymond. "Even in the Church, it's become rare. I suppose because the official line is that sorcery is dead. Why bother to read it if that's the case?"

"Why indeed," murmured Sam.

"I've been wondering, since you left Bridget's room, why so many of our leaders are so certain sorcery is dead," continued the Knife. "You are right, of course, that it was practiced in Harwick and Derbycross. There's no question it was, so why would the Church claim it was not, that it was impossible despite all evidence to the contrary? Before we even came to Enhover, I wondered who stood to gain from this knowledge being suppressed."

Sam tilted her head and waited.

"Bishop Yates was a scholar before he was an administrator," continued Raymond. "He spent his early years in the Church deep in the vaults below Romalla. He studied ancient texts, ancient languages. I know this because periodically those scholars come to our attention. They are the ones studying the guide posts to the dark path, after all, and some take the first steps. The Council has always been quick to act against those of our own who betray the Church's principles. Yates was one of the most promising young scholars, though at the time I do not recall any suspicions about him. He taught some of my classes, actually, when I was a young priest, just starting my own journey. I wish I recalled more of those lessons, now."

"If it makes you feel better, I never suspected him either," said Sam honestly.

She'd known Yates was a scholar, but that hadn't been enough to raise her suspicions. There'd been nothing else to tie it to, no other clue to connect. She'd never considered the possibility until the bishop had walked in to meet Raffles. What other clues had been lying in the open that she'd missed?

Shaking her head, she lied to Raymond, "A scholar, I did not know that. He's been an administrator for as long as I've known him. Do you think that's why he was recruited onto the dark path, or do you think he is the one who did the recruiting?"

"I'm not certain he is either, but..." Raymond flipped open the pack on the table, displaying a gleaming silver emblem, a quill bisecting the Church's circle. "I found it underneath of Bridget's pillow, right next to the knife she always keeps there. This is a symbol for a small cohort of scholars within the Church known as the Sect of Sages. They're given these emblems when granted a certain rank. It allows them access to the restricted archives, and it necessarily draws our attention. There are only two score men and women within the group, and I know all of them. Bishop Yates is one."

"Is he?" asked Sam.

Raymond asked, "Did you steal this from him?"

"If I could get close enough to steal that from the bishop, I'd kill him instead," said Sam with a snort. "Why do you think Bridget would have one of these symbols?"

"You knew it was there," he accused her.

"How would I know that?" she asked. "Under her pillow? How would I know Bridget keeps things there? How do you— Ah, of course. You slept with her as well."

"Years ago," admitted Raymond. He leaned forward. "Have you seen this emblem before?"

"Have you?" countered Sam. "I spent a night with Bridget. We were both swimming in the current. It was nothing more. She did not spill all of her secrets to me, and I did not share mine. I do not know why she would have this, unless she was conducting an investigation outside of your knowledge. Maybe, suspecting Yates, she was afraid to voice her concerns to you. Perhaps she collected this symbol on the airship from Romalla. Perhaps Yates learned of it, and that's why she's dead."

"Someone put this pendant underneath her pillow for me to find," stated Raymond.

"I didn't know what that was until you told me. Could Bridget herself have put it there?" questioned Sam. "Who else would know she kept something underneath of her pillow?"

Raymond stared back at her, his jaw clenched, his hands grasping the edge of the table. Finally, he said, "You led me into this."

"I thought I could warn Bridget, but I was too late. Once I saw she'd been killed, I knew you had to see it on your own," responded Sam. "If I'd told you everything I suspected, you'd be suspicious. You never would have believed me. If you came to understand yourself, though…"

Raymond nodded and drank deeply of his ale. "Bishop Yates and the new factions in the Church that align around him are the ones who proclaim most loudly that sorcery is dead. I thought he did it as a political ploy, as you hinted. It's no secret he's using Langdon's prolonged absence to grow close to the Wellesleys. In a few years, he probably would have been named cardinal, but perhaps there is more."

"The dark trinity," said Sam. "Set, Seheht, and Seshim. Three spirits, three sorcerers."

"What else do you know?" growled Raymond.

"There's a man, a director of the Company, Randolph Raffles," she said. "He's a sorcerer. I was following him and saw him meet with Yates. That's how I learned the bishop was involved."

"You want me to move against him?" questioned Raymond.

"No." Sam smirked. "The Crown is already taking care of that for us. I told you. They've been a step ahead of the Church."

"Duke Wellesley?" asked Raymond.

"I don't know if I can face Yates alone," said Sam, not bothering to confirm Raymond's guess. "You're right. I led you into this. I had to, once I saw Bridget was dead. Come with me, Raymond, and let us take care of our own."

The Knife glared at her, his fingers beginning a slow drum on the table. "Do you have proof?"

"Not yet, but I have a plan to get it," she answered. "I do not expect you to strike until you are sure. Is that a fair deal? Come with me and only act when you are certain?"

"It is what we do," replied Raymond. He placed a hand on the pack and pulled it into his lap. "I do not trust you, Sam, but I will go with you. I'll see if there is proof of this man's allegiance. I warn you, if you make a move toward him before I am convinced, I will kill you."

"You don't trust me. I understand that," said Sam. "I promise you. Before the night is over, you will."

THE KNIFE I

HE EDGED along the outside barrier of the estate, placing each hand and foot slowly so he did not lose his grip on the narrow wall. His fingers clung to the top, his body hung down. His boots, the toes dipped in tar, provided traction on the smooth stone. The wall had been designed for privacy and beauty, not security. It was thinner than those he was used to sneaking along. Still, it served the purpose, and he'd scouted the entire back side of the building before he swung over the top and let go to drop inside.

His soft boots landed with barely a thump on the stone courtyard. No plants, he noticed. Just statues, benches, a tinkling fountain, and... He paused. It appeared to be a sun-clock, but between the notches for the hours and the minutes, an intricate web of thin gold strips was inlaid in the stone. If the center of the clock was removed, the design would be suspiciously similar to ones he'd seen in sorcerous texts. It would not be unlike what that inspector had drawn depicting the scene in Harwick.

Had the infuriating girl been telling the truth? Earlier, he wouldn't have placed the odds at more than one in five, but the golden pattern inset in the stone courtyard was another weight on her side of the scale. He shook himself and moved forward.

Either Samantha was lying, and he'd be beside the bishop to

protect the old man when she attacked, or she wasn't lying, and the bishop truly was a sorcerer. Either way, he was going to be in the right place.

He grimaced and shifted, the contents of his pack rolling against his back as he tightened the straps. It made him uncomfortable, carrying it, but if she was telling the truth, her plan made sense. It was spirits-forsaken crazy, but he thought it would work. In another turn of the clock, he'd find out. Whichever way it went, he would avenge Bridget. One or the other was responsible for his dead partner, and they were going to pay.

Glancing over his shoulder, he wondered if Samantha was holding her end of the bargain and following in his footsteps as he snuck inside. If she'd lied, he would want to take her quickly. If she hadn't lied, and Yates really was a sorcerer, he might need her help.

Shaking his head and forcing himself back to the matter at hand, he left the curious sun-clock and scampered across the open stone of the expanse behind the bishop's mansion. It was no secret that Church leadership lived in opulent quarters, but the leaders in Ivalla at least had the decency to make those quarters part of the Church complex. Their comings and goings were known, and while they lived in luxury, they still lived within the bounds of the Church's domain.

This, though, was something else. Perhaps Sam hadn't been lying.

He found the back wall of the building and peered into a window. So far, he'd seen no guards except the two lumps at the front gate. As if anyone with seriously bad intentions would bother knocking on the gate. The fact that there was no obvious sentry in the back meant they were rather better at their jobs than he would have expected, or the bishop had fashioned another manner of security.

Frozen hell. What if she wasn't lying?

From the moment he'd opened the door and saw her sitting with Bridget's body to the shoddy acting and feigned surprise she'd shown at the emblem for the Sect of Sages, he had been so sure she was lying. He was so certain that he'd agreed to her ridiculous plan as a way of bringing her in. Yates had asked for her alive, if possible. Raymond au Clair, Knife of the Council, was walking the murdering, sorcerous bitch right in the back door.

He would have the bishop's favor, if the plan succeeded. All he had to do was keep Samantha from killing anyone important once they were inside. That was what he'd thought, at least.

Glancing over his shoulder again, he let his gaze slowly pass over the top of the back wall. If she was right behind him, she would be coming in that way. He didn't see her, though. Still, he was confident she would come, one way or the other. She wanted to kill the bishop, and he was her ticket inside. His role was to confront and distract Yates while she snuck in. She said she wasn't confident she could handle the bishop alone. Raymond believed that much of her outlandish tale, at least.

Giving up on trying to spot Samantha, he gripped the frieze work that decorated the pillars rising along the back of the building, and he climbed. Sure fingers finding easy grips, pitch-covered boots finding ample toeholds, he scaled the back wall like a spider.

He passed the ground-level floor, which he suspected the bishop never visited. It would be the laundry, storage rooms, and servants' quarters. The stairs out front passed by that level entirely. The second floor was the public space where Yates would host receptions for local peers or visiting dignitaries and showed off his devotion to the Church with whatever he could scavenge from the Church's galleries. The third floor held guest spaces which Raymond knew were unoccupied at the moment. He and Bridget had been offered lodging there before they'd agreed it would be better to remain in the city and away from the bishop while they looked for Samantha. He kept climbing. The fourth floor was Gabriel Yates' private quarters. Raymond knew this late in the evening, he would find the bishop somewhere on that floor.

Climbing the four-story stone pillar like it was a city street, the

Knife ascended quickly and paused at the top. He listened for sounds of guards, the bishop, or even Samantha behind him, but there was nothing, just the cold wind and the constant tinkle of water in the fountain. He looked down at the fountain and the moonlit sun-clock near it. From above, it was clear the sun-clock was in the direct center of the stone enclosure. Five granite benches, arranged equidistant from the pattern, were placed like they were distinct points of a star. The fountain lay at the base of the design, spraying water, a medium of both life and death.

He closed his eyes and hung on the stonework for a long moment, extending his senses, trying to hear any sound, feel any disruption that tickled the barrier between this world and the next. There was nothing, but he felt a creeping sense of wrongness. Samantha had wanted to enter this way. It was her plan, and he'd agreed to it as a means to draw her close, to make her show herself to the bishop. Had she suggested this because she knew the back of the estate was unguarded, or because she wanted him to see what lay behind the bishop's mansion?

Frozen hell, thought Raymond, shaking his head. The pattern... could it be coincidence? Perhaps some mason playing an unfortunate jest on the churchman? The stone workers were known to have a fascination with the occult. Had they done this independently? Did the bishop even understand what the arrangement below signified? Could Yates not understand it, being the scholar that he was?

Grimacing, Raymond traversed the back of the building, moving along the stonework like a monkey in the tropics, peering into each window he passed.

Most of them were dark, sleeping rooms and family rooms, had the bishop had one. At the far corner of the building, he could see a steady, yellow light bleeding from one bank of windows. He knew the bishop would be inside, and he grew sure the man would be waiting for him. If Yates was waiting... Raymond cursed silently. If the man somehow sensed his approach, was there an innocent explanation?

Finally, he reached the last window and peered inside. Bishop Gabriel Yates was sitting in a comfortable-looking chair. He had an open bottle beside him and a small glass at his elbow. Raymond had no doubt it contained a hearty pour of sherry. The bishop was aimlessly flipping through pages in a massive, leather-bound book.

Drawing a deep breath, Raymond scuttled a little farther down to the center of the window. Watching the bishop closely to see if the churchman's eyes ever looked up, Raymond slid a slender steel lockpick from a tiny pocket in the back of his wide belt.

Studying the window closely, he saw the thing wasn't locked. He simply inserted the pick and flicked it up, throwing the catch to the window. Raymond yanked it open, and the bishop glanced up, only appearing startled as he saw who was lurking outside of his fourth-story window.

"What are you doing here?" asked Yates, closing his book and setting it on the table near his sherry.

Climbing into the window and then closing it behind, Raymond turned to Yates. "Not going to ask why I came in the back window instead of the front door?"

Yates steepled his fingers. "Very well. Why did you come in the back window and not the front door?"

"I have a package I was sent to deliver to you."

"A package?" questioned Yates. "Sent by who?"

"Our mutual friend," remarked Raymond. He slung his pack off his back and spotted a silver tray on the side of the room. He collected it and walked back toward Yates.

"Is that..." began Yates, but he trailed off when Raymond emptied the pack and a severed head rolled out. "It is not, is it?"

"No, it is not," snapped Raymond.

"Bridget, then?" asked Yates calmly. "What happened to her?"

"Our friend did this, I believe," said Raymond, "but she blamed it on you."

Yates laughed. "No, not me. She must have found out you

were hunting... Wait, you said she blamed it on me? Did you speak to her? Did you kill her?"

"You asked me to bring her in alive, did you not?" responded Raymond. "Our plan is for her to follow me into this room. She should be here any moment."

Yates stood and strode across the room. The Knife's eyes followed his progress then widened when the man stopped in front of a yard-wide map of the mansion. Pale white lines glowed in complex geometric patterns on the paper surface of the map. They pulsed with energy, like the light of the fae. He'd never seen a map like it before.

"What is that?" he asked, walking to stand beside the bishop.

"It's a little experiment I rigged up," replied Yates. "It's a warning system, you could say. If anything crosses these barriers, I will know it. It's how I knew you entered the grounds and why I didn't leap out of my seat when I saw you. It seems your partner has not yet breached the barriers, though. You are sure she is coming behind you?"

"Why would she not be?" he asked. He glanced at the table where Bridget's decapitated head sat, the skin of her face peeled away. How had Yates known it was Bridget? Samantha had instructed him to watch the bishop's reaction to see if... Frozen hell. How had he known?

"Sam isn't my partner," muttered Raymond.

"Sam now, is it? She set you up, boy," said the bishop, still studying the faintly glowing map.

"How... how did you do this?" asked Raymond, gesturing at the map. "This is like nothing I've seen before. Is it... is it powered by technology?"

Yates smirked at him, turned, and headed back to his chair.

"Sir..." began the Knife.

"Bishop Constance was here just three months gone," said Yates over his shoulder. "The Whitemask has seen my map, and she had no qualms about it. It's important here, away from the seat of the Church, for those of us in leadership to protect ourselves. There was only one Knife in Enhover, you know, and that man was recently killed. I'm not like you, au Clair, able to hide in the shadows and strike from behind. I'm a public figure, an easy target for those like this girl." He shrugged. "I do what I must to survive. As do you. As do we all."

"You thought I was her, sneaking in over your back wall," guessed Raymond. "What would you have done if she'd been the one outside of your window?"

"Die, I suppose," said the bishop dryly.

Raymond shook his head. "I don't think so, Bishop. You weren't surprised to see me. You were calm. You had a plan. How did you know the head was Bridget's, not Sam's?"

"It's a dangerous world, Raymond au Clair," said the bishop, cutting his eyes to the lifeless head of Bridget. "One must always have a plan."

"You bound spirits to create the map," said Raymond, fighting the tension in his body. "What did you intend if Sam had turned up outside of your window?"

"What did you intend, coming in that way?" retorted Yates. "The guards out front have been instructed to allow you entry. There was no need for this. What did the girl say to you with her silver tongue and black heart? What did... Ah, I think I know. She did as so many women have done before her throughout history. You've been fooled, au Clair, by a pretty smile and a warm body."

Raymond shook his head. "No, Bishop, that's not—"

"You're not the first one she's slept with, you know," remarked Yates. "Not the first by a long way. You've been tricked, boy! That girl was trained from birth to fool the likes of you, and you fell right into her sultry trap. The Church employs legions of fallen women trained in the softer arts. Not all of our diplomacy is the cold steel of your dagger. I'm disappointed. One such as you should have seen through her temptation."

Blinking, Raymond stared at the older man.

"Well?" asked Bishop Yates, stabbing a finger toward

Raymond. "The girl tricked you. By your own admission, she killed your partner. What will you do about it?"

Against the bishop's chest, a glittering silver pendant swung with his movement. A quill bisecting the Church's circle.

"She did trick me," muttered Raymond, his eyes fixed on the symbol hanging around the bishop's neck. "She killed Bridget and pulled the wool over my eyes, all to get me here."

"Exactly!" cried Yates, smacking a fist into his palm. "Now go find that ruthless bitch and bring her back to me. You'll have your revenge, both for your partner and yourself."

Raymond, moving slowly, let his hand fall toward his hip. "I worry she is here, Bishop. I think that was her trap, to get me to come in and trigger whatever designs you had laid for her. She sacrificed Bridget, and she sacrificed me."

"Did she now?" questioned Yates, standing before his chair. He laughed, both hands holding his jiggling belly. "Was I meant to kill you, or were you meant to kill me?"

"I don't think she cared either way," replied Raymond. He glanced back at the glowing map. "I'll ask again. If it had been her outside of the window, what would you have done?"

"If she'd given me time, I suppose I would have shouted for the guards," said Yates. "Go on now. Do what you do and find her. A temptress and a murderer. A sorceress! If she does turn up here, I'll have my men handle it."

"Do what I do," murmured Raymond, his hands clenching involuntarily. "That's what she told me as well. Call your men, then, Bishop."

"What?" asked Yates.

"Call them," instructed Raymond. "Sam said she was going to be right behind me. Why not call the men now and have them waiting for her?"

"It's unnecessary," claimed Yates, moving from his reading chair and table toward the far wall of the room.

Raymond let his hand rest on his sword. "There are no men who will be rushing in, are there? You meant to deal with Sam yourself. You are what she said you were. A sorcerer, hiding within the ranks of the Church! How could you?"

Yates smirked. "It was quite easy, boy. There is no one easier to fool than those who are certain they are right. The Church, so sure their path to strength is the one, so sure the nations will fall under a populist tide, so foolish. What can the crowded masses do against the might of Enhover's technology, the airships, and their bombs? What can the crowded masses do against the strength of the underworld? Nothing, boy, they can do nothing. The Church has turned the wrong way, turned from the true sources of power. I saw as much in the histories, but no one would listen. When the opportunity arose to become a strength in my own right, I took it."

Raymond drew his rapier. "The Church does not seek… It does not seek power. Not like you say. The Church is there for—"

"You kill people!" shrieked Yates, his face locked in a rictus of mad glee. "You kill people! Maybe it helps you sleep at night to think they are all terrible sorcerers on the verge of calling dark power upon the lands, but you are wrong. The people you kill are innocents. Hedge-witches, healers, and a few of the foolishly curious. You think those people you murdered in Harwick had any idea what true sorcery is? They did not, boy. They did not even know they danced upon my strings. Those people had no idea what walking the dark path entails. They just liked getting drunk, having an orgy, and play-acting at serving some darker force. They had no forbidden knowledge, but you spilled their blood. You reveled in it, all while I watched from the shadows. I watched as you and they both conducted my bidding. Raymond au Clair, you're guiltier of sorcery than your victims ever were!"

From his belt, Raymond removed a thin glass vial and smoothly cracked it upon the steel of his exposed blade, tilting the weapon down so the liquid coated the surface. In the space of two heartbeats, it burst into shimmering red flame. The light from the blade cast an awful glow across the room, the flames burning furious and low, roiling up and down the edge of the sword like a jungle cat preparing to pounce.

"So be it," growled Yates.

The bishop shook his arm and out of his sleeve fell a fluted, crystal wand.

Raymond charged, his sword, the steel shimmering with crimson fire, thrusting ahead of him.

Yates tossed the wand into the air, and it spun, flashing with light from the fireplace and Raymond's sword. Halfway before it fell to the floor, it exploded. Crystal shards blasted out and then contracted, a punch of cold air mimicking the motion.

Raymond was knocked onto his heels by the wave of frigid air. He didn't let it stop him, though, and he charged back as soon as he regained his balance, lashing out with his sword, only to have it deflected by a flashing reflection of firelight. He staggered away, confused. The coruscating reflection moved, following him.

"Frozen hell," he gasped.

"Yes, something like that," chortled the bishop, his arms raised, his eyes fixed on the moving flickers of light.

Light, reflected as if it was shining upon animated crystal, stalked closer. Raymond, backing to the wall of the study, saw he was facing two constructs, seemingly formed of pure reflection. Despite their insubstantial appearance, from the way one of them had parried his blade, he knew they were devastatingly solid.

He circled backward, putting the bishop's desk between himself and the constructs. They pursued, and he could see from the reflected light that they were fashioned into humanoid shapes, bright orange-red flickering along their arms and legs. Their torsos were small, their heads barely visible shadow.

Knowing there was no other choice, he slowed his steps, letting one of the constructs draw closer. Then, he lunged.

The thing moved fast but not as fast as him. The tip of his burning rapier thrust past a swinging arm and struck the reflected shape of the chest. The steel point bounced off, like he'd struck it against a rock or hunk of glass.

The creature's arm smashed into his blade, catching against the side. With a sharp crack, the rapier snapped in two, crimson flames bleeding into the air where they drifted like bird feathers, falling to the floor and sputtering out.

"Spirit-forsaken..." muttered Raymond, back-pedaling and tossing his broken blade aside.

On the other side of the room, Bishop Yates watched, mumbling silently, his fingers dancing like a puppeteer commanding his marionettes.

The two monsters came closer, and Raymond gave up. If his spirit-blessed sword wasn't going stop them, then his dagger wasn't going to either. He needed to retreat, to prepare, and to come back when he had the upper hand.

He spun and darted to the bishop's door, grasping the handle and tugging on it. It didn't move. Behind him, he heard the churchman laughing. Raymond pulled again, but there was no movement, not even the door rattling against a locked bolt. Somehow, the bishop must have sealed the thing with sorcery. Turning, Raymond drew his dagger. It would be useless against the transparent constructs, but what about their master?

Flipping it, he caught the narrow steel blade and flung it between the two approaching shards of hell, straight at Bishop Yates.

Yelping, the sorcerer raised his arm, but he was too late to stop the flying weapon from thunking into his shoulder, a hands-length of steel sinking into his fatty flesh. The man screamed and his hold on his summonings wavered. The reflected light broke and fell to the floor like shattered ice, where it quickly melted into nothing.

Grinning, Raymond advanced.

He still had his boot knife left, but he didn't think he would need it for the portly churchman. Without his sorcerous tricks, Gabriel Yates would be no match for a trained Knife of the Council. Raymond would kill the man with bare hands.

Yates looked up, his hand clutching the bloody hilt of the

dagger, hatred in his eyes. Without blinking, the old priest yanked the blade free. His blood sprayed in a hot arc across the rug. With his other hand he swept his book and sherry from the reading table and stabbed the blood-covered blade into it.

"Ah, hells," muttered Raymond.

He sprinted forward, his pitch-covered toes stitching across the fibers of the rug as he ran. Just three running paces from Yates, the floor in front of him exploded, knocking him back, flopping him onto his bottom.

Over the sound of snapping floorboards and shredding fabric, he heard Bishop Yates calling loudly and shrilly. "Minion of Set, by my steel, I hold you! By my blood, I bind you! By my spirit, I command you! Kill that man."

An angry bellow sounded like that of an animal. The floor shook with impact as something beat against it. Raymond scrambled to his feet, watching in shock as the table grew like an awful tree stump, expanding and spreading, buckling the floor and nearly reaching the ceiling of the study.

"You have no power over me, life-breather," slavered a deep, booming voice.

Raymond wished he hadn't seen the thing, hadn't watched it transform from inanimate wood into... something horrible.

Standing in the middle of the room, its horned-head just a hand below the ceiling rafters, was a muscle-bound monstrosity. Its arms were nearly as long as its body. Massive knuckles rested on what remained of the flooring. Its legs were short and covered in coarse, black hair. Its skin was bright crimson except where more bristling hairs traveled from its neck to its rear. Tusks, as thick as his forearm, protruded from a mouth that trailed long, slimy streamers of drool.

The creature stepped toward Yates.

"I command you!" yelled the sorcerer.

A gurgling roar, which Raymond thought must be the monster's laughter, rattled the room. "You command nothing, life-breather."

The thing took another step toward the bishop, and the man yanked furiously at his cassock, tearing it where the dagger had punctured his flesh. Displaying strength Raymond wouldn't have believed the rotund man had, the bishop tore open his robes, exposing his blood-smeared chest and thick bands of black tattoos.

"I am a servant of Set," said Yates, his firm tone starting to waver. "I am a loyal servant."

The creature shook its head, strings of slobber snaking around the room. "You are not loyal, life-breather, but…" The monster turned to Raymond. "Are you the one? The one of prophecy? I feel it near. I feel… It is hard to sense what is real in this place." The creature turned back to the bishop. "Is that the one?"

Quaking, Bishop Gabriel Yates mumbled, "Yes."

The monster turned toward Raymond.

He crouched, one hand dropping to his boot and pulling the hidden dagger from there. He was ready to spring, to lunge around the side of the monster and try his luck throwing another blade at the bishop. If he could kill the man, the binding the sorcerer had formed would be broken, and both Yates and the summoning would head straight to hell. If he missed again…

The creature stretched, its heavily muscled, bright crimson arms spreading wide. Its mouth hung open, yellowed teeth filling its gaping maw. The giant creature blocked his view of the bishop.

Then, it charged.

Raymond flung his knife at the careening mass of muscle and flesh. He couldn't miss, but the small blade could do nothing to stop a creature like that, either. The steel embedded in its belly, and the summoning grasped him, thick fingers pressing his flesh, crushing his bones for a split second of pure agony. Its teeth closed on him, and Raymond felt cold, bitter, all-encompassing cold.

THE PRIESTESS XX

THE CREATURE FELL on Raymond au Clair, hiding the man with its
red-skinned, bristly black-haired back, but she didn't need to see
to know what the sickening sounds of snapping bones and tearing
flesh implied. She offered a silent thanks to the spirits that the
man's horrified scream was swiftly cut short, and his life merci-
fully ended. He was an arrogant ass, but he hadn't deserved that.
Not for long, anyway.

Turning away from the sickening scene, she tightened her grip
on Thotham's old spear and lunged out of the shadows, streaking
at the bishop's back.

The old priest never saw her coming.

The tip of her spear smacked into his back and neatly pene-
trated his flesh. The steel sank deep until the crossbar touched the
priest's cassock. She yanked it out and stepped back.

Warbling a pathetic cry, Bishop Yates collapsed to the floor,
motionless.

For a long moment, she stood there, looking down at the body
of the man she'd killed. A sorcerer, one who had been attempting
to bind the powerful dark trinity. Killing him seemed rather easy
in the end.

She looked up. The sounds of frenzied eating were slowing,

but the monster the bishop had summoned remained. Its binding was cut. The binding should have been severed with the bishop's death. There was no anchor for it in the living world. The creature should have been banished back to the underworld. It didn't make any sense. Why had it not been banished?

The gnashing and slurping stopped, and the giant monster turned to study her.

"You should not be here," she said, hating that her voice was breaking, hating that her palms were slick with nervous sweat.

"The man called me, but his ritual was imperfect," said the creature, wiping a hand across its bloody, drool-soaked mouth in an all-too-human gesture. "He opened the bridge, and I came across it, but I was not compelled. He did not force control on me with his foolish utterances. I am here freely."

The summoning's head fell back and it laughed, a grating rumbling cackle. The sound pounded through her like rocks fighting to burst from her torso.

Her breath stopped and she stood, stunned. A spirit of the underworld in the living world, manifested physically and unbound. It was the worst nightmare. Thotham had told her as much, and it hadn't taken much convincing. A creature like this, with no master, no bindings to manage it, nothing to stop it from doing whatever the frozen hell it wanted to do. It was an error on the part of the sorcerer, a bloody promise of destruction for the living. According to Thotham, a creature unbound was worse than one with a sorcerer commanding it. This was a denizen of the underworld. It knew nothing but death.

"You killed him," rumbled the creature, stopping its laugh and glaring at her. "I wanted to do that."

She blinked at the monster.

"Now, I will kill you," it said. Then, it lumbered toward her.

The thing was slow, but the room was small. There was no way she could avoid the clutch of its wide, powerful arms, so instead of trying to dodge it or fight back, she ran.

Bolting to the windows at the back of the room, she jumped,

kicking a boot at the clasp in the center, bursting open the iron-and-glass barrier. Moving quickly, she hopped into the window frame, one hand holding Thotham's spear, the other raised to steady herself. She glanced down. She was four floors above the stone patio. Four stories above certain broken bones and likely death. Four stories above the fountain, cold water tinkling, only unfrozen because of its cycle of constant motion.

She jumped.

She landed with a splash, her sprawled legs barely slowing her as they knifed through the waist-deep, winter-cold water. Her boots slammed against the bottom of the pool, followed by her bottom. Her teeth clacked shut at the impact. It jarred her body, and for a brief moment, she was immersed underwater, shocked at the jolt of pain and the bitter chill of the near-frozen liquid. She was stunned, but somewhere deep inside, she knew she had to move or she would die.

Bursting out of the water, flopping onto the edge of the fountain, she rolled over and dropped to the stones below. Her body numb from the cold water, she didn't feel the fall. She reached up and grabbed the rim of the fountain, pulling herself to her feet, forcing her ice-cold body to move. Miraculously, neither of her legs were broken.

A thunderous boom split the night air.

She stumbled back from the fountain, sparring a glance to the east, where an angry glow lit the night. Thunder rolled over West-undon, originating from Prince Philip's palace. Their timing was almost perfect. If all had gone well, Duke set off his munitions and was drifting to safety on the Cloud Serpent. If it hadn't, Ainsley had fired a barrage of rockets into the prince's study, hoping to incinerate the director before he could flee. Either way, no rescue was coming from that quarter.

Above, in the bishop's mansion, a crunching clatter and a rain of stone and mortar exploded from the back of the building. Whatever the frozen hell Yates had summoned merely punched its way through the masonry, opening up the back of the building where it stood, staring balefully down at her.

She stepped away and stumbled over Thotham's spear. Kneeling, she snatched it and kept backing away. The weapon burned hot in her freezing hands, coursing warmth through her ice-cold flesh.

The giant beast leapt from the shattered back of Yates' study and landed on the stones of the courtyard, slamming down hard with an impact that blasted the stones around it like they were water in the fountain.

The ground shifted under Sam's feet from the concussive impact, and she stumbled, but kept falling back. She'd need space for… for whatever the frozen hell she was going to do.

"What are you?" she gasped.

"Hungry," cackled the monster.

Its giant maw opened as it laughed its hideous, dragging laugh. Huge broken teeth, a bright pink tongue, and glistening saliva shimmered in the moonlight.

Thotham's spear smoldered in her hands, the heat doing nothing to injure her but to encourage her. She knew what must be done. The time for tricks and games was over. The time for fighting was now. This was what he'd trained her for. This was her purpose. He died so she could fulfill this mission.

She danced forward, the tip of the spear held in front of her. She let it bounce in her hands and then thrust half a yard and whipped it to the side, trying to draw the creature's eye to the razor-sharp steel.

It didn't work. The thing had eyes only for her. Burning, ravenous eyes.

Grimacing, she advanced closer. The monster took a step closer as well. Stone crunched underfoot, and it raised its hands, clutching fingers on each paw spread as wide as she was. If those caught her…

Like lightning, she darted forward, thrusting the spear in a blur of speed and agility. She jumped back, dexterous feet landing softly on the stonework. The monster looked down at its bleeding hand where her spear had pricked it. It frowned. She frowned as well and looked at the fire-hot spear in her hands. Even with Thotham's spirit imbued in the weapon, it wasn't enough. Evidently, this spirit wasn't going to be easy to banish.

Without word, the monstrosity lumbered after her, its short legs not carrying it far or fast, but in the wall-enclosed courtyard, anywhere near its giant arms could be fatal. Trying to climb out over the smooth stone would take too long. The monster lurched between her and the locked doors of the mansion. There was no way out.

She sped across the golden pattern Yates had arrogantly left exposed in his open courtyard, but she didn't know any rituals that made use of such a pattern, and even if she did, there was no time to prepare. There was no time for anything except desperate flight.

The monster reached for her, and she struck it again, using her superior speed and the extended reach of the spear to nick it and then escape. Again and again, she opened the thing's flesh, but it just kept coming, chasing her around the courtyard.

Its mouth hung open, but it no longer spoke. It was enjoying the chase, she thought and worried. The little scratches she kept inflicting did nothing to harm the monster. It barely even noticed them, though blood splatter was beginning to cover the stones of the courtyard.

To get close enough to put her spear somewhere deadly would mean she'd be well within the creature's grasp. Bleeding it to death from small wounds could work in theory, but it showed no adverse effects from the damage she'd done so far, and she was beginning to flag. Could a physically manifested spirit even bleed to death? She didn't know. Technically, the thing was already dead.

Her heart was hammering in her chest and her breathing was coming in ragged gasps. There had to be some way.

Above, Bishop Yates' mansion was silent and dark. The tall

stone walls of the estates around them showed no life. There was no help on the way.

Her speed was keeping her alive, but she couldn't trust it to win the day. Any miscalculation and she'd be dead. The way the thing had burst through the stone wall was like nothing she'd ever heard of. Not even the wolfmalkin had possessed strength like…

The wolfmalkin. They were both powerful and pitiful creatures, actual wolves captured, branded, and bound to spirits which twisted their bodies into something half-wolf, half-man. Half alive, half dead. This thing that was chasing her, it was all dead, a creature from the underworld, a denizen of that frozen place. What did it mean that it was here, physically manifested? What opportunity did that give her?

The thing lurched at her, brushing a solid granite bench aside like it wasn't even there. She sprinted away, escaping its outstretched fingers, but the creature paused, looking down at the heavy bench it had carelessly knocked over. Its mouth open in what she realized was a grin, the creature reached for another bench and broke off the long, single slab of the seat with an easy turn of its wrist.

"Frozen hell," grumbled Sam.

She launched into a reckless roll, narrowly avoiding the flung piece of granite furniture the monster had tossed her way. Tumbling across the ground, she heard another ear-shattering crack and knew another bench was going to come flying at her.

A denizen of the underworld. What did it mean? What could she do with that?

Rock shattered, peppering her with debris as she scrambled back to her feet.

She couldn't simply banish the thing. The bridge it crossed had closed with the death of Yates, and her odds of actually killing it were growing slimmer by the second. It was of the underworld, though. It could be forced to return there if there was a bridge.

A bridge. How could she form a—

She cursed as a fist-sized hunk of rock thudded into her shoulder. Pain radiated down her side, but she was fairly certain nothing had been broken, yet. She rolled her shoulder, wincing at the stabbing agony, knowing she'd lost much of her mobility on the left side. Limping away as the thing snatched up another bench, she knew she was running out of time.

A bridge. She had to fashion a bridge. The spear, smeared with the creature's blood, burned hot in her hands. It screamed for her attention. She dodged again as a two-yard-long block of granite went sailing over her head, thrown as easily as she would toss a dagger.

The monster roared and snatched up another bench and the iron centerpiece of the fountain, water splashing as the metal was wrenched free. It faced her, one missile held in each hand. The debris was as big as she was, and either object would smash her like a rotten cantaloupe if they landed on her.

Sam shifted her hands on the haft of the spear, feeling the pulse of heat. It radiated through her hands and up her arms, but it did not harm her. It was Thotham. He was with her. She knew what she had to do.

She raised the spear and then brought it down on a raised knee. The wood, ancient and hard enough to stop a razor-sharp blade, snapped like a winter-dead twig. The heat bled from it. Tendrils of drifting white mist spilled out of the broken ends.

The monster flung the iron flute of the fountain at her. She dodged, trying to avoid it, but she couldn't dodge the bench seat that came whistling through the air behind it. With a sickening thump, the corner of the granite clipped the side of her head. Milk-white fog rose from the snapped ends of the spear as it fell from her senseless fingers. Everything went black.

THE CARTOGRAPHER XXII

OLIVER STOOD before the menacing front of the building. He wondered if it had been built to look like a smaller, sinister version of the Church, or if Yates had enhanced those elements after he purchased it. Either way, the place loomed with a grim aspect, and Oliver was shocked he'd never noticed it before.

"You want me to get the airship?" asked Ainsley. "I still have those rockets. I can make a hole where this house stands."

"Sam could be in there," reminded Oliver.

"She might be, but if she is, why isn't she coming out?" questioned the airship captain. "I'm sorry, m'lord, but she wasn't at the meet—"

"She could be hurt and unable to get out," he insisted.

"And there could be traps," retorted Ainsley.

"Even if we knew Sam was not inside, I would not authorize bombing a building in the center of Westundon," snapped Oliver. "Go back to the airship if you want, but I'm going in."

He climbed Bishop Yates' wide, stone steps and went through the gate to the front door, ignoring Ainsley's cursing and muttering as she followed behind.

The airship captain might complain about the risk, but she hadn't brought her twin cutlasses and pistols for a peaceful stroll in the park. She'd come for action, she just wanted to complain about it first. Fair enough. It wasn't her fight.

The doors were shut, but when he tried them, they opened easily. He shoved both of the thick slabs of oak wide. In the low lantern light that illuminated the foyer, he saw two corpses wearing priest's robes. Halberds lay beside them and sheathed short swords hung on their belts. Wide streaks of blood showed where they'd been dragged inside.

"At least we know she made it through the door," offered Ainsley.

Oliver grunted and entered the soaring entranceway, his gaze darting around, looking for traps. Not that he had any clue what a magical snare might look like, but sure as hell was cold, he wasn't going to walk into a sorcerer's nest without looking for traps like some sort of idiot.

They quickly searched the entry level and found nothing amiss, but they could both smell dust hanging in the air, like from broken mortar. It wasn't until they ascended the wide, red-carpeted stairwell and found the bishop's study on the fourth floor that he saw why. The place looked like a tropical island after a violent spring storm — broken wood, shattered furniture, strewn books. The rug was torn in two where the floor seemed to have exploded higher, and other places had been crushed down. There was broken crystal and glass and blood, pools of blood.

"Spirits forsake it, what happened in here?" asked Oliver.

"Here's a body," remarked Ainsley grimly, kicking aside a small avalanche of debris near the doorway to reveal a pair of boots, a pair of legs, and nothing else above the knees. "Oh, never mind," the captain managed to utter before, bug-eyed, she lurched back into the hallway and got violently ill, splashing a foul shower of vomit across one of Bishop Yates' tapestries.

"I don't recognize him," called Oliver. When Ainsley didn't respond, he added, "Don't worry, Captain. Those aren't Sam's boots. These legs are not hers."

Oliver proceeded farther into the room, stepping carefully to avoid where the floor was buckled and broken. He couldn't fathom what had happened, what would have caused such destruction, and he grew even more concerned when he saw what used to be the back wall. He recalled peering out the wide windows when visiting the bishop, but now, the entire section of glass and stone was simply missing. The force it would have taken to blow out the stone wall…

"Spirits," whispered Ainsley, finally returned from spewing her breakfast all over the hallway. "What in this world could have done that?"

"Nothing from this world," remarked Oliver.

He saw the simple cotton of a priest's robe and hurried across the shattered floor to find Bishop Yates lying on his stomach. A deep puncture pierced his back and his robes were covered in dried blood. His face, tilted to the side when he fell, showed a look of startled confusion.

"Sam," he said, pointing to the wound in the man's back. "This had to be Sam. She killed him."

"The bishop is dead. The guards downstairs are dead. Whoever belonged to those legs is certainly dead, but where is she?" questioned Ainsley, nervous fingers playing with the triggers of her pistols. "If she killed the man, why did she not come to the meeting point?"

Oliver looked around. He walked to the back of the room and peered down into the courtyard. He cried out. Sam was there, lying dead still, a bloody gash on the side of her head obvious even from four floors up.

Oliver spun. He and Ainsley raced to the stairs and plummeted down, both of them nearly crashing as they whipped around the marble and carpet stairwell. In a frantic rush, they burst into the courtyard. Like the room above, it had been destroyed beyond belief with broken stone, smashed masonry, and what Oliver shuddered to think might be giant footprints.

Sam lay in the middle of it, motionless.

Oliver rushed to her side, kicking away the broken pieces of

Thotham's spear and kneeling next to her. He put a hand on her neck and felt she was cold to the touch, but not as cold as the ambient air, he thought. Bending down, he listened for her breath and felt the faint brush of it against his cheek. She was alive, barely.

"W-What should we do?" stammered Ainsley.

He gently slid his arms beneath Sam's prone body and carefully lifted her.

"Go to the Four Sheets Inn and ask the barman for Kalbeth," he instructed. "Don't take no for an answer. Use those pistols if you have to. Tell her what happened to Sam. She'll know what to bring. Find us in Philip's quarters. I'm taking her to his physician."

"M'lord," protested Ainsley, "when Philip sees you, it's not his quarters you'll be going to, it will be his gaol. You are his brother, and despite everything, I know he cares for you, but it's going to take more than a night to wiggle your way out of this one. You can't go back there, m'lord, not yet."

Oliver started back into the bishop's mansion. Over his shoulder, he called, "Captain, my brother has the best physicians in Westundon, so I'm going to the palace. Bring Kalbeth there, make sure she gets inside. My brother won't stop you from helping Sam, no matter how livid he is at me. With any luck, Philip hasn't been able to piece together what happened yet. When you've collected Kalbeth, send your crew underground. Do whatever you need to so that no one can find them. Winchester knows not to speak to my brother, and I hope you do as well. As long as we keep your crew quiet, my brother may not be able to prove our involvement. Philip is nothing if not a stickler for the law. As long as he can't find evidence, we could be in the clear, no matter his suspicions. If he can prove it, I'll get out when I get out."

Ignoring his captain's muttering, he strode quickly through the bishop's mansion then out onto the street where they had a mechanical carriage waiting.

Calling to the driver who was sitting atop the bench of the

puttering contraption, Oliver yelled, "The palace. An extra handful of sterling if you get us there in less than a quarter turn of the clock."

The man leapt down to help get Sam's limp body inside, and before the door shut behind them, he'd climbed back onto the driver's bench and kicked off the brakes. They lurched into motion, Sam's head lolling lifelessly. Dried blood covered her from scalp to navel.

Oliver bent over her as they rumbled through the streets, offering a hope to every spirit he could think to name. When he got to Thotham, he glanced at Sam's face. Thotham. He whispered the name over and over again as they rolled, hoping the spirit of her mentor could hear him, hoping he could do something.

THE PRINCE III

"FROZEN HELL," growled the prince, walking through the charred remains of what used to be his study. "It looks like an explosive device went off in here. Maybe several of them. Look at that, Shackles. The stone by the doorway is just gone!"

"Yes, m'lord," agreed the chief of staff. "It does appear a series of explosions happened in here late last night. The munitions experts surmised four distinct origins, meaning four bombs. They went off with equivalent force to some of the smaller explosives that are carried on airships. This is the type of device the Company kits, m'lord, when they are sailing fully armed. That coincides with reports of a darkened airship that was seen by hundreds of witnesses sailing low above the city shortly after the blast."

"Well, the airship couldn't have lobbed the devices inside my office door, Shackles!" snarled the prince. "How did they get in here? Was it an assassination attempt?"

"I, ah, I think not, m'lord," murmured Shackles, looking away from his prince.

"Bishop Yates killed in such... such unusual circumstances," continued Prince Philip, kicking a blackened leg of what used to be a chair out of his path. "Evidently, Director Raffles has gone missing as well. We are the three most prominent men in Westundon, Shackles. It doesn't seem like anything other than an assassination attempt to me. The United Territories, some faction that survives in the Coldlands? Perhaps even an enemy from farther abroad? The Southlands has never been a truly settled place, though, why they'd want anything to do with me I cannot tell you."

"I could make an argument that there's a fourth man who is just as prominent in Westundon," mentioned Chief of Staff Herbert Shackles. "Your brother, m'lord."

"You think he's a target as well?" questioned Philip. "He just arrived back in Westundon a few days ago, and I haven't… Oh. Oh, I see."

"Not a target, m'lord," confirmed Shackles, his gaze locked on his feet.

"I-I don't—" stammered Philip. "He's a royal. Do you have any proof, man?"

"I have no proof," replied Shackles, glancing up to meet the stare of his prince. "If the reports of an airship are accurate, then it's no great leap, m'lord. I'm certain the official logs will show that the Cloud Serpent was tied to the bridge last night, and I doubt we'll find anyone to say otherwise. It was a dark night, so none of the witnesses can identify which ship it was. There was the royal marine gunship and a Company vessel that were moving about last night, but neither reported seeing other traffic. The guards working the bridge seem to be missing. None of the palace staff reported seeing anything unusual until the explosion. All of Yates' household staff is dead, and evidently, his neighbors are in the south right now so no one heard anything. The Company still seems unsure what happened to the director, but I've confirmed he did not return to his home yesterday evening. There is no proof of the kind you could show a magistrate, and I imagine there never will be unless someone talks. Oliver's strange priestess, his airship captain…"

"The priestess and the airship captain," grumbled Philip,

pacing across the fire-charred stone floor. "They won't talk. I'm sure he's seen to that. What about the crew of the Cloud Serpent? I suppose you've rounded them up?"

"The crew is occupied elsewhere, I was told," said Shackles. "Word is that Oliver gave them a rather large bonus, and they're in the midst of spending it in every back-alley ale sink and flesh market in this city. I couldn't find a one of them. I did corner the officers though, Captain Ainsley and her first mate, a man named Pettybone. They claimed to have gotten blind drunk and had a tumble. Said they couldn't recall a minute of time between sunset and sunrise."

"Do you believe them?" wondered Philip.

"The first mate is fifteen years her senior, m'lord," answered Shackles. "She's a fine-looking woman with a choice position as the first female airship captain in history. He looks like a toad, and I suspect he may have head lice. Stranger matches have been made, but..."

"They're lying for Oliver," growled Philip, glancing around his ruined study and sighing. "Do you really believe my brother is somehow responsible for all of this, Shackles? An airship was reported flying above the city, but as you mentioned, there were other airships moving about. It's possible none of those vessels were involved in this attack. I can't imagine the reason Oliver would have to do something like this. Even for him, this is a lot..."

"I know, m'lord," responded the chief of staff slowly. "Your brother is a rogue of the first order, but he's loyal to the organizations that he serves. He's unquestionably personally loyal to you, m'lord. Whatever he's up to, it wasn't aimed at hurting you. I can't fathom any reason he, or anyone else for that matter, would want to set off explosives in your study."

"But you still think he was involved?"

"Who else?" asked Shackles, "But if he was, he couldn't have acted alone. The airship captain, his priestess, they must be guilty as well. The priestess had a terrible injury and just woke up in the infirmary this morning. Oliver told me she'd gotten it while engaged in rough bedroom play. I wouldn't put that past him, but she's a priestess, not a tavern wench. Oliver hasn't been by to see her since she awoke. Whatever the true cause of her injury and whatever lies she'd tell to protect him, it's likely she and your brother have not had a chance to coordinate their stories."

"In the infirmary, you said?" asked Philip. "You think I should question her, see if her story matches what my brother told us?"

"In the infirmary," confirmed Shackles. "I wanted to talk to you before you went to her, m'lord, to make sure you were prepared to ask the right questions."

Philip grunted. "I'm prepared, Shackles. Now, I am prepared."

HE PUSHED ASIDE THE CURTAIN AND STEPPED INTO THE SMALL SPACE it cordoned off. There was a bed, a table, and a chair. The only other feature was the woman in the bed, looking at him suspiciously.

"It's good to see you awake," he began, taking a seat in the chair. "I'm told the physicians weren't sure you'd recover."

"They told me that as well," said the woman slowly.

"Water? Anything I can get you?" he asked her. He continued without waiting for a response, "You know who I am, of course? My apologies for taking a seat without asking. It's not proper, but you're a friend of Oliver's. I imagine there is much that is not proper which you are accustomed to."

"No, ah, Prince Philip, I am quite comfortable," she murmured. "And the seat is yours, after all. I thank you. Your physicians have been taking excellent care of me."

"They are the best," he said.

He crossed his legs, studying the young woman. She was dressed in loose-fitting clothing unlike anything he'd seen her wear and unlike anything the physicians would have provided. Perhaps from her friend who had come barging through the palace halls and then disappeared just as quickly once the physicians started asking questions? The odd woman had been flagged to the guards, but she vanished before anyone could apprehend her.

He studied the priestess, wondering what she was hiding. Her face was bruised, vivid purple, just starting to fade yellow-brown at the fringes. The top of her head was wrapped in thick bandages, but he could see jet-black hair peeking out beneath. She was trim and athletic, as he remembered her, and he had no trouble seeing why his brother enjoyed her company. She had a darker mien, though, and the way she looked at him caused him to shift in his seat. This was no wilting flower that needed the like of the Wellesley brothers to protect her. She forged her own path, and he had no doubt that was the way she preferred it.

"Can I help you with something, Prince Philip?" she asked.

"Tell me," he asked, "how were you injured?"

"I…" She touched the bandages on her head, her sleeve falling back to reveal a thick band of black tattoos trailing from her wrist up her arm. "I don't recall. I'm afraid with the head injury it's all very fuzzy."

"My brother has not been to see you yet?" inquired Philip.

"Ah, not that I recall," she murmured.

"Does that sting?" wondered the prince. "That he's made time for other pursuits instead of coming to see you?"

"He is a busy man," she said. "Duke is all right, then?"

"Duke? Ah, yes. Why would Oliver not be all right?" asked Philip.

She shrugged.

"Let us skip the wrangling. Tell me what happened last night," requested Philip. "My study is destroyed, the staff in the palace is frightened half to death, Bishop Yates is dead, his guards are dead, and an important member of the Company is missing. I am certain my brother was involved, and I know you are in league with him. Make it easy on yourself, will you? Talk to me, and I can ensure the ramifications for what happened fall where they should. What, ah, what was your name?"

"Sam," she supplied.

"Sam, of course," he grumbled. Sam. Why wouldn't his brother be running around with a beautiful woman named Sam? "Sam, I can be a very generous man, and it would be worth a great deal for me to understand what transpired in my city — in my own study! Do you think you can help with that? Do you want to find out how generous I can be?"

"Oh, I am sure you are quite generous, Prince Philip," responded Sam. "If I may, a suggestion, why not ask your brother what occurred? Surely, if you think he was involved in… you said a death? Surely, he could explain the circumstances."

"Surely," said Philip, leaning back in the chair and re-crossing his legs. "Do you know what my brother said about your injury? He claimed you had gotten hurt during rough bedroom play."

Sam laughed and then quickly groaned, a hand shooting up to grip her head. "Sorry, m'lord. Some lingering effects…"

"Rough bedroom play. Is that how your injury occurred?" he pressed her.

"If Duke says it is, then I suppose it must be so," she replied, still holding her head. "My memory, you understand."

Prince Philip sighed. "I confess this is improper and beneath me, but I must press you. You are not aware of where my brother is right now, so I will tell you. I am sorry if this gives you some distress. At this very moment, instead of sitting by your side, my brother is lounging in the arms of one of Baron Child's twins. I couldn't tell you which one, but I can tell you it could be either of them. A beautiful baroness, with land and title, opportunities beyond imagining for a mere priestess… does that make you jealous, Sam?"

"Yes, it does," she said, letting her hands rest in her lap and nodding very slowly. Philip let out a sigh and sat forward, but before he could put a wedge into the opening she'd left, she added, "Those twins are quite lovely. What I wouldn't do to put myself in Duke's trousers right now, though, I suppose he's not likely wearing them, is he? Probably not wearing much at all. Given time with Isabella or Aria, I certainly wouldn't be wearing any more than I had to."

"What!" cried the prince. "I—"

"I prefer women," explained Sam.

Philip's jaw dropped open. He shook himself and then slowly closed his mouth. He didn't know what to say.

"Does that bother you, m'lord?"

"No, I-I assumed that you and Oliver…" He drew a deep breath and let it out. Sam folded her hands on the bedsheet, waiting. "If you prefer women, then this rough play did not involve my brother?"

"Oh, it very well could have," responded Sam. "Is that what he said? I prefer women, but I've found a properly trained man can do the job in a pinch. It's a big world, m'lord, and I was raised to try anything at least once before you declare you don't like it. Why limit oneself? Don't you agree?"

"I can see this isn't going anywhere," said Philip, rubbing his face in his hands. When he looked back at her, he shook his head. "I will never understand that man's way with women."

"Neither will I," admitted Sam, smiling pleasantly.

The prince stood, straightening this jacket, frowning at the woman. "I will let my brother know you're awake. Whichever Child twin has taken over nursing him, I imagine they've barely let him come up for air, much less to check on the news around the city."

"Thank you, Prince Philip," replied Sam. "And, m'lord, he is a good man, your brother."

"I'll never understand it…" said Philip, turning to go.

"Tell him the clock is ticking, m'lord," called the priestess as he pushed through the curtains.

He turned to look back at her, frowning. She met his gaze, stern-faced, entirely serious. Any doubt he'd had about whether his brother had been involved in the events of the other night vanished, but new ones crept in. This woman, this priestess, wasn't protecting Oliver because he'd engaged in some sort of wild drunken escapade that resulted in the prince's study exploding. She was protecting him because she felt they still had work to do.

"Sorcery," guessed Philip. "Neither of you dropped the investigation, did you? You don't think this is over. Tell me, and I can help you."

"The clock is ticking, m'lord," repeated the strange woman.

He turned to go.

THE CARTOGRAPHER XXIII

HE STUMBLED out of the bed and nearly crashed to the floor, slumping against the table and rocking the crystal stemware there. His breathing was raw and ragged. Sweat beaded his forehead and he could feel the chill of it on his back as he was exposed to the cool air in the room. His legs trembled, and raw scratches marred his shoulders and his arms. His lower back ached from vigorous activity that he was certain had eclipsed a full cycle of the day. His most tender bits felt like they'd been subjected to unending pummeling, though more often than not over the course of the day, he'd been the one doing the pummeling.

On the floor near the door was folded sheet of parchment. On wobbly legs, he walked over and picked it up. It was written in Winchester's jagged handwriting. Sam was awake, and his brother had gone to see her. Oliver scowled.

"I don't think I'll be able to walk for a week," called a voice from behind him.

He turned, taking in the vision that was Aria Child. Sprawled out on her silk sheets, her hair a mess, her makeup long since smeared away onto him or her pillow, her chest rising and falling in a failing attempt to get her breath, she couldn't have looked more beautiful.

"That was the idea," he muttered.

She snorted, the sound odd coming from her delicate features. "What? You plan to go see my sister while I'm incapacitated?"

He shook his head, walking back to the table. "I think she'd kill me if I did, one way or the other."

Rolling her eyes, Aria let her head fall back onto the pillow. "She would kill you, but you'd enjoy every minute of it. Go on, then. Run off to Isabella. I'll pretend I don't know."

"I'm not going to see Isabella," he insisted. "In fact, if I can, I aim to sneak out of here before she can track me down. I-I have something I must do, something I hope I can do now that... I have to go, Aria."

"I heard the knocking on the door," said Aria, glancing at him. He struggled to meet her eyes and not let his gaze rove over her naked body. "It was Winchester, wasn't it? Let me guess. The girl is awake, the common one you've been spending time with, a priestess? What do you see in that girl that you do not see in me or my sister? Isabella, I could live with. She looks just like me, for one, so I cannot fault you there. This other girl, though... Samantha, right? I do not like it, Oliver."

"It's not like that, Aria," he responded. "First of all, she's a priestess, and they, well, she does, ah... She's a priestess. Second, she prefers women. I suppose she's been with a man before, but it's only women she invites into her bed now."

Aria blinked at him. "Are you lying to me?"

"No," he answered, crossing his arms and realizing he was leaning against her table, stark naked. Not that there was any part of him she hadn't seen and thoroughly explored, but it did feel a bit uncomfortable to be standing in the cool air with nothing to drape over himself. "I tell you this true. I've never slept with Sam."

"Really?" asked Aria, rising up on one elbow. "You haven't even, I don't know, haven't done anything with her?"

"Not like that," said Oliver, letting his hands fall down so they covered his manhood and then shifting again as that felt entirely awkward.

"Interesting," murmured Aria, one slender finger tapping her lips.

"Why is that interesting?" wondered Oliver, suddenly nervous.

"Well, I can imagine there are certain activities where another woman may excel," explained the baroness. "You men, you think we only like one thing."

He frowned at her. "Sam said much the same."

"Perhaps I would enjoy this girl," purred Aria. "Will you introduce us when you have finished whatever it is you plan to do?"

"Introduce you?" exclaimed Oliver.

"Why not?" questioned Aria. "She is not attached, is she?"

"Well, no, not really," muttered Oliver. "She, ah, has a friend that… It's just not proper."

"Yes, propriety, something you've always been deeply concerned about." Aria laughed. "Introduce us, my sweet duke, and perhaps she and I will get along well. And don't worry, Oliver, I won't leave you out in the cold. Whatever the girl's preferences, I'm sure she and I could find some way to keep you happy."

Despite himself, he felt a stirring and decided if he was going to make it out of the room, he'd have to do it very soon.

"You like that, don't you?" teased Aria. "Come back to bed, and let's talk about it. Tell me what you'd like, what you're thinking about. I'm so curious."

"I-I have to go," he said hoarsely, shuffling toward his trousers.

"My father is beginning to wonder when Isabella and I will settle down, Oliver," she claimed. "He worries we'll grow old and all of our prospects will disappear. There's some truth to that, don't you think? Men want a young wife, one who is still nubile and eager to please. I kept you here so long, Oliver, because I need to convince you that I am what you want. If I am, then it's time to make it known. My father will not let me stay unattached for much longer."

Pulling his shirt over his head, Oliver turned to study Aria. For the first time in a day, she was serious about something. He could see she meant every word she was saying.

"I understand, baroness, but now is not the time," he insisted.

She let one of her legs slide up on top of the other, her knee pointing skyward, the space between those legs widening. "Maybe it is not, but it will be soon. The clock is ticking, Oliver."

Grunting, he turned to go.

"YOUR BROTHER IS LOOKING FOR YOU," MENTIONED SAM THE MOMENT he ducked through the curtain surrounding her bed.

"Yes, I imagined he would be," said Oliver. "I've been hiding out where he'd be loath to catch me. He spoke to you? What did you tell him?"

"I told him I couldn't remember anything," she replied.

"Can you remember anything?" asked Oliver.

"I remember enough to know we need to be moving," she said, shifting underneath of her blankets. "I think I can make my way out of here with a little help."

"I brought some of your potions," said Oliver, setting her pack on the bed beside her. "There's a few other things in there from Kalbeth. She stopped by, did you know? She began applying some tinctures and ointments while you were unconscious, but the physicians were getting suspicious. You seemed stable, so she left before they asked too many questions. I don't know which vials are which, but maybe there's something…"

"The stone vials," said Sam, rummaging through the open pack. "Philip told me you'd claimed I was injured during a bout of rough sex."

Oliver winced, rubbing his arm where one of Aria's nails had dragged deep. He coughed and then replied, "It can happen. I hope you're not offended."

"I'm a big girl," replied Sam, producing one of the stone vials he recalled her drinking on the train to Middlebury. She unstoppered it and downed it without pause. "That should help. These other mixtures, that is what Kalbeth applied? I owe thanks to Ivar val Drongko."

"Who?"

"The man I killed in Romalla," replied Sam.

"There's clothing in there as well," Oliver said. "The outfit you were wearing is rubbish now."

Pulling out a fresh pair of trousers, vest, and shirt, she remarked, "I need to get more clothes."

"Perhaps after we've…" He leaned in closer and lowered his voice. "After we've killed the last sorcerer in this dark trinity. Don't you think that would be a better time to go to the shops?"

"No time for shopping but time for sex?" questioned Sam. "Don't deny it. I can smell it all over you."

Frowning, Oliver stood and raised his arm, sniffing delicately.

"Not there," said Sam with a sigh. "It's… Never mind." She flipped back the blankets and levered her legs over the edge of the bed. "Help me get dressed, will you? Until that potion has had time to work, I'm going to be a bit woozy. The bench nearly cracked my skull, I think."

"Bench?" wondered Oliver. "You fell on a bench?"

"No, it was thrown at me," she claimed.

He blinked in confusion.

"We have a lot to catch up on," she said. "The monster was gone, I take it, or you would know how a stone bench was thrown at me."

"Nothing like that has been reported," he said, letting his voice drop even lower. "The only things I found at the bishop's mansion were dead bodies and you. When you didn't arrive at the meet, I went looking for you. What caused that kind of destruction, Sam?

There was a man missing everything but his legs and feet. What happened to the rest of him?"

She shrugged, evidently unsurprised a dead man was missing everything but his lower limbs. "Later, when we can speak privately."

Nodding, he helped her up, and trying not to look too hard at her naked body, he helped her get dressed.

"How was the baroness?" she asked.

He shot up, frowning at her. "How did you... Ah, Philip told you. It... I wasn't going to leave without you, and I didn't want to try to wake you until your body was ready. Truth be told, I didn't want to sleep in my own bed, either. I did my best to keep your location secret, and, well, I did a bit of hiding of my own."

"Hiding the sausage." Sam snickered.

He rolled his eyes, muttering, "Childish..."

"I don't know how you keep those two so interested," she continued. "In my experience, you men have one trick, and you insist on using it every time. With a creative woman, the possibilities are endless. It's about a journey, a range of experiences, and not just the sausage you have hanging between your legs. You're missing out, Duke, but the biggest crime is what your partners are missing."

"I haven't had any complaints," snapped Oliver.

"Don't let those two ever experience another woman, then. They won't be the same afterward," advised Sam. She must have noticed his startled jump. "What? What did I... Ah, a woman. Perhaps you can introduce me to the baronesses one day? I think I'd enjoy that."

"We need to go," growled Oliver, helping Sam shrug into her vest and then collecting the belt with her kris daggers. He stuffed them into her pack and slung it over his shoulder. "Let's get out of here before my brother— Oh, hello, Philip."

His brother was standing outside of the curtain with his arms crossed and an annoyed look on his face.

"What did you hear?" asked Oliver.

Philip snorted. "Nothing, but spare me your lies about whatever it is you're going to claim you were discussing. You are leaving, is it, without talking to me?"

"We did talk..." mumbled Oliver, glancing back at Sam then to his brother.

"You did this, all of it!" said Philip, his voice quiet but tight with palpable tension. He stepped close and glanced around the infirmary to ensure they were alone. "Somehow, you're responsible for what happened in my study. You know what happened at Bishop Yates' mansion as well, don't you? What is going on, Oliver? Do you know where Director Raffles is? He's gone missing, and the Company is going to be apoplectic if we cannot find him."

Oliver drew his shoulders back and forced his arms to hang loosely by his side.

Philip reached out and gripped his brother's shoulder. "I know you, brother. I trust you, but to maintain that trust, you have to tell me what is happening! Is it sorcery again?"

"Yates and Raffles were sorcerers, brother," confirmed Oliver quietly. "They're part of a trinity that is trying to bind a dark, terrible power. They planned to sacrifice Middlebury, Philip. They would have killed everyone within the city. It'd be Northundon all over again. They were going to use the power from those captured souls to penetrate the barrier to the other side and bind spirits stronger than you or I can imagine. Tens of thousands of people would have died, and that'd just be the beginning. That's why we did what we did. We had to."

"You expect me to believe—"

"What do you think happened to Northundon, Philip?" interjected Oliver. "The city was sacrificed, and it would have happened again. These men would have brought down Enhover, would have brought down everything. Everything!"

His brother shook his head like he was trying to keep out the information Oliver was sharing with him. Finally, he tightened his grip and looked into his brother's eyes. "You have proof?"

"Go to Bishop Yates' mansion," suggested Oliver. "Look for yourself what happened there. Decide if you think that destruction could have come from anything in this world. If you cannot fathom it, Philip, then that is your proof."

"I've heard the report," growled the prince. "How do you know? What if—"

"We serve the Crown, brother," said Oliver, interrupting the prince in a whisper, "both of us in our own ways, we serve the Crown. Trust that I serve the Crown, Philip. That night, Sam and I killed two of the three sorcerers. I heard the words from Raffles' own mouth. He is what I say he was. Yates was as well. There were three of them, Philip. The third is in Southundon."

Philip let go of Oliver's shoulder and stepped back. "Who is it?"

"I don't know yet," admitted Oliver, shaking his head. "I don't know, but we have the means to find out. We can follow the taint of the underworld to whoever it is, and once we've identified them, we will prove it. Then, we will act."

"I'll let Father know," said Philip, pinching his chin with his fingers. "Between him, Admiral Brach, and William, we can support you—"

"No," said Oliver. "In Westundon, it was Yates and Raffles, two men almost as close to you as I am. I don't know who we'll find in Southundon, but if Father begins to alert his top echelon of advisors…"

"If those men were almost as close to me as you are, you'd be in gaol right now," remarked Philip. "The Crown and the family, there is nothing more important. Father taught us that. Family, we are nothing without each other. Let me tell—"

"I'd never turn my back on our family," insisted Oliver. "I do this for us. The Crown and the Wellesleys."

"I hope so," said Philip, stepping back. "Is there anything I can do? There must be some way I can help."

"No one must be allowed inside Bishop Yates' of Director Raffles' homes. There could be things in there, books or materials, which can be used in sorcery. Anyone who sees it is in danger of starting the dark path. It must all be destroyed without anyone knowing the truth. And, Philip, don't tell Father we're coming," said Oliver. "Don't tell anyone. If we fail… Let us hope we do not fail."

"Spirits bless you, brother."

"Spirits bless Enhover, the Crown, and our family," replied Oliver.

Then, he led Sam out of the infirmary, the palace, and down to the airship bridge. They had a mystery to solve.

THE PRIESTESS XXI

"Middlebury, he said?" she asked Duke.

"That's what he said," replied the nobleman. "The moment I told him I knew of the sacrifice, he thought that's what I meant. It was the only thing he was truly concerned about. He aimed to torture me until I told him how I found out about it."

"They did not achieve what they aimed for in Northundon," mused Sam. "Your mother escaped, for one. Do you think they've been fiddling with the ritual since then? Both men were getting on in years, and if they hoped to obtain immortality, I know I'd much rather live it as a young woman than an old one."

"Do you think they could do it in Middlebury?" asked Duke. "Bind the dark trinity to their bidding?"

Sam shrugged. "I don't know. It doesn't matter. Whether it worked or not, Middlebury would be gone, as dead as Northundon. That, Duke, is what matters. That's why the Church formed the Council of Seven so long ago. For years, I did not understand it, but now, I do. Nothing can be allowed to sink to those depths of evil. Someone has to stop it."

"We will," said Duke with more conviction than she thought was earned, but she didn't disagree with the sentiment. Whatever they had to do, they would stop it.

Sitting at the small table in the captain's cabin of the Cloud Serpent, Ainsley noisily cleared her throat and then refilled the copper cup sitting in front of her. She'd kept none of the fine wine Captain Haines had traveled with, unfortunately. Ainsley preferred her grog. She said it got the job done quicker, which Sam supposed was true, but there was such a thing as getting the job done, and getting the job done in style.

The captain had her own sense of finesse, though. Laid in front of her were her two cutlasses, her two pistols, two empty glass bottles that had once been full of rum, and a sinister-looking clay orb that made Sam want to cry out every time the tilt of the airship shifted, and the thing rolled across the table. More than once, Ainsley caught it before it crashed to the floor.

"Is that, ah… What…"

"Grog," slurred Ainsley, a hand on what really looked an awful lot like a grenado. "I'm drinking grog."

"We know," mentioned Duke, glancing between Sam and the captain. "You… Shall we bring Pettybone in?"

"What? Just because he's sober?" muttered Ainsley.

"Well, yes," replied Duke slowly.

Ainsley snorted.

Grumbling to himself, Duke tried to continue the conversation. "Raffles acted like he did not know where my mother was."

"He likely doesn't know," said Sam. "If he did, I think he'd capture or kill her, right? She's the missing piece in completing the sacrifice. That's what the spirits told you, isn't it?"

Duke frowned. "Sacrifice, bargain, yes, that's what they told me."

"If they knew where she was, their plan would be to capture her and complete the original ritual, not start all over again," said Sam. "They were going to bind the dark trinity, and from what I gathered, Set's minion was not happy about it. If I hadn't killed Yates myself, that creature would have done the work. They've gone a long time with those spirits angry at them."

"I understand that," said Duke, frowning, "but why would my mother not return? She would not have any idea she was a target of the attack, much less a piece of some dark bargain."

"No," agreed Sam, looking away, "not unless…"

"Unless what?" asked Duke coldly.

"It's a good line of questions. How did she escape? Why hasn't she returned to your father?" said Sam, not wanting to say what was obvious to everyone but Duke.

"Because someone close to him is who we seek," guessed the peer.

Sam glanced at the furcula that lay on the table next to all of Ainsley's clutter. It pointed in line with their heading to Southundon.

Without sorcery, could his mother have known of the dark bargain? Was there any other rational explanation for why she had not returned? Having a healthy fear of sorcerers was common sense, but the King and Queen of Enhover were the most powerful leaders in the known world. Edward had stood up to what he had thought was the Coldlands' invasion, and if he was anything like Duke, he wouldn't back down no matter the threat. If there was a hidden hand close to the throne that Lilibet feared, would she leave her children behind? No matter the threat, would she have allowed her four sons to remain in danger? The more Sam thought about it, the less likely it seemed Lilibet merely fled. But, they were trying to piece together a mystery twenty years old that no one back then had even realized was a mystery.

It was too much. Sam sat back, frowning in frustration. There was too much they just simply did not know. They did know one thing, though. Someone carried the taint of the underworld, and the furcula was leading them there.

She looked to Duke. "If it is someone close to the throne, Southundon makes sense."

"My uncle led the incursion into the Coldlands twenty years ago," said Duke quietly. "He was the one responsible for exterminating those people. He's always been a regular visitor to Westundon, and I know he was close with Raffles and Yates."

"Let's not jump to conclusions," said Sam. "It could be... It could be anyone."

"We'll find out soon enough," replied Duke.

THE SOLDIER I

HE TOUCHED the edge of the copper knife, sliding his finger down to the point. He let the tip of the knife touch his flesh, feeling it press against his skin but stopping short of puncturing it. He would not draw his own blood. That was dangerous, though the time for hiding in the shadows, for minimizing risk, was at an end. It was time for danger, time to gamble.

He'd seen the glae worm transmissions. His nephew, the prince, had been panicked, sending concerned tidings to King Edward, worried that something awful had happened in Westundon. It had. Edward had shown the messages to William, curious what he would make of them. William had acted confused, as if he couldn't understand what he was reading.

Most wouldn't have understood, but he did.

Director Randolph Raffles. Bishop Gabriel Yates.

His partners. Something deeper than mere business associates or romantic flings. They'd intended to bind themselves together for, well, forever. Had their plans come to fruition, they would have become nearly immortal. Supported by the power and the longevity of the dark trinity, they could have gained control of the shroud between this world and the other. They could have siphoned strength to sustain themselves, to make themselves impervious to wounds that would fell another man, impervious to old age.

The trinity was a collection of spirits more ancient than the oldest texts, older than the oldest evidence of writing in Enhover, which took some thinking about. Spirits that, due to their tenure on the other side of the barrier and their incredible ability to avoid the grinding of the wheel, would impart near limitless power on anyone who could command the force to their will. Power that was, frankly, unimaginable even for him.

He guessed that in the early days of ascension, they wouldn't be able to comprehend what it was they controlled. He imagined it would take years, decades, even centuries to fully realize the strength of those three spirits. They would have the time, though. He knew that with the power of the trinity, they could interrupt the pull of the barrier, the tug of the underworld, just as the dark trinity had avoided the wheel, rebirth, and life. Everything in balance.

It was so simple, except he was now one. He was one, and he needed three. Without three souls, the ritual they had designed would not work. Without a reflection in the pattern, the trinity could not be bound. But there was one hope that he clung to. It was irrational. It was risky, and it was foolish, but it was all that he had.

His nephew. Oliver would come to Southundon and confront him. He could feel it. The boy had never backed down in his life. Oliver didn't know how. It might not even occur to him that he could fail, that he could lose. He certainly hadn't experienced loss often.

That, ironically, was what William was counting on.

Three souls. Himself, his nephew, and the priestess who was certain to be in tow. Three souls. Himself, Raffles, and Yates. Then there was the dark trinity. Three interlinking groups of three, arranged in a pattern, bound together. He could use his nephew's death, the family blood within his veins, to tie him to Raffles and Yates. Even dead, the partnership could continue.

William hadn't had time to test his theory, but he was confident it would work. The logic was sound. The ritual was supported by similar bindings and examples within the literature, and he could place himself in position to control it. He only needed his nephew's blood. His nephew's blood, and that of so many others. To power to the pattern, to lock the binding, the blood would have to flow like a river.

That was for another day, another place. First, Oliver would come striding in, shouting righteous platitudes and expecting certain victory. He'd achieved it against Raffles and Yates, somehow. He'd vanquished those sorcerers who commanded power greater than Enhover had seen in four centuries, yet they were shadows, shadows of the true leader of their mirror trinity.

That was what he'd learned that they never had. Every group needed a leader. Every pattern needed a strong point supported by the weaker ones. Each triangle had an apex. Whatever Oliver had done to defeat those two, he would find a tougher opponent with William Wellesley. He smiled, turning the bone-handled, copper-bladed knife in his hands.

"What are you laughing at, you sick bastard?" screamed a man.

He glanced at the man and his smile only grew broader.

"Stop toying with us, you monster. If you're going to kill us, do it!"

He shrugged. "As you wish."

Taking three quick steps forward, William plunged the copper blade into the speaker's chest, instinctively slipping the tip between the man's ribs and stabbing directly into his heart.

With the practice of a man who'd done the same motion hundreds of times, he twisted the blade, opening the wound and the hole in the man's heart, then withdrew it. He held a copper bowl, forged from the same vein of metal as the knife, underneath the puncture in his victim's chest. He watched as blood pumped furiously out, splashing into the bowl, filling it halfway to the rim.

William turned to the two other captives that he'd brought up for the ritual. Both of them stared at him, stunned.

"Anyone else in a hurry?" he asked calmly.

Neither responded, which was too bad. He had left them ungagged purposefully. He enjoyed hearing their pleading. Alas, these two were too frightened, and he knew from experience that wasn't about to change. To be fair to them, it shouldn't change. They should be frightened. They were going to die soon.

Their arms and legs were locked in place by thick iron manacles. They were spread eagle against giant iron crosses, bound naked. They were exposed to the winter elements and entirely helpless. They'd just witnessed one of their fellow captives murdered in front of their eyes, and no one did anything about it. No one was going to do anything about it. No one had for two decades.

William shook the knife, flinging a stringer of blood onto the ancient stone floor where so many other spots of the sanguine liquid had fallen. Occasionally, a powerful storm would sweep the roof of the old druid keep and wash the blood away, but until it did, William left it there. The dried blood gave him a sense of accomplishment, of progress toward a goal.

He grinned, looking from his fortress, across the river to his brother's city.

The prime minister. A plum position. One he'd earned by both birth and merit. It was the envy of almost every person in the nation of Enhover and, he imagined, the world. It was as far as he would ever rise, though, by conventional means. His brother was king, and he had a line of healthy sons. They were having their own children now. With every birth, William's proximity to the throne lessened.

He knew his nephews respected his judgement and experience, but in time, they would have their own loyal advisors. They would have their own sycophants whispering into their ears. In time, William would be sent to the country for a comfortable retirement.

It was wonderful, he supposed, but he'd never known less. Ever since birth, he'd been destined to be his brother's prime minister. It didn't matter that he deserved it. He would have had the role anyway. His entire career had been about avoiding catastrophic failure. That was all he'd ever needed to do — simply do not fail so spectacularly that his brother had to send him away or bury him. It soured the sweetness of having the position, knowing that it was through no great skill of his own.

William had avoided demotion, for what that was worth. He'd avoided it and achieved heights that few men could dream of. But he was a Wellesley, and their blood did not flow through the veins of servants. He was not meant to be a mere advisor, whispering and bowing to his older brother's whims. No, he was destined for something grander. He had always felt that. He'd spent twenty years crafting a design which would earn it.

He experienced a brief moment of doubt.

The other two points in the pattern had fallen. Weaker ones, of course, but weaker did not mean weak. Raffles and Yates had both been accomplished sorcerers, though they'd rarely used their skills in outright battle. Still, they'd known what was coming and had been ready. It made him nervous that he had heard nothing. He hadn't known what had occurred until he'd felt their souls almost crossing the shroud.

Almost. He smiled, shaking aside the cloud of doubt.

He'd laid a snare along that barrier years before. Their cabal had worked decades studying, taking their time, and designing a pattern to bind the dark trinity. He had left nothing to chance. If his partners had backed out, if they were somehow discovered and killed, if they'd had a simple accident, he would not allow his work to be for naught. In the moment their souls had made the transition from one world to the next, he'd captured them.

It was a difficult bit of sorcery. First, he'd spent years unravelling the mysteries the ancients had left in the frozen wilds of the Coldlands. Then, for months he'd prepared the rituals which set the net between the living world and the other. The fact that his partners never realized he'd tied those bindings to their souls demonstrated which of the three was the key point in their trinity, and that justified his actions.

Preparation. It was what the game was about, and he'd prepared for everything.

Now that he had Raffles' and Yates' souls in his custody, he had to sustain them. The pull of the underworld was constant, and without the strength of the dark trinity, he couldn't avoid it forever. He could delay the transition, though, and for long enough, he hoped. Long enough to complete the ritual and bind the dark powers. Then, he'd let his partner's souls go to the other side where he could only imagine they would suffer eternal torment. The dark trinity would take revenge where they could, and William couldn't protect the other two in the underworld.

No matter.

He turned back to the two captives behind him.

"Take one last look around," he suggested. "Remember this place when you are on the cold other side. The stronger your memory of this world, the quicker the wheel will grind your soul, and the sooner you will be reborn. Consider it one last friendly piece of advice."

Shocked, the red-haired youth stared at him, ignoring the instructions to take in his surroundings, to try and remember this place as he passed through barrier. Ah, the folly of youth. William hadn't listened to his elders either when he had been the boy's age.

He stepped forward and plunged his copper knife into the red-haired boy's chest, finding his heart and letting that blood spill into the copper bowl he placed underneath the wound. More life-blood, enough to keep Raffles' soul anchored in the living world for another two days.

Sighing, the prime minister realized he would need to spend more of his captives to keep Raffles' and Yates' souls secure. Captives he was in short supply of, but he couldn't risk letting his partners slip away. He had much to do in the next several days, much to prepare before the ritual, and he was certain it would not be long before his nephew came looking for him.

Sliding his blade into the third victim and collecting the dying woman's blood, he thought about his nephew and wondered how the impatient boy would come at him. Would he charge straight in, or had he learned wisdom in his travels? Would he fabricate a distraction and come from behind?

However Oliver came, William was ready.

THE CARTOGRAPHER XXIV

"SEHEHT IS the physical strength of the dark trinity," explained Sam. "The society was known as the Feet because the entity was the strength and power that moved the union forward. Set is the spoken knowledge, the Mouth. Seshim is the apex of the trinity, the master manipulator, the Hands. I believe Raffles was associated with Seheht and Yates with Set. Whoever the third point of the triangle is, they must be affiliated with Seshim."

"Then we've got the strongest one left to defeat?" asked Oliver.

"So it seems," agreed Sam.

In front of her, the black-leather bound Book of Law was open. She had spent the last several hours leafing through its ancient pages. Evidently, much of the grimoire was indecipherable for the priestess, but Kalbeth had agreed to translate a portion relating to the makeup of the dark trinity. Despite Sam's angry demands, the palm reader had refused to translate any of the rituals.

"This book deals primarily with the spirit Seheht," continued Sam, "though there is mention of Set and Seshim. I don't know how much it will help us. It seems even in the lore of the trinity, Seshim is an unknown factor. To use a popular analogy, Seshim is the one behind the curtains directing the action, while Seheht and

Set are on the stage drawing all of the attention. We should plan for the unknown, whatever that means."

Oliver grunted. "One thing I do not understand, how does this all relate to Ca-Mi-He? That's what got us started down the trail, right? Hathia Dalyrimple somehow made contact with that spirit. It tainted a dagger, and the bodies started to fall."

"I know," murmured Sam. "Here's another mystery. The dark trinity and Ca-Mi-He are frequently noted as opposing each other. Two lords of hell, I guess you could say. I don't think Ca-Mi-He would bless an artifact that was being used by disciples of the trinity. If Raffles and Yates were behind Northundon, then why would they change tact? It makes no sense, unless..."

"The master manipulator," said Oliver. "It all comes down to that, doesn't it? Even Raffles and Yates were being played. When I mentioned sacrifice, that could be why Raffles jumped to their plans in Middlebury, not Northundon."

"I don't know, maybe," said Sam. "It's possible after the ritual in Northundon failed, this unknown third sorcerer aimed to strengthen the pattern by recruiting help. Three is always stronger than one. Everyone knows that. I don't think Raffles and Yates had any clue who, or what, they were dealing with."

"Southundon is just over the horizon," called Ainsley from the doorway to the captain's quarters. "We can update our heading or drop you down. Either way, the time to decide is now."

Oliver stood and picked up the furcula. With Sam and Ainsley in tow, he stepped out onto the deck, holding a hand over his eyes in the bright morning sun. He marched to the foredeck and stood beside First Mate Pettybone.

"Which way is Southundon?" Oliver asked.

The first mate pointed dead ahead.

Holding the furcula in his hand, Oliver waved it slowly back and forth until he was certain the tug was centered, tracking a few points starboard.

"Damn," he muttered.

"Not in the city?" wondered Ainsley from behind him.

"No," said Oliver. "It's tracking west."

"West of the city," said Sam. "What's west of the city?"

"An old druid keep," said Oliver. "Raised before my family took power, like the one in Northundon except it's… bigger and wilder, I guess, like it wasn't built for men as we know them. It's been occupied periodically over the centuries, but no one has stayed long. Rumor is that it is haunted. Of course, that's always the rumor around those places. It is true, though, that anytime someone moves in, something awful has happened to them or those they love. It'd been abandoned for decades until my uncle purchased it a few years after returning from the Coldlands."

"Oh," said Sam quietly.

"Maybe he can help us… Oh," said Captain Ainsley.

"Set us down," instructed Oliver, his voice heavy with dread. "If we have any chance of stealth, we can't arrive in an airship. On foot, we might be able to sneak in. After Northundon, I spent a lot of time in that keep, exploring the ruins, drawing maps for my… for my uncle. Being inside felt comfortable to me, the only place that did after my mother disappeared. I know this place."

Grimly, Sam nodded.

"You certain you don't want me coming with you?" asked Ainsley.

"I need you to go to my father," said Oliver. "King Edward has to know what is happening. He has to know about the knife poised at his back. He's dealt with sorcery before. He'll know what to do if we fail."

"Should you not wait for his assistance?" questioned the captain.

Oliver shook his head. "I have to do this. I have to. I was always out of place in my family. My brothers have provinces to run. They have wives, families, heirs to the throne. I was always trying to find my calling, whether it be in the bowels of a druid keep or over some far horizon in the tropics. I'm still searching, I think, but I know where I need to look next. I have to do this. It feels right."

"Thotham's prophecy," murmured Sam. "He foresaw this."

"It feels right," stated Oliver. He turned to Sam. "If it is my uncle we seek, I think I know where he'll be. Do you think those tattoos will keep you undetectable by the spirits?"

"I think so," she said. "If they have no reason to suspect I'm there, the designs will help me avoid notice."

"Come on then. I have a plan," he told her. "First, I need to draw you a map."

The two of them scurried into the captain's cabin.

Behind them, Ainsley called out, "Bring her down. Prepare to put two over the side. Quickly, now, boys! There's work to do."

THE FORTRESS, A SINGLE MASSIVE BLOCK OF STONE, SAT AMIDST THE green hills and surrounding forest like a giant tree stump that some farmer hadn't bothered to yank from the field. The structure was of the land, as if it always had been, but not a part of the current arrangement. The trees and open fields seemed to have grown around the uncompromising stone instead of the fortress being built amidst the foliage. Beside the forest, a river ran wide and sluggish, so near the coast. On the other side of the slow-moving water was a dusky smear in the sky which marked Southundon.

From the distance, they could not yet see the tops of the tallest towers in Enhover's capital city, but Oliver knew they would see them when they got closer. More times than he cared to count, he'd sat in airy rooms in his father's palace, ignoring some blab-bering tutor, staring out over the rooftops and walls to look at the countryside and the old druid's keep in the distance. That scene, still vivid in his mind after so many years, was his strongest recollection from his studies, the pull, like iron to a lodestone, drawing him from the palace and civilization into the wilderness.

No one quite knew what to think when William Wellesley had purchased the old keep from a family of peers that was on the decline, but everyone assumed there was some element of sibling rivalry. It was a joke, amongst those close enough to the royal family to speak assuredly, but not so close that they actually knew anything, to say that William wanted a place that adequately reflected his status — within sight of the royal line but not a part of it.

Oliver wondered if there was some truth to the sibling rivalry speculation. Why else would William pursue the dark path? He was prime minister, the most powerful administrator in the empire. He'd been named a duke as well, though his land holdings were paltry. Still, it was enough to make Lannia an excellent match, but not so much he would be distracted tending to it. King Edward had ensured William's family would be well provided, which was not always the case with offshoots of the Wellesley line, and William had been given true control over his offices, which was even rarer. What else could a man ask for?

King Edward Wellesley always thought like that, always a step ahead. He'd placed his brother close. Oliver had assumed because William was a capable manager, but what if there'd been more? Had his father suspected something about William and made efforts to assuage his ego or keep an eye on him? If he'd had suspicions, why hadn't Edward acted? If anyone had known of William's secret studies, it would be Edward.

"Rather grim, isn't it?" asked Sam, holding a hand above her eyes to block the afternoon sun, staring at the keep in the distance. "For practitioners associated with life spirits, the druids built some pretty imposing buildings."

"They did, didn't they?" muttered Oliver. "I wonder why."

"I have no clue," said Sam. "I thought that would be the kind of thing you would have studied, you know, history of this land before your family's empire?"

Oliver shook his head. "There are few written records from the time when the druids held sway in Enhover. It was a century or more before the rise of the Wellesleys. That much is known. It's clear from these structures that they must have run some sort of government, but it's not known why the druids fell. By the time scholars began keeping track, the druids were no more than roaming vagabonds."

"All empires fall," remarked Sam.

"So they do," agreed Oliver.

He started hiking again. They knew where they were going and there was no reason to delay. William would know they were coming, and any time they granted him was time likely time spent preparing a defense.

Sorcery was an art of preparation, and they were planning on assaulting a powerful sorcerer within his own keep. It was foolish when thought about so plainly, but the alternatives were even worse. If they left William to his own devices, they could only guess at what he had in store. Would he sacrifice the city of Middlebury as Raffles had said? Would he do something even more vile? They had no way to knowing, but they knew he would not merely sit on his hands and wait. They'd killed his two counterparts, and that begged a response. Oliver was certain William would give one. The man wasn't in the line of succession, but he was a Wellesley.

If they ran to King Edward for assistance, his father would send the fleet against the old druid stronghold. He would bomb the place into nothing but gravel and dust. Not even a powerful sorcerer could stand against the full might of Enhover's military, the Coldlands had proved that, but what if William escaped? What if he had some other design? There was only one way to be sure he was defeated, and that meant looking into his eyes as it happened.

And there was one other reason Oliver wanted to confront his uncle, one reason Ainsley had not guessed at, but as soon as they were on the ground, Sam had.

"You think he knows something of your mother?" she'd asked.

In truth, he did not know, but it was a hope, and hope was all he had. Sam had earned his trust, so he'd admitted his own selfish reason for pursuing his uncle in person. She'd simply nodded and gestured for him to lead the way.

Sam was willing to risk her life to support his desperate gamble for knowledge, but he suspected she may have had her own reasons as well. Whatever her motivation, he was grateful. He knew he had no chance without her. Without the arcane knowledge in Sam's head, he would be dead before he had a chance to ask his uncle about Lilibet.

Not speaking, Sam and Oliver marched across the open fields toward the forest that surrounded the ancient druid keep, a forest that was dark and full of brambles, a forest that had sent chills down his spine when he had been younger. Now, he knew there was no lurking danger underneath the looming boughs of the trees. He knew the scattered rocks and undergrowth hid no skulking attackers. He knew the place wasn't haunted. No, the forest no longer held any of those fears that he'd faced as a child. The forest wasn't haunted. Not at all. The keep, though… He worried they were about to find darker horrors than his childhood imagination ever could have conjured.

They had one advantage, though, and he could only hope to the spirits it was enough. As a young man, in the years after his mother passed, he'd spent countless hours running from his tutors, escaping to the environs around Southundon. The forest and the druid keep it enclosed had been his favorite haunt. No history tutor was going to follow an active young boy through those netted branches and into the dark corridors underneath of the trees. It was a place Oliver could escape to, and only his older brothers had the wherewithal to track him down in the wild expanse.

After his uncle purchased the keep, William had encouraged Oliver's exploration of it. He'd been Oliver's first patron, commissioning rough maps of the sprawling interior. Like roots of a tree stump, the twisting pathways inside seemed to follow no formal logic. Nothing like Oliver's geometry and engineering tutors would understand. Instead, the pathways followed a deeper schematic, something long lost to current wisdom. He could never explain it, but somehow, Oliver had felt a semblance of order to the chaos inside of the keep. He had mapped those branching paths, explored the depths and the heights. He had stood upon the living rock of the roof of the place and looked across the forest to his father's city. He'd sat in what he believed to be the ancient throne room, showed his uncle the maps, and taught his uncle what he'd discovered.

William had been amazed, and Oliver wondered uncomfortably if it had been his uncle's praise that had set him on a course to a position as the Company's lead cartographer. Even then, Oliver had displayed a knack for the art. He'd mapped the twisting warrens of the druid keep while others failed to find a path to ascend to the top. Oliver had understood the place, like those strange tunnels were veins in his own arm. He'd felt it, and while he couldn't put it into words, he'd been able to put it onto paper. His first maps.

He knew the keep, knew it nearly as well as Southundon across the river. He knew the main entrances as well as the secret passages. He knew, no, he hoped, the knowledge would lead them safely into that old throne room, where he suspected they would find his uncle. Somehow, in his soul, Oliver could feel that was where the man was.

And it would be his uncle standing in that room. The signs and coincidences had not been obvious before, but now, they were too much to be ignored. William Wellesley, defender of the realm, the man who'd spent years crushing every remnant of the Coldlands people. The man responsible for finding and disposing of the shamans' sorcerous knowledge. William Wellesley, ascended to near the height of power in Enhover but one impossible step below the peak. William Wellesley, a close companion to both Randolph Raffles and Gabriel Yates. William Wellesley, the owner of an ancient keep that they were being inexorably pulled toward by the furcula. It simply didn't make sense that anyone else could be the sorcerer they were seeking.

They made good time through the low hills west of Southundon, and it was sunset when they reached the forest that clustered around the base of the druid keep. Another league through the tangled woods and they'd be there.

To the east, Southundon had finally appeared, rising from the bank of the river, obscuring the expansive harbor which had made it such an attractive capital. The city glowed in the evening sun, and Oliver pined to cross the river and find comfort there. His father, his brother John, he yearned for the chance to tell them what was going on and to gain their support, but he knew it was only a dream. This was his fight. That certainty pulsed through his body.

Prophecy or not, it felt right.

"It's just a league farther," he said to Sam. "Even in the woods, we should arrive at the base of the structure a few turns before midnight. Moving cautiously, we could be to the throne room right as the clock chimes the new day. I've got to admit. The timing makes me a little nervous. Approaching a sorcerer at midnight?"

Sam shook her head. "That's the perfect time. The change from one day to the other at midnight is a construct of man. I'd expect a true sorcerer to be most powerful during a natural change, like sunset or sunrise. At midnight, we'll be there at the darkest of night, the smallest moment of change. The pretenders practice then so no one will see them or because they don't understand. I know it's creepy, but it's for the best."

"Onward, then," he said, gripping the hilt of his broadsword.

She nodded and untucked a vial of fae light from within her shirt. "Onward."

THE PRIESTESS XXII

AHEAD OF THEM, she could hear the telltale rattle of a large body moving through winter-dry forest. In the black of night, underneath the skeletal, bare branches of the towering trees around them, the small noises were like firecrackers. The wind blew into their faces, still carrying the heavy scent of the sea. She guessed it was the only reason that whatever was out there had not yet caught their scent.

She glanced back at Duke. In the pale light that suffused through the branches, she saw him scowling. They'd planned to approach stealthily, to slip into the bowels of the keep unnoticed. A violent confrontation with whatever was in the forest may ruin that chance.

The prime minister likely knew they were coming or at least suspected that they would. That didn't mean they wanted to let him know they were coming right then. It was a big difference, him being on his toes and listening for them versus him waiting with a blade in hand.

She wondered if it wasn't best for them to turn around. They could still slip away undetected before it was too late, take their time, and come up with a better plan. Perhaps they could lurk in

King Edward's corridors, waiting for the prime minister to show up to work? A quick knife to the back and they'd be done.

Except, what if he didn't return to his duties at prime minister? What if he went to Middlebury instead and began the ritual to bind the dark trinity? What if tens of thousands of people died because they were too scared to confront a sorcerer in his own nest? What if the ritual worked, and he gained control of one of the oldest and most powerful entities in the underworld?

She shuddered at the thought. They couldn't wait. They had to strike now. Of course, that still left the problem of whatever was moving around in the forest. The time to strike was now, but for the last quarter hour, they'd been still, listening and waiting.

A low huffing made her twitch. Then, in the quiet, she heard the creature inhale, drawing a long breath. Had it finally caught their scent?

She glanced back at Duke, and he voiced, "Wolfmalkin."

Grimly, she nodded back. Physical, large, able to operate independently, and hunting by scent. It made sense. They knew the cabal of sorcerers had the capability to call upon the things, though she still hadn't figured out how they did it.

Sam nearly jumped when Duke's hand rested on her arm. He reached down and gripped the basket hilt of his broadsword, raising an eyebrow at her.

She nodded. If it was a wolfmalkin, they would have no chance of slinking away. It would could hear them moving through the forest, and the creature would have little trouble tracking them by sound or by their scent once it was on their trail. She tapped Duke's arm and pointed to the right, then touched her own chest and pointed left. They would come on either side of it.

She did not risk whispering to him, and she did not explain she thought it likely one of them would draw the creature's attention and then the other could attack while it was distracted. He would either figure it out or he wouldn't.

As he began to stalk away, barely catching himself before tripping over a fallen log, she guessed he was the one who was going to draw the wolfmalkin's attention. Silently, she crept the opposite direction, her feet falling silently on the forest floor.

For a moment, she recalled her lessons with Thotham, sneaking through the woods around the farm they had lived on, but she forced herself back into the now. Her mentor would have switched the younger version of herself had he seen her so distracted.

Ahead of them, the wolfmalkin had gone silent. She tried to move quicker, getting herself in position to charge its back when it went after Duke. Hopefully, the man would survive long enough on his own for her to get there.

Keeping her daggers in the sheaths for now, she ghosted through the trees, her feet finding solid ground to move across, her shoulders ducking and dipping as she maneuvered around low-hanging branches. Then, there was a crash, and a large body started moving rapidly.

Sam darted ahead, trusting the wolfmalkin's own noise to cover her footfalls. She barely dodged a wrist-thick branch that hung at chest height, almost invisible in the dappled light of the moon bleeding through the bare canopy. She ducked under it on the run, and when she rose, she caught sight of the tall frame of her quarry. It was a wolfmalkin, as she'd guessed, and it was now smashing through underbrush with no care of stealth.

She sped up but quickly slowed when a dark form sprang from atop a boulder. Steel gleamed in the moonlight, and Duke swept his blade down into the neck of the charging beast. The wolfmalkin whimpered as the sharp edge of the broadsword caught it, biting down to the bone.

Duke crashed heavily onto the ground, rolling across twigs and leaves before leaping back onto his feet. The wolfmalkin had already collapsed and was stone dead by the time she arrived.

"Nice work," she whispered.

"I threw a rock to distract it," he explained. "I figured if it went after the sound, I could come at it from behind."

She coughed, rubbing the back of her neck. "That's smart."

Duke glanced around. "I think we need to—"

"Grimalkin," she cried, jerking the nobleman off his feet and out of the way of the silent, pouncing, sleek black cat.

Stumbling, Duke fell to the side, and the giant feline landed lightly where he'd been standing.

Cursing, Sam jumped away as a paw swept at her face, claws the length of her hand extended, nearly raking her eyes out. Her two sinuous kris daggers held in her hands, she was so focused on the animal in front of her she nearly didn't hear the one coming from behind. Only a hiss in the air as it lunged gave warning.

She ducked. Instead of catching the back of her neck with its open jaw, the second big cat pounded into her, silken fur, heavy muscle, and bone impacting the back of her head and shoulders. Sam sprawled forward, her fists landing on the soil, daggers still in hand. She pitched away, rolling over her shoulder, across the forest floor, a disturbance in the air the only sign she'd narrowly avoided a second clawed paw.

From the corner of her eye, she saw Duke swing his broadsword and sever the paw that had so closely missed her, eliciting a terrible wail from the first cat. Hissing at him, the second cat prepared to spring while Duke lashed his sword at the first one, trying to force the injured beast back, nicking it on the side of the head but not delivering a fatal blow. Blood pumped from the stump of its foreleg. It would be dead within moments, but until then, the enraged animal was a threat.

Duke dodged as it reared up and batted at him with its good paw, the second foe evidently forgotten behind him.

She launched herself off her knees and crashed into the side of the second cat, plunging a dagger into its throat, feeling the grimalkin jerk in surprise and then in agony as she ripped her sinuous blade free.

The giant cat took two steps and collapsed.

The one facing Duke teetered as well, held at bay by his broadsword, and unable to retreat quickly due to its missing foot.

She and the peer eyed it cautiously. They watched as it dragged itself painfully backward.

"Should we go after it?" he wondered.

"I don't think it can follow us, and it's not going to make it to the keep before we do," she said. "Without that foot, it's not much of a threat to sneak up on us. It should bleed out in minutes."

"Live and let live, then," said Duke.

"If you say so," replied Sam, looking over the dead grimalkin and wolfmalkin. "I didn't think these things could work together, but that must have been what they were doing. One to distract us, the other two to close on our backs."

"Not so different from my plan," acknowledged Duke.

She nodded, not looking into his eyes. "We have to assume William will know we're coming, now."

"He will," agreed Duke. "We already thought that he'd be on guard. Surely, he knows about Raffles and Yates. He has to think we might be coming for him next. He will have other watchers around the place. If our plan works, that could help us."

"Depends on what the watchers are," challenged Sam.

Duke shrugged. "It's a simple idea that my uncle would have summoned shades to guard the entrance to his keep. They'll have no problem finding me as I have no protection and I share a blood bond with the man. But those tattoos Kalbeth gave you? They'll let you slip in behind me unnoticed. It worked against Yates, didn't it? He didn't sense you when you crossed his sorcerous trip wires. This is an almost identical plan."

She grunted. Duke was right. Yates hadn't sensed her approach. She hadn't told the peer the full details of her plan against the bishop, though. She shivered, hoping that this wouldn't end the same way. Instead, she suggested, "We're putting a lot of faith in chance."

"We can run to my father, enlist the help of the royal marines, but neither one of us wants to do that, do we?" asked Duke. "You want this as badly as I do."

Frowning, she realized it was true. For him, it was personal.

For her… she didn't know. Duke was right, though. Despite the risks, despite the holes she could see in their plan, she wanted to do it. It was the path she'd been set on since she was a girl, and it was impossible to turn back now.

SHE SKIRTED THE EDGE OF THE TOWERING STONE STRUCTURE, LOOKING for the entrance Duke had promised would be there. Beside the massive keep, without the full tree cover, she'd hidden her fae light and was navigating solely from the light of the moon. There was plenty illumination to keep the huge fortress in sight, but not enough to read the map Duke had drawn out for her while they had been back on the airship.

There. Fifty paces ahead, she saw a black patch on the dark gray rock. It had to be the way in. Stepping cautiously, she approached it and leaned around the corner, peering inside. The tattoos inked on her back would limit shades' ability to notice her, but they would do nothing to hinder a living guard. A wolf-malkin, grimalkin, or whatever else the prime minister could call upon would spot her as easily as she would see them. With luck, the living sentries were out in the forest, and it was only spirits from the underworld which barred the paths inside. If so, they had a chance.

It would be impossible for Duke to go unnoticed stalking through the halls, but the shades would be hesitant to attack him. He shared blood with William, the same blood that would have been used to call and bind the spirits. Whatever geas the man had laid on his summonings to protect himself would afford Duke some safety as well. The shades couldn't help but see him, though, and when they did, they would alert their master. They were counting on William's iron control of his minions. It was a dangerous gamble, but what else was there to do?

The pathway into the keep seemed clear, so she stepped inside the dark tunnel. Ahead, the way quickly disappeared with the little bit of moonlight that poured into the opening. She removed her vial of fae light and shook the lazy creatures awake.

Their glowing bodies brightened quicker than they had in the forest, and the light filled the glass and spilled out in front of her. With the illumination from the tiny life spirits, she saw two drifting shadows just ten paces ahead of her. The shades did not react to her appearing in the entrance of the tunnel or to the supernatural light of the fae. The tattoos Kalbeth had inked on her back were working, and the spirits of life were invisible to the denizens of the underworld. Swallowing nervously, she edged into the cylindrical tunnel then tiptoed in between the two hanging patches of darkness.

If she touched them, they would sense her. Once they did, not even her tattoos would keep her hidden. Kalbeth had explained that she would be more difficult to notice, but once noticed, she would have no protection at all.

Sam paused in the tunnel, staring at the shades. Could they hear? She didn't know. A curious thing for Thotham to leave out during his instructions on how to battle the summoned spirits. Holding her breath, she moved farther down the tunnel, and they didn't hear her. Twenty paces past them, she glanced back. They were still hanging there, floating listlessly, just like when she first spotted them.

So far, so good.

She turned and started up the pathway. The floor changed from dirt, likely debris the wind blew into the opening, to raw stone. The floor, walls, and ceiling were all made of the same dark rock that Northundon's keep had been built from. There were no signs of joints and no tool marks. It gave her the uneasy sensation of passing up an artery, something built to transport fluid or another substance that she could not fathom. Maybe it was a drain, though certainly it couldn't be active with so much sediment accumulated at the bottom. It was smooth and easy to walk along, though, and as she ascended there were no branches, no ways she could get lost.

She kept her fae light out because otherwise, the tunnel would be pitch black. Shades from the underworld would not be able to detect the light from the life spirits, but anything from the living world would. She strained, trying to listen ahead, but all she could hear was her own breathing and soft footsteps. If there was something alive with her in the tunnels, it was certain to see her light flickering in the pitch-black long before she came into view. Nothing that could be done about it, though. She had to see to know where she was going. Muttering to herself, she hurried. If she was going to be found, there was no sense taking it slowly.

THE CARTOGRAPHER XXV

A BRUSH of bitter cold touched his shoulder, like icy fingers tracing his collarbone and down his arm. He swallowed and kept walking. It wasn't the first frozen stroke he'd felt, and he was driving himself mad trying to determine if they were becoming more frequent. Shades were tracking his progress as he climbed higher inside of the ancient fortress.

It was awful, knowing the summonings were shadowing his footsteps, hanging close beside him. It reminded him of his progress through Northundon, except now, the spirits did not keep their distance. They passed around him, through him, causing him to shiver constantly, both from the cold of their touch and the fear of their presence.

This was the plan, though, and somehow, it seemed to be working.

His broadsword in one hand, the basket-hilt icy against his bare skin, a globe of fae light taken from the Cloud Serpent in the other, he continued his ascent. The road he followed was one of the largest that bored through the structure. He'd thought of it as the main entrance when he had been younger. It was cylindrical, like all pathways through the lower third of the towering stone edifice, but this one was broken by frequent openings. Other tunnels, twisting and winding away, led to other parts of the fortress.

There were rooms there, giant, open ones that his light would not reach the end of, and tiny ones that would quicken his breath. There was no reasoning to the layout that he'd been able to determine. Paths snaked about randomly like roots of a grand tree. Rooms opened beside or above each other, rarely connected in any rational way. Few of the spaces retained purpose that he could understand. They'd been fashioned hundreds, maybe thousands, of years earlier. Much of the organic material that had been inside was long ago rotted to dust. In other places, it was curiously preserved. The stone gave few clues to the past, aside from a few obvious points where there was seating or a table. The entire keep was a nearly endless maze of jumbled, untouched passageways.

Or at least, it had been. As he walked higher, he saw evidence it was not as it once was. There were the signs of man, now. His uncle or his minions had left their mark.

There were stands sprouting unlit torches, and some of the larger rooms showed evidence where huge fires had burned. Markings and patterns graced some of the walls, drawn in white chalk that blazed with the reflected light of the fae globe he carried. Most of the chalk patterns obscured older ones that seemed to be naturally formed as part of the rock, except nature never formed with such intent. He did not know if the new designs were meant to counteract the ancient ones below or somehow enhance them. It did not seem to be chance.

As he walked, he found other grim testimonials of his uncle's occupation of the place including scattered bits of rope and iron. Bindings, he realized after seeing several of them. Blood was smeared on some walls and the floors where captives might have struggled and had been overwhelmed. Newly installed steel gates spanned several of the passages.

Higher into the keep, Oliver had a horrible realization. There was no way his uncle, busy with his duties as prime minister, did all of this alone. Perhaps he had drawn a few chalk patterns, but the man had little time for construction work in an abandoned keep. The blood on the walls and the broken bindings hinted at a steady flow of captives through the passageway, and one man could not be responsible for all of that.

Sorcerous minions, perhaps adherents to another secret society. Oliver hated to guess who else had been involved. He dreaded finding out his uncle was not alone in the ancient druid fortress.

Alone. He shivered. Clinging to him like lines trailing from a fishing fleet were countless shades. He could feel the chill of their touch, and his skin crawled as they watched him continue upward.

Halfway up the structure, the nature of the tunnels and rooms began to change. Where below the paths were organic, above some sense of logical structure was evident. Rooms were connected to each other rather than only through the tunnels. Space was delineated in ways that made sense for human occupation. The strange artifacts he recalled from his youth became prevalent.

In one room, high on the wall, moonlight shone through crystal-covered windows. It sparkled, reflected and refracted by the crystal, illuminating giant contraptions of wood, glass, and raw metals. They were fitted together seemingly seamless, suspended a dozen yards above the stone floor. He remembered looking for hours at the odd constructs, wondering what their purpose was, but alone as a youth, he couldn't carry a ladder tall enough to reach the objects. His one attempt to pack climbing gear and scale the glass-smooth stone walls had ended nearly the moment it started.

His uncle, it seemed, had not been so easily deterred. One of the strange devices lay on the floor, broken open, showing nothing inside but wadded tufts of what looked like stripped tree bark. Some of it was scattered on the floor, as if a person had tossed it down in frustration after making the considerable effort to retrieve the worthless artifact.

Oliver glanced at the debris, but his innate curiosity was overwhelmed by the urge to keep going, to keep climbing, to find his uncle.

He came to an enormous room, one he recalled speculating whether it was a grand reception chamber, a ballroom, a sports court, or perhaps something he could not imagine. His light made it only halfway across, but he knew the room was braced by twenty-yard-tall openings on each of its four sides. Four doors for four compass directions, arranged perfectly in the circular room. He didn't know if the druids had a talent for cartography, but according to his measurements, they'd accurately situated the room on north, south, east, and west axes.

Oliver paused. In the distance, he heard the first sounds of life that were not his own. Wails of desperation, shouted orders, the noise of strife. Captives, he guessed, and their guards.

He stood in the entrance to the huge room and frowned. If he was able to free the captives, perhaps they could assist him. If he left the noises unexplored, guards might come after him from behind. Knowing there were people there but ignoring them seemed contrary to everything he thought and every instinct he had.

After a moment, he decided he had to ignore them, though.

Sam was ascending through the twisting tunnels and open rooms just as he was, taking a different path, the one he'd sketched out for her. If he paused and went off on another mission, what would happen when she reached the top of the keep? Would his uncle be there? Would she have to face him alone, without the element of surprise they hoped their plan would bring?

No, he had to keep going. He had to ignore the sounds of suffering coming from down the unexplored hallways.

Oliver traced the wall of the room until he found the door to his right, to the south. He wondered if the direction had any relevance to sorcery.

He stepped through the looming opening and glanced up the slope. From his previous exploration, he knew the path spiraled several times to a room hundreds of yards up, directly above the one he was leaving.

And in that opening, he ran into his first serious problem.

THE PRIESTESS XXIII

SHE LET HER BREATHING SLOW, inhaling and exhaling through her mouth to minimize any chance of noise. She flexed her toes, feeling the soft boots resist as she did. She opened her hands, her fingers spread wide, stretching the joints and tendons but stopping short of letting them pop. Slowly, like ice melting, she drew one of her kris daggers. The steel whispered softly against the leather of the sheath as, inch-by-inch, the sinuous blade emerged. With her other hand, she unwound a thin wire from her waist, a yard and a half long, terminating on both ends in weighted, wooden handles.

Ahead of her, facing down a dark hallway, were two wolfmalkin.

The creatures' ears were twitching and their heads were tilted back. She heard snuffing and knew they were smelling something, trying to understand what they were sensing. It wasn't her, though. They were watching a pathway ahead of them, one she knew Duke was to climb up. The intersection was one of the few where he'd marked that they might meet. It was lit, unlike the tunnels she'd been traveling. Did that mean William was waiting for them, or was it merely illuminated for the convenience of the prime minister and his minions? She didn't know.

She'd hidden her light in anticipation of passing the main thoroughfare, and between that and the lights ahead, the wolfmalkin hadn't noticed her approach. Were they waiting for Duke in ambush? Had they already let him pass unmolested? She could not tell, but it was clear they were aware someone was inside the keep and that they'd been stationed as watchers.

It didn't matter what their intentions with Duke were, because they were blocking her way forward. It was critical to their plan she adhered to her route and was able to approach the top independently, away from the notice of the shades they expected would be clustered around Duke.

Moving as silently as the shades scattered throughout the tunnels, she crept behind the creatures. They stood half again as tall as her and three times as wide. They held massive battle axes. Swung with their muscle-bound arms, the axes would surely cleave her in twain. The creatures were alert, waiting for a trespasser in their domain. The heavy slabs of muscle on their backs and necks prevented her from simply tossing a blade into them from behind and making a quick kill.

She supposed an assault on a sorcerer's stronghold shouldn't be easy, but she'd been trained to attack from behind. This was something she could do.

Half-a-dozen paces from the backs of the wolfmalkin, she knew she couldn't draw closer without alerting the beasts to her presence. Thotham had taught her how to sneak up unnoticed on a victim, and had taught her that no matter how good she was, there was only so close one could approach before being noticed.

So, she charged.

Three quick steps and then she leapt into the air, slinging one end of her wooden-handled garrote around the neck of the wolfmalkin on her left. The weighted handle whipped around the surprised creature's throat, and when it came back, she looped the wire she was holding around the flying bit and yanked it tight, the flung handle snug against the back of the wolfmalkin's neck, the wire digging into the beast's flesh. She set her feet against the creature's back and leaned hard, hauling on the garrote with all of her weight. Then, she stretched toward the other creature as it was spinning around, raising its axe, its eyes wide in surprise.

Lashing out with her kris dagger, she brought the blade across the unprepared beast's throat, slicing open a deep laceration that cut nearly to the bone. The blow severed the wolfmalkin's windpipe, and it fell back, gargling an attempted howl.

Hanging from the back of the first wolfmalkin, she kept the pressure on the garrote and felt it pull tighter, the thin wire cutting into the monster's neck, choking it and slowly slicing through the thick muscle protecting its airway.

A battle axe clanged to the floor, and clawed hands scrabbled to get underneath the wire of her garrote, but it was too late. The metal thread was already embedded in the thing's flesh, and even if she lost her grip, it was twisted tight.

The second wolfmalkin fell against the side of the tunnel and slumped down, its axe in its lap, stunned confusion on its canine face.

She jumped free as the first creature collapsed to its knees, still futilely grasping at its throat. It fell forward, feet twitching, arms flopping uselessly. She waited, watching both creatures die, then cleaned her dagger and retrieved her garrote, unwinding the thin wire from the monster's neck, wincing as she had to shift its head to free the weapon. Even dead, the wolfmalkin's finger-length teeth made her cringe.

With weapons back in hand, she waited quietly, wondering if the falling axe would draw any attention, wondering if any shades would happen across the dead bodies and flee to their master.

So far, the apparitions had not seen her. Kalbeth's work was holding up, but they could definitely see the dead wolfmalkin. Had William thought to instruct the summonings to alert him for something like that, or were they merely looking for living intruders? Shades, bound and forced to a sorcerer's bidding, would not be inclined to go beyond their specific instructions, but there was no telling what he'd assigned them to do.

The huge wolfmalkin were too heavy for her to move alone, so one way or the other, she would find out soon enough.

Moving quickly, she crossed through the lighted intersection and walked back onto her path and into the darkness.

THE CARTOGRAPHER XXVI

"MASTER?" asked a shocked voice.

Another exclaimed, "You're not—"

Oliver didn't bother to hear what else the man had to say. He hurled the heavy glass fae globe at the face of one of the speakers and charged the other, lunging with his broadsword. The two robed figures didn't have time to react. One of them caught the fae light in the face, the globe smashing against his chin with the sound of breaking bone. The other stared in surprise as Oliver's broadsword pierced his chest, the steel driving deep.

The fae globe fell to the floor, and the thick glass cracked, releasing the dozen glowing green spirits. In the light of the frenzied flying creatures, Oliver saw a third masked and robed shape and barely danced out of reach as a dark blade slashed toward him.

He staggered away, yanking his broadsword clear and parrying another strike from the new attacker. The fae swarmed in the face of his assailant, blinding his opponent, slowing them, and Oliver lunged, stabbing the robed figure in the shoulder.

Wounded, his attacker retreated, but Oliver advanced, striking at the arm, the chest, and then the head of his opponent. His steel smacked hard against his assailant's skull, and Oliver could see the life fading from his attacker's eyes in the swirling dance of the fae light.

An arm wrapped around his neck, and Oliver realized the first man, the one he'd stunned with the fae globe, was not done. Oliver swung his head back, impacting the man on the chin and feeling the shattered bones there grind together. The arm around his neck went limp, and the man uttered a pathetic whimper.

Spinning, Oliver lashed out with his broadsword, burying the steel in the man's neck. Eyes glassy from the pain in his jaw and the steel in his throat, the man rasped a final, pained groan and fell to the floor.

Glancing around, ready to fight, Oliver saw there was no one else in the corridor. Just him, the three motionless bodies, and the drifting shadows of the shades that had been following him. None of them were fleeing, rushing to tell his uncle what had transpired. Instead, they just floated nearby, watching.

Grimacing, Oliver knelt and cleaned his steel before sliding the blade into the sheath. He pulled the masks off of his attackers, seeing two men he did not recognize and a woman that he did. He knelt there for a long moment, looking at her red hair and scattered freckles. She had been attractive, a friend of Lannia's. They'd danced together, once, at a gala years before. Had they done more? He couldn't recall how the night had ended.

He closed his eyes and tried to calm himself. When he opened them, he glanced up and saw the fae still swirling around. In Enhoverian air, they should have quickly expired once released from their glass prison, but if anything, their glow was burning brighter than before. When he stood and continued up the spiraling slope of the pathway, the fae followed him like the shades did, the glow from the tiny life spirits illuminating the way ahead.

WHEN HE REACHED THE TOP OF THE SPIRALED RAMP HE STEPPED OUT

into an open room, blinking in the startling light of a dozen burning braziers. They lined a room that was covered in thick carpets, couches, and tables. The far end was open air. Beyond the stone pillars that framed the opening, he could see the twinkling lights of Southundon. Standing in the center of the space was his uncle.

Turning as Oliver entered, William Wellesley crossed his thick, scar-covered arms. He was shirtless. His pale skin gleamed in the firelight. Dark tattoos twisted across his skin, snaking like smoke from his shoulders down his arms. Oliver couldn't tell if it was flickering shadow from the fires or if the ink itself was moving, slithering across his uncle's naked torso like shades trapped behind glass. On his forearms, clasped by the opposite hands, he wore shining golden bracers. The bands gleamed liked he'd just finished polishing them, and even from a distance, Oliver could see intricate designs etched into the metal.

"I've always loved this view of the city," said William, his voice calm and steady. "It's nearly as good as the one up top."

"I knew it would be you," growled Oliver.

"When?" wondered the prime minister. "Raffles and Yates claim they did not give me up."

"They did not," responded Oliver. "I knew it would be you when we were led here. Who else would build a nest in a place such as this? It had to be you. That you were friends with the two of them, that you were the one who led the expedition against the Coldlands… it all fit."

William nodded, his fingers tapping on his golden bracers. "Friends, I'm not sure I would… You said you were led here?"

"We followed the taint of sorcery," said Oliver, stepping toward his uncle, hoping he could get close enough to attack the man. "Hathia Dalyrimple's dagger, the one you and your partners killed her for."

"Ah," said William. From behind his back, he drew a long, curved dagger. The firelight reflected on the steel, mirroring the shine of his golden armbands. "That priestess was able to sense this? I am impressed."

Oliver smirked, still edging closer, trying to distract his uncle. "We followed your movements to the Coldlands and met one of their elders, one you failed to eradicate so long ago. He gave us a device that we followed here. The guilt of Northundon, William, the unnecessary slaughter in the Coldlands, how do you live with it? Lilibet was like a sister to you. I was young, but I remember that much."

His uncle snorted. "You were too young, and you don't remember. Your mother may have been kind to you, but you were the only one. Neither I nor Edward shed a tear when we heard she'd been lost in Northundon. You came to talk, so ask me your questions. I am curious what you want to know."

"You sacrificed her for what? For what, William?" demanded Oliver. "You were destined to be prime minister at my father's side. What did Northundon's souls buy you? That is why I am here. I must know. Where is my mother, and what did her death buy you?"

His uncle frowned. "Northundon's sacrifice? I did not sacrifice Northundon, nephew. As to where your mother is, I do not know. She did not care for him, you know? Your father was only a means to an end, for her. That is why she was in the north so often, to get away from Edward. It was years before I gained enough skill in the dark art to discover she had not died in Northundon. I could barely believe it when I found her soul had not breached the barrier to the other side. By the time I found out, I could only assume she had fled the attack from the Coldlands. Like a coward, she must have seen those sails on the horizon and ran. I wish I knew, but I have no idea where she fled to. I promise you this, if I find her, I will kill her."

"The Coldlands," growled Oliver. "They did not attack Northundon. They came to liberate it from you. I met their elder, he told me everything!"

"A sorcerer you found in the wilderness told you this?"

William snickered. "Where do you think I learned the secrets that I know? What I've spent studying the last twenty years, they already knew. I tell you true, I had nothing to do with Northundon or with Lilibet's disappearance. If this shaman told you that, it must have been so you'd come looking for me, to grant them vengeance. An unfortunate coincidence if that's what led you to discover our plans."

Shuffling his feet slowly, Oliver had advanced to within a dozen paces of his uncle. "Do not lie to me."

William shrugged, his heavy shoulders rolling with the motion, the gleaming dagger held loosely in one hand. "What would I gain from lying to you?"

Oliver frowned. "What would you gain from telling me the truth?"

With a laugh, William admitted, "You make a fair point. Believe me or not, I had nothing to do with Northundon. Back then, I had no knowledge of the dark path outside of the blind fumbling the societies engaged in. It was only during the war that I discovered real truth. Our men uncovered a trove of artifacts and scrolls. When they were brought to me, I recognized them for what they were. I sent trusted lieutenants on the hunt for more. I recruited those I needed and killed those who had learned too much. I found a Church scholar with a thirst for ancient secrets and a young merchant who had access to a global network of agents. We formed a partnership, you could say, and we spent the last two decades preparing. You nearly ruined those plans, but I managed to salvage the situation. Our work, not so different from what the Coldlands tried to do in Northundon, will continue."

"I will stop you," declared Oliver.

"No, no, you won't," assured William. "I allowed you up here because I was curious what you'd say to me. It seems they tricked you, nephew. The Coldlands attacked Northundon, not I. You saw the aftermath from the deck of the same airship that I did. I was in Southundon when the attack occurred. We spoke that day, Oliver. Don't you remember?"

Oliver frowned.

"They tricked you so that you would stab me in the back," continued William, shaking his head. "You might have done it, had you not bothered with the churchman and the merchant first. Now, I'm afraid it's too late. You know too much, and this can end only one way."

"If you don't know where my mother is, then who does?" cried Oliver.

"I don't know. I can't tell you anything about her." William glanced down at the dagger in his hand and then back to Oliver. "I can tell you this. Whoever gave you the means to find me is the same one who sacrificed Northundon. A Coldlands shaman or someone made up to make you think they were. This dagger is tainted by Ca-Mi-He. That's the same spirit that enshrouds Northundon, both in this world and the other. Whoever you encountered in the Coldlands, whoever facilitated Hathia's contact with the great spirit, and your mother, they're all tied together. But not to me. For all I know, Lilibet is the one who did it. Without sorcery, how else could she escape while everyone else died? Think about that, Oliver."

"You claim you are not a sorcerer?" Oliver sneered.

"No, I am exactly what you think," responded William coolly. "My hands are stained with blood, and within the next week, I will spread that blood like an ocean across Enhover. I am evil, nephew, if you want to call me that. I am what you think, but I am not the one to answer for Northundon."

Oliver reeled, stunned by what his uncle was telling him. He tried to disbelieve it, to find reasons his uncle would lie, but there were none. William was right. He'd been in Southundon when the Coldlands sailed. Oliver had seen him there. Besides, the man was admitting to a plan to sacrifice Middlebury. Why lie about Northundon but not that? What did William have to gain from it?

"Who..." asked Oliver.

"I wish I knew, boy, I really do," remarked William, true concern in his voice. "The Coldlands making one last desperate gambit for revenge, your mother, someone else? Whoever they are, there is another on this dark path. I've no doubt they tracked your movements here. When I'm done with you, they'll come for me. Twenty years ago, they had direct contact with the great spirit. Twenty years ago, they achieved power I can only dream of. I'm afraid I won't survive a direct confrontation with them, not yet at least. One result of your foolish quest to find me is that I must flee. But before I do..."

Oliver raised his broadsword and assumed a fighting stance.

"I'm sorry, boy. I did like you. You're the best of your father's brood. It's unfortunate it has come to this." William raised the dagger, aiming the tip of the shimmering steel blade directly at Oliver.

Behind the prime minister, Sam sprang out of hiding, streaking directly at William's back, her kris daggers held wide, ready to plunge into the unsuspecting man's throat and side.

THE PRIESTESS XXIV

SHE PATIENTLY WATCHED the scene unfold in front of her. William Wellesley, Enhover's prime minister, a distant successor to the throne, was spewing out his plans like some sort of mad villain on the stage. Evidently, family ties complicated things for him as well as Duke. The men held real affection for each other, and it appeared neither one of them wanted to be the first to admit the truth. They were going to have to fight, and one of them was going to die.

There was no other way out of the scenario. William was a sorcerer, and Duke was hunting and killing sorcerers. Bloodshed was the only resolution. She just had to wait for her moment.

"I'm sorry, boy. I did like you. You're the best of your father's brood. It's unfortunate it has come to this," declared the prime minister.

Then, he pointed the curved dagger at Duke. His arm was steady, the gleaming golden band on his forearm shimmering in the light of the fire. The steel of the dagger blade seeming to quiver, thirsting for blood.

Did the dagger have powers? She didn't know, but she couldn't wait a moment longer. She attacked.

She sprang from behind one of the huge, burning braziers,

leaving the heat of the blaze for the cold of the open air. Beads of sweat froze on her forehead as the passage of time seemed to slow to a crawl. Her two daggers were held steady in firm grips, arms wide, prepared to plunge steel into the sorcerer's unguarded flesh.

Behind her, she felt the swirl of the shades that had been stationed at the narrow chute she'd climbed through. They noticed her as she plunged past, but they were too late. Duke's recollection and hastily drawn maps had been correct. She'd climbed up some sort of staff entrance to the room, narrow and circumspect, the perfect place to stage an ambush, and William had helpfully strolled right in front of her.

The world crept by, carpets passing beneath the achingly slow steps of her feet. The firelight flickered at quarter speed, reflecting on the brilliant shine of the tainted dagger that had started all of this mess.

Then, William Wellesley turned, moving quickly, while she and the world moved slow. She opened her mouth to curse, but she didn't get the chance. William closed with the confidence of an old soldier, a man who'd spent years on the battlefield and decades sacrificing victims. He stabbed his dagger into her gut.

Agonizingly slow, she felt the tip of cold steel pierce her skin. She felt the razor edge slice flesh as the blade dug deeper, each inch gradually cutting into her, driving deep from her momentum and William's thrust. He grinned at her, not hurrying, letting her impale herself on the blade.

Long moments passed, and all she could think of was the incredible pain of the steel plunging into her, stabbing deep and slow until she wondered that it hadn't burst out of her back yet.

Then, she was by him, and she felt William shove her away, catapulting her into a dreadfully slow tumble. Spinning in the air, she saw Duke, a dozen steps away, his mouth hanging open. She heard a high-pitched drone that might have been a shout. Duke's broadsword was rising, his foot creeping through the air as he charged toward her, moving like he was running in cold honey.

Suddenly, her shoulder cracked against the floor, and she sped up, smashing into another brazier across the hall, the hot metal scalding her, a shower of embers cascading down over her. She rolled away, her hands clutching her gut, feeling the gush of blood that poured from the terrible puncture. Her daggers were forgotten on the floor. She could only think of the one that had stabbed into her, spilling her blood in a six-yard-long fan across the floor.

Looking down, she saw the wine-red fluid pumping around her fingers. The slick, crimson digits doing nothing to stop the furious flow.

"Sam!" cried Duke.

Through tear-filled eyes, she saw him running to her, one arm reaching out, like there was something he could do.

"Your uncle, you spirit-forsaken fool!" she cried through gritted teeth.

THE CARTOGRAPHER XXVII

"YOUR UNCLE, YOU SPIRIT-FORSAKEN FOOL!" Sam rasped, her voice barely audible through her pain.

Oliver turned to face William and saw the older man was merely watching him, shaking Sam's blood from the horrific dagger clutched in his fist. The old soldier knocked his two golden bracers against each other. Oliver struggled to comprehend what had just happened, the blaze of motion he'd seen, the—

An ice-cold arm wrapped around his neck and squeezed.

He swung his broadsword back, hoping to catch his attacker's head, but the weapon sailed through empty air.

"Sorcery, Oliver, is about creating bridges through the shroud to the underworld and then fashioning patterns to channel and control what can be found there," remarked William, studying him. "There is an order to both our world and the other one. By understanding that order, recreating those natural designs and then manipulating them for our own purposes, sorcerers are able to achieve incredible things. But no matter the skill of the sorcerer, no matter how complex and involved the patterns they invoke, the results are only as good as the strength of the bridge. A strong bridge requires familiarity, proximity, connection. The strongest bridges require a passage, a change. Life transitioning to death. Life becoming from nothing. These changes naturally breach the shroud, you understand?"

Oliver wheezed, unable to respond, unable to free himself from the relentless arm wrapped around his neck. He thrashed with his sword again, but a transparent hand caught his arm, gripping tight until his fingers spasmed and his broadsword clattered to the stone floor. He was held rigid, one arm around his neck, others clamped onto his limbs.

"My own blood would help fashion the strongest bridge, but I don't want to die for my cause," explained William. "You, however, are going to die anyway. I let you come here, Oliver, so I could use your blood to fashion my bridge. You will die so I never have to."

Tugging, kicking, and struggling with his invisible attackers, Oliver fought the entire way up to the rooftop of the ancient druid fortress. The arm wrapped around his throat never relented. When he was dragged through passages narrow enough, he pushed himself off the floor and against the wall, kicking hard, trying to dislodge the unceasing pressure on his neck. He was rewarded by a series of vicious blows to his ribcage and more hands squeezing him tight, dragging him onward.

Finally, they emerged into the clear, night air. In the distance, Southundon sparkled. Nearby, it was dark. Only light from the moon above illuminated the battlement-ringed rooftop of the ancient fortress.

William turned and grinned at Oliver, spreading his arms wide, his pale skin white in the light, crawling with black tattoos. He declared, "The chill reminds me of the underworld. I prefer it like this, when it's bitter cold outside. I wish I could stand here and revel in it, but you and your priestess delved too deep. You interfered with our plans, and I have to act now or the other will take advantage of my weakness."

"Interfered with you," growled Oliver, finding barely enough air to spit out a retort. "We killed your partners. Your ritual cannot be completed without them. Without three of you, you have no hope of binding the trinity!"

William smirked and then nodded behind Oliver.

His head was forced around by the invisible shade that gripped him, and Oliver found himself looking at two fist-sized hunks of amber sitting on waist-high block of stone. An altar, Oliver thought. The amber glowed softly, lit from within. He could see the rocks were streaked with black stains. He uncomfortably decided those must be dried blood. Both hunks of amber sat in shallow copper bowls that were filled with the same dark liquid. Around the bowls, he could see iridescent white chalk lines marked in dizzying patterns that turned his stomach to look at. The low light of the moon seemed to be drawn to the chalk and held there, shining within the design.

"Raffles and Yates." William laughed. "I believe you've met? That is what is left of their souls."

The shade jerked Oliver back around to face his uncle. He drew a ragged breath as the arm loosened around his neck, and he kicked back with a foot, catching nothing. He struggled, helplessly.

"I had a snare waiting on the shroud," explained William. "When you killed them, I snagged their souls before they passed into the underworld. It is not ideal, I admit, but I believe it will work. With the help of your life blood, it is worth the risk. Eternal life, or eternal damnation? If it works, at least I will not have to suffer those fools any longer. I will rule alone, forever. A risk, yes, but such a prize…"

William turned, seemingly losing interest in Oliver for a moment and staring across the night-black river to Southundon.

"It's all about my father, then?" questioned Oliver, glaring at his uncle's back. "Jealousy? You're willing to kill tens of thousands to settle some feud with my father?"

William looked back. "Jealousy? No, I wouldn't term it like that. I thought you might understand, actually. It is why I'm even bothering to speak with you, Oliver. I don't want the throne, not the way Edward sits upon it. It seems a rather large bother, doesn't it? No, it is not that I want to be my older brother or to be the king. It is that I want to be more than I am. I am destined for more than this, Oliver. Once, I thought you might be, too."

Oliver blinked at the older man. "You're trying to turn me?"

"No." William chuckled, shaking his head. "I'm not trying to turn you. I was just… I admit it would be nice to be understood, to speak to someone who realizes what it is like to be the younger brother of the first in line. You are not jealous of Philip, are you? I cannot imagine you would want to live his life, but don't you want to live your own life? Don't you feel bound by the expectations of your family? Being a Wellesley is a great honor, or so we are told by those who use us. You never would have lived your own life, Oliver. You would have always been in the shadow of your brothers, dancing to their whims. For the Crown, they tell you." William shook his head. "Not for me. Not anymore."

"Enhover is more than a crown and a throne, William," argued Oliver, struggling against his formless captor. "It's about—"

"Save the speech," remarked William. "You think after this we'll shake hands and agree to leave each other alone? Besides, even if you do not realize it, you were sent by another to distract and delay me. I'm not going to let that happen."

From beside the hunks of amber on the altar, William collected a third copper bowl, the outside gleaming, the inside dull and stained black. His uncle removed a dull hunk of amber from the bowl and placed it on the altar, in the center of a matrix of white chalk symbols.

By invisible hands, Oliver was shoved back against an iron cross. His arms were forced up by his head along the lifeless metal spars. Across from him, he saw two similar devices. The three of them were arranged in a triangle. Three crosses where his uncle would bind his victims, where he could take his time sacrificing them. The floor of the rooftop was covered in old blood, and Oliver shivered, thinking about how many souls had been taken in the place. He shivered from the biting cold in the air and the iron behind him, and he shivered from the implacable hands of the spirits that pressed him back. Ice-cold nothing, pinning him down while he watched his uncle approach with the bowl and the dagger.

A look, somewhere between regret and anticipation, marred his uncle's face. In the cold light of the moon, he wasn't the boisterous, jolly soldier Oliver had always known, but a strange shining apparition, not far different from the shades that he summoned.

William stepped toward Oliver, raising the tainted dagger.

THE PRIESTESS XXV

Duke was dragged away, a shadowy wisp half a yard taller than him clinging to his back, dozens more surrounding him. William, haughty and laughing, led the way.

Between her fingers, she could feel her warm blood seeping out. The dagger had pierced her deeply, and when William had drawn it from her, a torrent of blood had followed. Even if she was lying on a surgeon's table, the prognosis would not be good. Alone, in the middle of a forest, leagues from Southundon and the physicians there, she had no chance. She was going to die.

Cursing under her breath, she untucked her shirt and wadded it beneath her vest, pressing the fabric against the furiously bleeding wound. It was too wide, too deep to completely stop the flow, but she could slow it and maybe follow William to where he'd taken Duke.

There wasn't much fight left in her, but thanks to Kalbeth's ink, her death would not be in vain. When her soul breached the barrier, it would unleash a torrent of power. That deluge would sweep away any nearby shades, banishing them to the underworld.

It was just as her mentor had done for her when he had died beneath Derbycross. He'd sacrificed himself to save her and Duke, to give them the opportunity to defeat the evil that they faced. She had hated Thotham for it, that he'd taken the easy way out and convinced Duke to strike the killing blow. She had hated that he didn't fight, didn't find some other way, but now, she understood.

Weak, blood gushing from her abdomen like water from a pump, she couldn't fight. She didn't even think she could stand. Gritting her teeth, one hand pressed against her stomach to stanch the flow of blood, she reached out with her elbow. Kicking her feet, she dragged herself ahead. Inch by inch, she crawled across the stone floor.

Sweat popped out on her forehead. Her jaw ached from how tightly she gritted her teeth. Her stomach... She couldn't think about that, couldn't consider the pull and tug, the fresh warmth of new blood with each yard she traveled.

She was going to die. If only she could get close enough that her spirit's passing would help. Perhaps Duke would still be in good enough shape he could fight back against his uncle. Perhaps without his minions, William would fall to the younger Wellesley.

Perhaps.

She closed her eyes, her mouth forming wordless curses.

Three more yards to the doorway. Then, if she guessed correctly, maybe she could find where they went. Maybe...

She slumped on the floor. The only sounds in the room were the crackling of the fire in the braziers and her own pained breath. Wherever William was taking Oliver, they were already out of earshot. They were already hundreds of yards away and well out of her reach.

She smacked a hand on the raw stone of the floor. Thotham did not raise her to quit when she was needed. He'd raised her for this moment — for now. His prophecy was about right now. She had to keep going.

She looked up at the doorway, trying to decide which way to go, wondering how far she could make it.

In front of her, barring the doorway, was a wall of insubstantial shadows.

Refusing to give in, she reached out her elbow and dragged herself forward again. A foot crashed down on her head, slamming it against the stone floor. Another kicked her shoulder and then her arm. More blows fell on her legs. Invisible strikes rained down on her, but still, she crawled forward until finally a toe swept underneath her side and pounded into her gut, right where William had stabbed her. Wheezing, she flopped over from the force of the kick, landing on her back, staring at the rock of the ceiling, gasping and choking.

Shadows surrounded her. One settled down on top of her, wrapping ice-cold fingers around her throat. It squeezed, and her head pounded. Specks of white flooded her vision, spinning dizzily. She could feel the hands around her throat, but when she swept her arms, trying to dislodge them, she felt nothing, nothing but the pressure on her neck. She kicked wildly, trying to find her daggers, knowing they could banish the shades, but she'd dropped them and didn't know where they were. The weight of the thing settled on her chest, the unrelenting hands strangled her.

The shades. William had not made a foolish error by leaving her alive. He'd left his minions to finish the job.

Her vision wavered and then went black. Only the agonizing pressure on her neck and the throb of blood in her head were real anymore. She couldn't feel the cold opening in her stomach where William had stabbed her, where her blood leaked out freely. Somewhere deep inside, she knew that when blood loss or the shades finally killed her, it meant their own banishment, but in the sea of agony, the thought had no power. There was no spiteful joy that they'd pay for her demise, just the dull pressure, the sharp pain as she wrenched her body on the stone floor, struggling impotently.

In the black, the utter darkness and despair, she felt cold. Ice cold. Was it the underworld? Was she approaching the shroud? She was slipping. She could feel motion. She grew colder, and while she couldn't see, she could sense something. A wall extending to the sides beyond imagination, rising higher than she could fathom. A wall between everything. The barrier between her old world and her new one. She was drawing closer, distance-less, timeless.

She was dying… dead?

All she could feel was cold.

The motion stopped, and she floated, suspended in front of the barrier. How far, she couldn't say. How long, she didn't know. There was no time or space. She stayed there, insubstantial, form-less, like one of the shades, floating before the barrier. Darkness flowed all around her, swallowing her whole.

THERE WAS INCREDIBLE PAIN. THE WOUND FROM THE TAINTED DAGGER in her stomach burned fire hot. Compared to the cold of death, it was the hot of forge fire. It scalded her, scoured her. Her veins filled with terrible heat. Piercing agony enveloped her skull. Needles jabbing, heat burning. Her flesh felt like, inch by inch, it was peeled away and then seared back down by orange-hot iron. Tingles, like pinpricks, tens of thousands of them, cascaded from the tip of her head to her toes, stabbing her with new agony. Pain was all that she knew, all that she was.

WITH AN AGONIZING, UNEVEN LURCH, HER HEART STARTED TO BEAT. Squeezing cooling blood through her body, it thumped and then thumped again. Her eyes flicked open and she gasped, drawing a long breath of air, filling still lungs. Her body, in fits and starts, was waking back up.

She was alive.

IF THE SHADES AROUND HER HAD FACES, SHE KNEW SHE WOULD SEE confusion there, and knew they could see it in her face as well.

They were not attacking. They were hesitant. These shades, they knew death, and they knew her soul had passed from her body. They must have seen it transitioning to the same plane they'd been summoned from. Death was what they were. The shades knew another.

Now, her soul was back.

She sat up, her eyes drawn to the floor beside her. Her hand, painted crimson with her own blood, had drawn a pattern on the stone floor.

A triangle, inverted, three slashes passing through it.

Her heart hammered, and her breath came fast and panicked as her mind struggled to adjust, to rationalize that she'd been dead, but now, she was not.

Somehow, her hand, operating without her direction, had drawn a pattern representing the great spirit Ca-Mi-He. She touched her stomach, feeling a knotted scar where William had stabbed her. The fabric of her vest, her shirt, her trousers, were soaked in her still-wet blood. The vest and her shirt were torn where the steel had slid into her. They were torn, but her flesh was not.

Ca-Mi-He, the spirit that had tainted the dagger, its name drawn in her blood. The same blood that had leaked out, killing her from the wound the dagger had given her, sending her soul to the barrier where it would have passed through the open shroud.

She'd been killed by Ca-Mi-He's dagger. She'd drawn the spirit's name in her blood.

Frozen hell.

Her soul had made it to the shroud. It had opened to take her, and then she had returned. Ca-Mi-He had used her, but used her for what?

She scrambled to her feet, unnatural energy suffusing a body that moments before had been dead. Around her, the shades were gone. They'd simply vanished. Either the surge of her death had finally caught them, or they'd fled before a spirit more terrifying than themselves. She glanced around the room, gaping in confusing, then back down at the bloody symbol on the floor.

Ca-Mi-He.

Frozen hell.

Ca-Mi-He had stopped her passage, had prevented her from going to the other side. He'd… She didn't know. She didn't know what was happening, but she knew she was alive. She wasn't dead. She was in the fight, and Thotham hadn't raised her to quit.

She strode across the stone floor, wet with her own blood, and bent to retrieve her kris daggers.

She wasn't dead. Not yet.

THE CARTOGRAPHER XXVIII

THE BLADE of the tainted dagger, slick with Sam's blood, raised into the air, poised to swing down and plunge into his chest. William held the copper bowl in his other hand, ready to catch the fountain of life he would spill from his nephew. Oliver's eyes were locked on the tip of the dagger, watching as crimson drops dripped from the edge. Sam's blood, smeared along the entire length of the sharp steel.

The blood curled, writhing on the blade, like a silken sheet twisted into a pattern.

Oliver, trembling with terror, straining against the invisible hands that held him, wasn't sure what he was looking at. Along the edge of the dagger, the blood seemed to move on its own, forming into crimson lines, complex designs, revealing the steel beneath. Steel that gleamed brighter than the reflected light of the moon warranted.

William noticed it as well and his hand froze. He stared at the animated liquid.

"What the hell is this?" he asked, like he was wondering at their mechanical carriage coming to a stop in unexpected traffic.

The pressure on Oliver's arms and legs vanished. Arms still raised above his head, he blinked at his uncle.

William shrugged and then swung the dagger down, aiming for the center of Oliver's chest.

Flinging himself to the side, Oliver stumbled out of the way, the steel dagger striking iron, a shower of sparks garishly lighting the cold rooftop.

"Spirits forsake it!" cried William.

Oliver scrambled back, glancing around wildly, unable to spot any of his uncle's shades in the dark of the night. He couldn't find any weapons, either, or anything at all he could use to defend himself. Out of the corner of his eye, he saw his uncle place the tainted dagger between his teeth and clap his hands on the golden, rune etched bands he wore on his forearms.

Nothing happened.

William's eyes were wide, and Oliver stared at him for half a breath. Then, he charged.

Opening his mouth, William let the dagger fall from the grip of his teeth and caught it one-handed. He slashed at Oliver.

Oliver skidded to a stop, narrowly avoiding the razor-edge of the blade. He raised his fists in a boxer's stance and began to circle his uncle, uttering a continuous stream of mumbled curses as he eyed the tainted dagger.

The older man, flexing muscles earned from years of campaigning and maintained in the palace's practice yards, circled as well, Ca-Mi-He's blade held in one fist.

"Did you do that, or did..." William wondered, his voice trailing off nervously.

Oliver, guessing his uncle was referring to the suddenly missing spirits, didn't answer. He certainly hadn't done anything to get rid of them, and he wasn't going to take the time to speculate on what did happen. Instead, he danced forward, punching a tentative jab at his uncle.

The old soldier swiped at Oliver's hand, and Oliver barely pulled it back in time to avoid a deep laceration along his wrist.

He knew from years of arms training, when unarmed against a man with a blade, it was best to accept that you were going to get hurt and to charge in and grapple your opponent. Oliver's old instructors would have demanded he launch himself into the face of the steel now, but he wondered if those old men, so confident in the practice yard, would take the same action when faced with the certainty of their own wounding. He wondered whether they would ignore the taint of the dagger, the stain of the underworld. He wondered what properties the weapon might have and what even a small nick might do to him.

At the moment, volunteering to get stabbed certainly sounded stupid.

William wasn't going to let him make the decision, though, and his uncle advanced, blade held ready. Oliver punched, and William slashed. Neither one landed a blow, and Oliver began a cautious retreat across the rooftop of the druid fortress. Unable to look behind where he was walking, he offered a hope to the spirits that he wouldn't trip over anything or bump against the waist-high battlement and go toppling over the side.

In front of him, behind his uncle's approaching figure, were the three iron crosses and the copper bowl his uncle had dropped. Not much, even if he could get to them, but it was better than his fists and his wits, neither of which were doing any good at the moment.

He was younger and faster, and he knew his uncle had a bad shoulder from a wound he'd earned in the United Territories. Edging to his uncle's left, Oliver forced the older man to turn. Then, Oliver lunged, faking an attack that his uncle defended by swiping across his body with the dagger.

Oliver sprinted around the older man, ducking as William unleashed a brutal backhand chop at him. The tip of the dagger caught the sleeve of his jacket, and Oliver shivered, thinking of how close the tainted steel had come to parting his flesh. Then, he was racing toward the copper bowl which he stooped picked up. He spun around, facing his uncle.

William laughed uproariously. "You stupid boy, why didn't you just run down the stairwell we came up?"

Oliver blinked. Now that he was by the iron crosses, he saw they were situated in a narrow corner of the old fortress. On the other side of his uncle, he could see the dark opening they'd come through and hundreds of yards of open rooftop he could have run around in except now, he was pinned in one sliver which jutted out toward the river.

Still chuckling, his uncle advanced. "When I cut you, Oliver, do me a favor and catch some of your blood in that bowl?"

Oliver waited, letting his uncle draw close.

The former soldier was moving cautiously, certainty evident on his face, but he knew Oliver had been in a brawl or two. Even with the advantage of the dagger, William wasn't going to take chances against his younger nephew. The prime minister touched a wrist to the golden bracer on his forearm again and, cursing, kept moving forward. Whatever he was trying to do, whatever spirits he wanted to call upon, they weren't answering. He kept coming, though. With or without sorcery, William intended to end the fight.

Oliver retreated until his back hit one of the iron crosses, the cold of the metal bleeding through his jacket. He held the copper bowl in front of him, like it was some sort of shield.

"Perfect," growled William.

His hand brushed against the golden bracer on his arm another time, and a flicker of concern crawled across his face, but it was replaced by fiery determination. The old soldier lunged, swinging the dagger at his nephew.

Oliver blocked it with the bowl, the metal ringing as steel struck copper. Again, William thrust, and Oliver blocked, the tip of the dagger coming uncomfortably close to his fingers gripping the edge of the bowl.

Oliver was pinned against the iron cross, and William feinted and then struck low. Oliver had been waiting for it. He dodged to the side and snapped the bowl down on his uncle's wrist, cracking the rim against the bone of William's hand.

Yelping, William involuntarily dropped the dagger.

Oliver swung the bowl backhanded and smashed it against his uncle's face. The older man stumbled back. Oliver cracked him again, using the copper bowl like a club, beating William over and over with it until one strike too hard knocked the bowl from Oliver's hands.

William was reeling back, cursing, gripping his bracers then raising his hands to box, panic in his eyes.

Oliver advanced and jabbed at his uncle with his right fist then swung a quick hook with his left, catching William on the side of the head. Two crosses, a jab, and another hook and William staggered away, blinking, trying to shake his head.

Jumping after him, Oliver grabbed his uncle's bare shoulder, swung him around, and shoved him, smashing William face-first into the arm of one of the iron crosses.

Crying in pain and clutching his head, blood seeping through tight fingers, William fell to his knees.

Oliver kicked him, catching William in the chest and sending him staggering back to fall against the battlement surrounding the rooftop. Oliver pounced, punching his uncle like the man was one of the stuffed boxing bags the marines kept in the practice yard. He pounded his uncle while the man helplessly tried to hide behind his gold-covered forearms.

Oliver felt his knuckles crack painfully against the metal. He cursed, shaking his fist, and hooked William's arms aside with his left hand. He punched him in the face with his right fist, catching the prime minister square on the nose. Oliver felt the fragile bone crunch beneath his blow. Breathing heavily, Oliver stood, glaring at William.

The older man sagged against the wall, his hands clutching the raw stone. His breathing was heavy, and his head was down. Blood leaked from where his scalp had been split by the copper bowl or the cross, and it poured from his broken nose. Half-a-dozen other scrapes and cuts dribbled blood, masking his face crimson.

Oliver saw William could no longer summon the energy to

defend himself. The prime minister had practice and muscle left-over from years before, but he didn't have his nephew's vigor. He was done. Oliver knew it, but to be safe, he reached down and tore off the man's golden bracers, tossing them over the edge of the rooftop.

William, blood dripping from his chin onto his bare chest, looked up at Oliver.

"What do you know of my mother?" Oliver demanded. "Where is Lilibet?"

His uncle smiled bitterly at him, baring blood-stained teeth. "Ask the other."

"The other? Who is the other?" cried Oliver.

Suddenly, behind him, Oliver felt a cold, malevolent presence.

"O-Oliver," stammered William, his knuckles white from gripping the stone wall, his voice hoarse with fright. "Don't let it… don't let it take me."

Oliver turned and saw nothing, but he felt it. On the stone floor, fifty yards away at the entrance to the rooftop, brilliant white hoarfrost formed as something approached.

"Oliver," babbled his uncle, his voice a harsh whisper in the cold night air, "I've prepared myself for a binding. It can invest itself in me. Ca-Mi-He will be in our world, in the flesh!"

Instinctively, Oliver spun and lunged at his uncle. He had no way of dealing with whatever was coming for them. Ca-Mi-He, if his uncle was telling the truth. There was nothing Oliver could do about that, nothing he could do to fight such a powerful shade from the underworld.

But there was something he could do about his uncle.

Oliver dove forward, sliding on his knees to crash against the older man. He wrapped his arms around William's legs and then hurled himself up, shoving to lift his uncle, tossing the man like a heavy sack of potatoes over the battlement of the ancient druid fortress.

With a startled scream, William flipped over and fell into the night air.

Bitter cold assailed him, and Oliver's muscles locked. On the battlement in front of him, large crystals of ice formed instantly in front of his eyes. William's terrified scream was followed by a whistle and a burst of frozen air as something, a shade, swept by Oliver.

The cold rolled away, chasing over the edge of the battlement.

Barely audible, William's body thumped on the ground far below.

Oliver staggered back. In front of him, the stone of the battlement cracked with cold, fissures forming in the raw rock. Hanging in the air, steps off the battlement, the presence returned. Oliver felt pure terror in his bones and stumbled into one of the iron crosses, stopping there and leaning against it, waiting for what was next. The presence moved closer, seeming to crouch in the crenellations of the battlement, ice webbing down the short wall and across the rooftop.

Oliver was paralyzed. His body would not respond to his commands. He could do nothing but look at… at nothing, but it was there. The spirit was there. He could feel its weight on the world like a rock laid atop him. Pinned, he could do nothing but wait.

———

Sam burst out of the entrance to the rooftop, racing across the icy stone and skidding to a stop in front of Oliver. Her daggers were in her hands, but she made no move to attack. He supposed it wouldn't have done them any good. No mere swipe with an inscribed blade was going to banish this spirit. Instead, she simply stood there, drawing herself upright, and waited.

The presence rose, towering half-a-dozen yards tall, invisible but apparent. It moved down from the battlement onto the rooftop, the hoarfrost signaling where it was going, and it stood, looking at them.

"What the frozen hell is that?" gasped Oliver.

Sam just shook her head, evidently speechless.

Oliver moved to stand beside her, clenching his fists, feeling foolish for trying to stare down something he couldn't see, wishing he had some weapon to hold, though, against an insubstantial opponent, he knew it would be an empty comfort.

"Hells it's cold," gasped Sam, her breath billowing from her mouth.

Suddenly, she cried out and doubled over, clutching her stomach where William had stabbed her. Her daggers clattered to the stone, and she fell to her knees.

Oliver knelt beside her, putting an arm around her and a hand on the stone rooftop to steady them. He looked up, a snarl on his lips, a hope to the spirits in his heart, but there was nothing there, nothing to shout at, nothing to defend Sam against. Just the terrible cold and the raw, physical sense of dread.

Warmth soaked from the stone of the ancient druid keep into his hand, crawling across his skin, passing from him to Sam. Warmth, like hot water pumped through a pipe, cycled through him, pouring into her.

She looked up, staring toward the presence, a scowl on her face.

He stayed crouched, touching the stone of the old fortress, touching her, waiting for something to happen, waiting for the shade to move in and kill them.

Slowly, like watching the sun crest the far horizon, he felt the pressure of the spirit fade, and the unnatural cold passed. Warmth pulsed through him and then returned to the world. He didn't move, though, not knowing if the thing was truly gone or if it would come back.

They stayed like that, silent, for a long moment. Then, Sam gathered her daggers and stood, sliding the sinuous blades into their sheaths. "I think it's gone."

He stared up at her.

"What?" she asked.

"How, ah, why aren't you dead?" he asked, rising beside her.

"I'm sorry. I didn't mean it like that. It's just… I saw him stab you. That dagger sank to the hilt in you, Sam."

She shrugged, looking around. Near the iron crosses, she saw the tainted dagger his uncle had wielded, and she picked it up.

"I had some of Ivar's ointments left," she claimed. "For a moment there, I wasn't sure I was going to make it. Thought I was going to die, but… I didn't. It still hurts something awful, but I managed to get up here."

"I'm glad you made it," he said, his gaze darting between the tainted dagger in her hand and the bloody tear in her vest and shirt. "Ivar's mixture was more potent than what Thotham used?"

"What happened up here?" she wondered, not answering his question.

"He was going to sacrifice me," replied Oliver, shaking his head and looking around the rooftop of the fortress. "He was ready to plunge that blade into my chest. Then, all of a sudden, it was like his shades were banished. They just disappeared, and I was free. We fought, and I won. I was asking him… I was trying to question him when… something, I guess, came up that ramp. He said it was Ca-Mi-He."

"I felt it, too," murmured Sam. "I can't explain it, what that was, but Ca-Mi-He… Yes, I think that's correct. I think somehow, the spirit manifested. It's not here physically, but it's no mere shade like those we've battled before. I need to read, to research…"

"William claimed the spirit could invest in him," added Oliver, "so I tossed him off the roof."

Sam blinked at him. "You threw your uncle over the battlement?"

Oliver ran his hand over his hair, feeling the leather thong at the back. "I didn't know what else to do. I figured if he was dead, the spirit couldn't invest in him. Like the footmen, you know? Once we struck them down, the spirits fled. Are we… are we safe?"

She shook her head, glancing at the empty air where the spirit had hung. "No, not safe. Not at all. But maybe, for now, we are. William might have been right, Duke. If he prepared a binding with the dark trinity, it's possible some other spirit could use the design and fill the pattern he had created. Ca-Mi-He might have been able to take over him, to control William like a hand within a glove. If that spirit had been here physically, I don't think there's anything we could have done to stop it. I don't think there's anything anyone could have done. Throwing your uncle off of this rooftop might have been the smartest thing you've ever done."

"I couldn't reach the dagger," said Oliver, still looking at it in her hands. "If I could have, maybe... I don't know. I could have used it."

Sam tucked the blade out of sight behind the back of her belt. "It's probably for the best that you didn't. The dagger was tainted by the great spirit, remember? It was... It's for the best, Duke. I think I should study this later, when we've gotten out of here. The shades are gone, but there could still be wolfmalkin, grimalkin, people... We need to leave as quickly as we can, get help from your father, and come back in the daylight to clean this place out."

"What do you think happened to the spirits?" wondered Oliver. "How did... how did Ca-Mi-He, or whatever that was, how did it get here? Where did it go?"

She shrugged, glancing over her shoulder at where the presence had disappeared. When she looked back at him, her face was blank. "I don't know."

"There's a lot we don't know," muttered Oliver, hugging himself in the cold night air.

Sam only nodded.

Drawing himself upright, feeling the scrapes and bruises he'd gotten, Oliver said, "There were acolytes in the keep. I killed three of them. I think they had prisoners as well, but... I think they're gone. I don't, ah, I don't feel them here, in the keep."

"You don't feel them?" questioned Sam, a skeptical look on her face.

He shrugged. "I don't know. I just think they're gone, or dead. We should look, though, to be sure."

"Of course," agreed Sam. "It's possible the acolytes, the wolf-malkin, whatever your uncle had here, felt that presence and fled. Duke, it's possible that when they ran, they didn't leave any captives alive. Anyone still breathing had a chance to identify them. I wouldn't have left witnesses if I was them."

He grunted. "We have to look. Then, we have to speak to my father."

A DOOR SLAMMED, SHOCKING HIM AWAKE. STARTLED, HE SAT forward in the chair, blinking blurry eyes, his hand reaching instinctively for the half-empty glass of whiskey on the table in front of him.

"Drinking, Oliver, really?" questioned King Edward. "It's just two turns after dawn."

"It seemed appropriate," muttered Oliver, covering a yawn with a fist and then taking a slug of the whiskey.

"A physician, perhaps, might make more sense?" wondered his father, looking with concern at his youngest son. "Shall I call for one?"

"I've had worse," remarked Oliver, poking tentatively at a painful bruise on his face. "I'm just tired now. I've been up nearly a full day, I think. A lot of hiking in that time."

"Your Captain Ainsley demanded to see me yesterday evening," said his father. "She was a little tipsy, and claimed you were going into that old dump of rocks across the river to battle a sorcerer. Does this have anything to do with the frantic messages I've been getting on the glae worm filament from Philip? Many of those had to do with you, and then suddenly he stopped communicating. What happened last night, Oliver?"

"Uncle William," said Oliver quietly, his gaze on his nearly empty whiskey glass instead of his father. "He was part of a cabal of sorcerers, along with Director Randolph Raffles and Bishop Gabriel Yates. They had a plan to sacrifice Middlebury, to bind a spirit known as the dark trinity. They said it would have given them immense power, perhaps even eternal life."

Frowning, King Edward tugged on his slender goatee. He began pacing the room, reminding Oliver uncomfortably of himself. "William, you are sure? Is he…"

"I am sure," responded Oliver. "He's dead. I killed him."

"You have evidence he… he did these things you say?"

"The old druid fortress across the river is filled with his things," said Oliver. "His minions were there, but they fled. Still, there are writings, sorcerous implements, bodies… scores of bodies, people he held captive and used in sacrifices, creatures that he summoned. Nothing was left breathing in that place."

"And William," asked his father, "where is he?"

"Outside of the walls, at the base of one of them," whispered Oliver. "What's left of him, anyway."

"I will send men to investigate," remarked the king, turning to Sam.

She was sitting across from Oliver, and he saw her pinching her wrist hard, trying to force herself awake.

"You are the one Bishop Yates originally assigned to assist my son with the investigation in Harwick?" asked the king. "If what Oliver says is true, then your master was a sorcerer. Are we to trust you, now?"

Her face twisted into a grimace, and Oliver thought it quite possible she was literally biting her tongue. Finally, she was able to respond, "King Edward, Bishop Yates was never my master. I served a mentor named Thotham, a Knife of the Council of Seven. He was killed beneath Derbycross. But yes, your son and I have been seeking those behind Hathia Dalyrimple's murder and… and I cannot even count how many other murders. We knew the sorcerers were out there, but we didn't know who they were until the last few days."

"Surely not so simple as that," remarked the king, setting his hands on his hips and looking between Oliver and Sam.

"Not simple," agreed Oliver, "but it was what we had to do, Father. I heard it from their own lips, both Raffles and William. They admitted to a plot to sacrifice the city of Middlebury. They would have killed every man, woman, and child within that city."

King Edward nodded, his hand floating up to tug on his chin hair again. "From their own lips… The dark trinity? You are certain you heard correctly?"

"There is no doubt," replied Oliver, studying his father's sedate reaction. "Are… are you mad, Father?"

"At you?" replied Edward, letting go of his facial hair and beginning to pace again. "No, of course not. I knew you were still investigating this matter. You're like me, boy, more so than your older brothers. I am not mad at you. At William, though… I knew he was not happy as prime minster, but I'd given him everything I could. I'd shared more power with him than has been done in generations. I granted him lands, income. With more responsibilities, a marriage for Lannia coming up, I thought he would be content as prime minister, at least long enough until you or one of your brothers was ready to assume the role, and then William could pursue his personal ambitions. He was my brother, and he would do this to the Crown, to Enhover?"

"I loved him as well," murmured Oliver. "Part of me didn't believe it until I saw him with my own eyes. He tried to kill me, Father. He told me so, that he was going to sacrifice me. He meant to capture my soul and use it in his ceremony. I was just a step on his path. A step toward sacrificing all of Middlebury. I—"

"Enough," said Edward, pacing back and forth across the room. "We will talk of this. We will, but for now, we need to discuss what is next. You said some of William's acolytes fled. What about spirits, conjured creatures?"

"Yes," said Oliver, glancing at Sam. "There were people there, I don't know how many, but they've fled. We saw, ah, we saw wolf-malkin and grimalkin and killed some of them. Do you know of them? I do not know if we killed all of the beasts or if there were more. We did not see any as we left. There were shades, but they were banished, I think. They are gone, now."

Pacing again, the king murmured, "Interesting."

"Father," Oliver said, "I did what I thought I had to. My proof is what I heard from the sorcerers' own mouths. Not everyone may see it that way. In front of the Congress of Lords, in front of a magistrate—"

"Not everyone needs to know," stated King Edward. "In fact, they shouldn't. Your brother Philip, of course. Edgar and Herbert Shackles. Your captain and crew know. Can they be trusted to remain silent?"

Oliver nodded. "I believe so."

"Good," replied the king. "We keep quiet, but we have to offer some explanation for everything that has happened. I believe from what Philip has sent, there will be restitutions to make. There will be difficult discussions with the Congress of Lords, the Church, and the Company. Even more difficult conversations with Philip. He's livid."

"He will understand," claimed Oliver, fairly certain it was true.

The king nodded. "It's best if you deal with Philip in person. I'll have Edgar Shackles speak with his son, Herbert. Shackles the younger can keep Philip subdued until you have a chance to meet. Both of the Shackles can begin addressing other matters which do not require our direct attention. I'll inquire with Admiral Brach and Will — with Shackles — about getting some experienced investigators assigned to hunt down the missing acolytes. The royal marines also have some special squadrons that I believe may be suited for this. Unfortunately, it is not the first time we've had to keep information close at hand." The king looked to Sam. "In my experience, informing the Church of these matters is a certain way to have them whispered in every corner of the empire. Is that your view as well?"

"I think it best the Church knows as little as possible," agreed

Sam. "If it becomes necessary, I can inform them of what has happened, but…"

"I understand," said the king. "I will trust your judgement."

Oliver nodded, slowly. "Father, I am sorry…"

"You did not do this, Oliver. It is not you who should be sorry," said King Edward. He looked to Sam. "I am confident we can manage the political difficulties, but what of sorcery? What other threats remain?"

"There were three in the cabal, and I have absolute faith we got the right men," declared Sam, "but some of their people escaped. We do not know who they are or what they are capable of. I think it's best to assume they are dangerous, but not as dangerous as the bishop, the director, and, ah, your brother. And… Oliver and I both felt a… a presence. It was powerful and malevolent. It left, but I do not know where it went. I do not know if it returned to the underworld or if it is still in our world."

"A presence?" asked the king.

"We believe it was a powerful spirit called Ca-Mi-He," said Oliver.

The king blinked. "You are sure?"

"We are fairly certain," said Oliver, running a hand back over his hair, feeling the leather thong that tied it back. "Certain enough. The creature was not manifested physically, but it felt more robust than a mere shade."

"I've heard the name," said Edward, walking to the window of the room and staring out at the morning sun. Shaken, he turned to his son and Sam. "What can be done about this spirit?"

"We don't know," replied Sam. "We need to research, to learn more about it."

"Yes, it's best to understand what we'll be facing," acknowledged Edward. He turned to Oliver. "Do you have a plan?"

Oliver shrugged. He drew a deep breath and then said, "Father, there is one more thing. Mother is alive. She did not die in Northundon. She's not in the underworld."

Edward crossed his arms, frowning. "Oliver, it's been twenty years. How could she not be… be dead?"

"I am sure," declared Oliver. "I do not know where she is or why she disappeared, but Father, I mean to find her."

"If she is not dead, then… then where is she?" asked the king. "Why has she not returned to Southundon? Why has she not sent me a message, or to you and your brothers? If she is alive, do you think she abandoned us, son?"

"I don't know," said Oliver. "Perhaps she was scared. Maybe she knew William was on the dark path."

"Son, if Lilibet is alive, she would not have simply left us," declared Edward. He shook himself, as if trying to come to terms with what Oliver was saying. "It's been twenty years. If she was alive, she would be here. If she thought William or anyone was on the dark path, she would have come immediately! You were old enough to know your mother. If she thought I was in danger, if you and your brothers were in danger, wouldn't she have come running? If she is alive as you propose, you understand what that means, right? She abandoned us, Oliver. For whatever reason, she abandoned us. That is not the woman I knew. The Lilibet I married would never turn her back on family."

Oliver opened his mouth and closed it. He knew she lived, and because she lived, he had to look for her. He knew it deeper than he'd ever known anything, but his father was right. Why had she not returned?

"I do not believe it," murmured the king, finally ceasing his pacing. "I know you do, though. If-If Lilibet was alive, where would she be? Where would you even begin looking for her?"

Oliver winced. His father was right about that. He had nowhere to start looking, no idea where she could be.

"The Darklands," said Sam quietly.

Both the king and Oliver glanced at her in surprise.

"In Northundon, there was evidence of powerful sorcery," remarked Sam, looking apologetically to Oliver. "Not just the sacrifice of the city. A ritual was performed that anchors the summoned spirits to the ruins of the city. That is why they have not spread across Enhover. They are bound to that place. The ritual wasn't conducted by shamans from the Coldlands. It wasn't William and his cohort. Who else but the Darklands is capable of such a feat? If someone was in Northundon with the knowledge and ability to do such a thing, it stands to reason that same someone helped Lilibet flee, or maybe they captured her. She's known throughout Enhover. I imagine in many circles in the United Territories as well. She could not hide out in the colonies for long. Where does that leave?"

"Captured," whispered Oliver.

Captured. Held prisoner for twenty years. That could explain why she had not returned. It could explain much, except why. Why would his mother be held captive for so long without any demands? What purpose would that serve?

"Do you truly think this is possible, priestess?" demanded the king. "I know nothing of the rituals which you describe, but I know my wife. She had no involvement with the Darklands. She'd rarely left Enhover, and the Darklands have very little involvement with us. In my rule, we've never sent a diplomatic mission there, and in history, they've never sent one to us. Why would they kidnap Lilibet? If—"

"It makes more sense than anything else, Father," interjected Oliver, his gaze locked on Sam. "She's right. Where else could Mother be undiscovered for twenty years? The Darklands is the only place Crown and Company representatives do not go. Where else would a sorcerer come from who has the skill to perform such a powerful ritual as what happened in Northundon?"

"Northundon? I am sorry, son, but I do not believe it," stated the king. "The Coldlands attacked us there, and we retaliated. If that was not the case, if some other sorcerers snuck in and performed such a heinous act, why did the Coldlands elders not tell us back then? Why wait until twenty years after we destroyed them?"

Oliver opened his mouth and then closed it. He had no

answer. If what the shaman told him was true, they'd attempted to make contact with Enhover. Had the old man been lying? Had William been right, and the old man wasn't even a Coldlands shaman?

His arms still crossed, the king began pacing again. "I do not like this. Your brothers will like it even less."

"We don't tell them, not about Mother," declared Oliver suddenly. "Father, you are right. They would not understand. I know I am not wrong, but if I am…"

"If you are wrong, it's quite likely you'll perish in that strange land," mentioned Edward.

"Even if we're right, that's not exactly unlikely," Sam said.

"Thanks," grumbled Oliver. He looked to King Edward. "We can come up with a story to tell my brothers. They would believe I was sent out of Enhover until things settle. That will give us the time we need. Sam and I will travel to the Darklands and search for Mother. If I don't find her, the only thing we lose is time."

"And maybe your life," reminded the king.

"The world is a dangerous place anywhere you go," said Oliver, his face earnest. "The Darklands cannot be much more dangerous than the last several days in Enhover."

"What about the acolytes who fled William's keep?" asked Edward, glancing at Sam. "What about this terrible spirit you told me of? You do not plan to hunt them down?"

"The inspectors and Admiral Brach's marines can handle that," insisted Oliver.

Sam shot him a look, but he did not meet her eyes. He knew she would want to find the acolytes personally. He knew she would want to confront Ca-Mi-He herself. She didn't think the Crown was capable of handling the matter, and she was probably right, but if they lost themselves in the hunt, they might never get a chance to go to the Darklands.

Edward looked to Sam. "You will accompany him?"

Oliver held his breath, wondering if she'd say no, if she would remain in Enhover trying to locate the rest of William's organization.

"Of course," she said. She offered Oliver a small smile. "I do not have the knowledge or skill to confront a spirit like Ca-Mi-He. Perhaps in the Darklands, they do."

"And how do you plan to get there?" questioned the king. "Company airships will not go to the Darklands. I will be honest, son, I do not think this is a good idea. With the unrest in the United Territories, pirates sprouting all over the tropics, I will not send you with a royal marine vessel."

"Captain Ainsley and the Cloud Serpent," said Oliver. "She'll take us."

"You haven't even asked her," retorted the king. "No matter how loyal, you cannot force a private captain and crew to sail to such a dangerous place."

"I have a way with women," claimed Oliver.

Shaking his head, King Edward walked to the doorway. "We have much to think about, and you've been awake far too long. I suggest you get some sleep, and then we will discuss this again. It's not the woman I knew, and if she was taken captive and held for twenty years, what possible motivation is there? Let's get the report from the inspectors once they've explored the druid fortress. We can cover up whatever we need to cover up, bribe whoever we need to bribe, and ensure this is resolved before we move on. Even if I eventually agree to let you leave on this foolhardy errand, I need your assistance in finding the rest of William's entourage first. You two are better suited for this than anyone else in the empire. So, sleep on it, spend some days doing what must be done, and then we will talk again about your mother. Agreed?"

Oliver nodded curtly. "Agreed."

Without further word, the king swept out of the room.

"If he has time to think about this, he's going to say no," warned Sam.

"I know," replied Oliver. "I wasn't planning to wait while he mulls it over. I think he'll give us four or five days and then give a direct order. If he issues an edict, it'd be a crime for us or anyone assisting us to disobey."

"Four or five days until he commands us, so we've got three days to figure a way out of here?"

"Three days," agreed Oliver.

"Do you have any idea of how drunk Ainsley's going to have to be to agree to this?"

Oliver grinned. "I think I have some idea."

"We'd better rest while we can, then," advised Sam. "It's going to be a long three days."

GLOSSARY

MEMBERS OF THE CROWN:

Edward Wellesley - King of Enhover

Lilibet Wellesley – wife of Edward & Queen of Enhover

Philip Wellesley – son of Edward & Lilibet, Prince of Enhover & Duke of Westundon

Lucinda Wellesley - wife of Philip, Princess of Enhover & Duchess of Westundon

Franklin Wellesley - son of Edward & Lilibet, Duke of Eastundon

John Wellesley - son of Edward & Lilibet, Duke of Southundon

Oliver "Duke" Wellesley - son of Edward & Lilibet, Duke of Northundon, the Cartographer

William Wellesley - brother of Edward, unlanded earl & Prime Minister of Enhover

Lannia Wellesley - daughter of William & unlanded countess

MEMBERS OF THE PEERAGE (CONGRESS OF LORDS):

Josiah Child - widower & Baron of Eiremouth

Aria Child - daughter of Josiah, twin of Isabella

Isabella Child - daughter of Josiah, twin of Aria

Nathaniel Child - brother of Josiah & unlanded baron
Rafael Colston – unlanded marquees
Ethan Brighton - unlanded viscount
Adelaide Boughton - Countess of Swinpool
Vassily Resault - unhanded earl

MEMBERS OF THE CHURCH:

Joshua Langdon - Cardinal of Enhover
Gabriel Yates - Bishop of Westundon
Timothy Adriance - priest & scholar
Thotham - priest & Knife of the Council
Samantha "Sam" - apprentice of Thotham
Constance - bishop & leader of the Council of Seven, the Whitemask
Raymond au Clair - Knife of the Council
Bridget Cancio - Knife of the Council

MEMBERS OF THE MINISTRY:

Richard Brach - Admiral of the Royal Marines
Brendan Ostrander - Commander of the Royal Marines in Archtan Atoll Colony
Edgar Shackles - Chief of Staff for King Edward Wellesley
Herbert Shackles - Chief of Staff for Prince Philip Wellesley
Walpole - minor bureaucrat in Westundon
Winchester - valet to Oliver Wellesley

MEMBERS OF THE COMPANY:

Randolph Raffles - member of the Company's board of directors, Company representative in Westundon
Alvin Goldwater - President of the Company, Marquess of Southwatch

Alexander Pettigrew - member of the Company's board of directors, finance committee

Sebastian Dalyrimple - Earl of Derbycross & Governor of Archtan Atoll Colony

Hathia Dalyrimple - wife of Sebastian & Countess of Derbycross

Isisandra Dalyrimple - daughter of Sebastian & Hathia

Jain Towerson - Governor of Imbon Colony

Ethan Giles – senior factor (merchant) in Imbon Colony

Charles - personal secretary for Director Randolph Raffles

Catherine Ainsley - Captain the airship Cloud Serpent

Pettybone - First Mate on the airship Cloud Serpent

Samuels - crew on the airship Cloud Serpent

OTHERS:

Pierre De Bussy - Governor of Finavia's colonies in the Vendatt Islands

Goldthwaite - proprietor and madam of the Lusty Barnacle

Kalbeth - daughter of Goldthwaite, tattoo artist

Rance - barman at the Lusty Barnacle

Lagarde - former barwoman at the Lusty Barnacle

Ivar val Drongko - perfume merchant

Duvante - historian & author

Andrew – barman & owner of the Befuddled Sage

LOCATIONS:

Nation of Enhover

Southundon - home to King Edward, Duke John & capital of Enhover / Southundon province

Westundon - home to Prince Philip, Duke Oliver & capital of Westundon province

Eastundon - home to Duke Franklin & capital of Eastundon province

Northundon - capital of Northundon province, destroyed
in war

Middlebury - city in Eastundon province & major rail
transit hub

Swinpool - city in Westundon province & cod fishing village

Harwick - city in Eastundon province & whaling village

United Territories – allied nations, tribute states to Enhover

Ivalla - home of the Church's headquarters

Romalla - capital of Ivalla, home of the Church

Valerno - port city

Finavia – wealthy merchant nation

Rhensar – forested nation known for hedge mages and wood
witches

Coldlands - subjugated and largely destroyed by war

Archtan Atoll - colony of the Company & famous for levitating
islands

Archtan Town - location of Company House

Eyies – island in Archtan Atoll

Farawk – island near Artchtan Atoll

Imbon - colony of the Company

Westlands - largely unexplored & location of Company
outpost

Southlands - largely unexplored & location of Company
outpost

Darklands - largely unexplored, religious state known for
worship of the underworld

THANKS FOR READING!

If you liked this book, please tell a friend!

Thanks to Shawn T King for the cover design and the graphics you see on my social media and website. Bob Kehl for much of what is on my website's art page. Soraya Corcoran created the maps — which was a bit crucial in this one. Nicole Zoltack is back yet again and my proofreader, and James Z is my lone beta reader. Without their help, this would be a very different experience.

If this book was your first experience with my stories, I encourage you to check out my completed series: **Benjamin Ashwood**. It follows a young man who embarks on a dangerous quest with mysterious strangers.

On my website, accobble.com, you can sign up for my newsletter to get a free prequel novella and short stories, you can check out my art page, see all of my books, my blog, and get in touch.

I save the best stuff for Patreon (www.patreon.com/accobble). I share exclusive updates, you get my books EARLY, it's the only place to have signed copies, I share audiobook codes, and you can even help direct what I write.

Thanks again and hope to hear from you!

AC

Printed in Great Britain
by Amazon